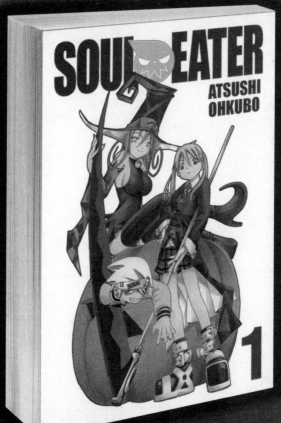

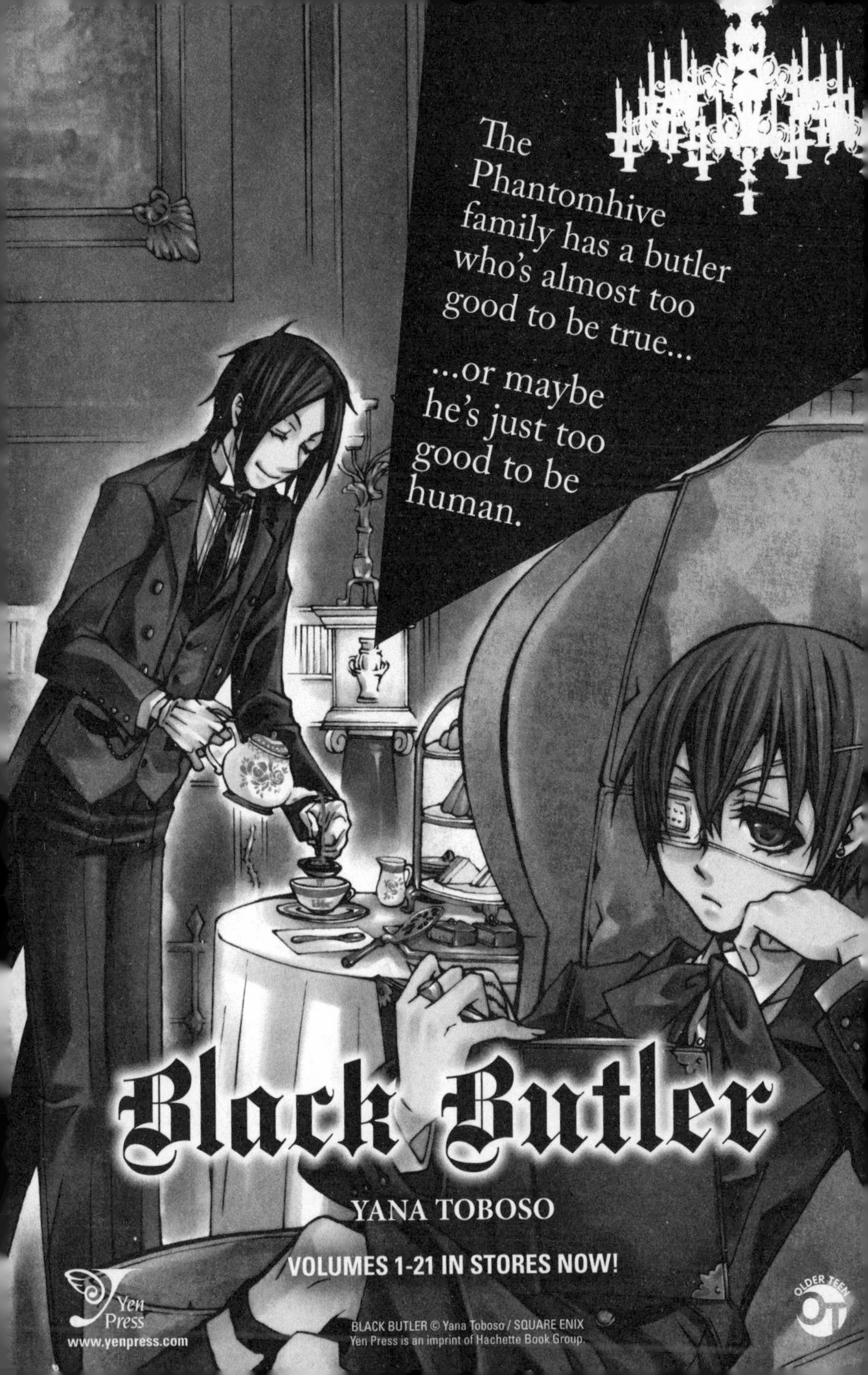
The Phantomhive family has a butler who's almost too good to be true...
...or maybe he's just too good to be human.
Black Butler
YANA TOBOSO
VOLUMES 1-21 IN STORES NOW!
Yen Press
www.yenpress.com
BLACK BUTLER © Yana Toboso / SQUARE ENIX
Yen Press is an imprint of Hachette Book Group.
OLDER TEEN
OT

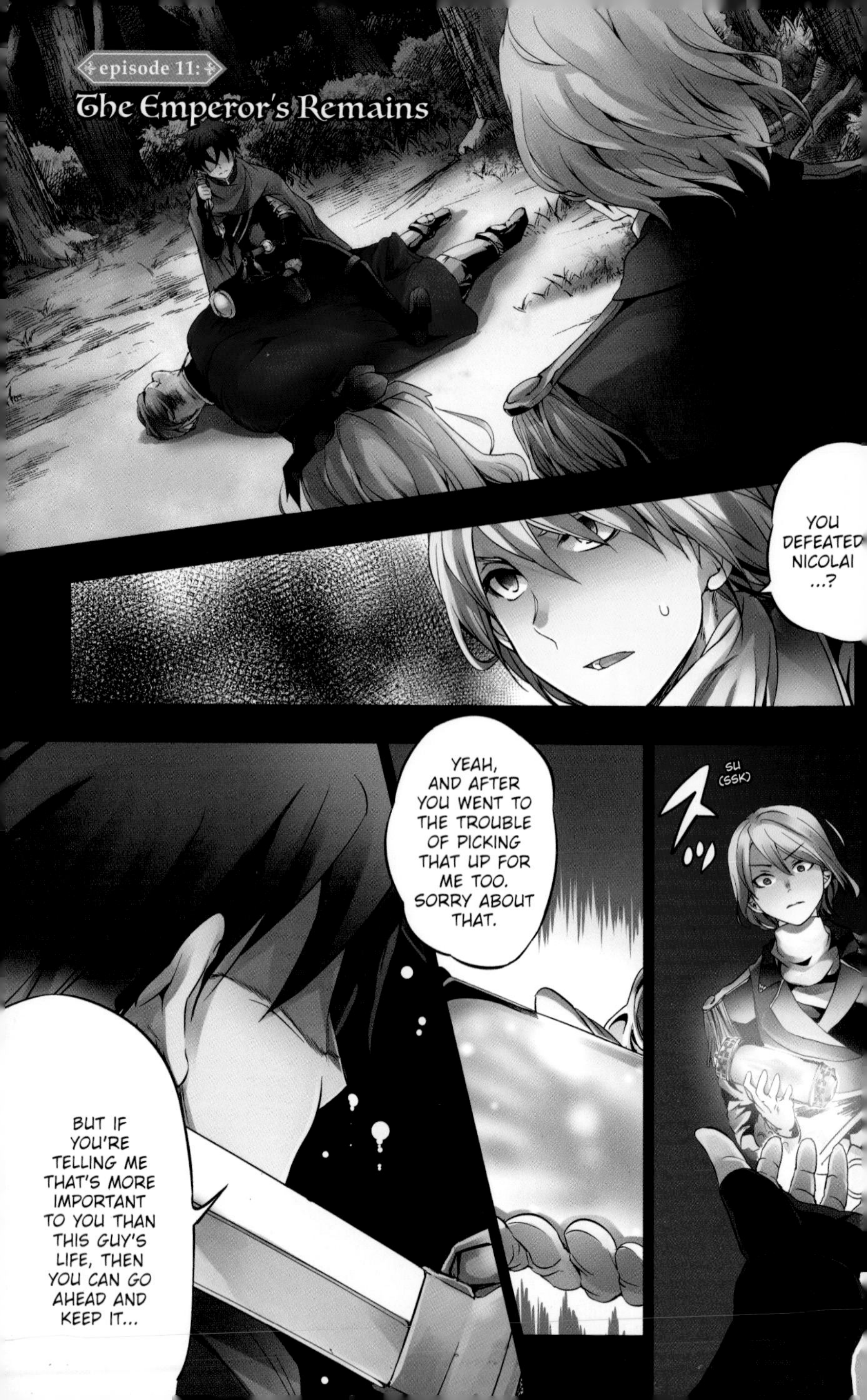
episode 11:
The Emperor's Remains
YOU DEFEATED NICOLAI ...?
SU (SSK)
YEAH, AND AFTER YOU WENT TO THE TROUBLE OF PICKING THAT UP FOR ME TOO. SORRY ABOUT THAT.
BUT IF YOU'RE TELLING ME THAT'S MORE IMPORTANT TO YOU THAN THIS GUY'S LIFE, THEN YOU CAN GO AHEAD AND KEEP IT...

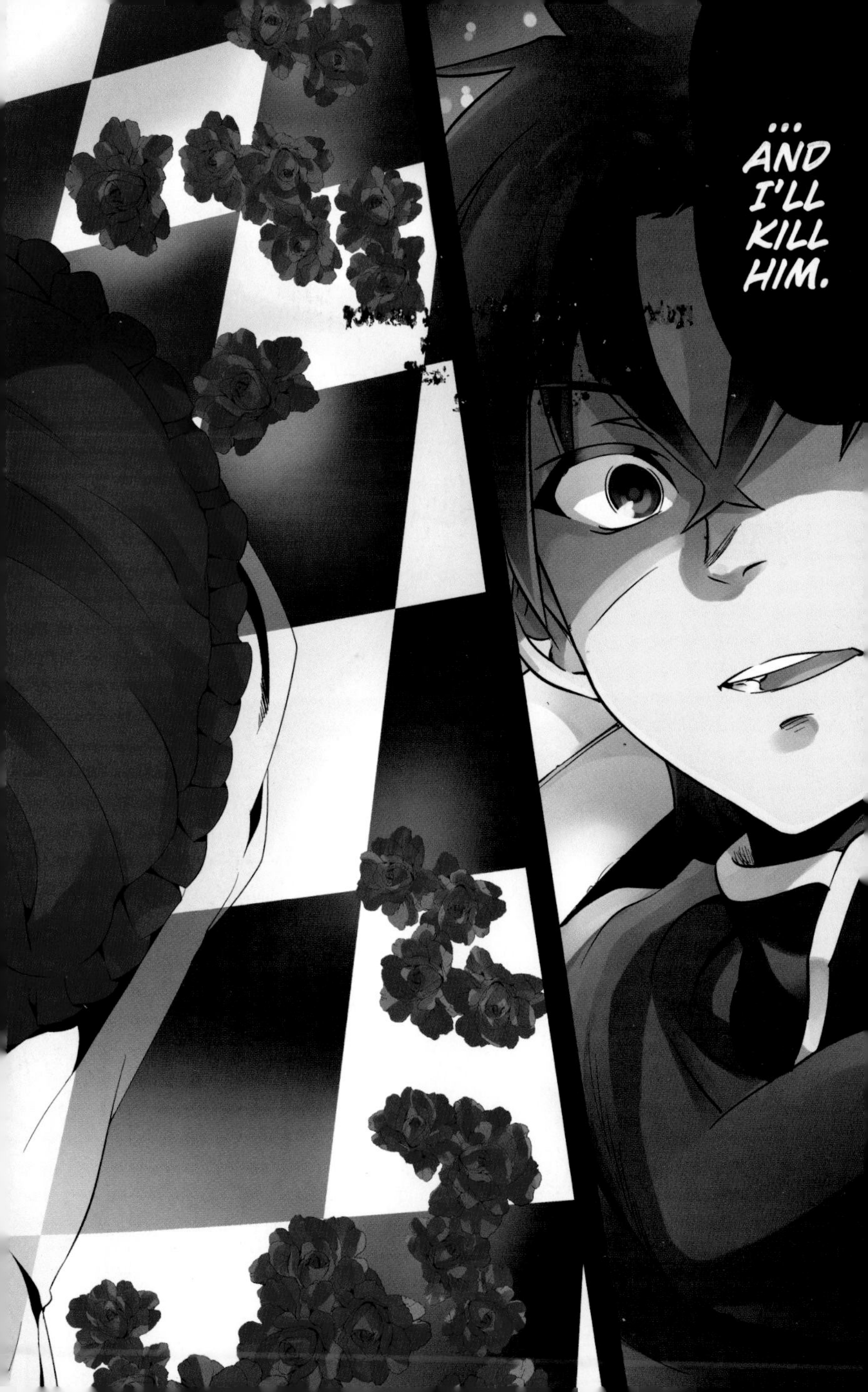
...AND I'LL KILL HIM.

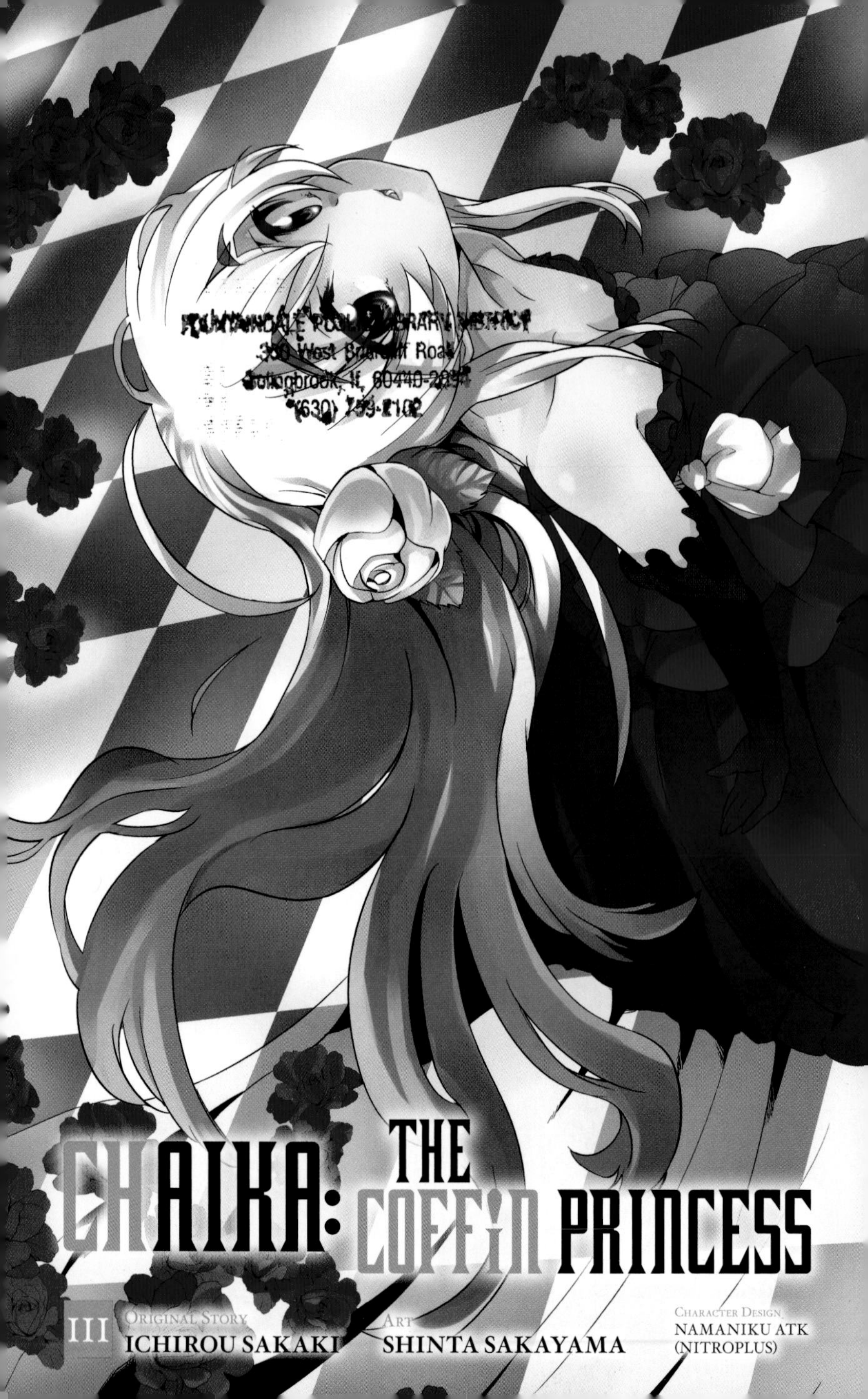
CHAIKA: THE COFFIN PRINCESS
III
ORIGINAL STORY
ICHIROU SAKAKI
ART
SHINTA SAKAYAMA
CHARACTER DESIGN
NAMANIKU ATK
(NITROPLUS)

CONTENTS

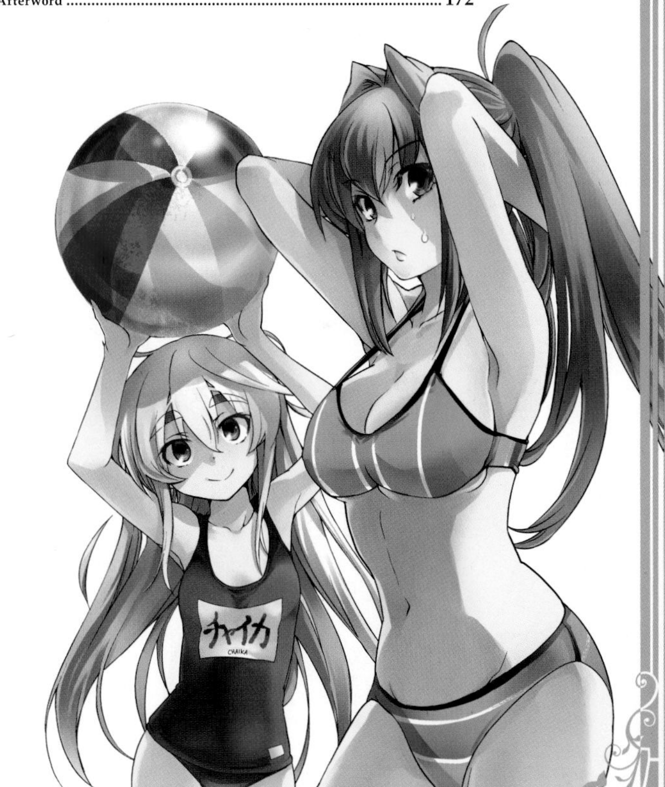

チャイカ
CHAIKA

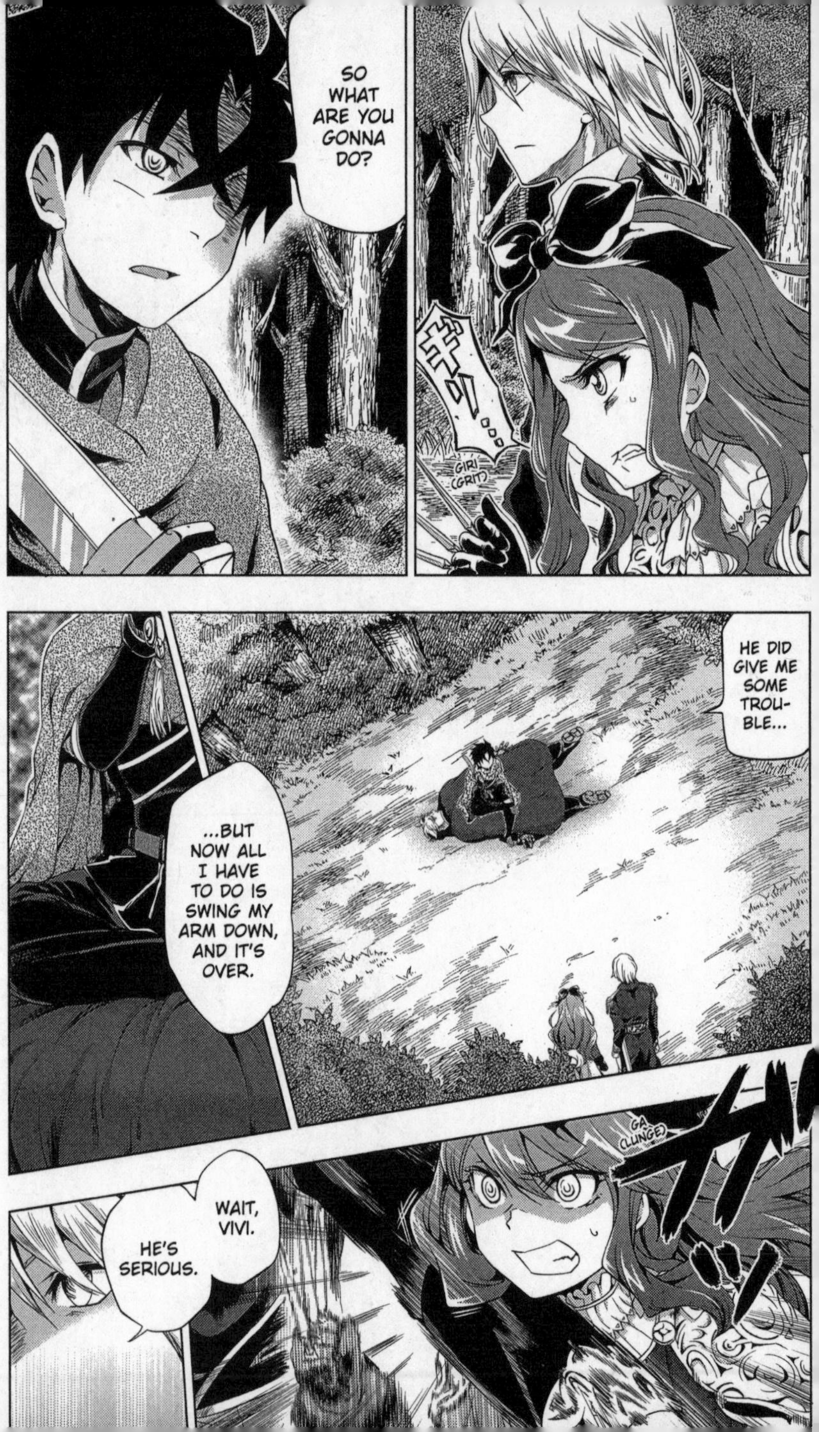
GIRI (GRIT)
SO WHAT ARE YOU GONNA DO?
HE DID GIVE ME SOME TROUBLE...
...BUT NOW ALL I HAVE TO DO IS SWING MY ARM DOWN, AND IT'S OVER.
GA (LUNGE)
WAIT, VIVI.
HE'S SERIOUS.

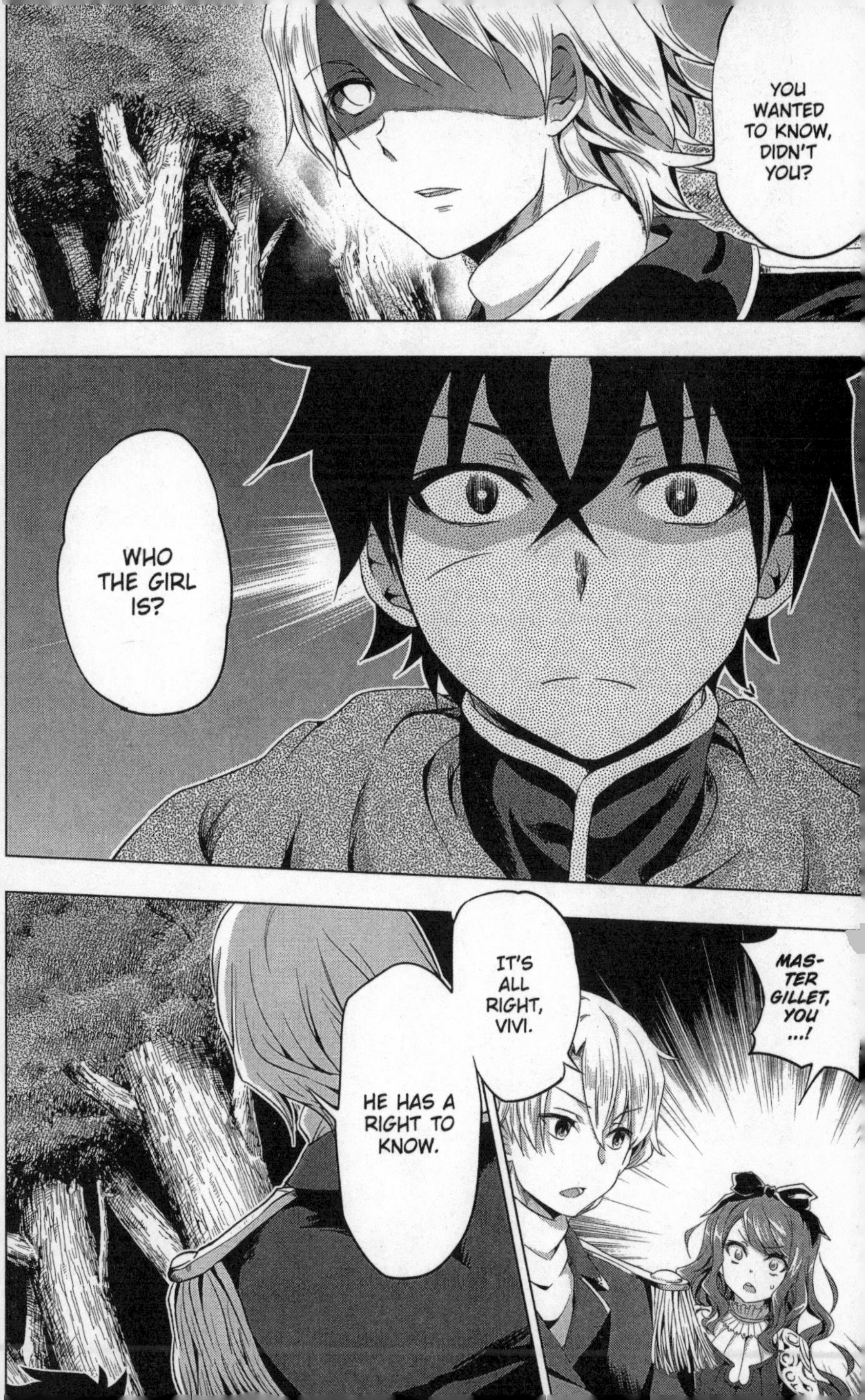
YOU WANTED TO KNOW, DIDN'T YOU?
WHO THE GIRL IS?
MAS-TER GILLET, YOU ...!
IT'S ALL RIGHT, VIVI.
HE HAS A RIGHT TO KNOW.

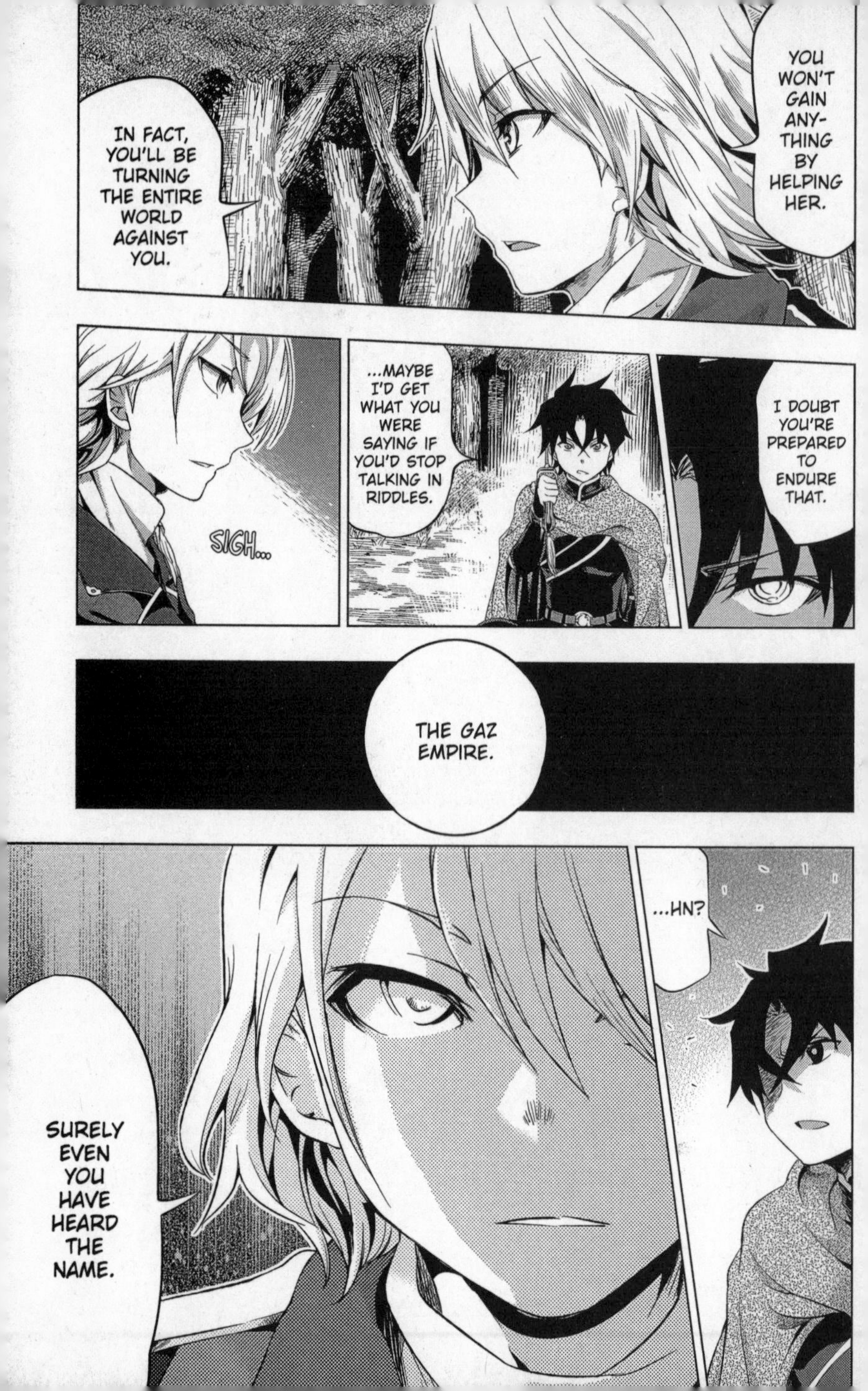
YOU WON'T GAIN ANYTHING BY HELPING HER.
IN FACT, YOU'LL BE TURNING THE ENTIRE WORLD AGAINST YOU.
I DOUBT YOU'RE PREPARED TO ENDURE THAT.
...MAYBE I'D GET WHAT YOU WERE SAYING IF YOU'D STOP TALKING IN RIDDLES.
SIGH...
THE GAZ EMPIRE.
...HN?
SURELY EVEN YOU HAVE HEARD THE NAME.

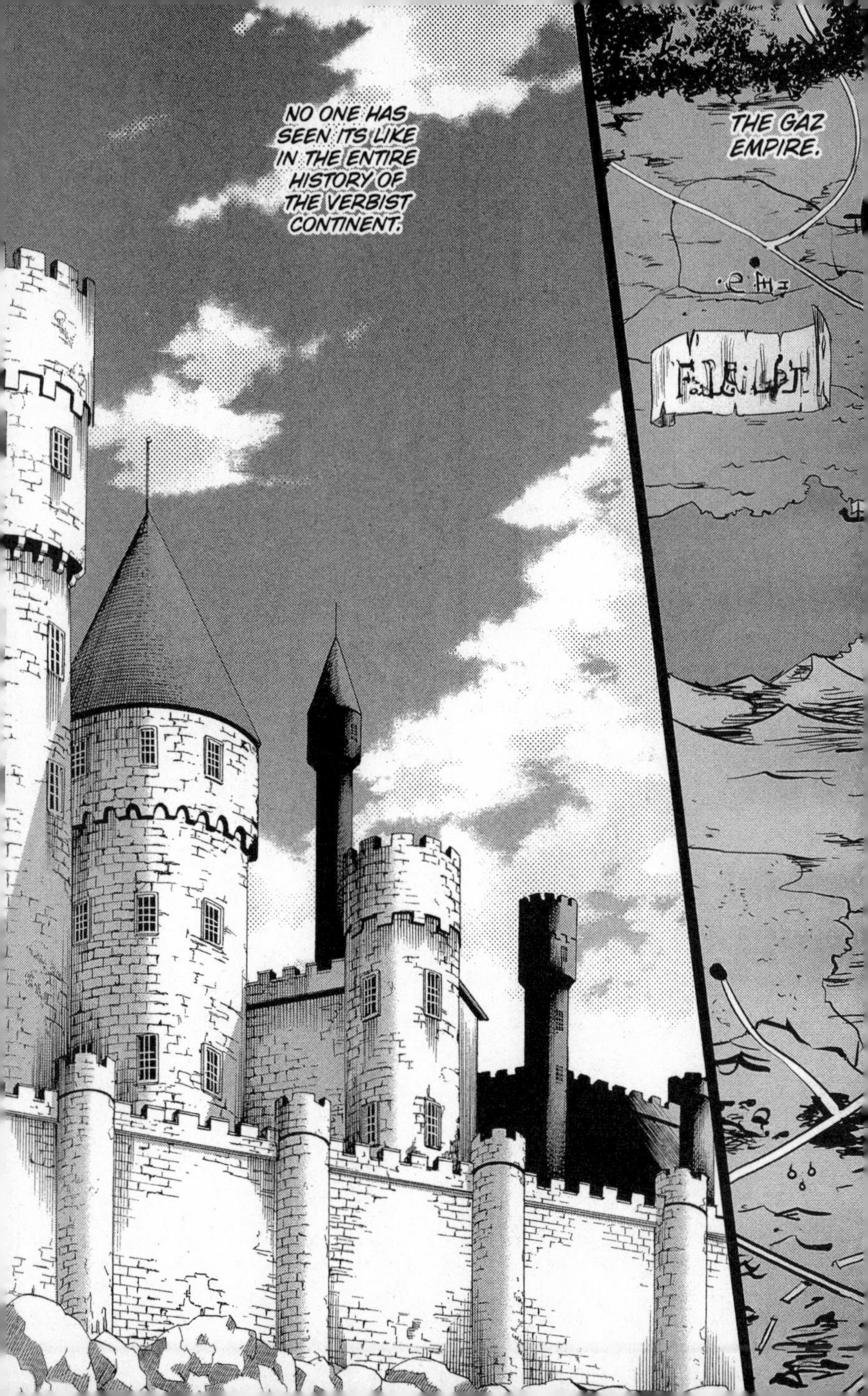
THE GAZ EMPIRE.
NO ONE HAS SEEN ITS LIKE IN THE ENTIRE HISTORY OF THE VERBIST CONTINENT.

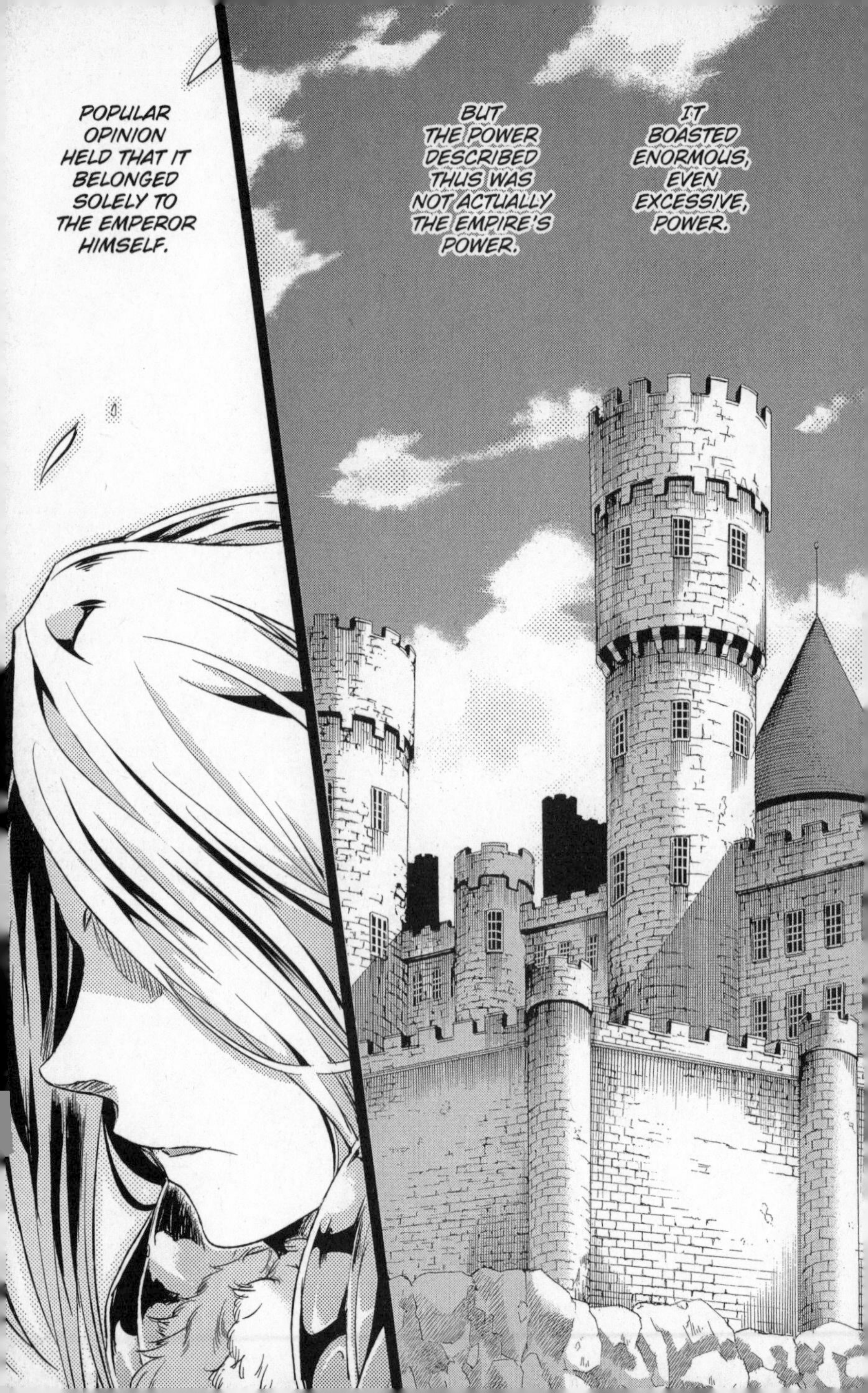
IT BOASTED ENORMOUS, EVEN EXCESSIVE, POWER.
BUT THE POWER DESCRIBED THUS WAS NOT ACTUALLY THE EMPIRE'S POWER.
POPULAR OPINION HELD THAT IT BELONGED SOLELY TO THE EMPEROR HIMSELF.

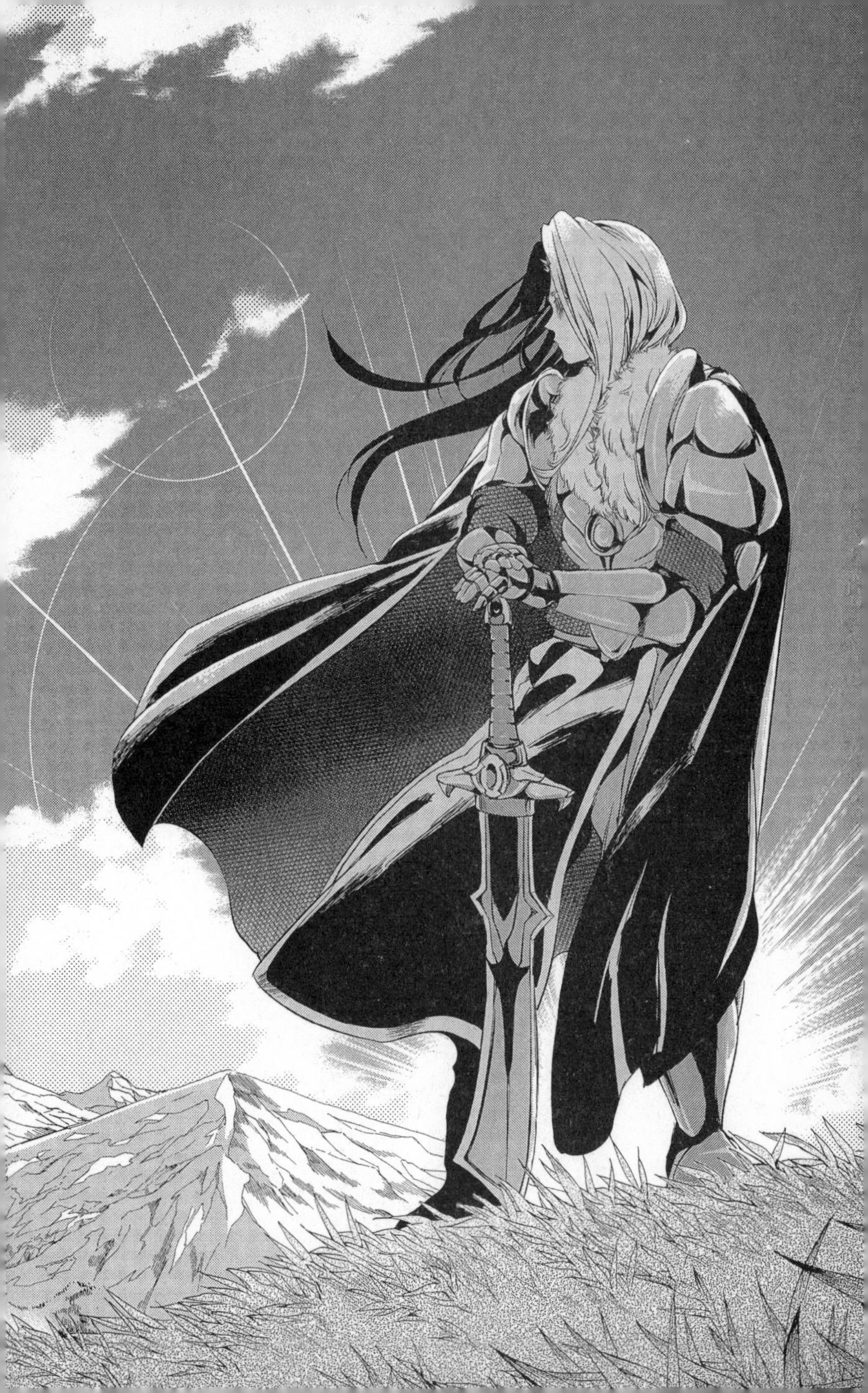

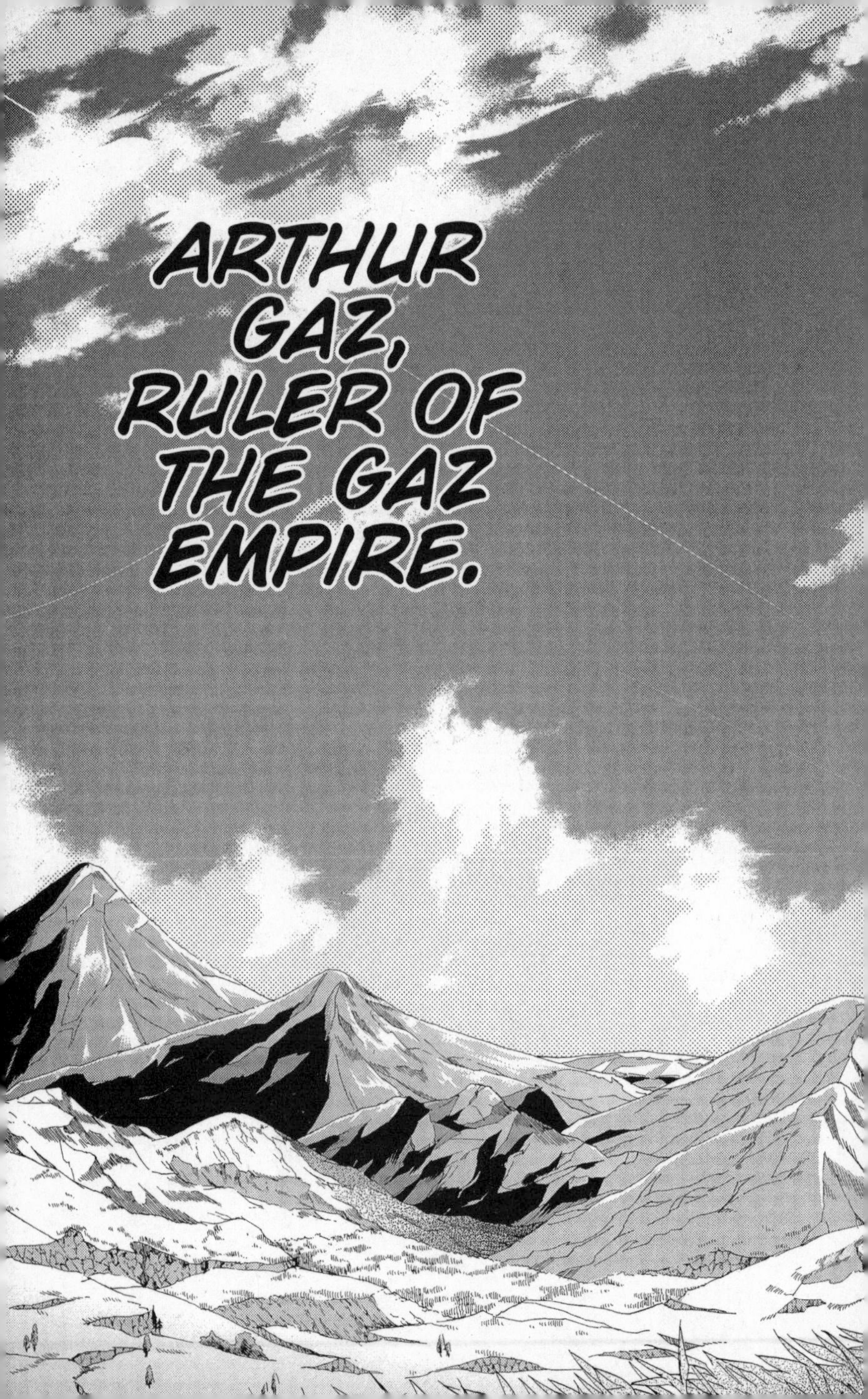
ARTHUR GAZ, RULER OF THE GAZ EMPIRE.

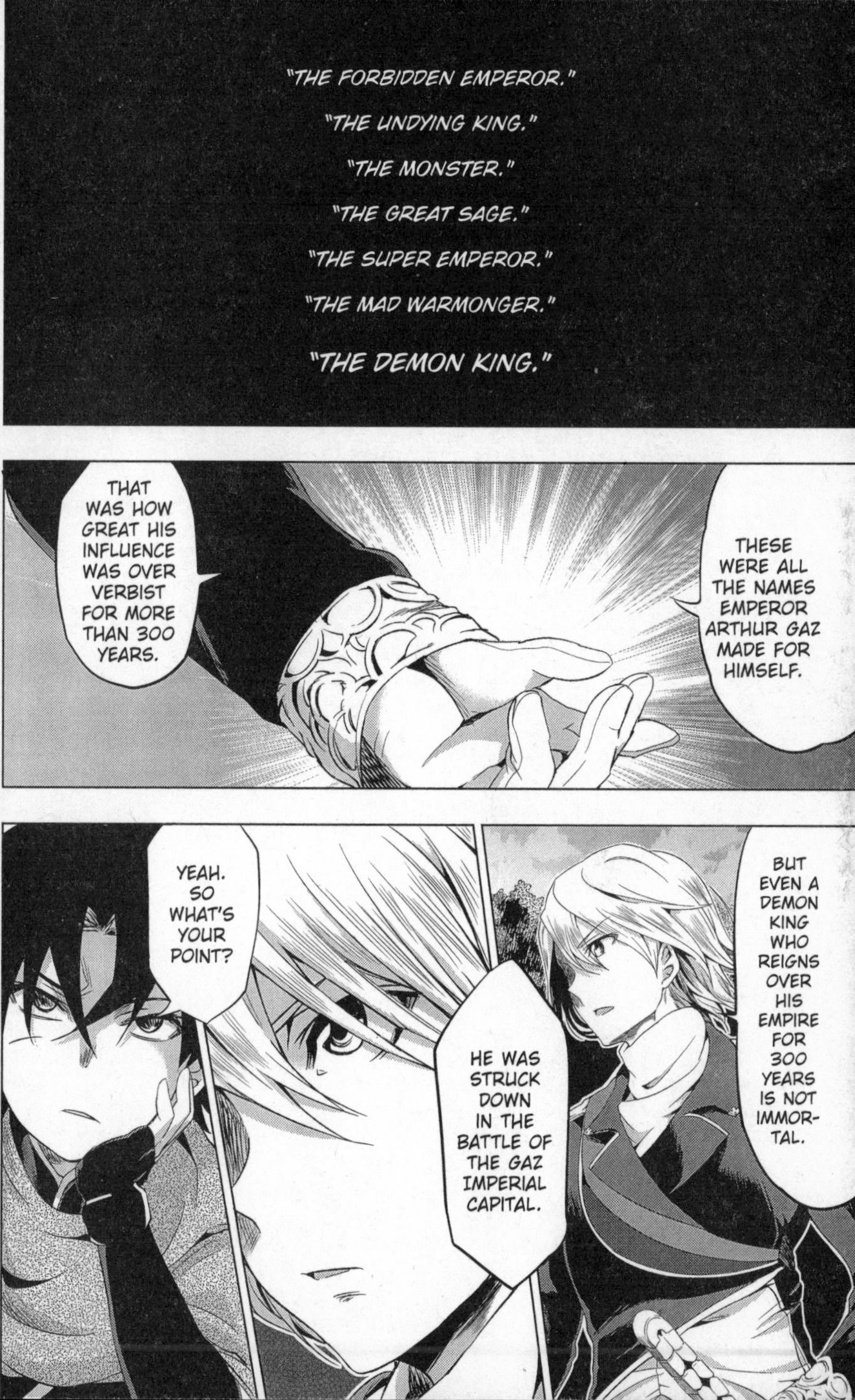
"THE FORBIDDEN EMPEROR."
"THE UNDYING KING."
"THE MONSTER."
"THE GREAT SAGE."
"THE SUPER EMPEROR."
"THE MAD WARMONGER."
"THE DEMON KING."
THESE WERE ALL THE NAMES EMPEROR ARTHUR GAZ MADE FOR HIMSELF.
THAT WAS HOW GREAT HIS INFLUENCE WAS OVER VERBIST FOR MORE THAN 300 YEARS.
BUT EVEN A DEMON KING WHO REIGNS OVER HIS EMPIRE FOR 300 YEARS IS NOT IMMORTAL.
HE WAS STRUCK DOWN IN THE BATTLE OF THE GAZ IMPERIAL CAPITAL.
YEAH. SO WHAT'S YOUR POINT?

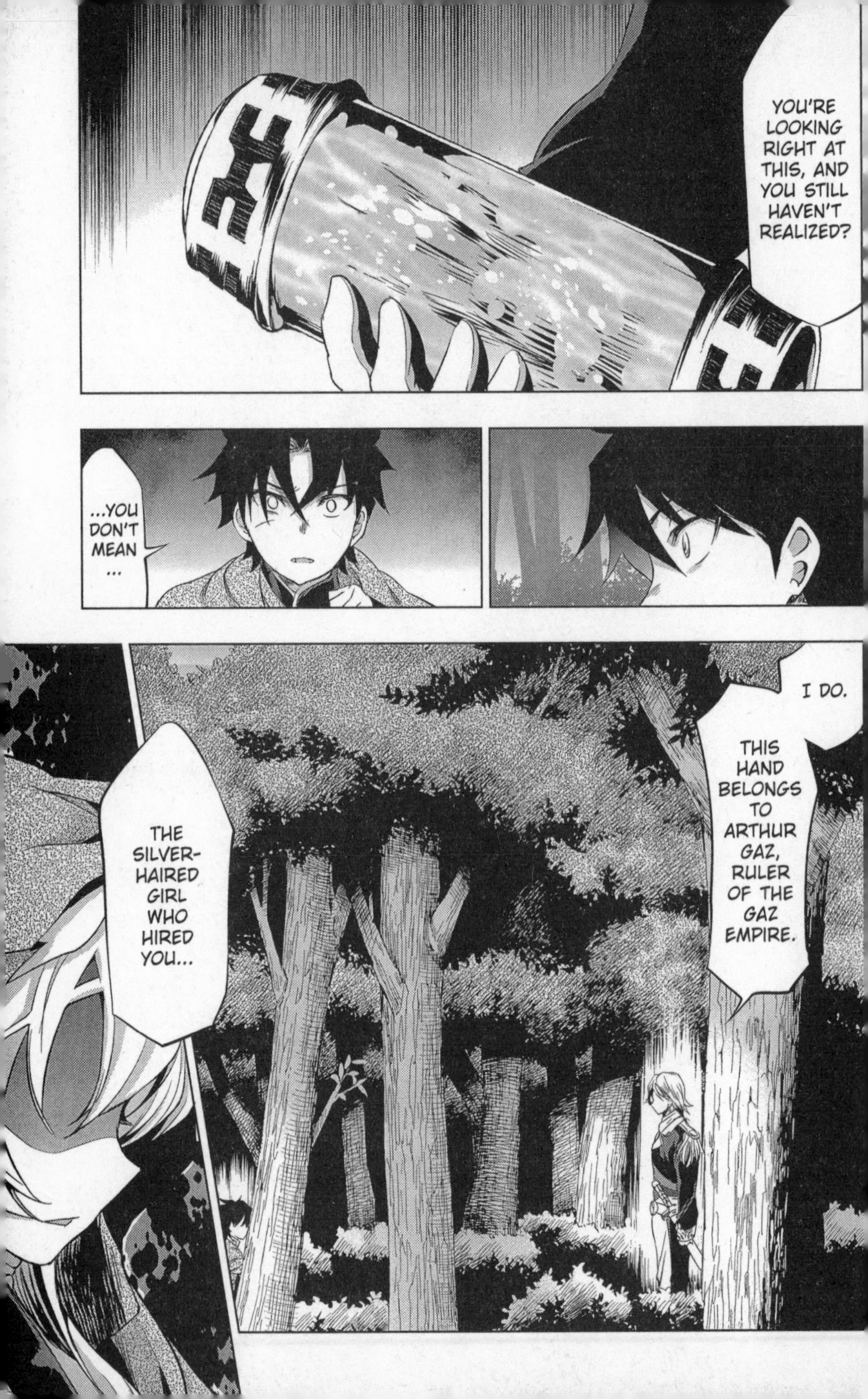
YOU'RE LOOKING RIGHT AT THIS, AND YOU STILL HAVEN'T REALIZED?
...YOU DON'T MEAN ...
I DO.
THIS HAND BELONGS TO ARTHUR GAZ, RULER OF THE GAZ EMPIRE.
THE SILVER-HAIRED GIRL WHO HIRED YOU...

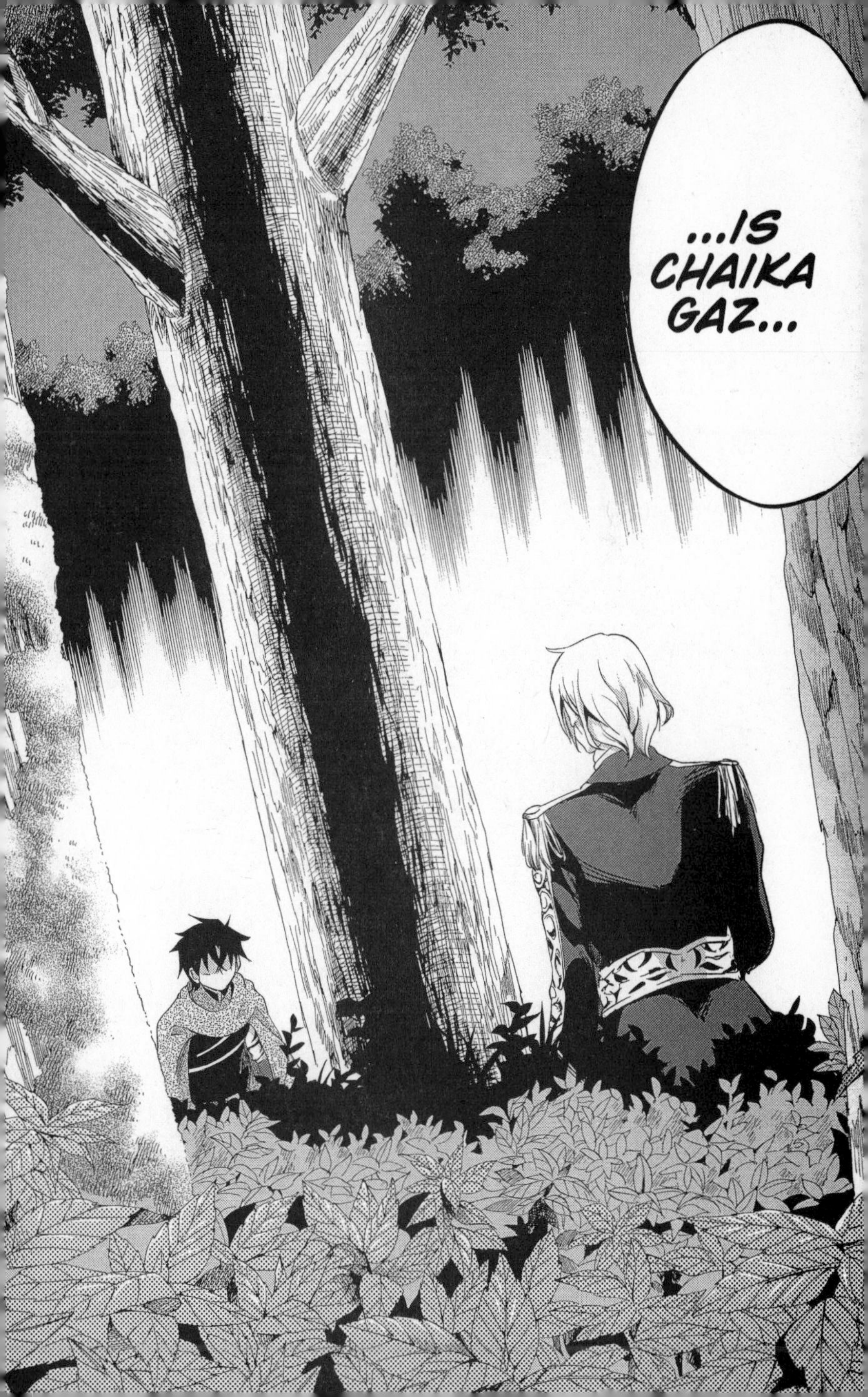
...IS CHAIKA GAZ...

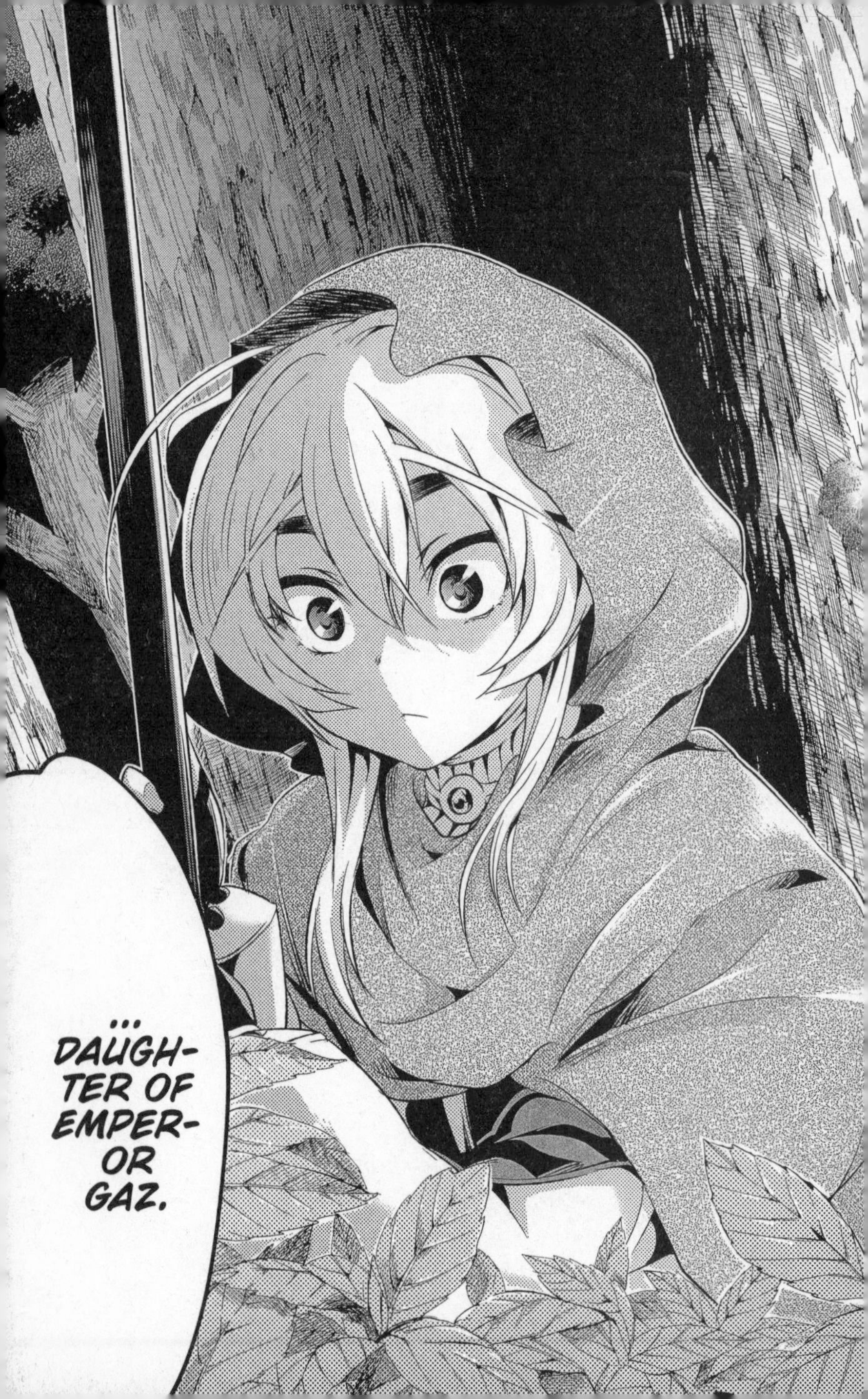
...DAUGHTER OF EMPEROR GAZ.

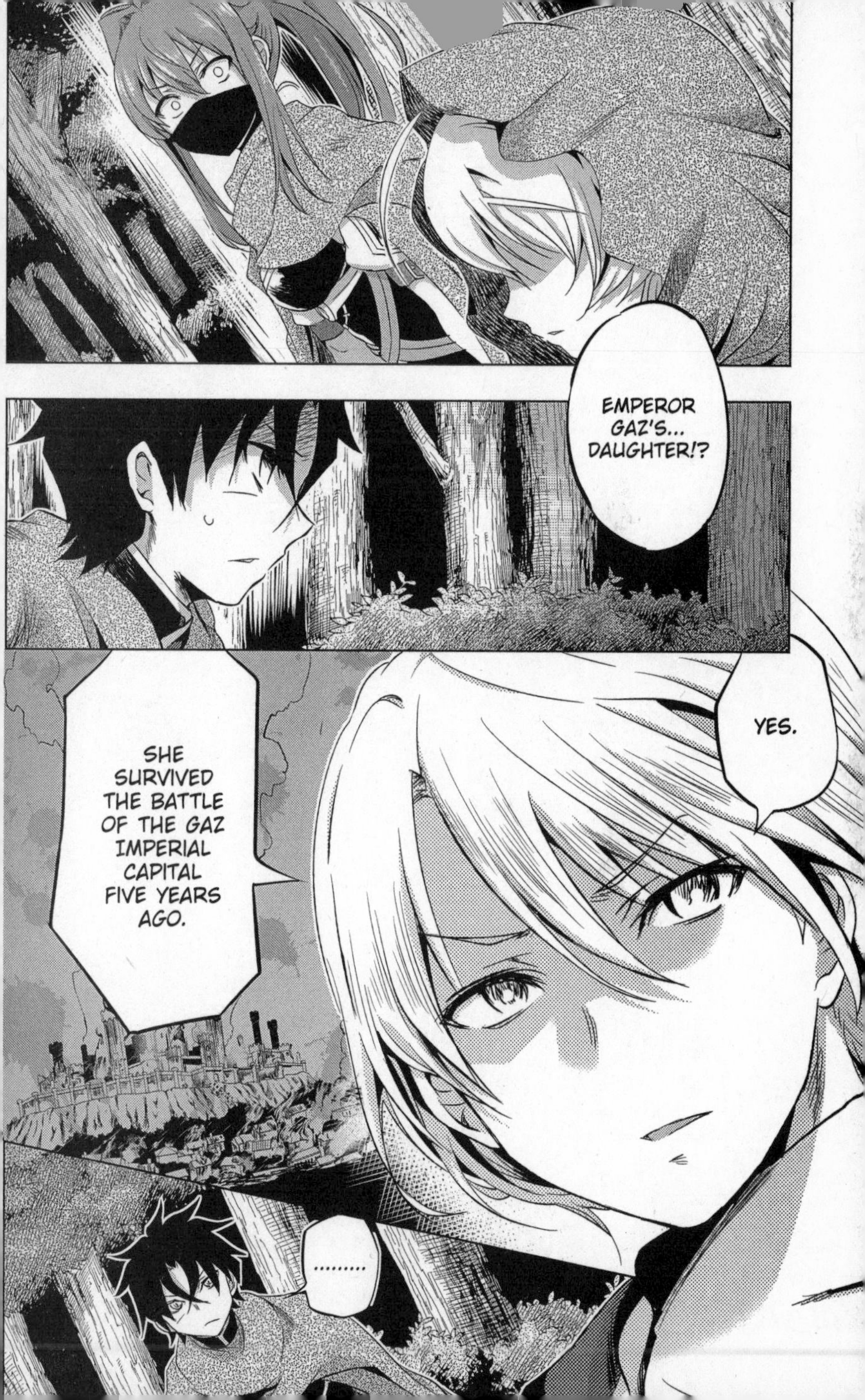
EMPEROR GAZ'S... DAUGHTER!?
YES.
SHE SURVIVED THE BATTLE OF THE GAZ IMPERIAL CAPITAL FIVE YEARS AGO.
....

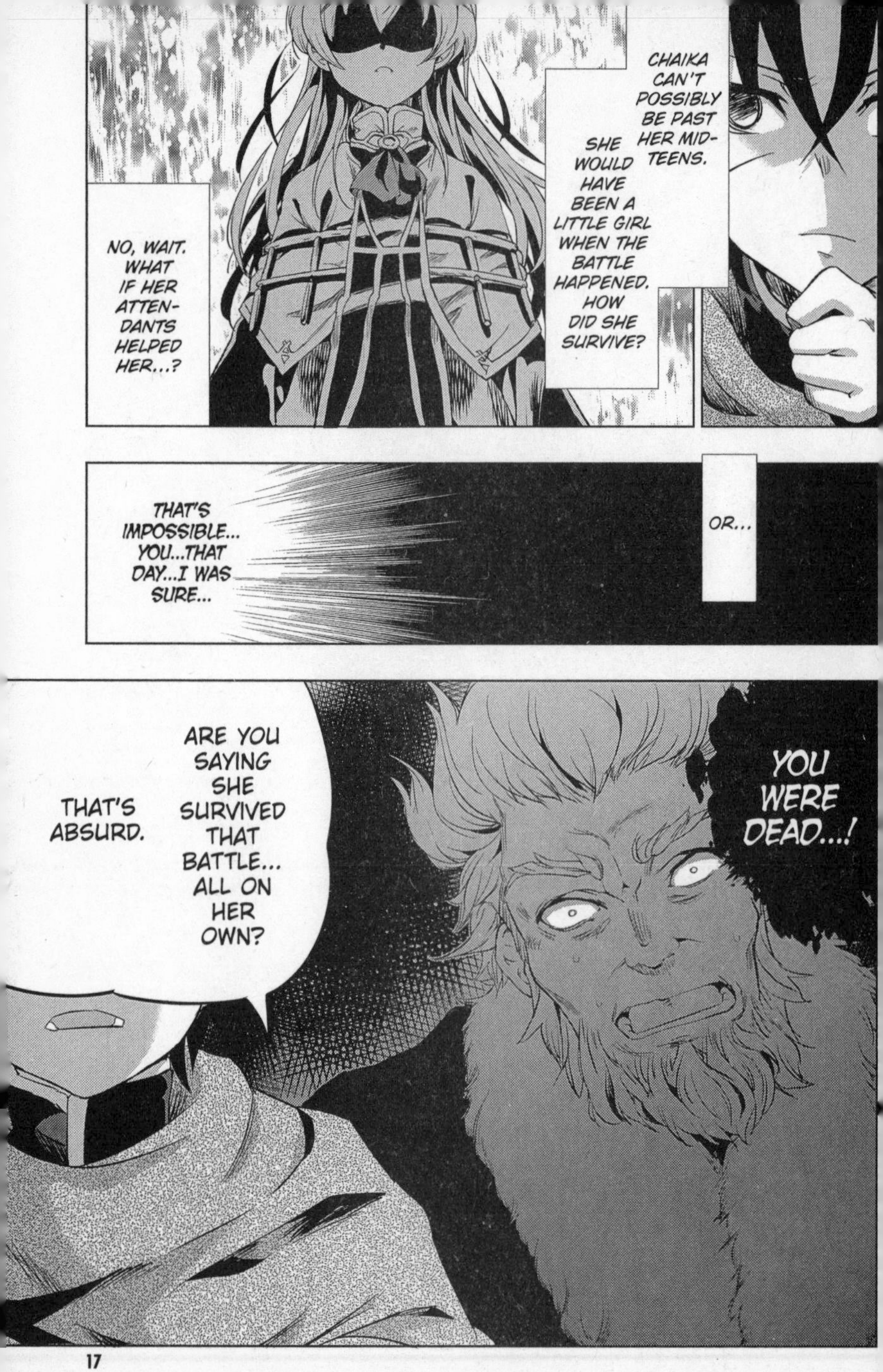
CHAIKA CAN'T POSSIBLY BE PAST HER MID-TEENS.
SHE WOULD HAVE BEEN A LITTLE GIRL WHEN THE BATTLE HAPPENED. HOW DID SHE SURVIVE?
NO, WAIT. WHAT IF HER ATTEN-DANTS HELPED HER...?
OR...
THAT'S IMPOSSIBLE... YOU...THAT DAY...I WAS SURE...
YOU WERE DEAD...!
ARE YOU SAYING SHE SURVIVED THAT BATTLE... ALL ON HER OWN?
THAT'S ABSURD.

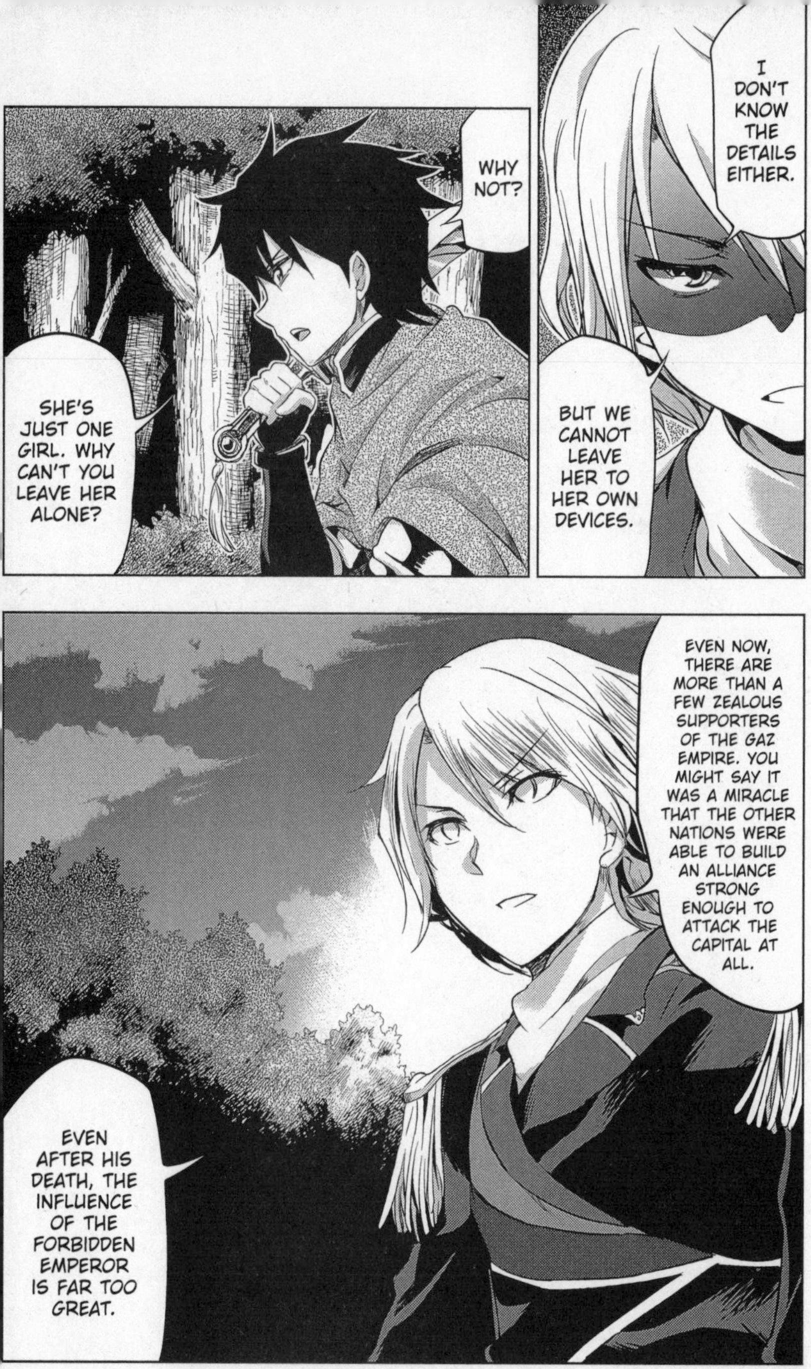
I DON'T KNOW THE DETAILS EITHER.
BUT WE CANNOT LEAVE HER TO HER OWN DEVICES.
WHY NOT?
SHE'S JUST ONE GIRL. WHY CAN'T YOU LEAVE HER ALONE?
EVEN NOW, THERE ARE MORE THAN A FEW ZEALOUS SUPPORTERS OF THE GAZ EMPIRE. YOU MIGHT SAY IT WAS A MIRACLE THAT THE OTHER NATIONS WERE ABLE TO BUILD AN ALLIANCE STRONG ENOUGH TO ATTACK THE CAPITAL AT ALL.
EVEN AFTER HIS DEATH, THE INFLUENCE OF THE FORBIDDEN EMPEROR IS FAR TOO GREAT.

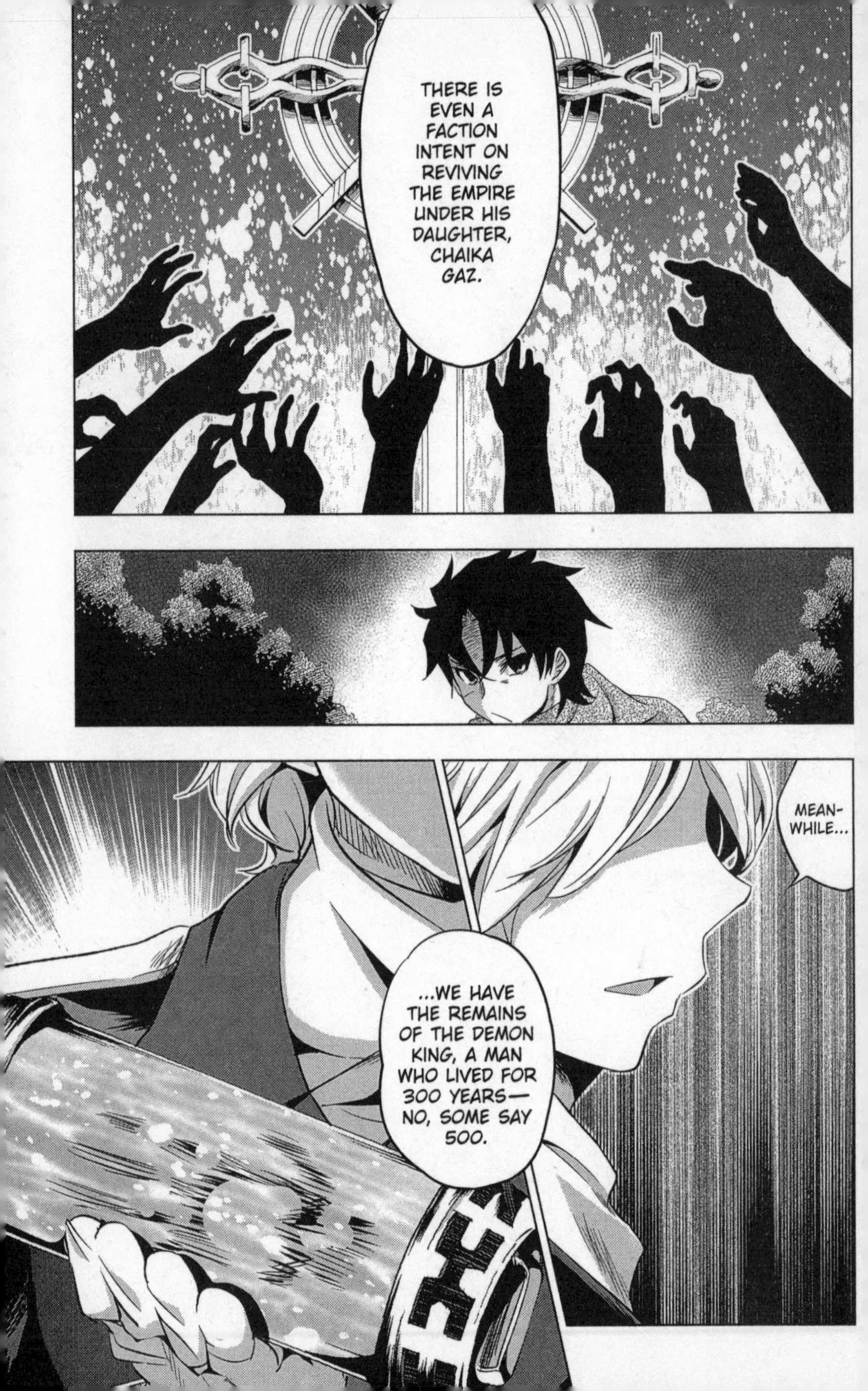
THERE IS EVEN A FACTION INTENT ON REVIVING THE EMPIRE UNDER HIS DAUGHTER, CHAIKA GAZ.
MEAN-WHILE...
...WE HAVE THE REMAINS OF THE DEMON KING, A MAN WHO LIVED FOR 300 YEARS— NO, SOME SAY 500.

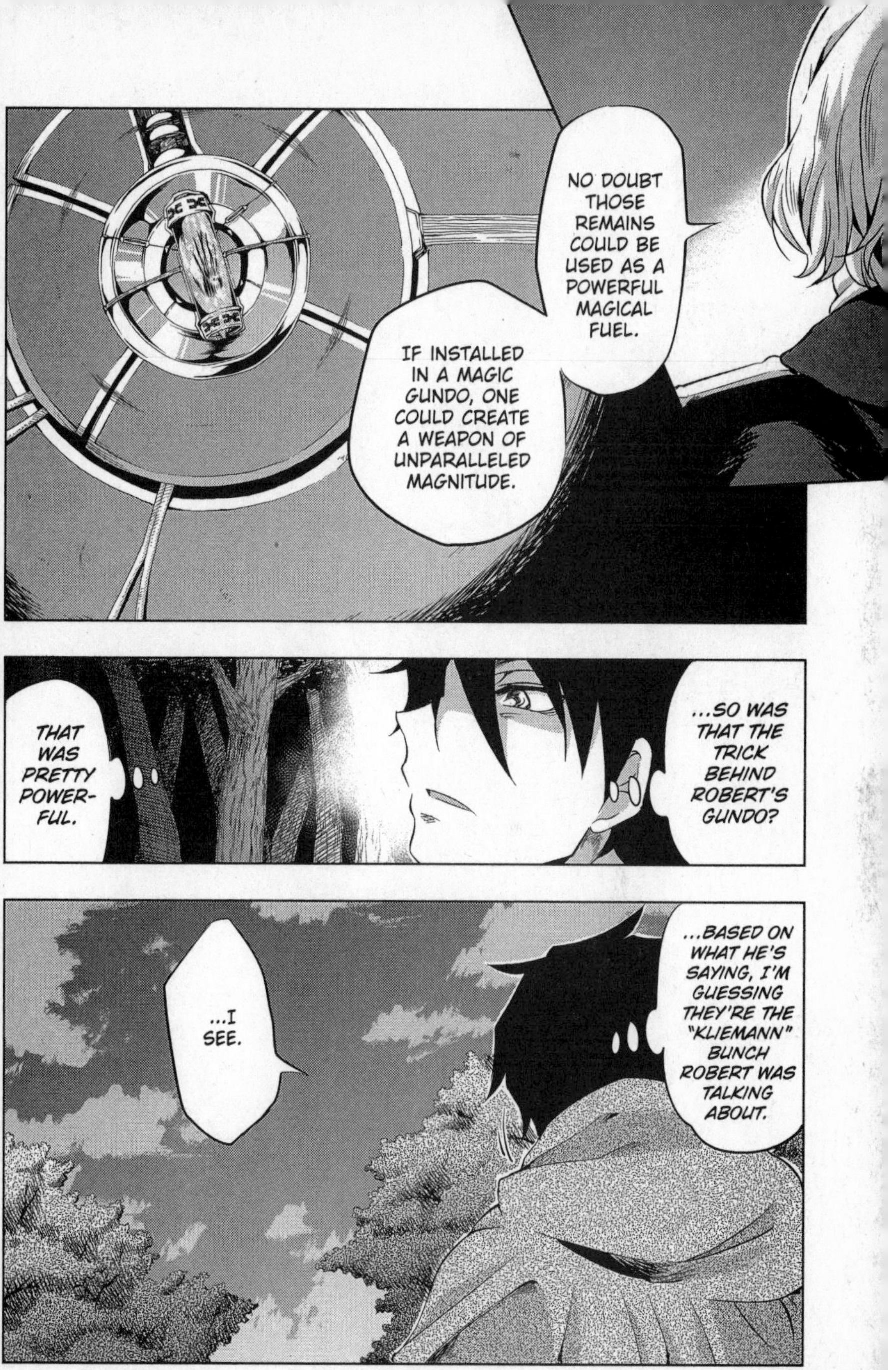
NO DOUBT THOSE REMAINS COULD BE USED AS A POWERFUL MAGICAL FUEL.
IF INSTALLED IN A MAGIC GUNDO, ONE COULD CREATE A WEAPON OF UNPARALLELED MAGNITUDE.
...SO WAS THAT THE TRICK BEHIND ROBERT'S GUNDO?
THAT WAS PRETTY POWER-FUL.
...BASED ON WHAT HE'S SAYING, I'M GUESSING THEY'RE THE "KLIEMANN" BUNCH ROBERT WAS TALKING ABOUT.
...I SEE.

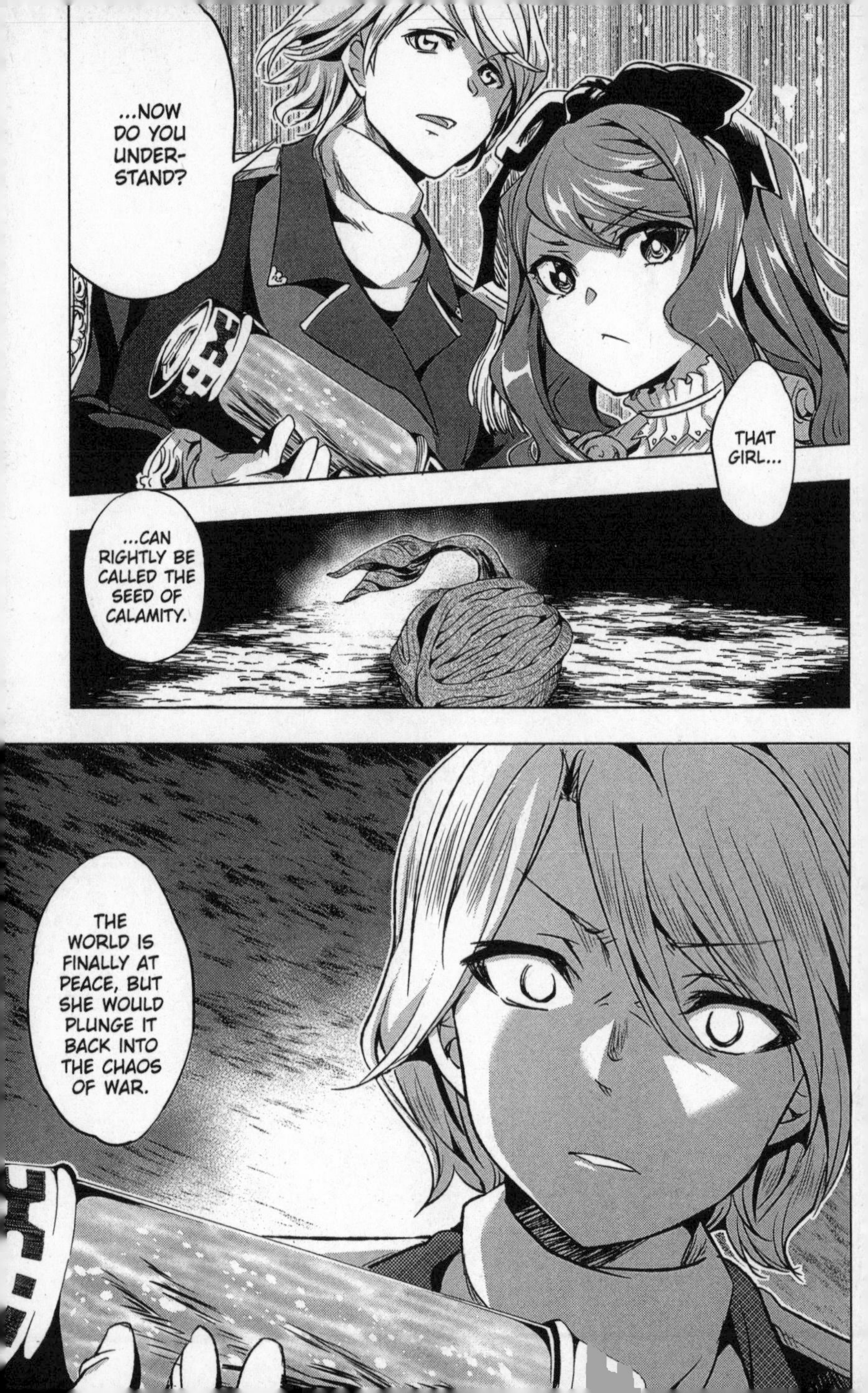
...NOW DO YOU UNDER-STAND?
THAT GIRL...
...CAN RIGHTLY BE CALLED THE SEED OF CALAMITY.
THE WORLD IS FINALLY AT PEACE, BUT SHE WOULD PLUNGE IT BACK INTO THE CHAOS OF WAR.

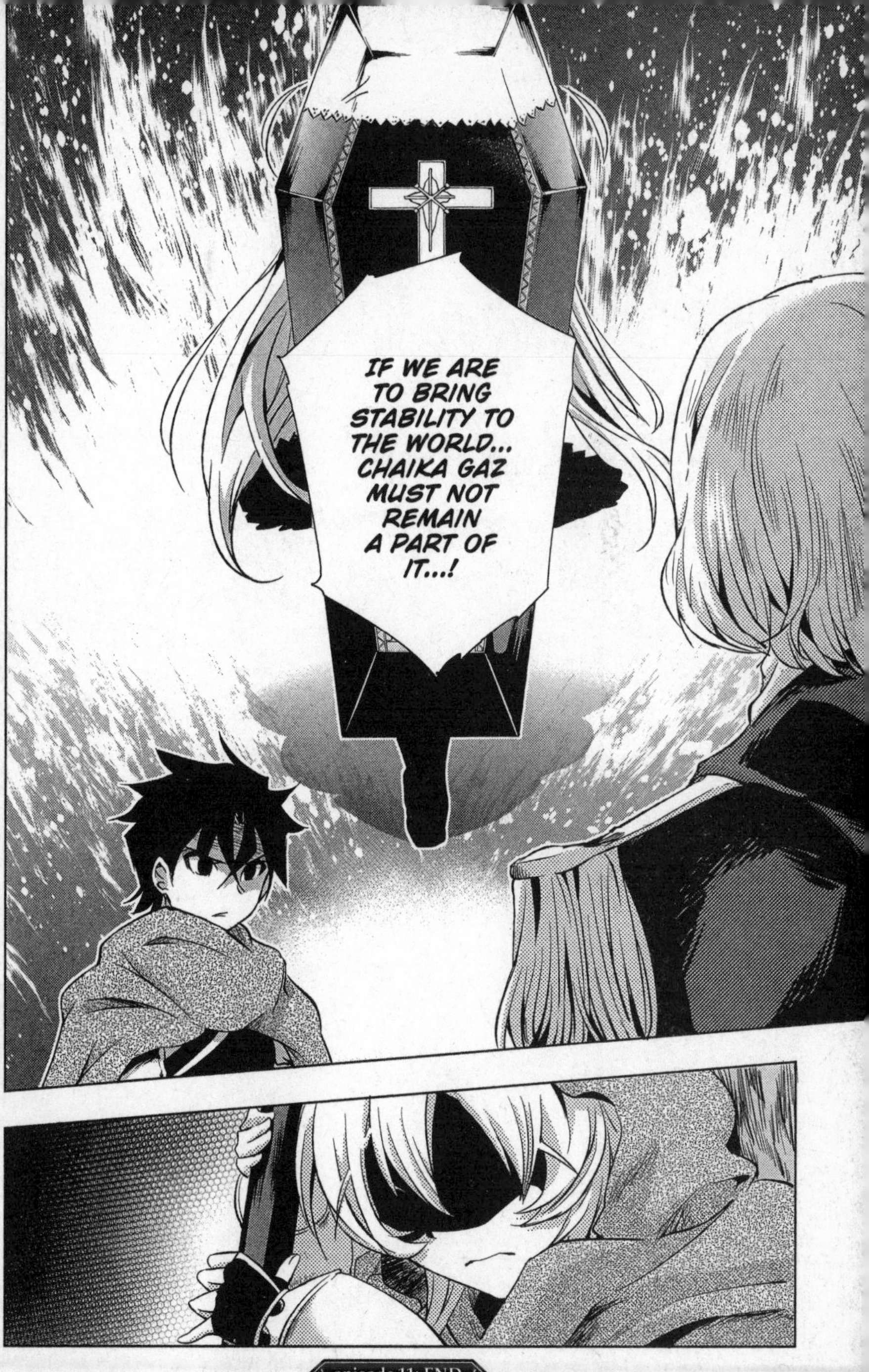
IF WE ARE TO BRING STABILITY TO THE WORLD... CHAIKA GAZ MUST NOT REMAIN A PART OF IT...!

episode 11: END

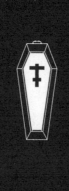

CHAIKA: THE COFFIN PRINCESS

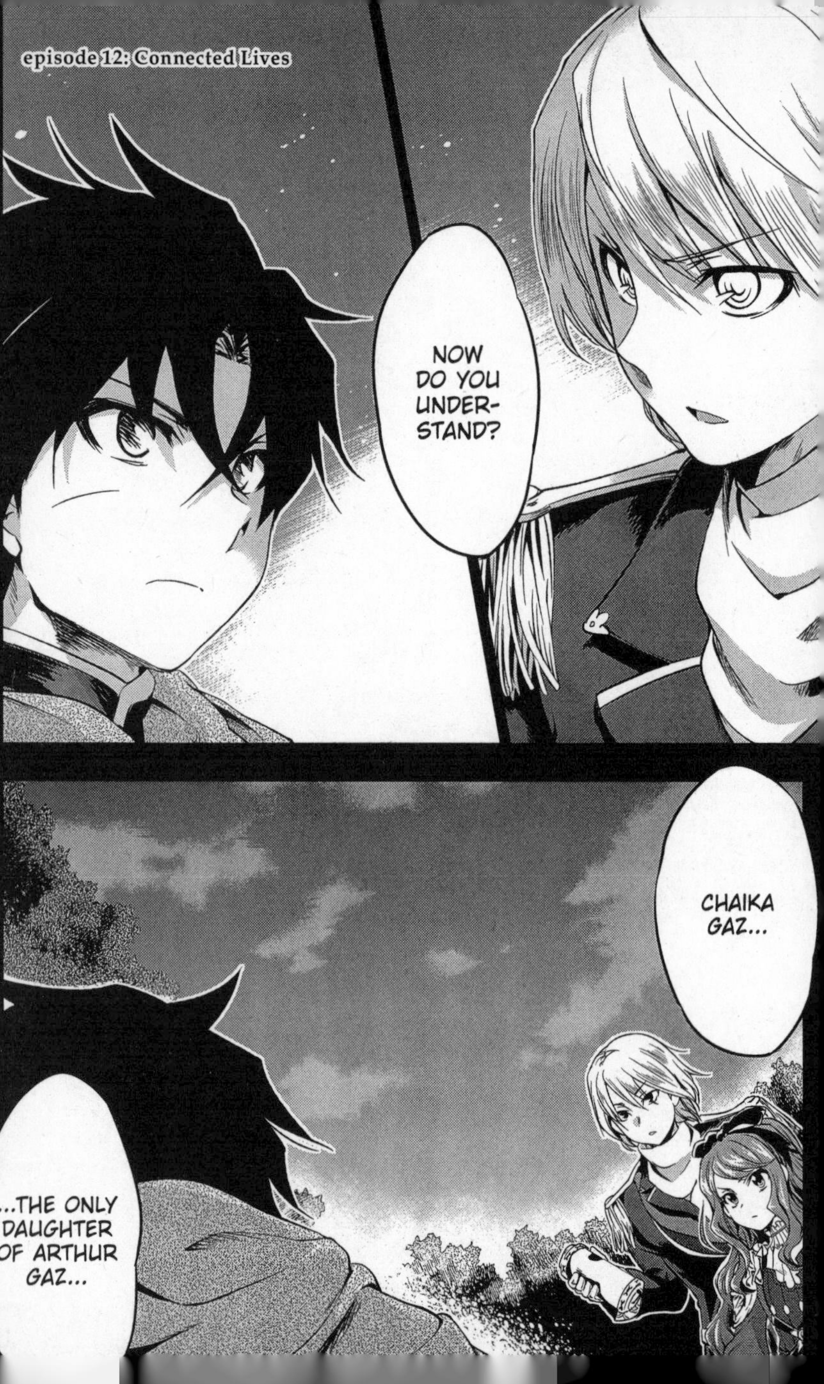
episode 12: Connected Lives
NOW DO YOU UNDER-STAND?
CHAIKA GAZ...
...THE ONLY DAUGHTER OF ARTHUR GAZ...

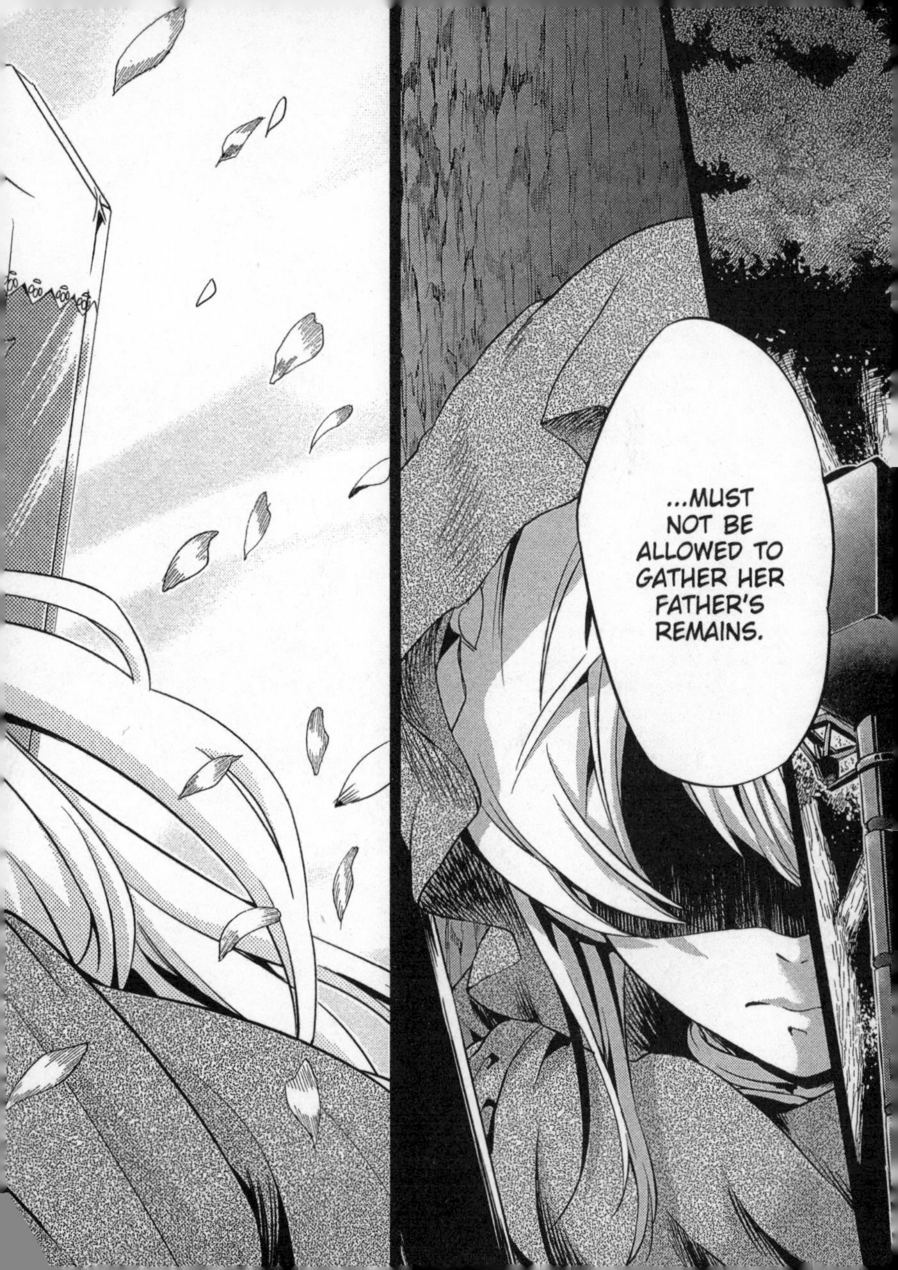
...MUST NOT BE ALLOWED TO GATHER HER FATHER'S REMAINS.

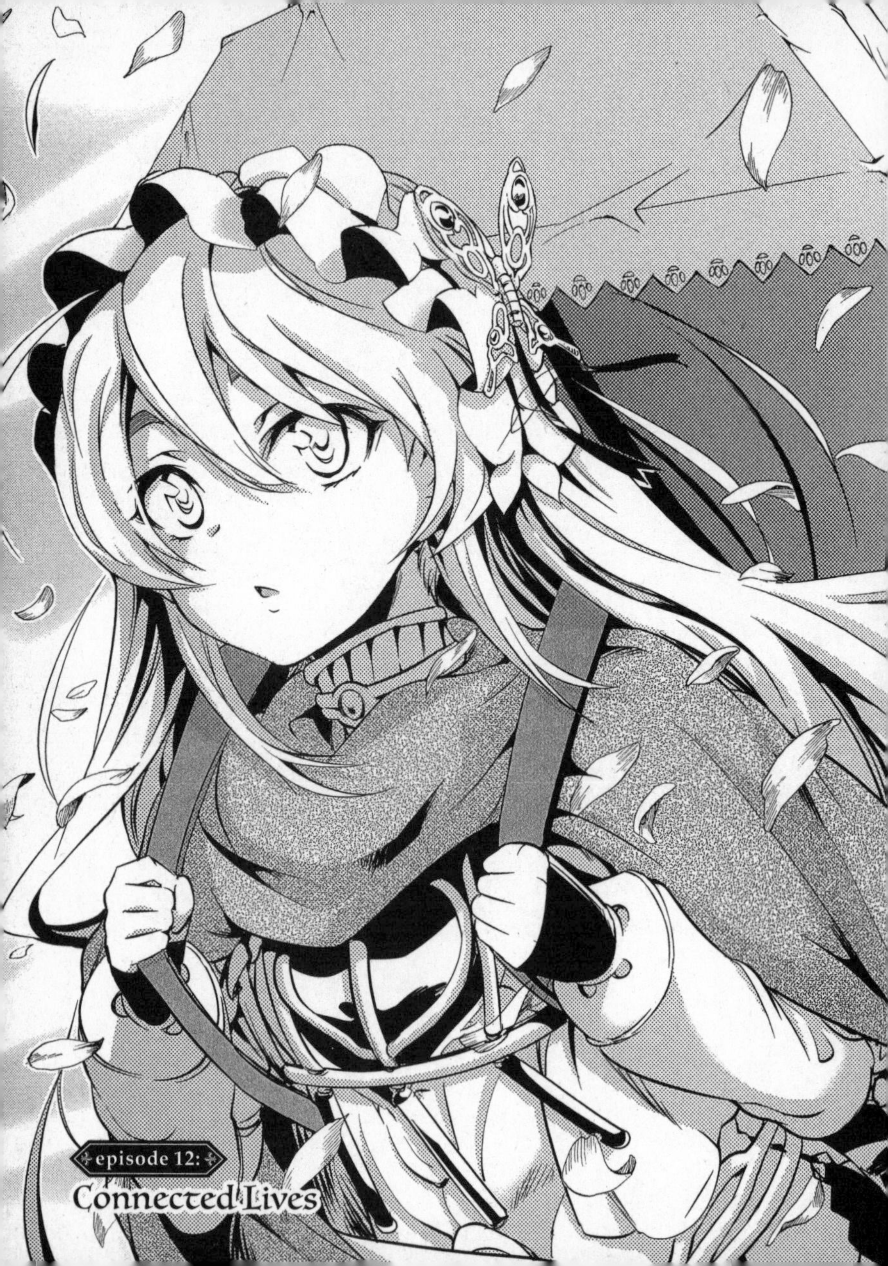
episode 12:
Connected Lives

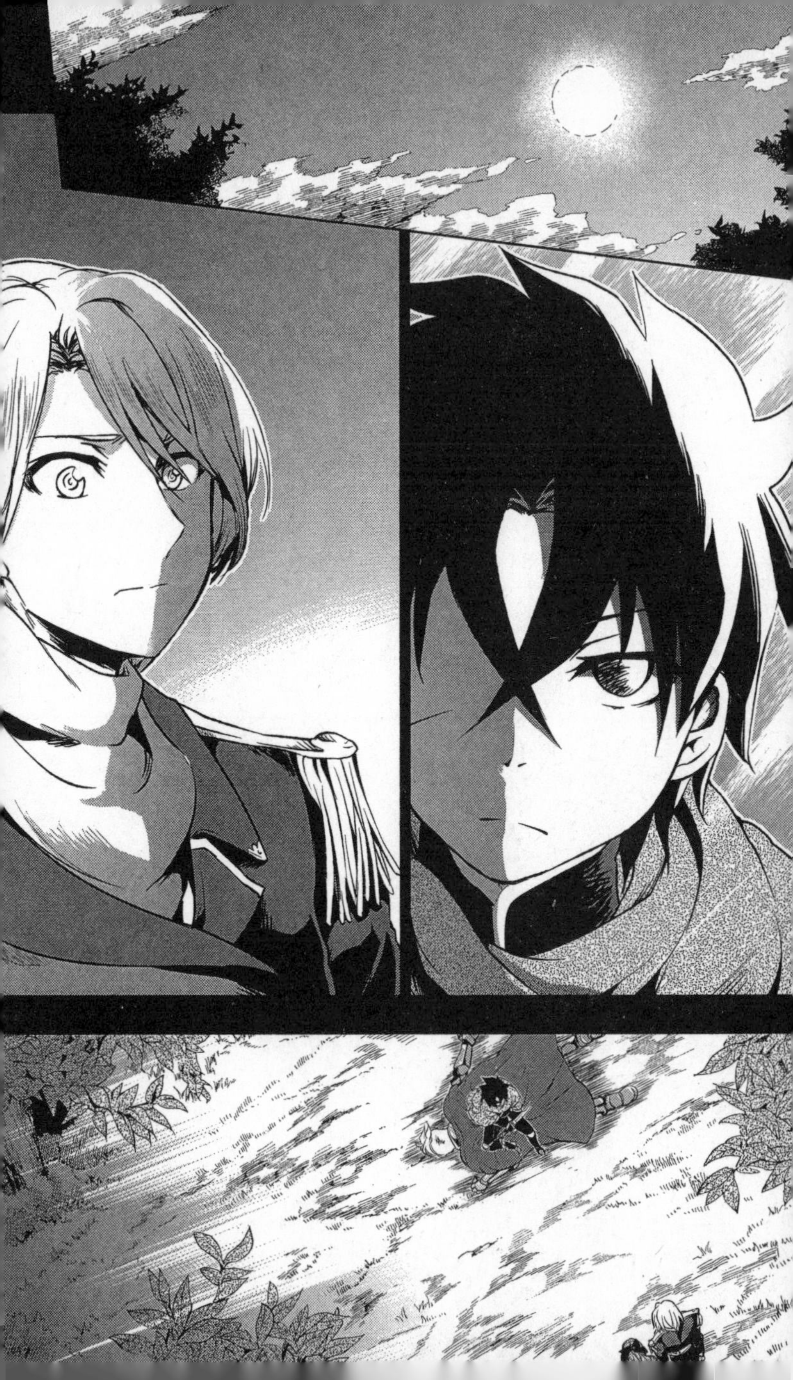

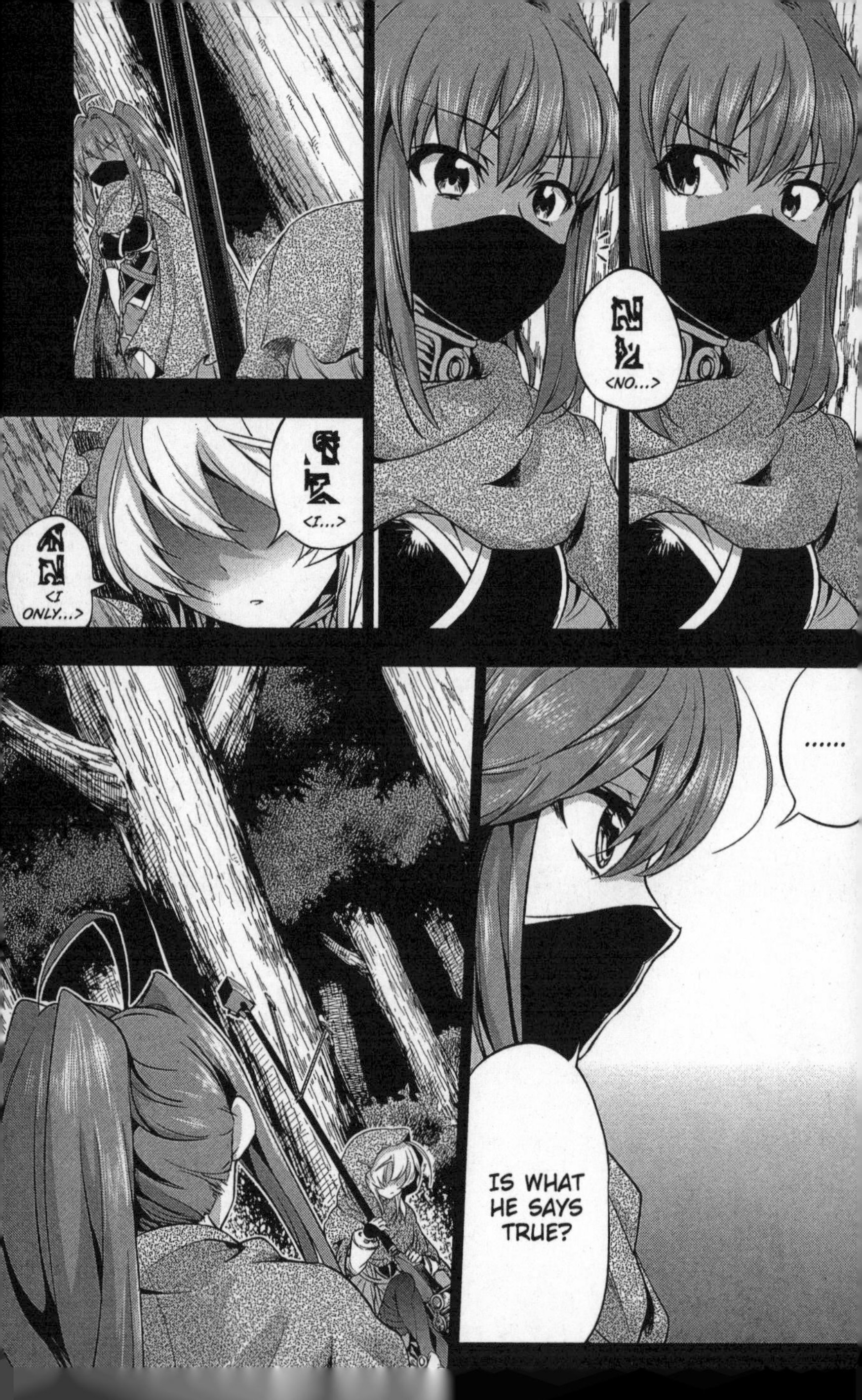

<NO...>
<I...>
<I ONLY...>
......
IS WHAT HE SAYS TRUE?

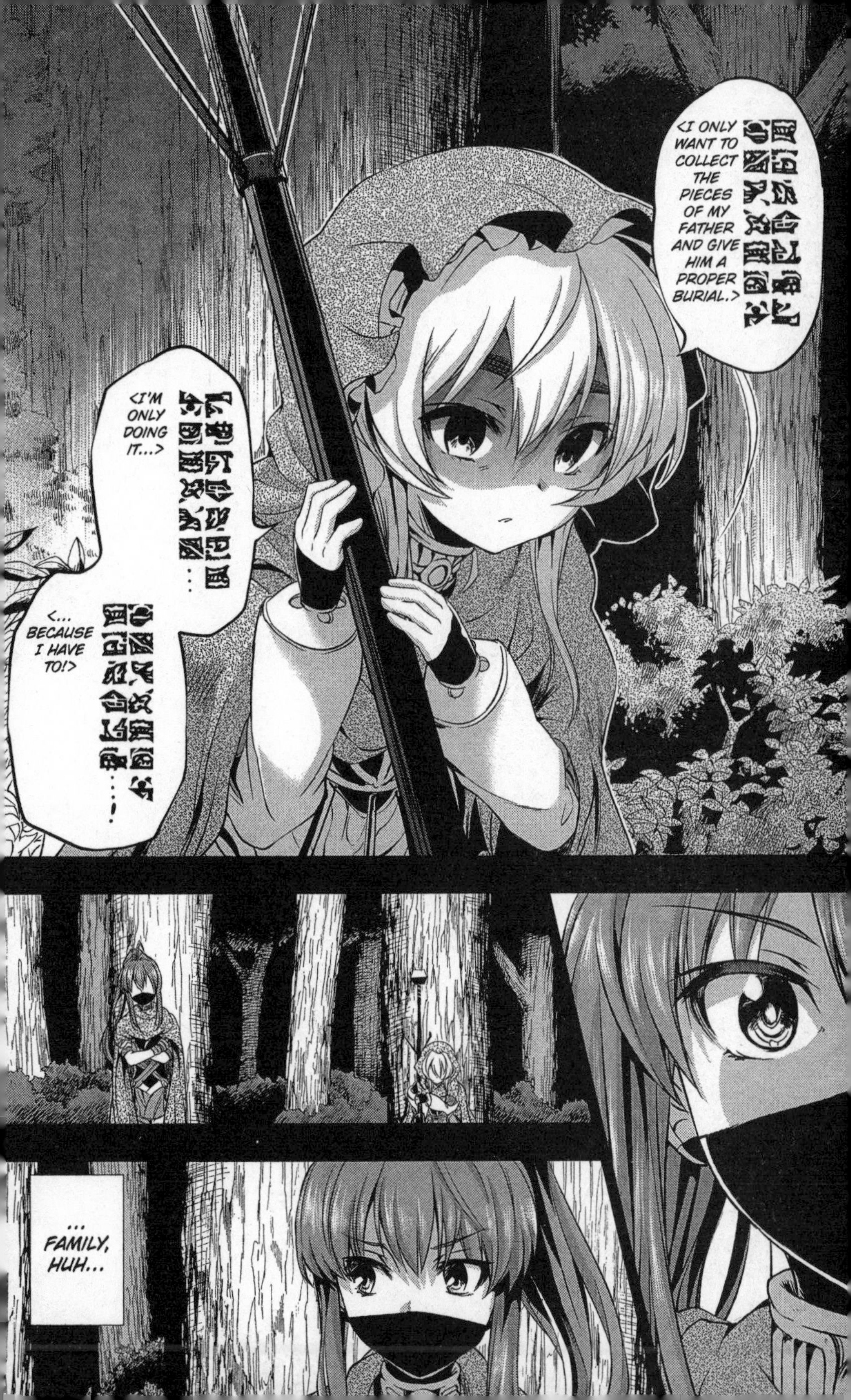
<I ONLY WANT TO COLLECT THE PIECES OF MY FATHER AND GIVE HIM A PROPER BURIAL.>
<I'M ONLY DOING IT...>
<...BECAUSE I HAVE TO!>
...FAMILY, HUH...

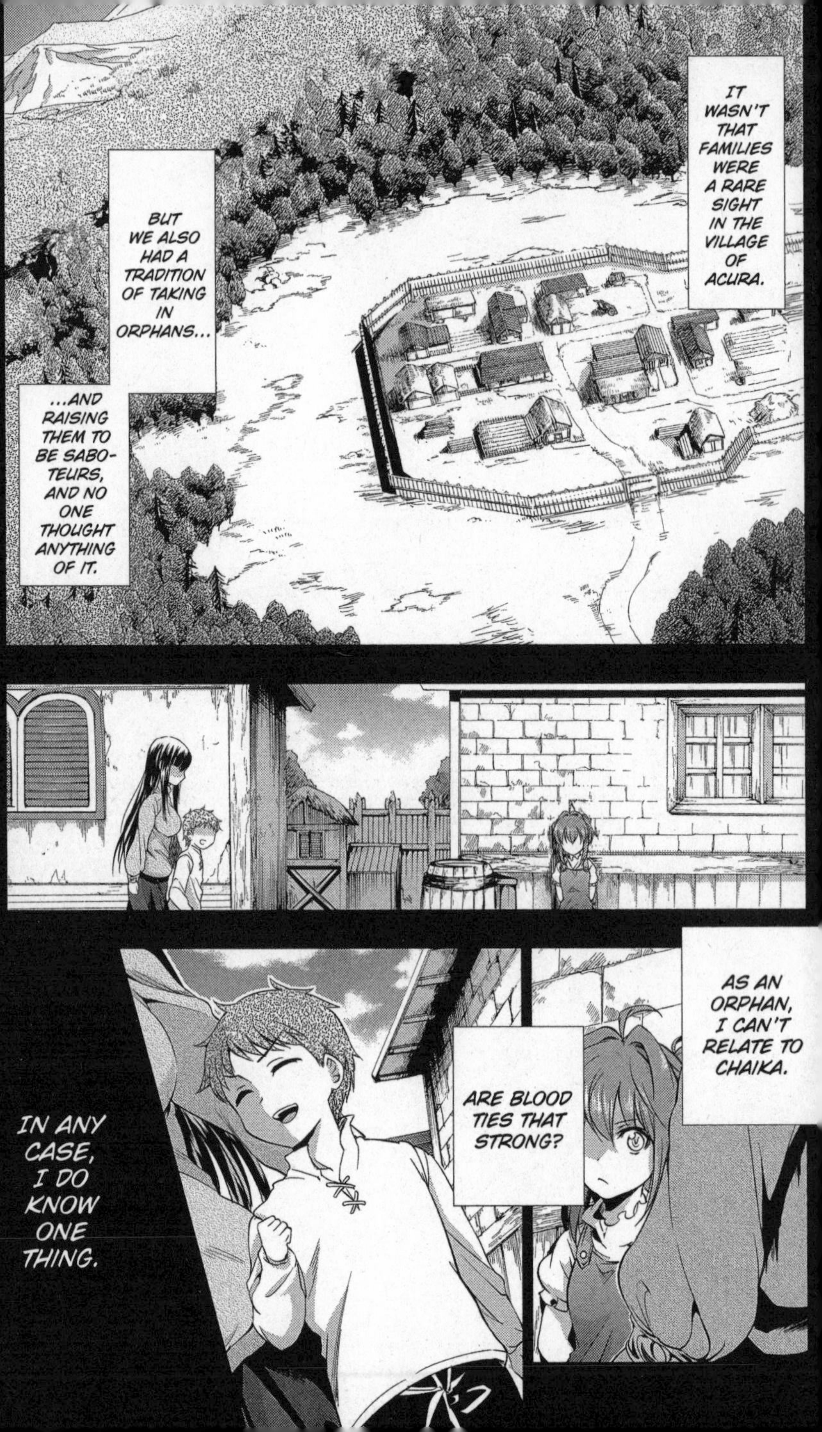
IT WASN'T THAT FAMILIES WERE A RARE SIGHT IN THE VILLAGE OF ACURA.
BUT WE ALSO HAD A TRADITION OF TAKING IN ORPHANS...
...AND RAISING THEM TO BE SABO-TEURS, AND NO ONE THOUGHT ANYTHING OF IT.
AS AN ORPHAN, I CAN'T RELATE TO CHAIKA.
ARE BLOOD TIES THAT STRONG?
IN ANY CASE, I DO KNOW ONE THING.

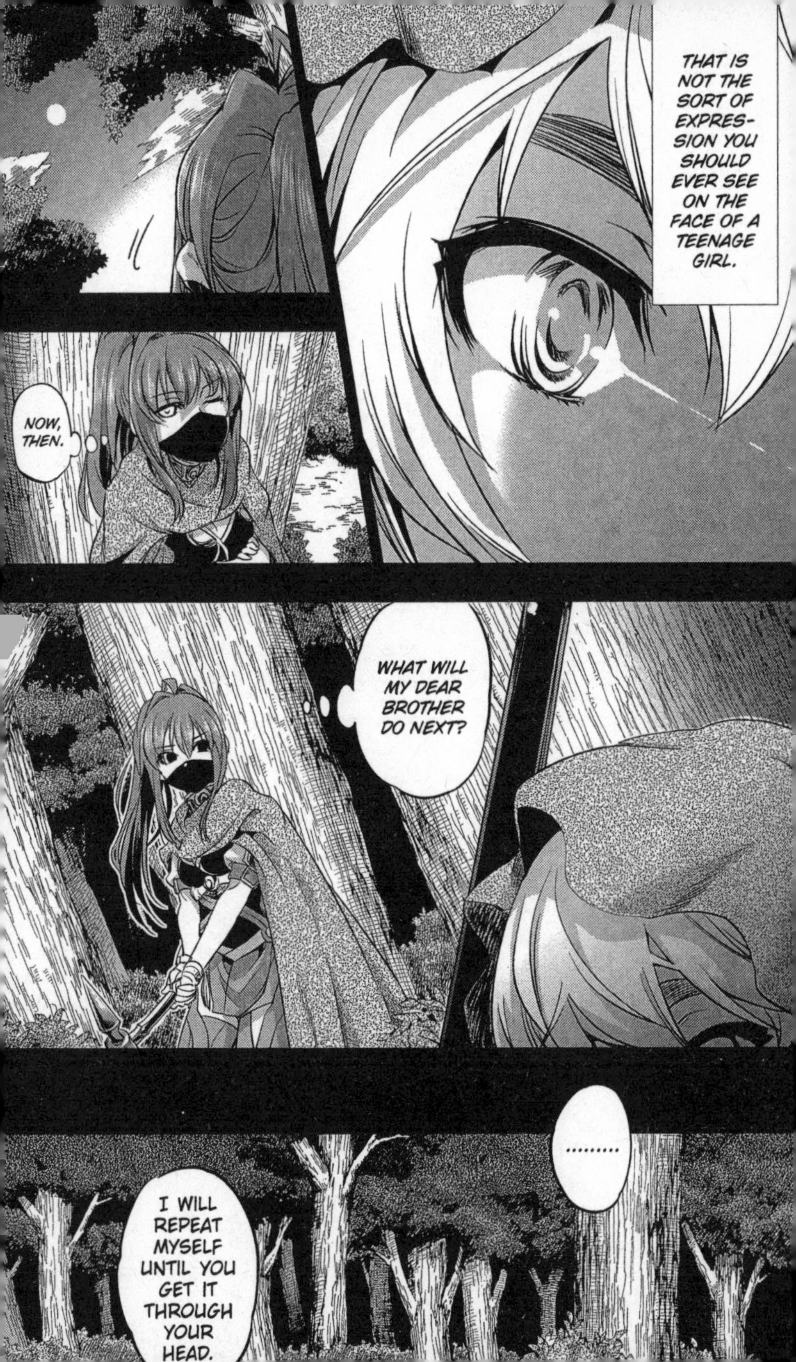
THAT IS NOT THE SORT OF EXPRESSION YOU SHOULD EVER SEE ON THE FACE OF A TEENAGE GIRL.
NOW, THEN.
WHAT WILL MY DEAR BROTHER DO NEXT?
....
I WILL REPEAT MYSELF UNTIL YOU GET IT THROUGH YOUR HEAD.

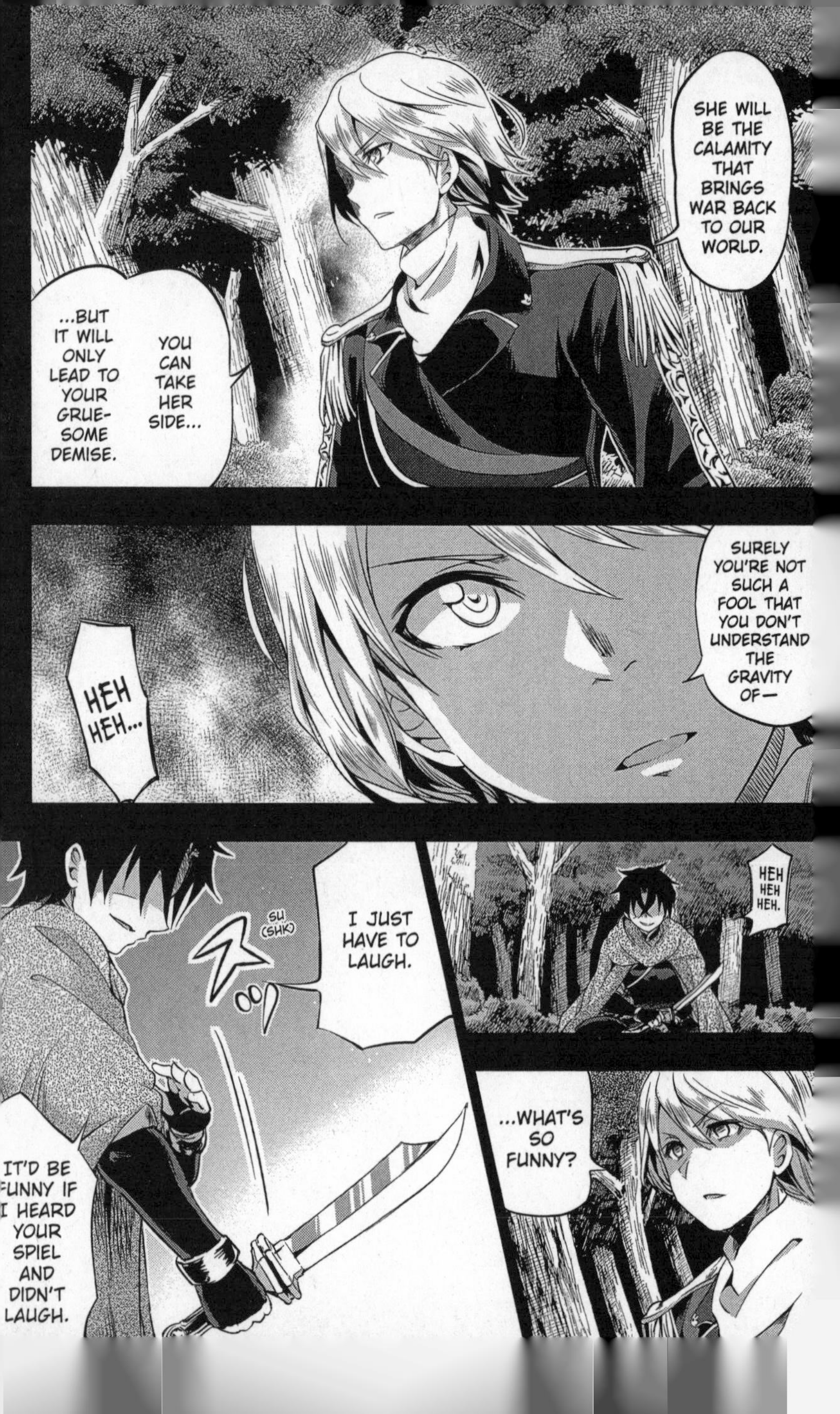
SHE WILL BE THE CALAMITY THAT BRINGS WAR BACK TO OUR WORLD.
YOU CAN TAKE HER SIDE...
...BUT IT WILL ONLY LEAD TO YOUR GRUESOME DEMISE.
SURELY YOU'RE NOT SUCH A FOOL THAT YOU DON'T UNDERSTAND THE GRAVITY OF—
HEH HEH...
HEH HEH HEH.
...WHAT'S SO FUNNY?
I JUST HAVE TO LAUGH.
SU (SHK)
IT'D BE FUNNY IF I HEARD YOUR SPIEL AND DIDN'T LAUGH.

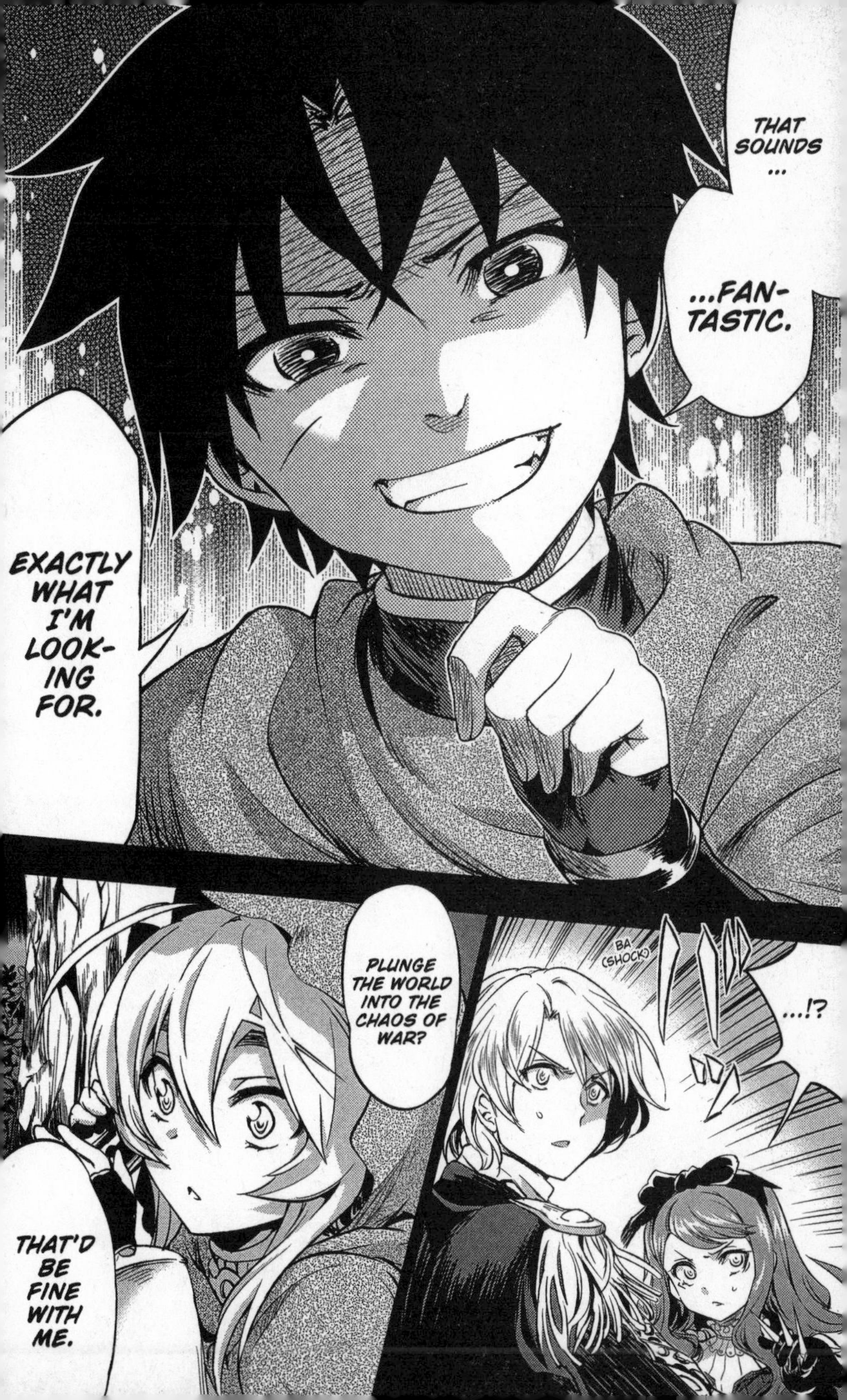
THAT SOUNDS ...
...FAN-TASTIC.
EXACTLY WHAT I'M LOOK-ING FOR.
BA (SHOCK)
...!?
PLUNGE THE WORLD INTO THE CHAOS OF WAR?
THAT'D BE FINE WITH ME.

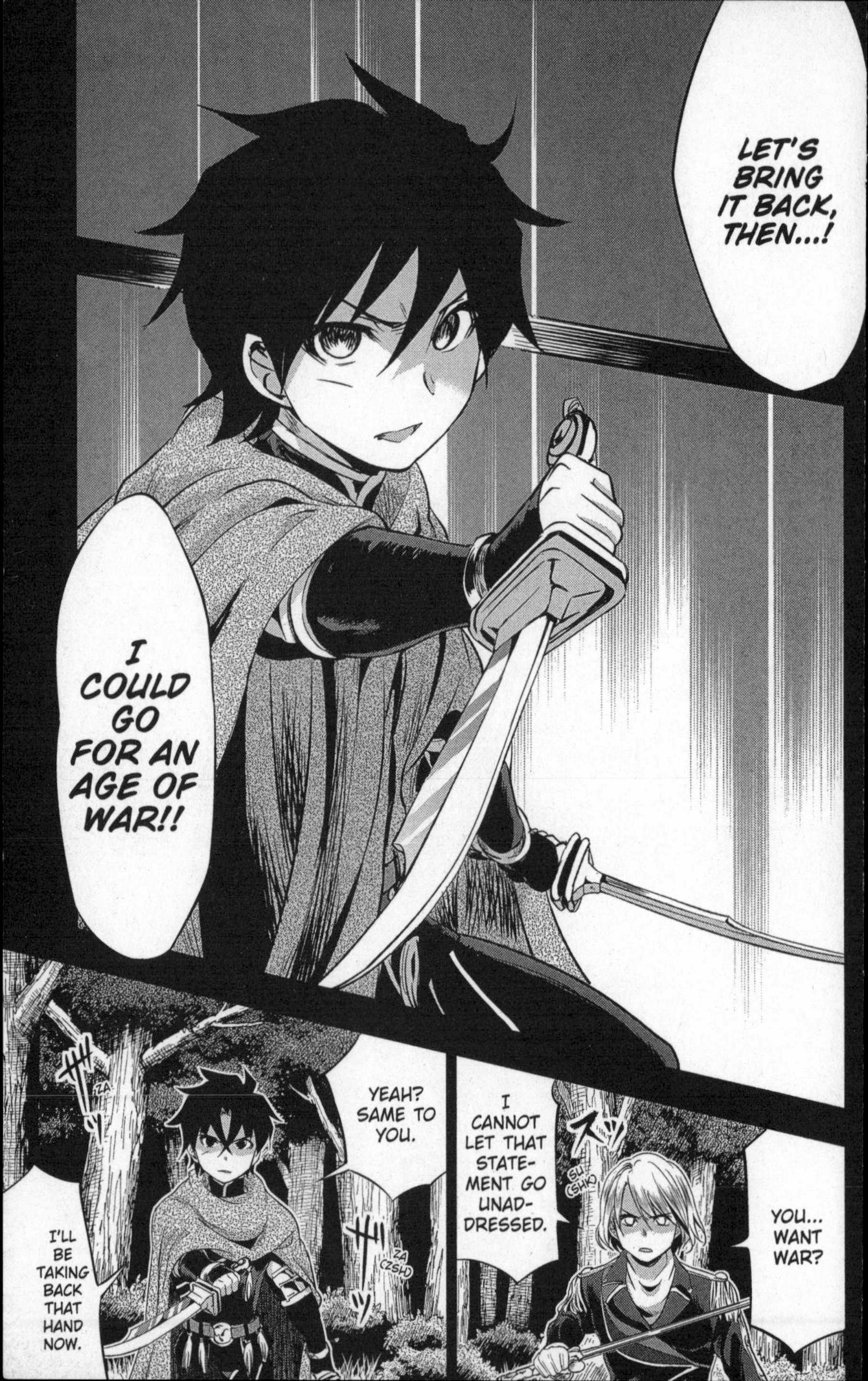
LET'S BRING IT BACK, THEN...!
I COULD GO FOR AN AGE OF WAR!!
YOU... WANT WAR?
SU (SHK)
I CANNOT LET THAT STATE-MENT GO UNAD-DRESSED.
ZA (ZSHD)
YEAH? SAME TO YOU.
ZA
I'LL BE TAKING BACK THAT HAND NOW.

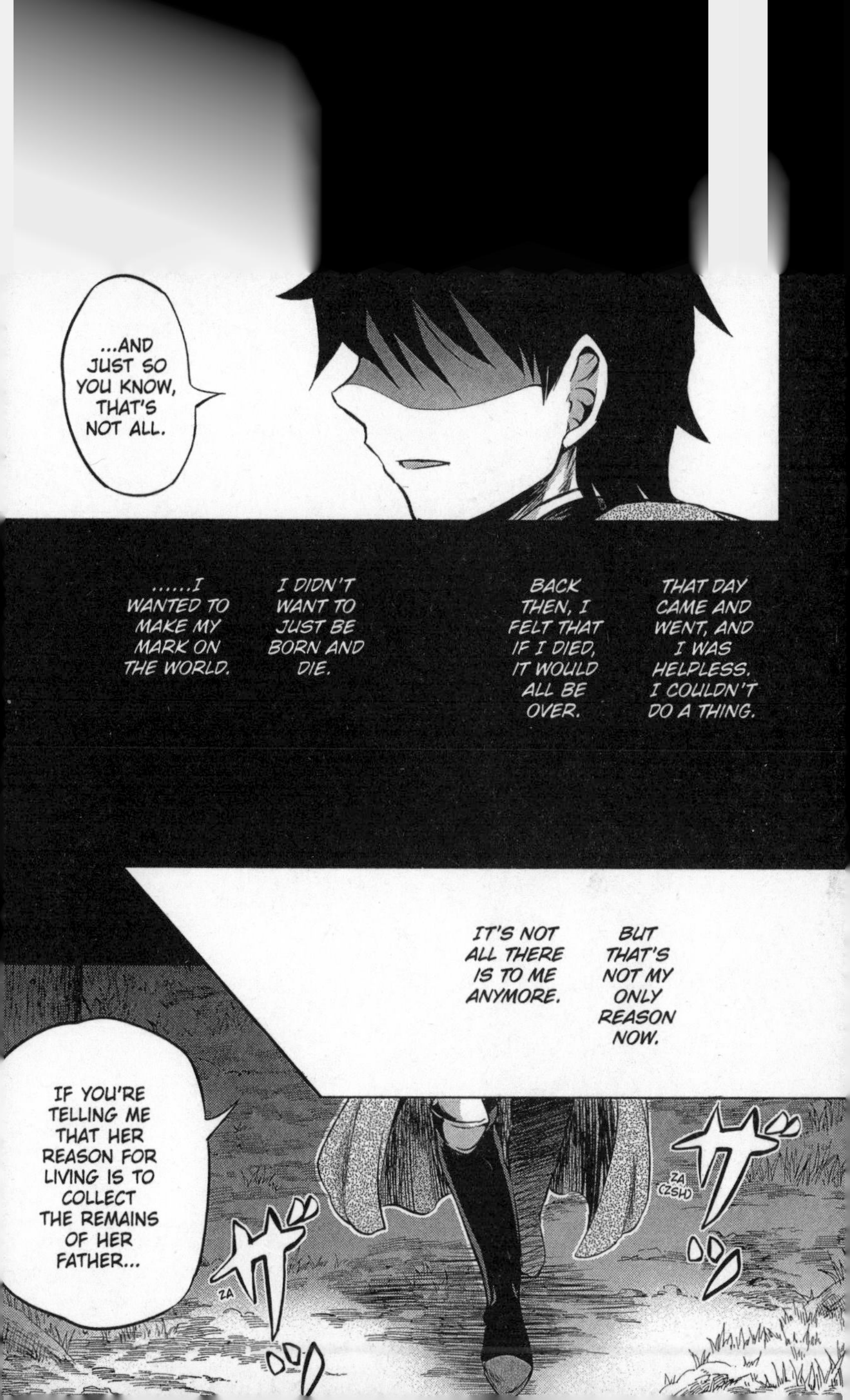
...AND JUST SO YOU KNOW, THAT'S NOT ALL.
THAT DAY CAME AND WENT, AND I WAS HELPLESS. I COULDN'T DO A THING.
BACK THEN, I FELT THAT IF I DIED, IT WOULD ALL BE OVER.
I DIDN'T WANT TO JUST BE BORN AND DIE.
......I WANTED TO MAKE MY MARK ON THE WORLD.
BUT THAT'S NOT MY ONLY REASON NOW.
IT'S NOT ALL THERE IS TO ME ANYMORE.
ZA (ZSH)
ZA
IF YOU'RE TELLING ME THAT HER REASON FOR LIVING IS TO COLLECT THE REMAINS OF HER FATHER...

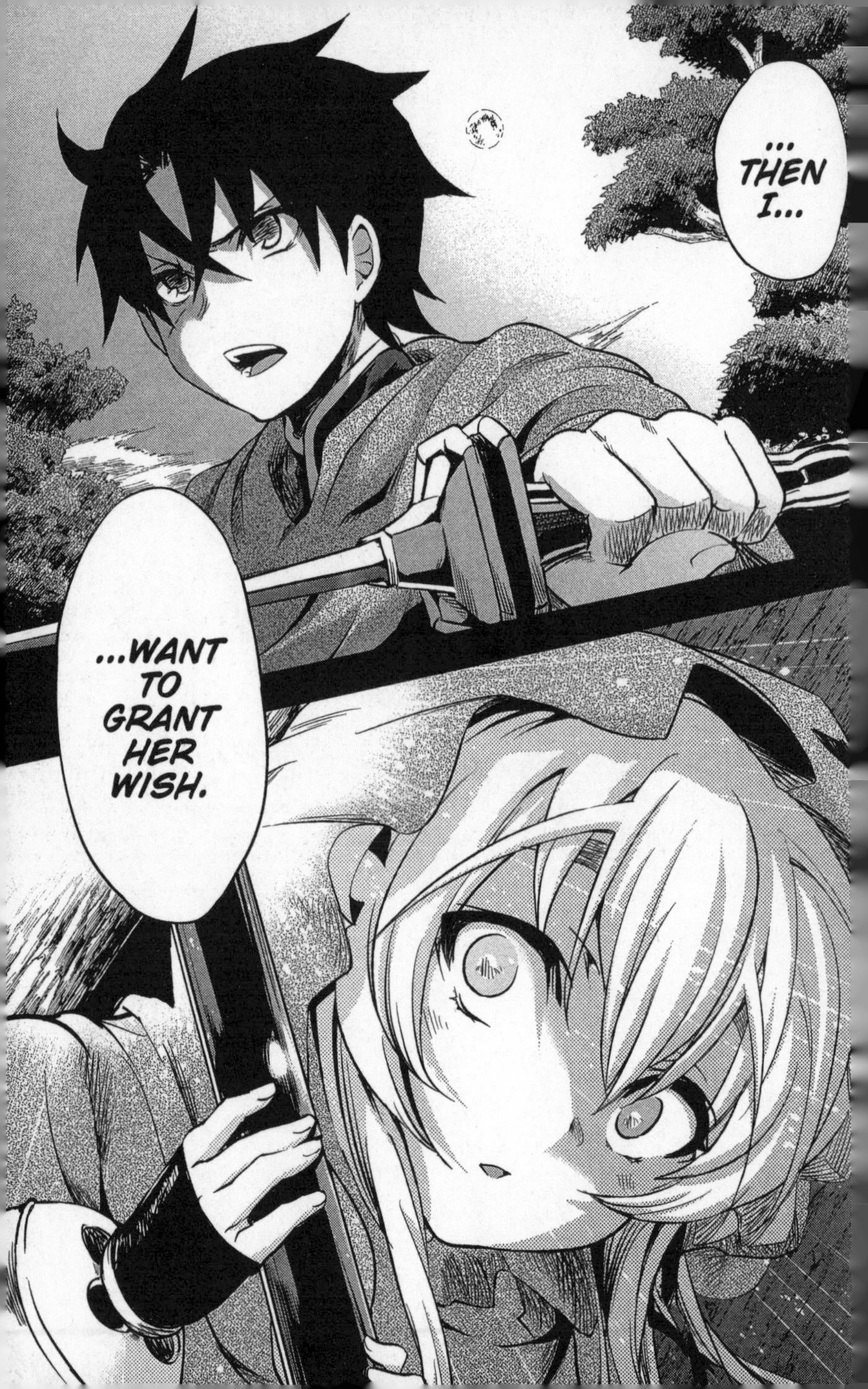
...THEN I...
...WANT TO GRANT HER WISH.

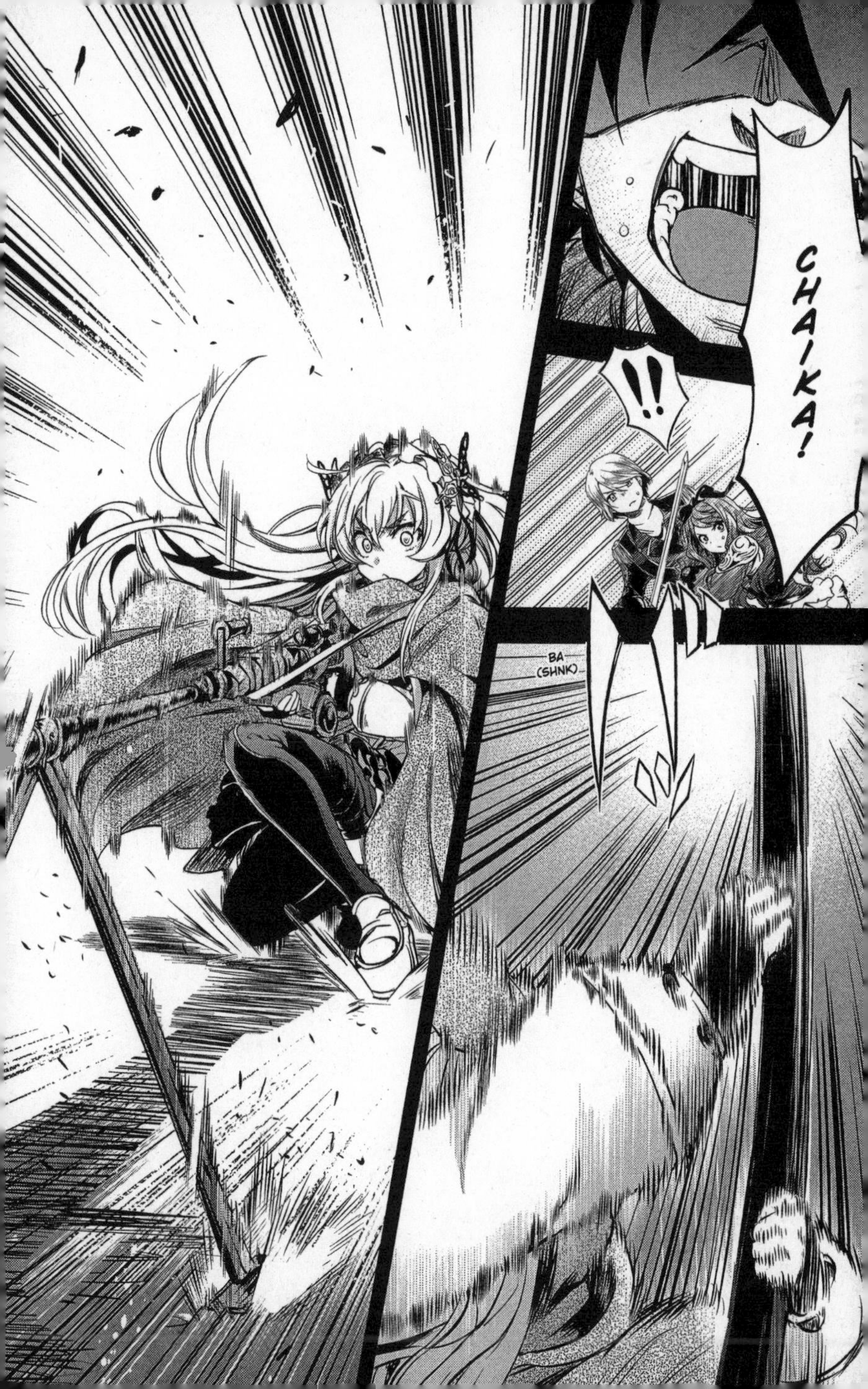
CHAIKA!
!!
BA
(SHNK)

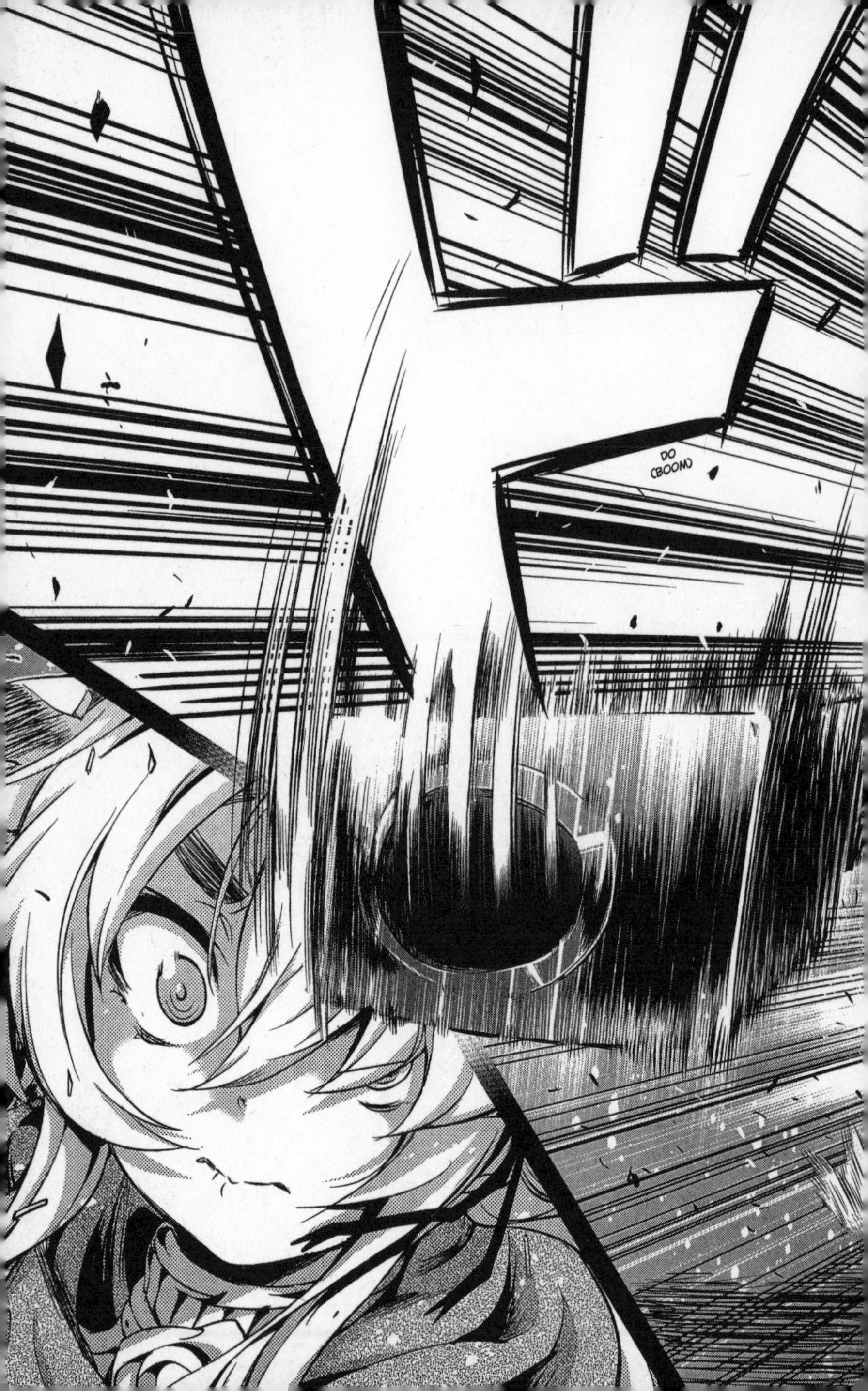
DO
(BOOM)

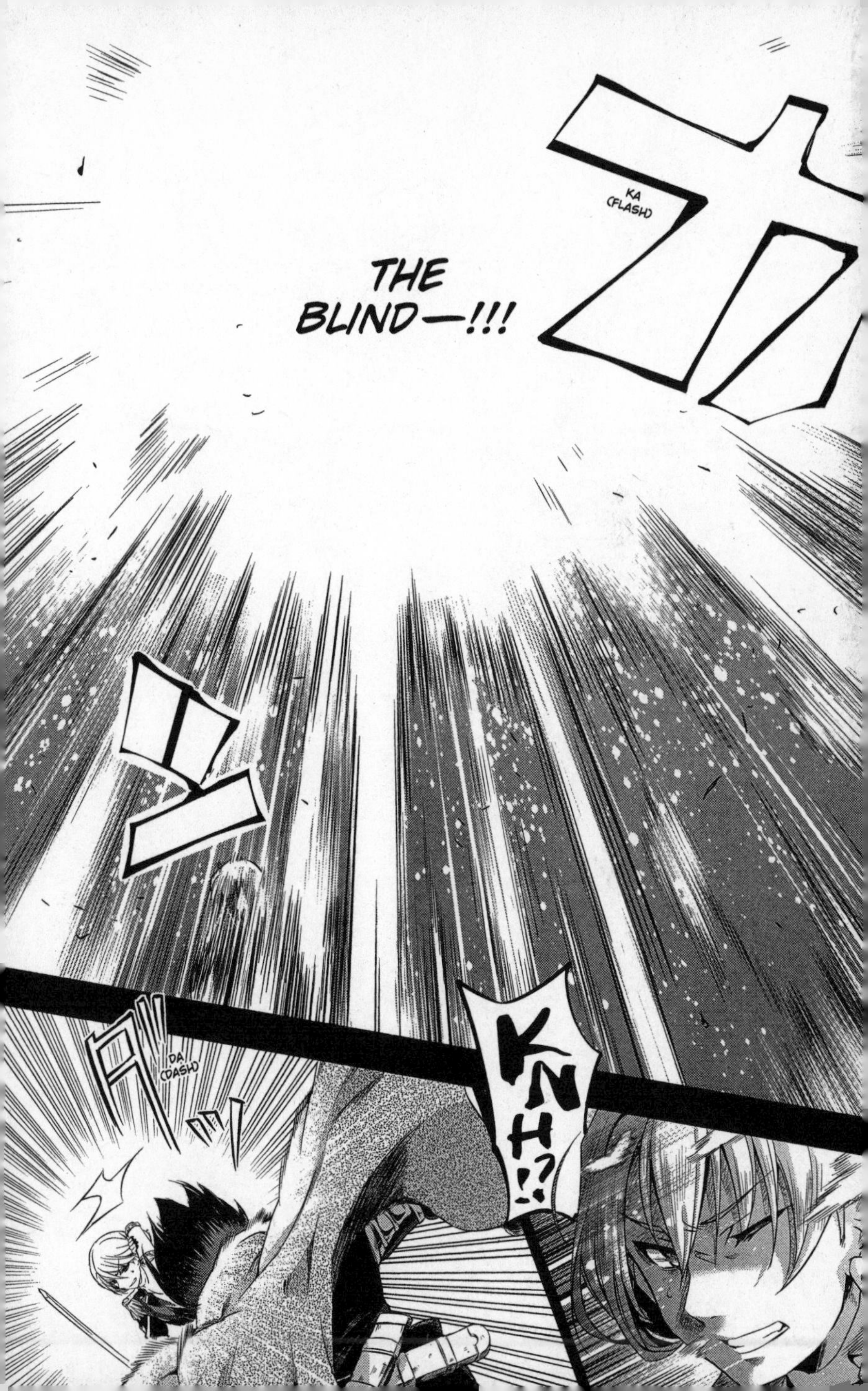
KA (FLASH)
THE BLIND—!!!
DA (DASH)
KNH?!!

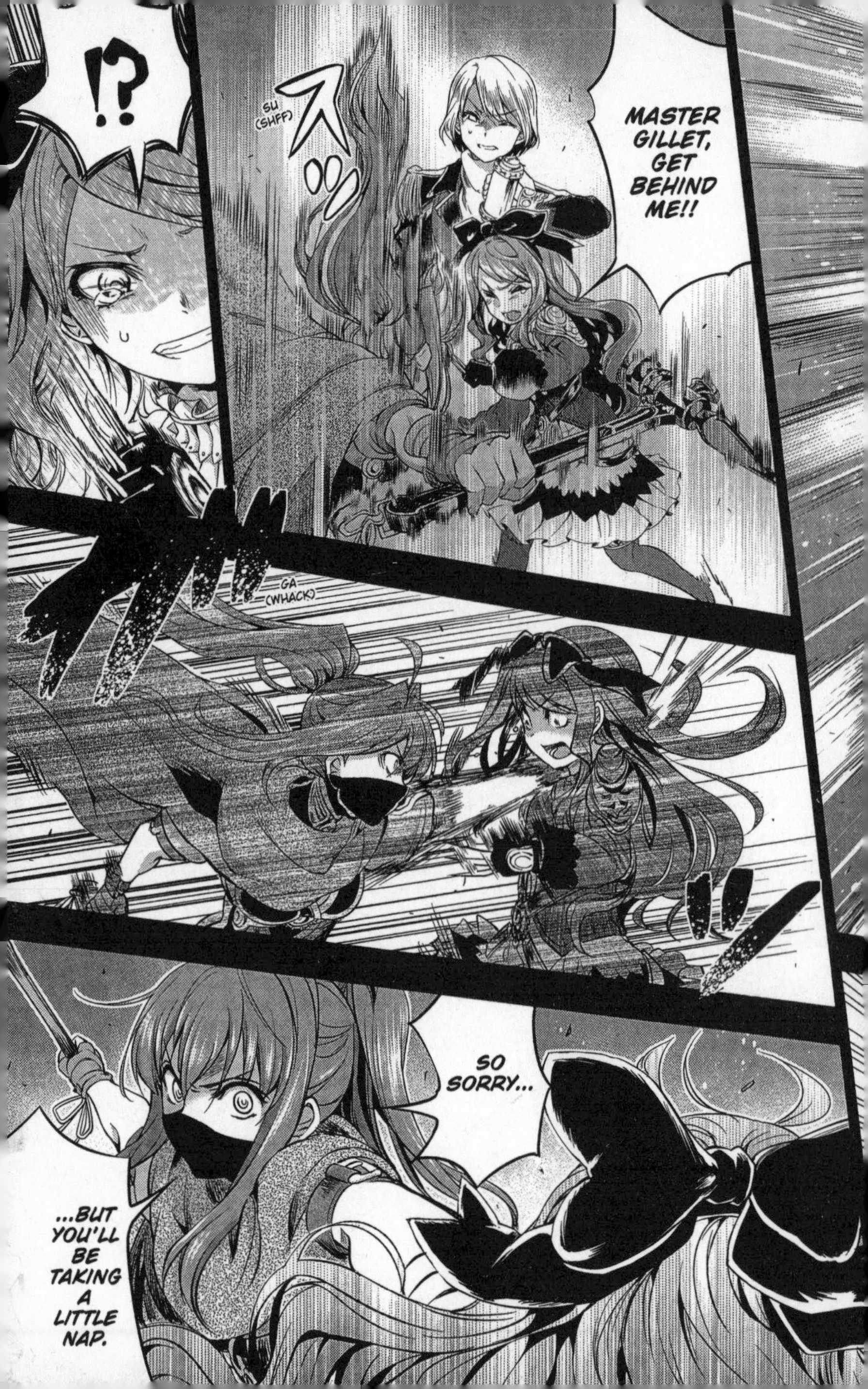
MASTER GILLET, GET BEHIND ME!!
SU (SHFF)
!?
GA (WHACK)
SO SORRY...
...BUT YOU'LL BE TAKING A LITTLE NAP.

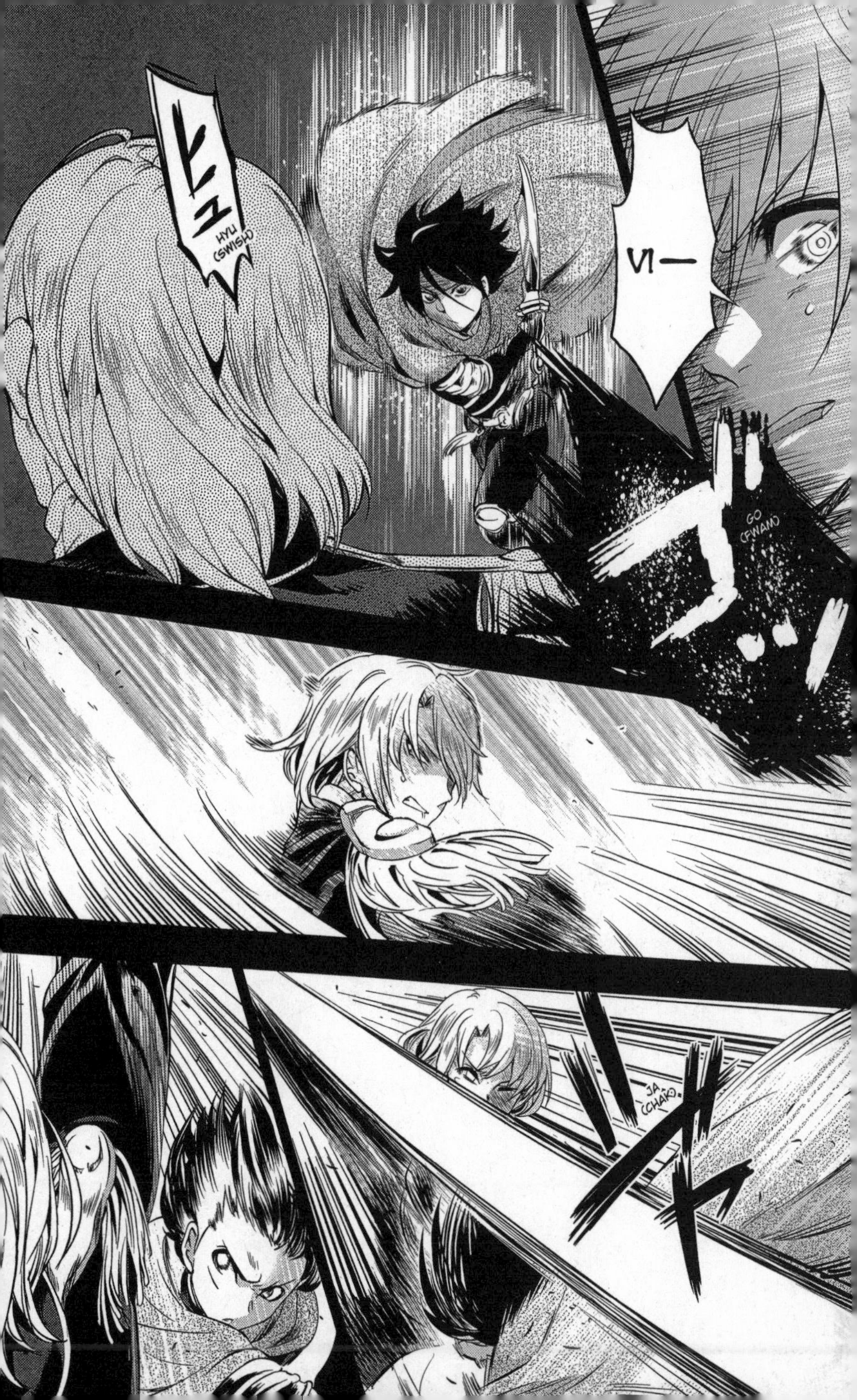
VI—
HYU (SWISH)
GO (FWAM)
JA (CHAK)

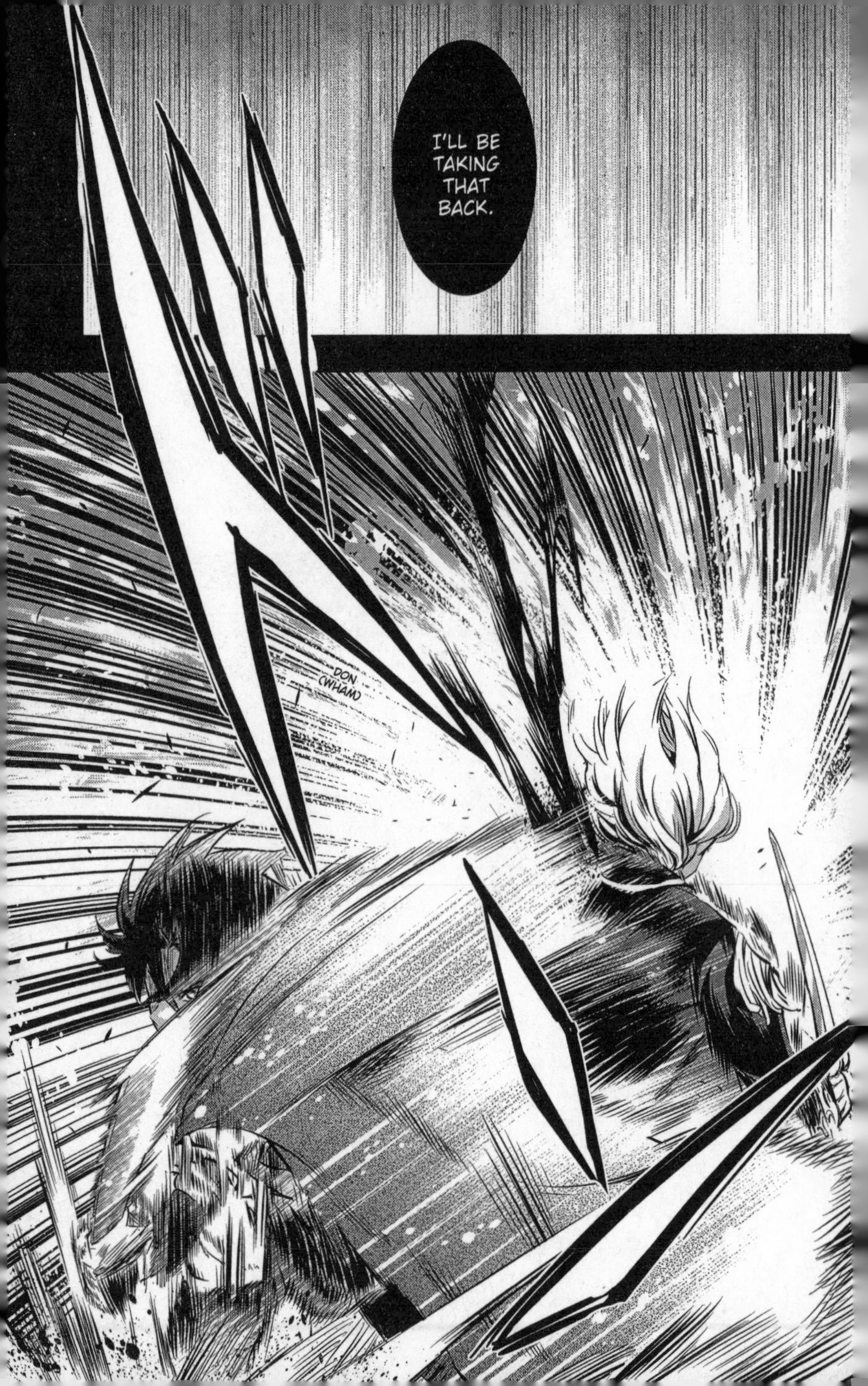
I'LL BE TAKING THAT BACK.
DON (WHAM)

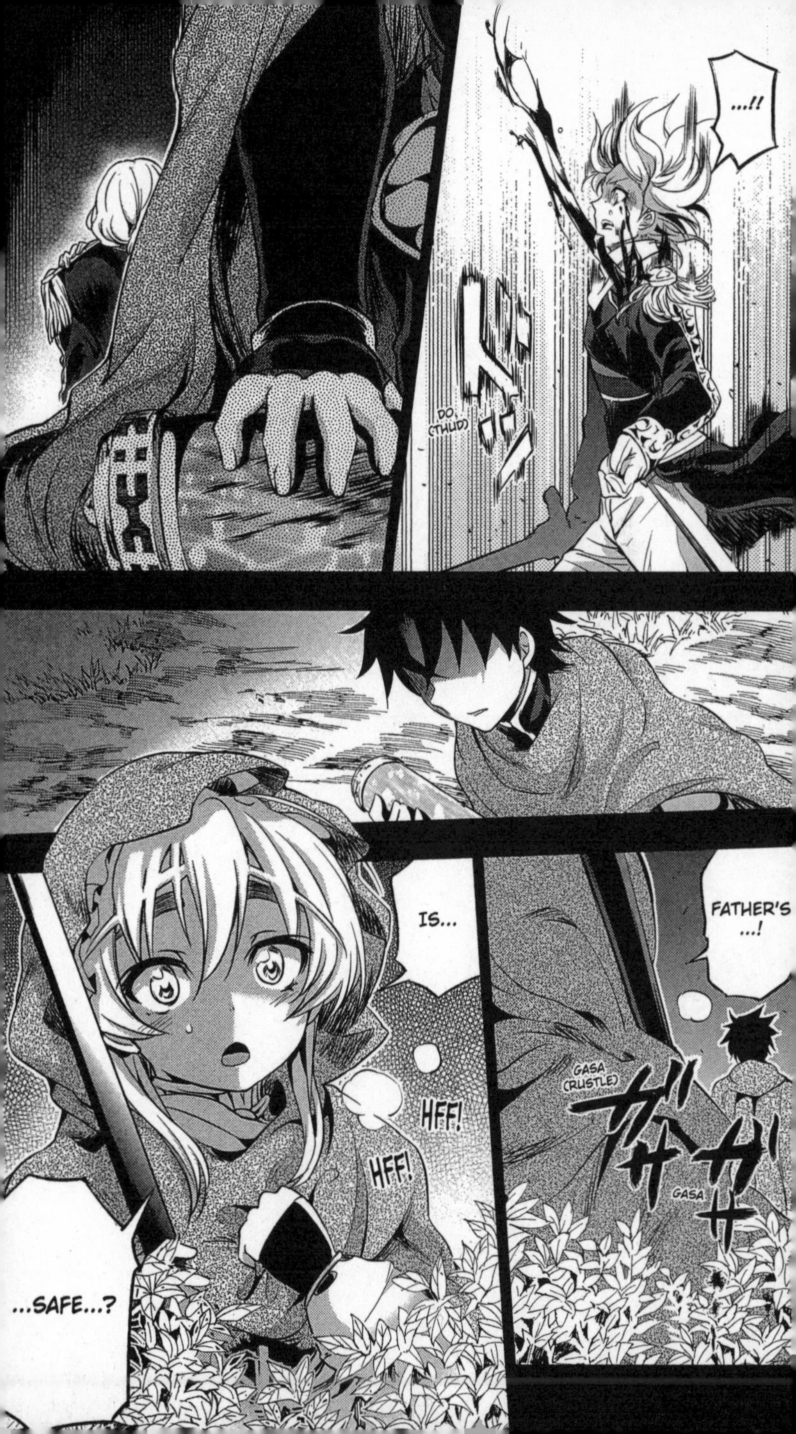
...!!
DO (THUD)
FATHER'S ...!
GASA (RUSTLE)
GASA
IS...
HFF!
HFF!
...SAFE...?

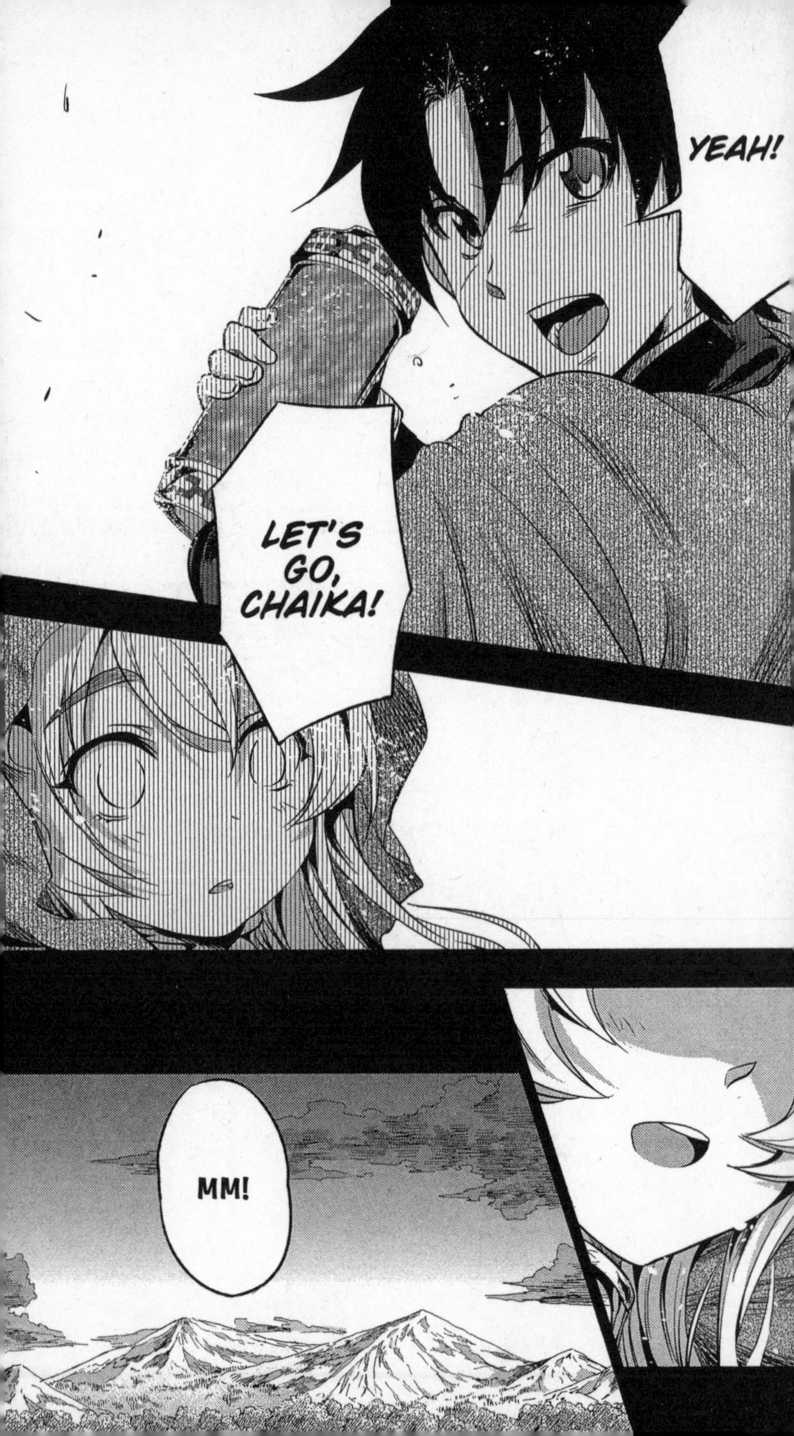
YEAH!
LET'S GO, CHAIKA!
MM!

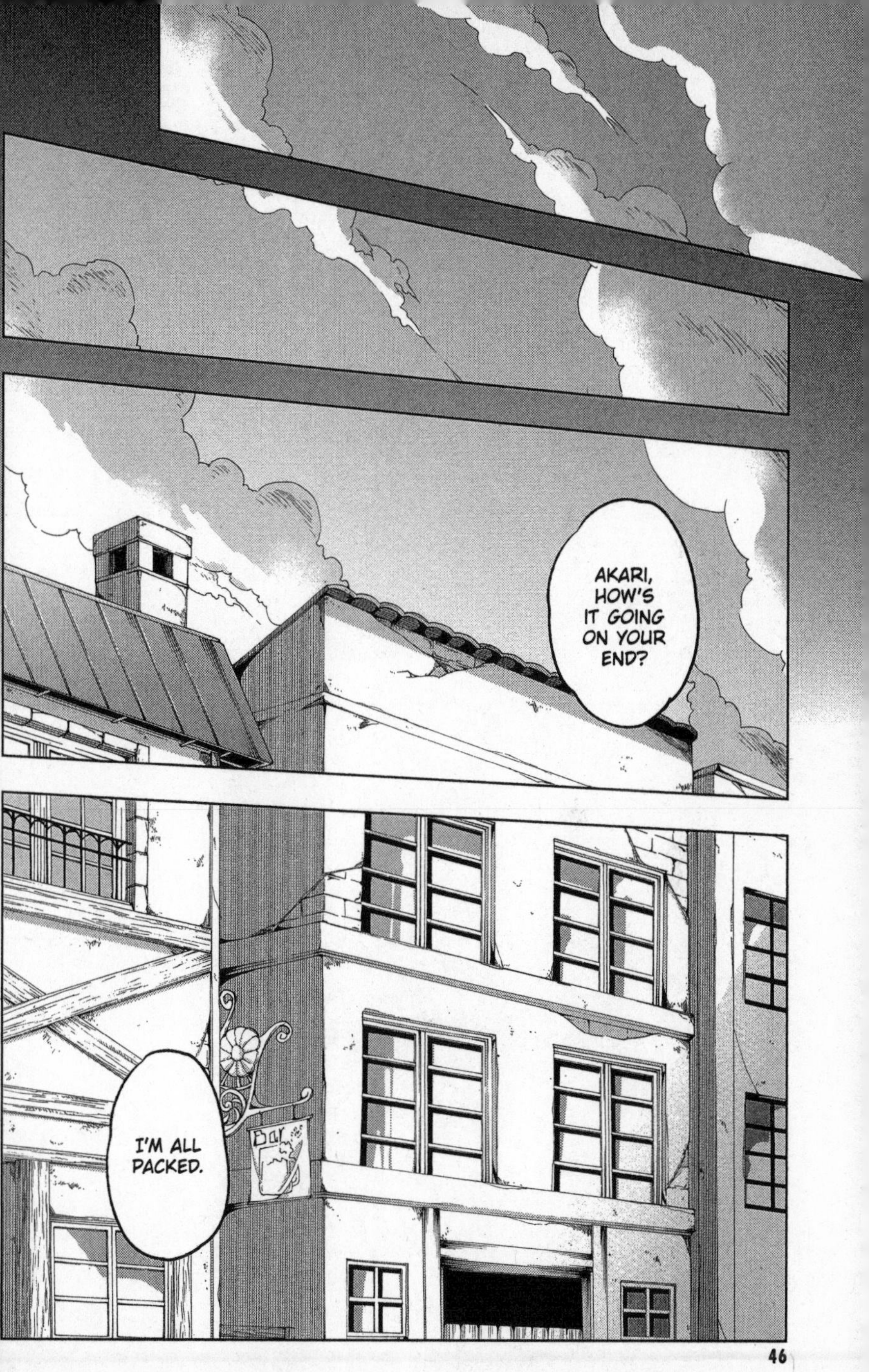
AKARI, HOW'S IT GOING ON YOUR END?
Bar
I'M ALL PACKED.

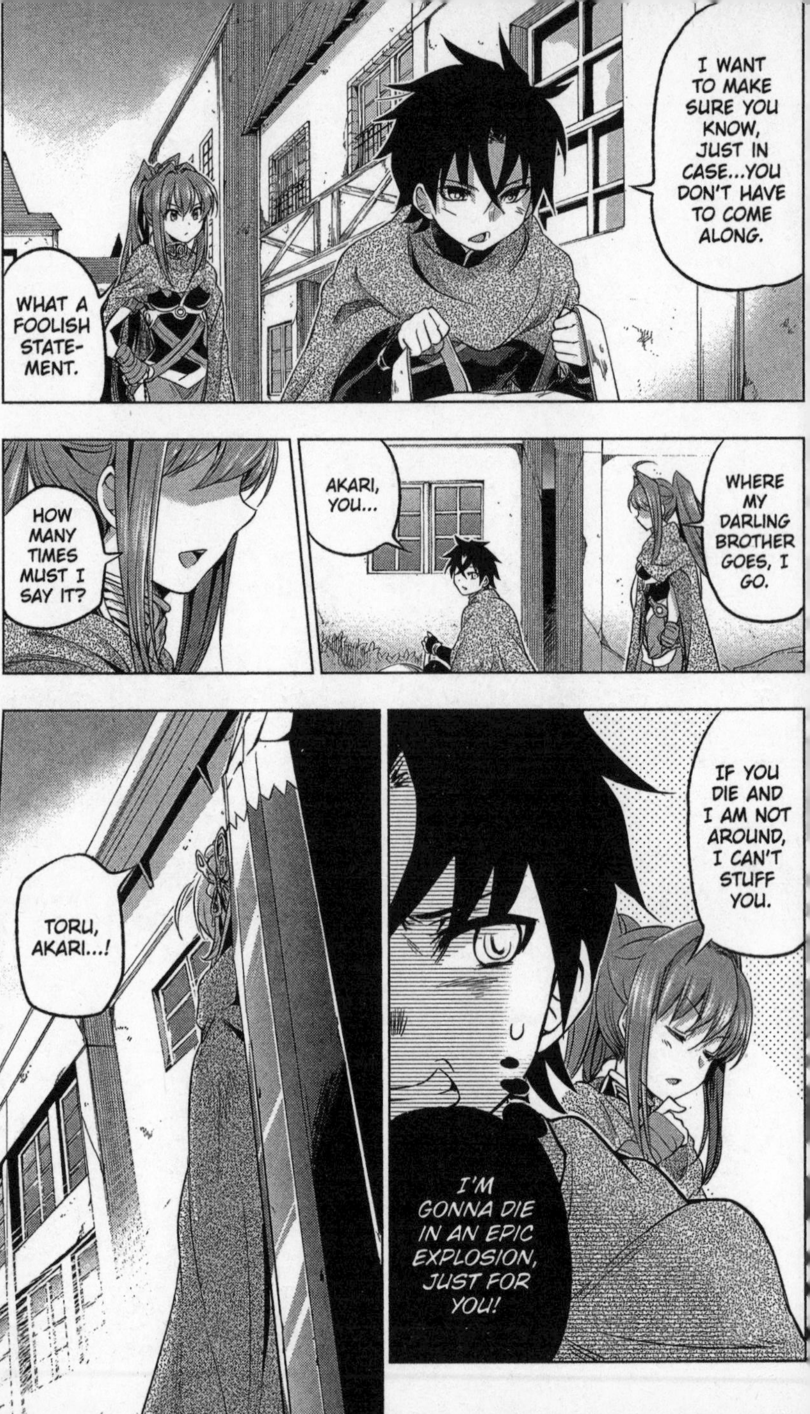
I WANT TO MAKE SURE YOU KNOW, JUST IN CASE...YOU DON'T HAVE TO COME ALONG.
WHAT A FOOLISH STATE-MENT.
WHERE MY DARLING BROTHER GOES, I GO.
AKARI, YOU...
HOW MANY TIMES MUST I SAY IT?
IF YOU DIE AND I AM NOT AROUND, I CAN'T STUFF YOU.
I'M GONNA DIE IN AN EPIC EXPLOSION, JUST FOR YOU!
TORU, AKARI...!

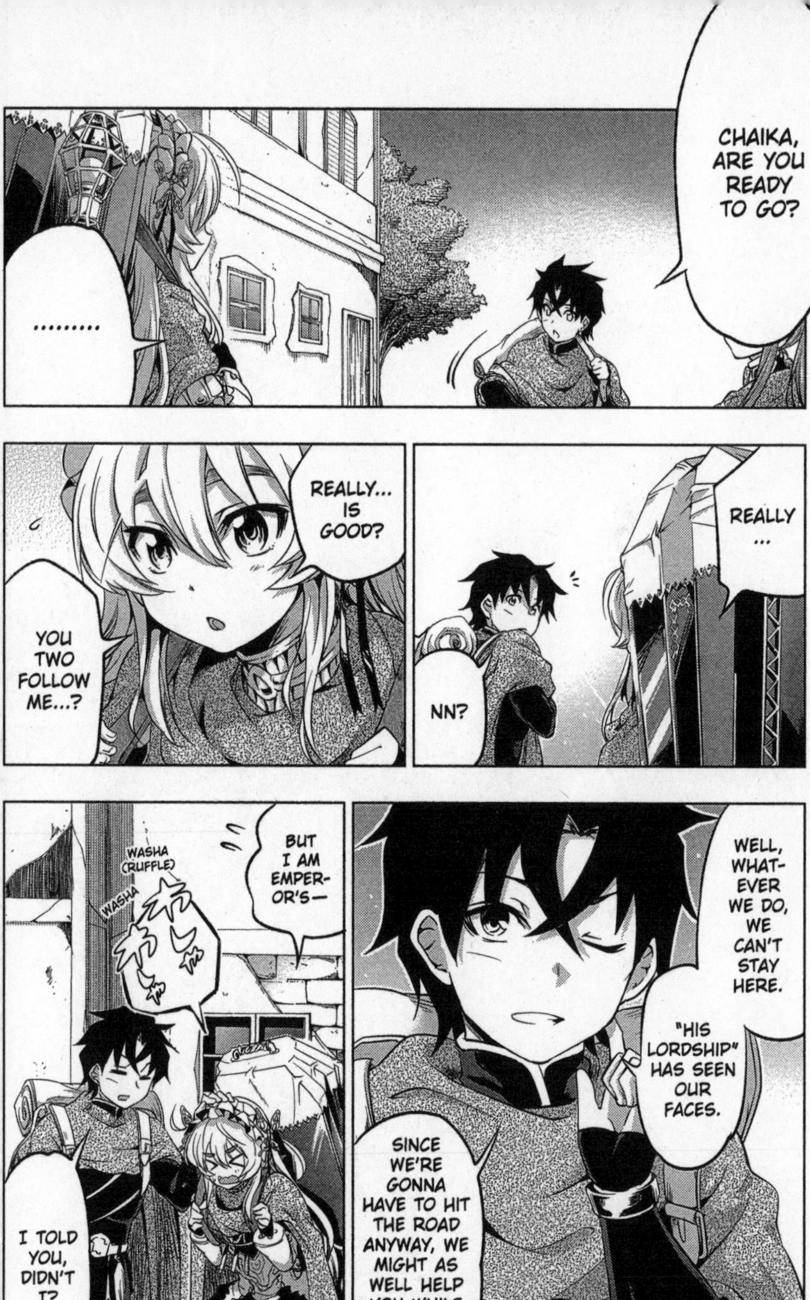

CHAIKA, ARE YOU READY TO GO?
....
REALLY...
NN?
REALLY... IS GOOD?
YOU TWO FOLLOW ME...?
WELL, WHATEVER WE DO, WE CAN'T STAY HERE.
"HIS LORDSHIP" HAS SEEN OUR FACES.
SINCE WE'RE GONNA HAVE TO HIT THE ROAD ANYWAY, WE MIGHT AS WELL HELP YOU WHILE WE'RE AT IT.
BUT I AM EMPEROR'S—
WASHA (RUFFLE)
WASHA
I TOLD YOU, DIDN'T I?

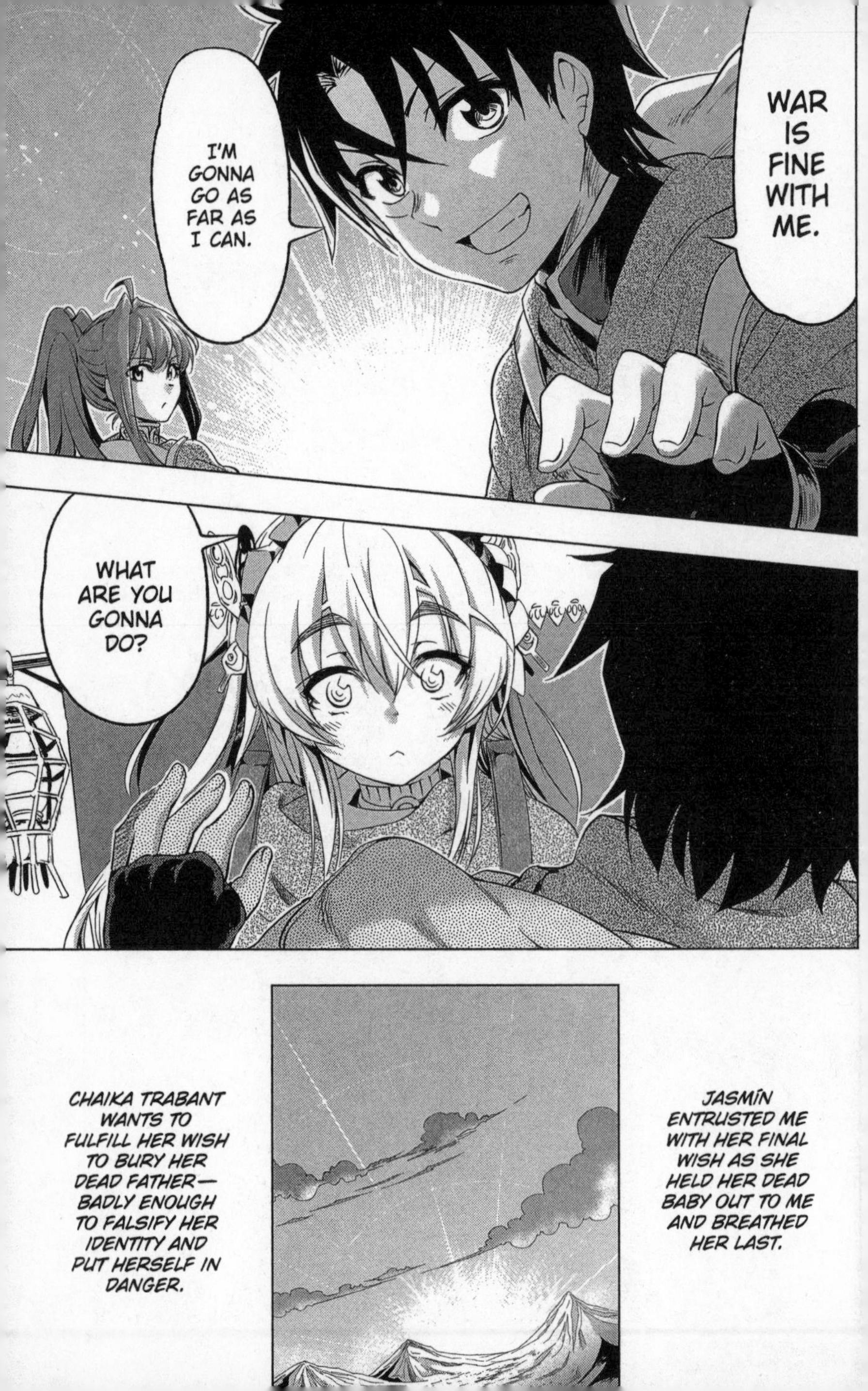
WAR IS FINE WITH ME.
I'M GONNA GO AS FAR AS I CAN.
WHAT ARE YOU GONNA DO?
JASMÍN ENTRUSTED ME WITH HER FINAL WISH AS SHE HELD HER DEAD BABY OUT TO ME AND BREATHED HER LAST.
CHAIKA TRABANT WANTS TO FULFILL HER WISH TO BURY HER DEAD FATHER— BADLY ENOUGH TO FALSIFY HER IDENTITY AND PUT HERSELF IN DANGER.

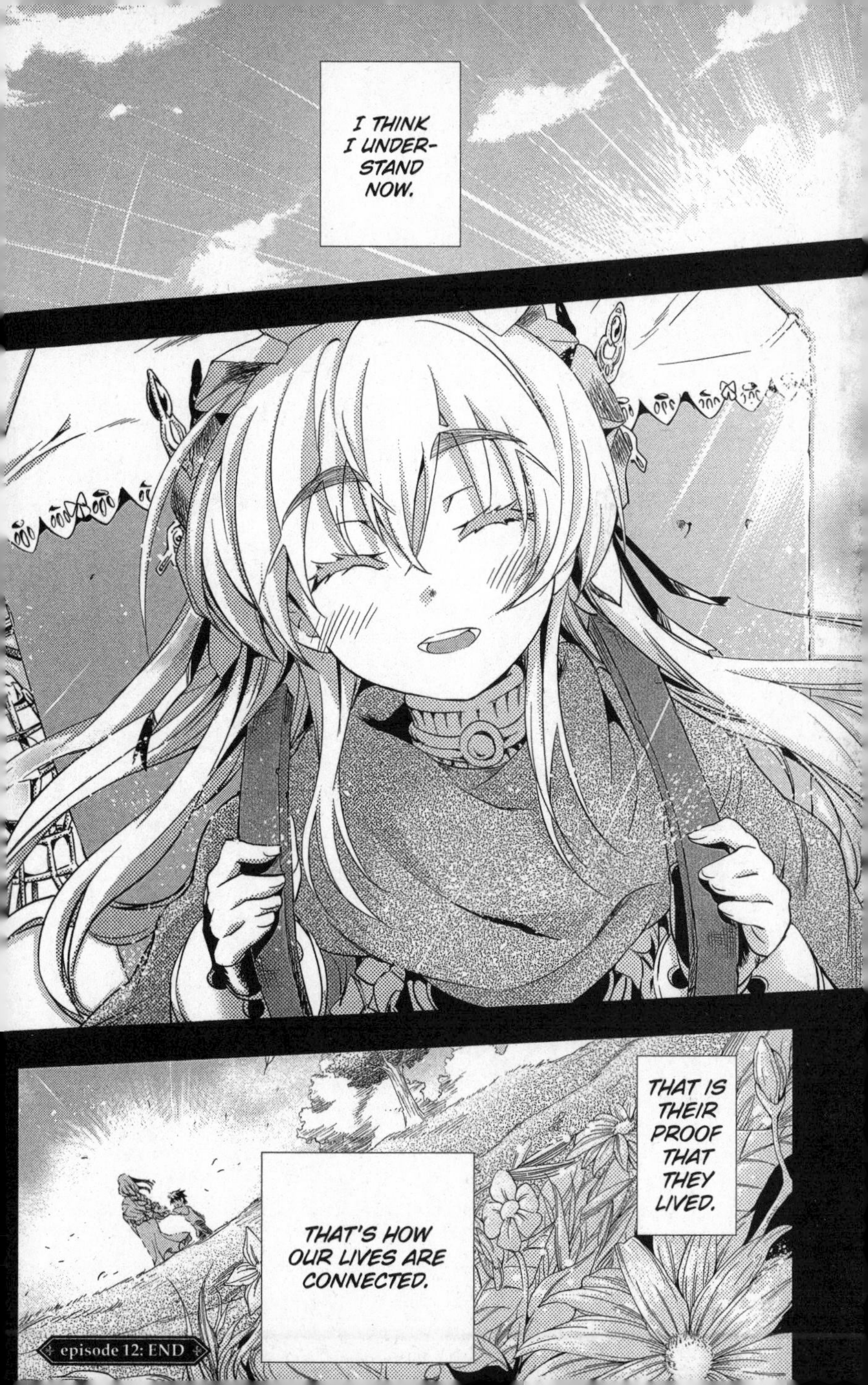
I THINK I UNDER-STAND NOW.
THAT IS THEIR PROOF THAT THEY LIVED.
THAT'S HOW OUR LIVES ARE CONNECTED.
episode 12: END

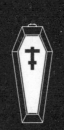

CHAIKA: THE COFFIN PRINCESS

episode 13:

The Devastation of Bygone Wars

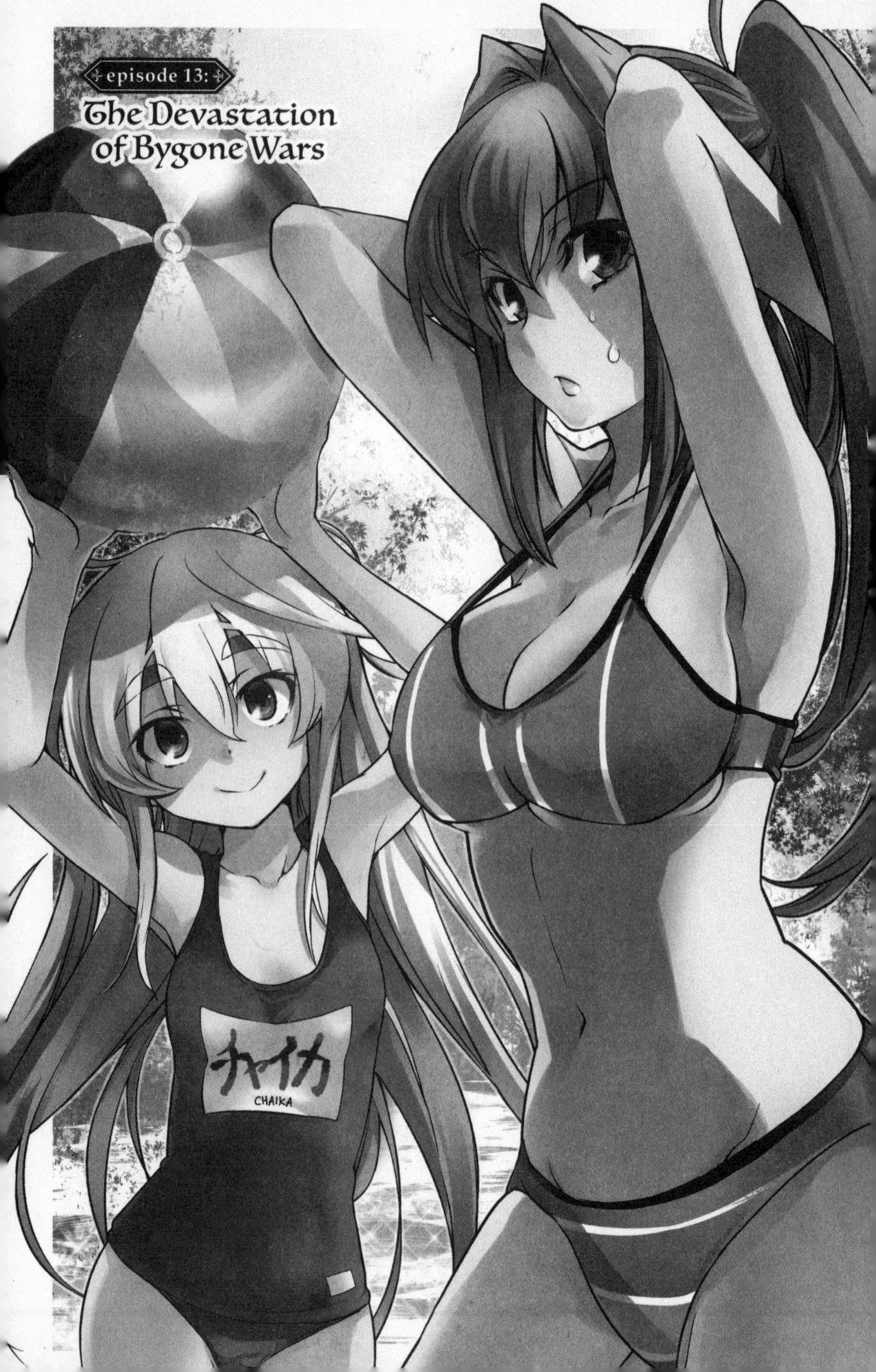
チャイカ
CHAIKA

CHAIKA: THE COFFIN PRINCESS

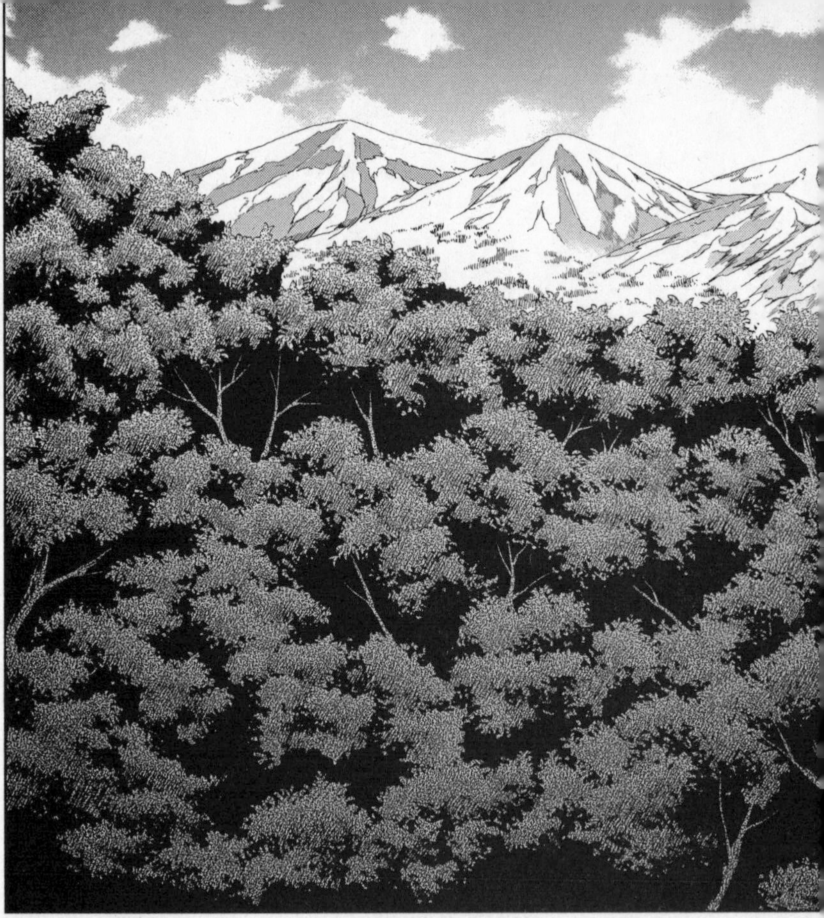

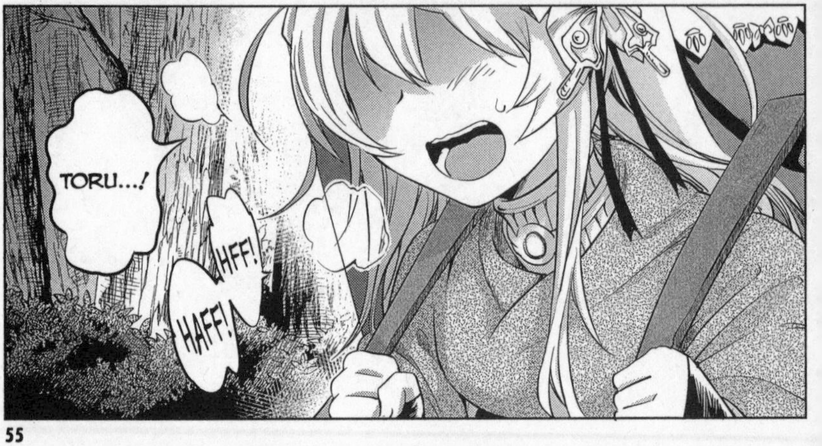
TORU...!
HFF!
HAFF!

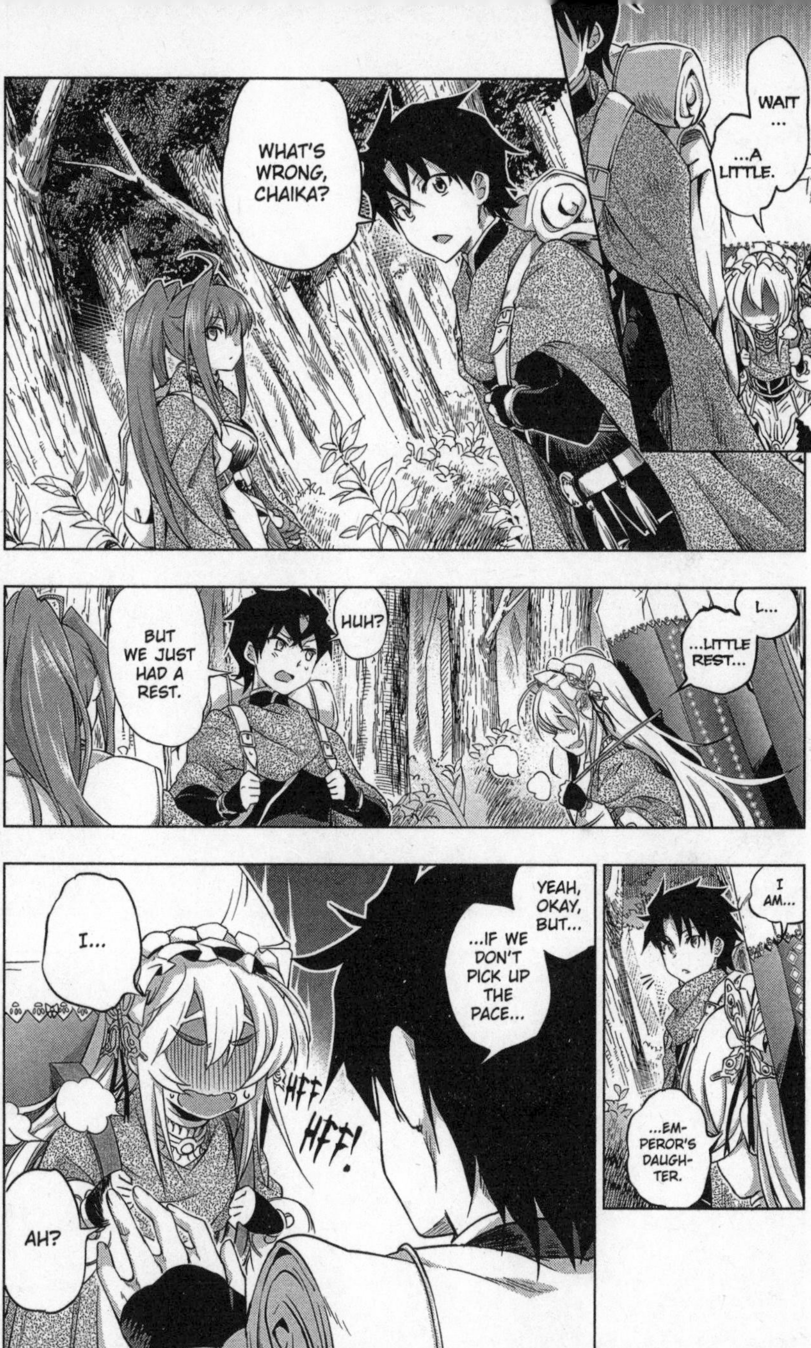
WAIT... ...A LITTLE.
WHAT'S WRONG, CHAIKA?
I... ...LITTLE REST...
HUH?
BUT WE JUST HAD A REST.
I AM...
...EM-PEROR'S DAUGH-TER.
YEAH, OKAY, BUT...
...IF WE DON'T PICK UP THE PACE...
I...
HFF HFF!
AH?

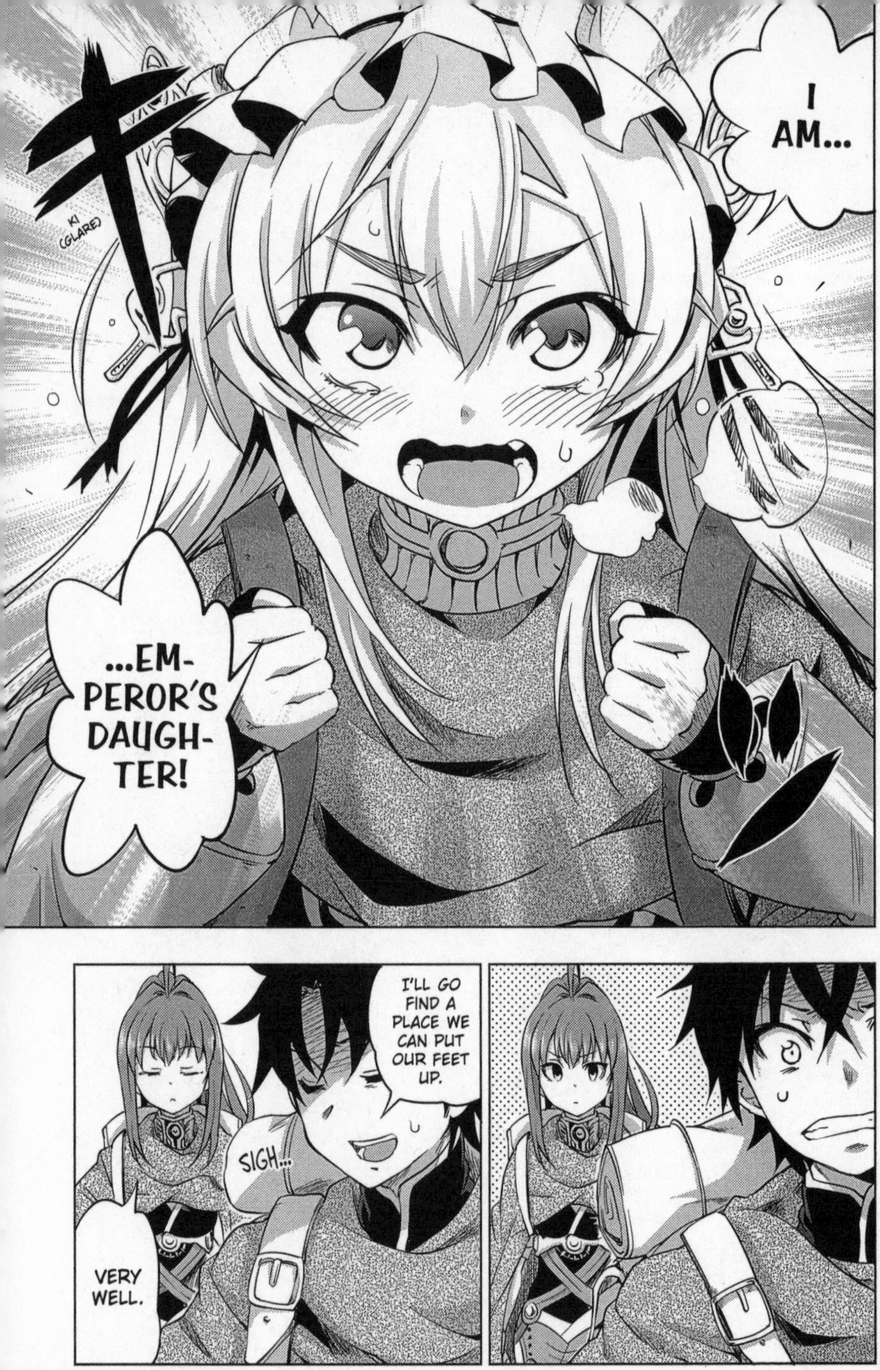
I AM...
KI (GLARE)
...EM-PEROR'S DAUGH-TER!
I'LL GO FIND A PLACE WE CAN PUT OUR FEET UP.
SIGH...
VERY WELL.

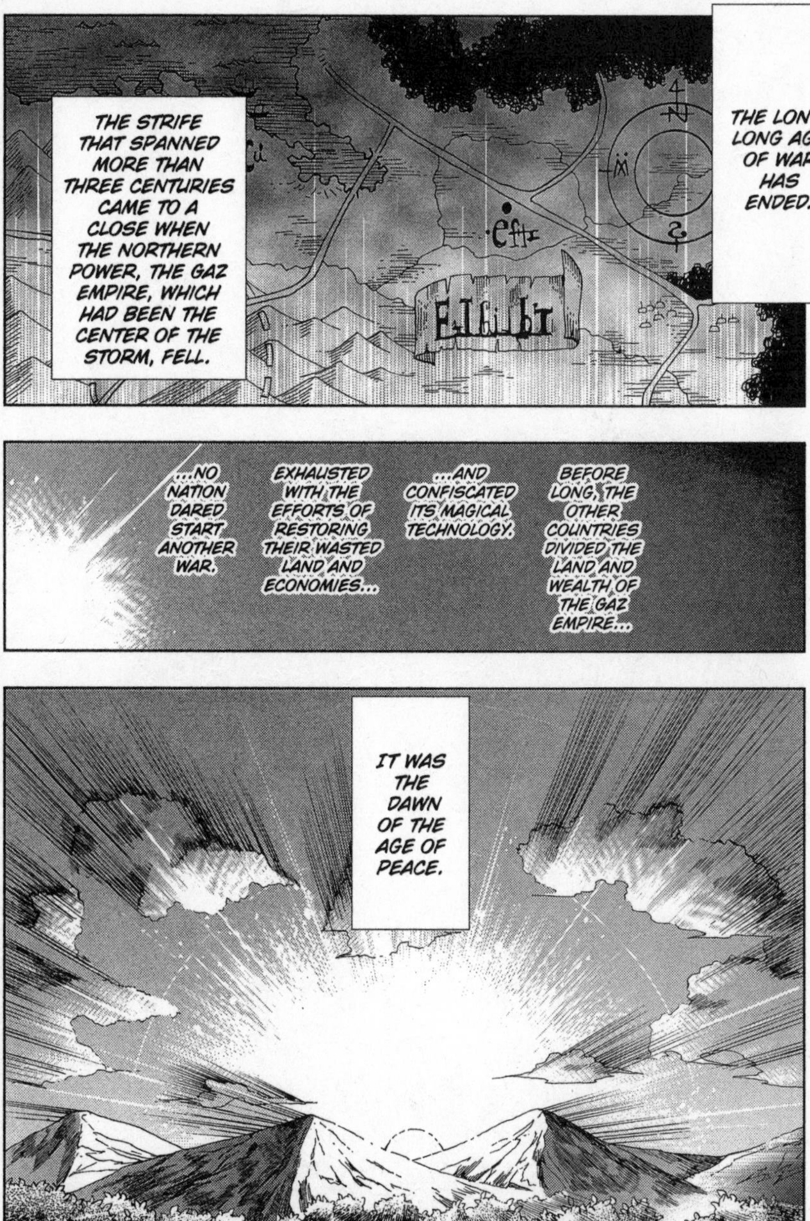
THE LONG, LONG AGE OF WAR HAS ENDED.
THE STRIFE THAT SPANNED MORE THAN THREE CENTURIES CAME TO A CLOSE WHEN THE NORTHERN POWER, THE GAZ EMPIRE, WHICH HAD BEEN THE CENTER OF THE STORM, FELL.
BEFORE LONG, THE OTHER COUNTRIES DIVIDED THE LAND AND WEALTH OF THE GAZ EMPIRE...
...AND CONFISCATED ITS MAGICAL TECHNOLOGY.
EXHAUSTED WITH THE EFFORTS OF RESTORING THEIR WASTED LAND AND ECONOMIES...
...NO NATION DARED START ANOTHER WAR.
IT WAS THE DAWN OF THE AGE OF PEACE.

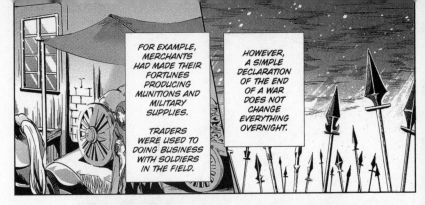

HOWEVER, A SIMPLE DECLARATION OF THE END OF A WAR DOES NOT CHANGE EVERYTHING OVERNIGHT.
FOR EXAMPLE, MERCHANTS HAD MADE THEIR FORTUNES PRODUCING MUNITIONS AND MILITARY SUPPLIES.
TRADERS WERE USED TO DOING BUSINESS WITH SOLDIERS IN THE FIELD.
TORU AND AKARI WERE TRAINED IN THE VILLAGE OF ACURA TO BE SABO-TEURS, MEN AND WOMEN WHO SHINED BRIGHTEST IN THE MIDST OF BATTLE.
THEY HAD LIVED TO FIGHT SINCE BIRTH; THEY COULDN'T CHANGE THEIR WAY OF LIFE SO EASILY.
ALONG WITH CHAIKA TRA-BANT...

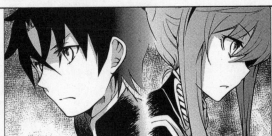

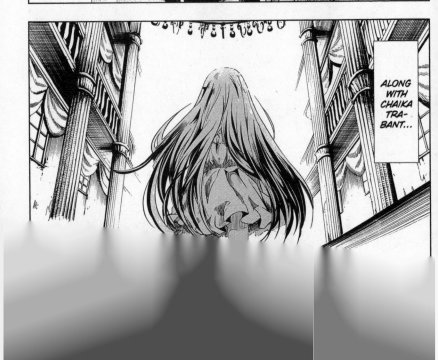

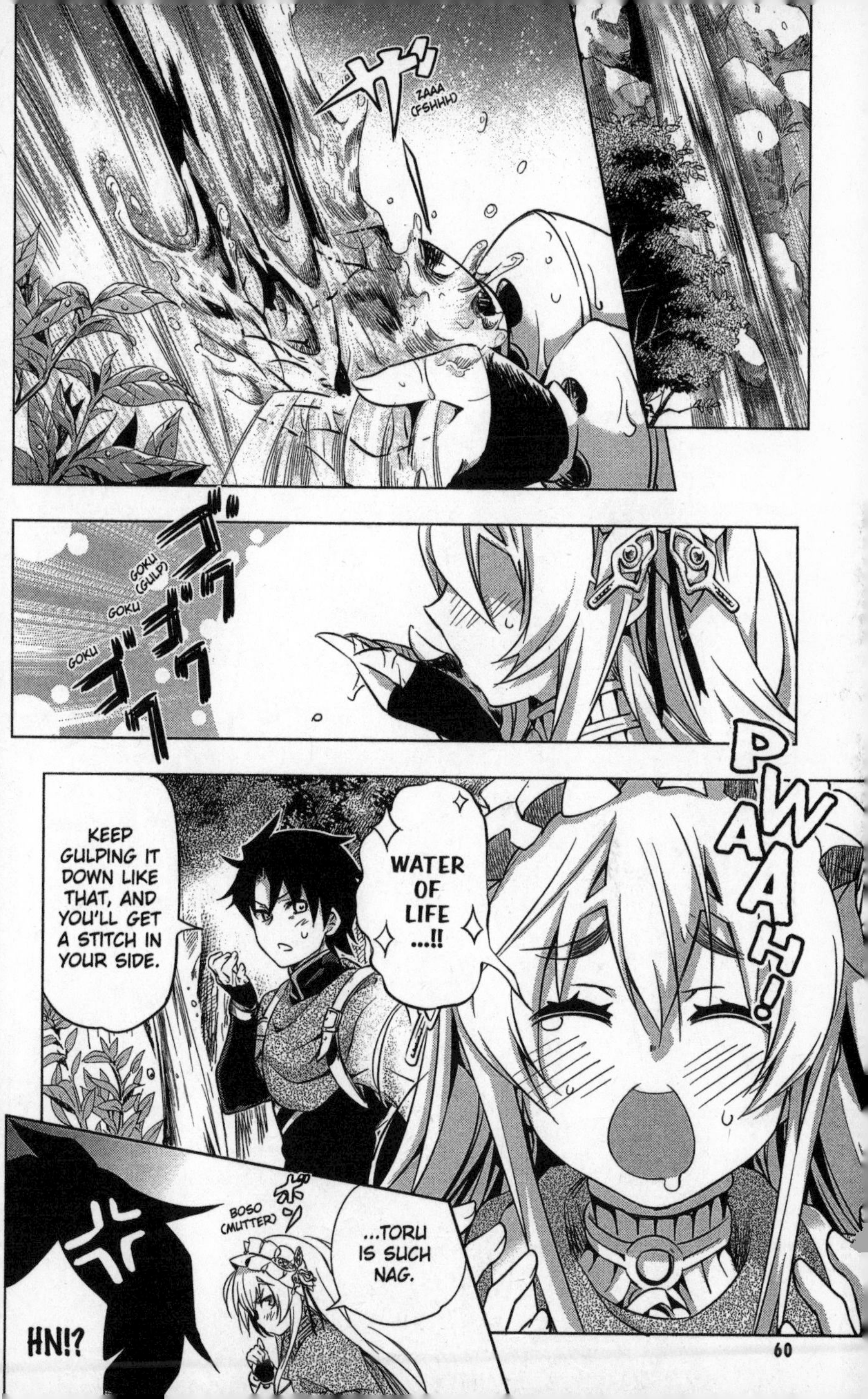
ZAAA (FSHHH)
GOKU (GULP)
GOKU
GOKU
PWAAH!
WATER OF LIFE ...!!
KEEP GULPING IT DOWN LIKE THAT, AND YOU'LL GET A STITCH IN YOUR SIDE.
...TORU IS SUCH NAG.
BOSO (MUTTER)
HN!?

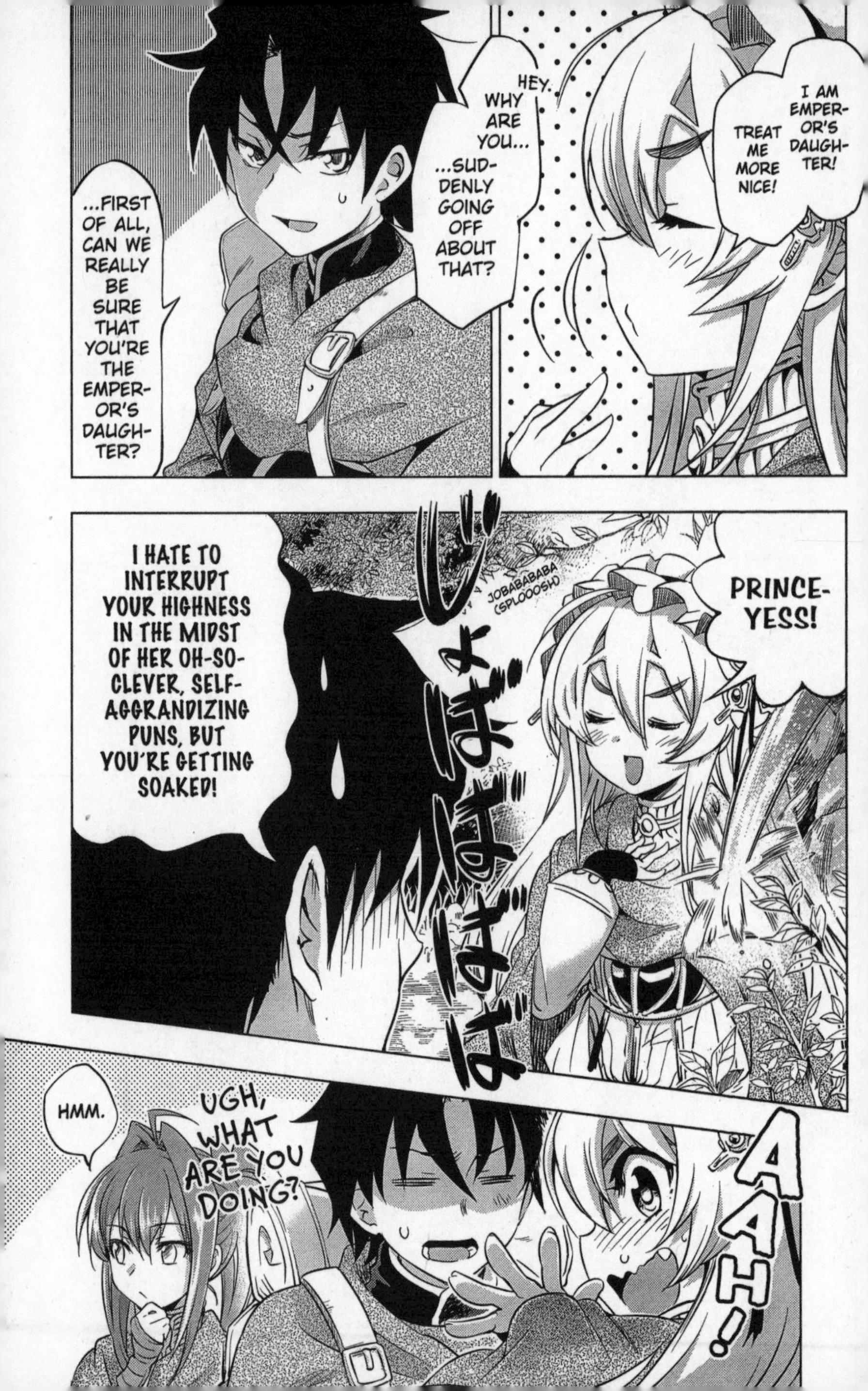
I AM EMPEROR'S DAUGHTER!
TREAT ME MORE NICE!
HEY. WHY ARE YOU...
...SUDDENLY GOING OFF ABOUT THAT?
...FIRST OF ALL, CAN WE REALLY BE SURE THAT YOU'RE THE EMPEROR'S DAUGHTER?
PRINCE-YESS!
じょばばばば
JOBABABABA (SPLOOOSH)
I HATE TO INTERRUPT YOUR HIGHNESS IN THE MIDST OF HER OH-SO-CLEVER, SELF-AGGRANDIZING PUNS, BUT YOU'RE GETTING SOAKED!
AAAH!
UGH, WHAT ARE YOU DOING?
HMM.

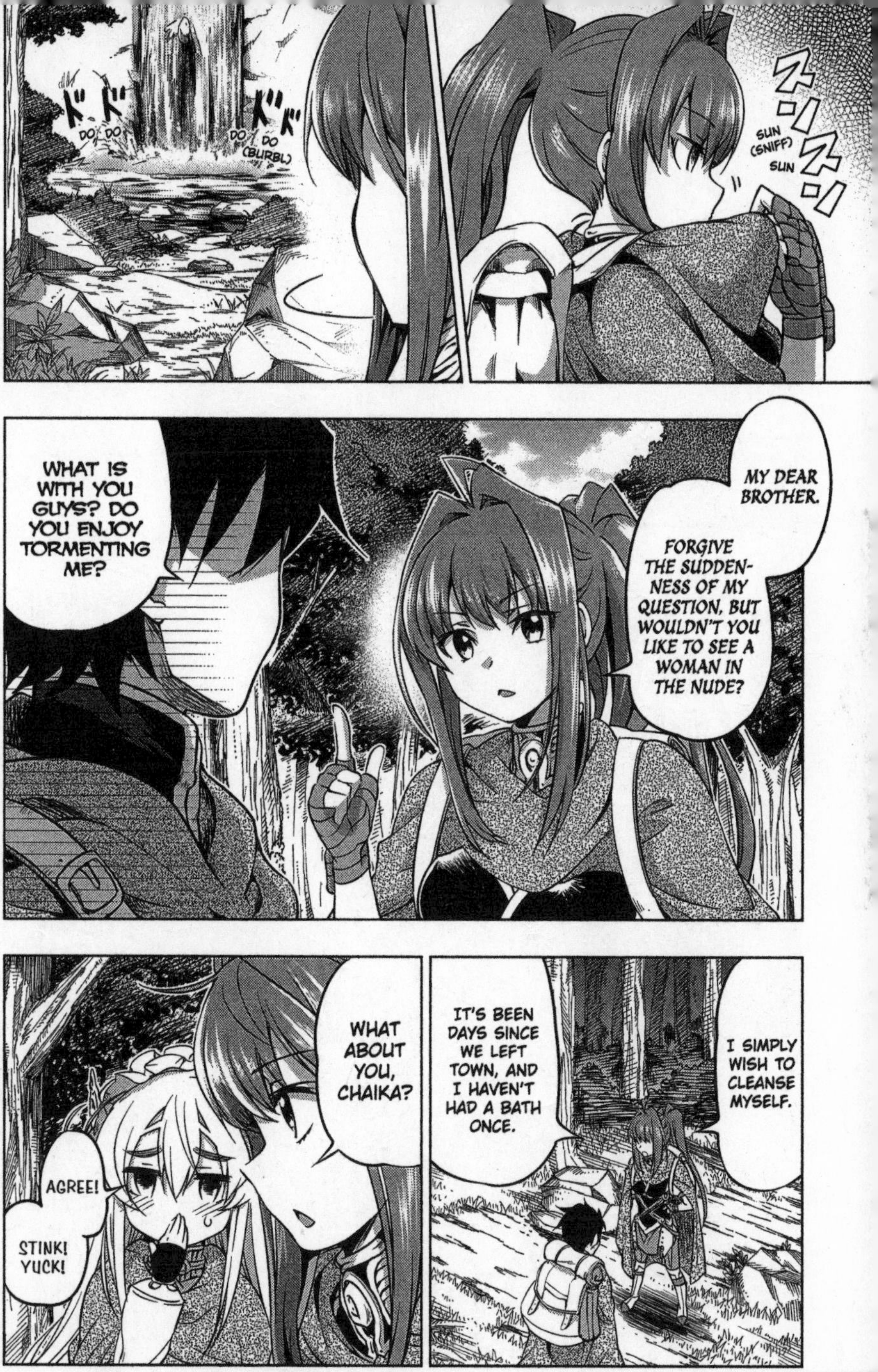
スンスン
SUN (SNIFF) SUN
ドドドド
DO DO DO DO (BURBL)
MY DEAR BROTHER.
FORGIVE THE SUDDEN-NESS OF MY QUESTION, BUT WOULDN'T YOU LIKE TO SEE A WOMAN IN THE NUDE?
WHAT IS WITH YOU GUYS? DO YOU ENJOY TORMENTING ME?
I SIMPLY WISH TO CLEANSE MYSELF.
IT'S BEEN DAYS SINCE WE LEFT TOWN, AND I HAVEN'T HAD A BATH ONCE.
WHAT ABOUT YOU, CHAIKA?
AGREE!
STINK! YUCK!

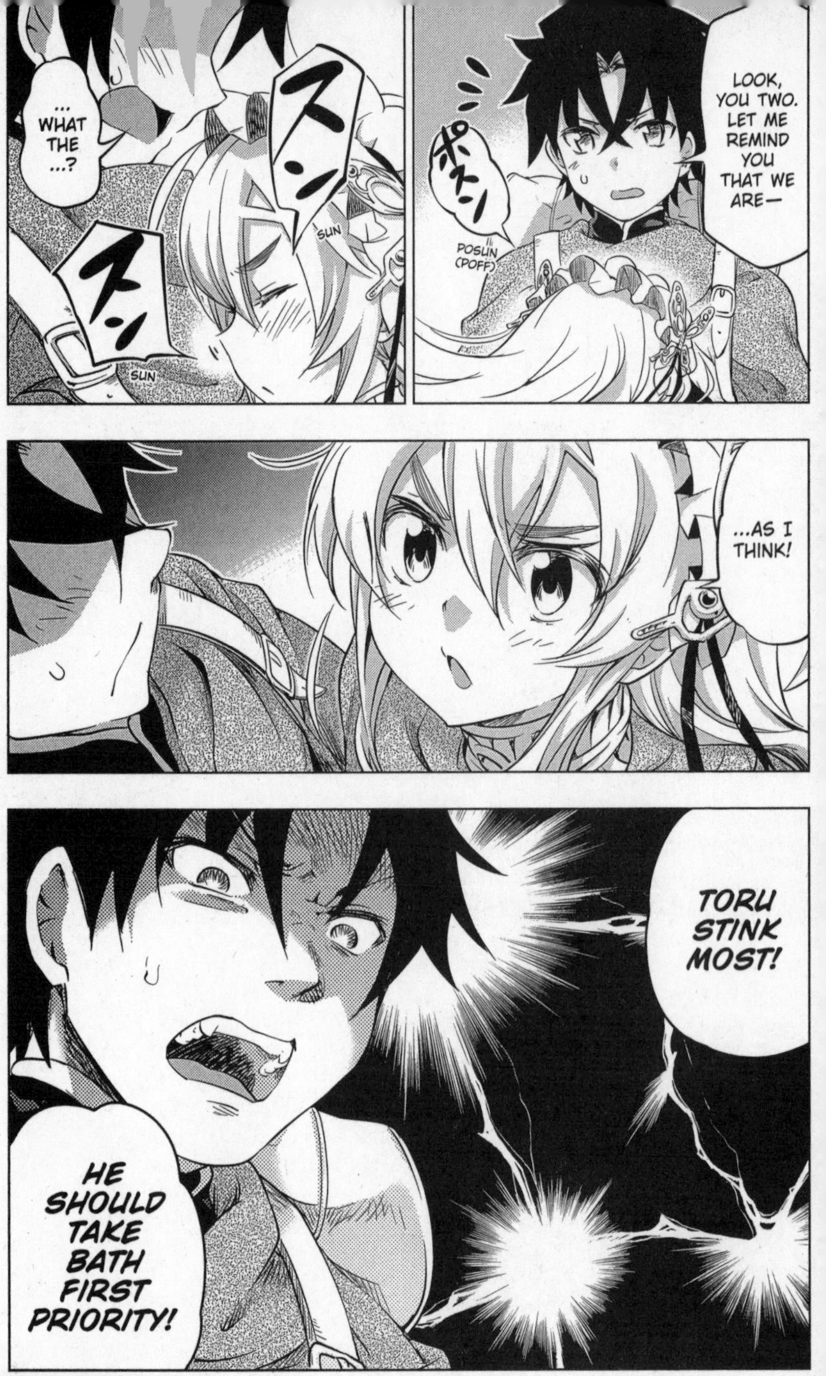
LOOK, YOU TWO. LET ME REMIND YOU THAT WE ARE—
ポスン
POSUN (POFF)
スン
SUN
スン
SUN
...WHAT THE ...?
...AS I THINK!
TORU STINK MOST!
HE SHOULD TAKE BATH FIRST PRIORITY!

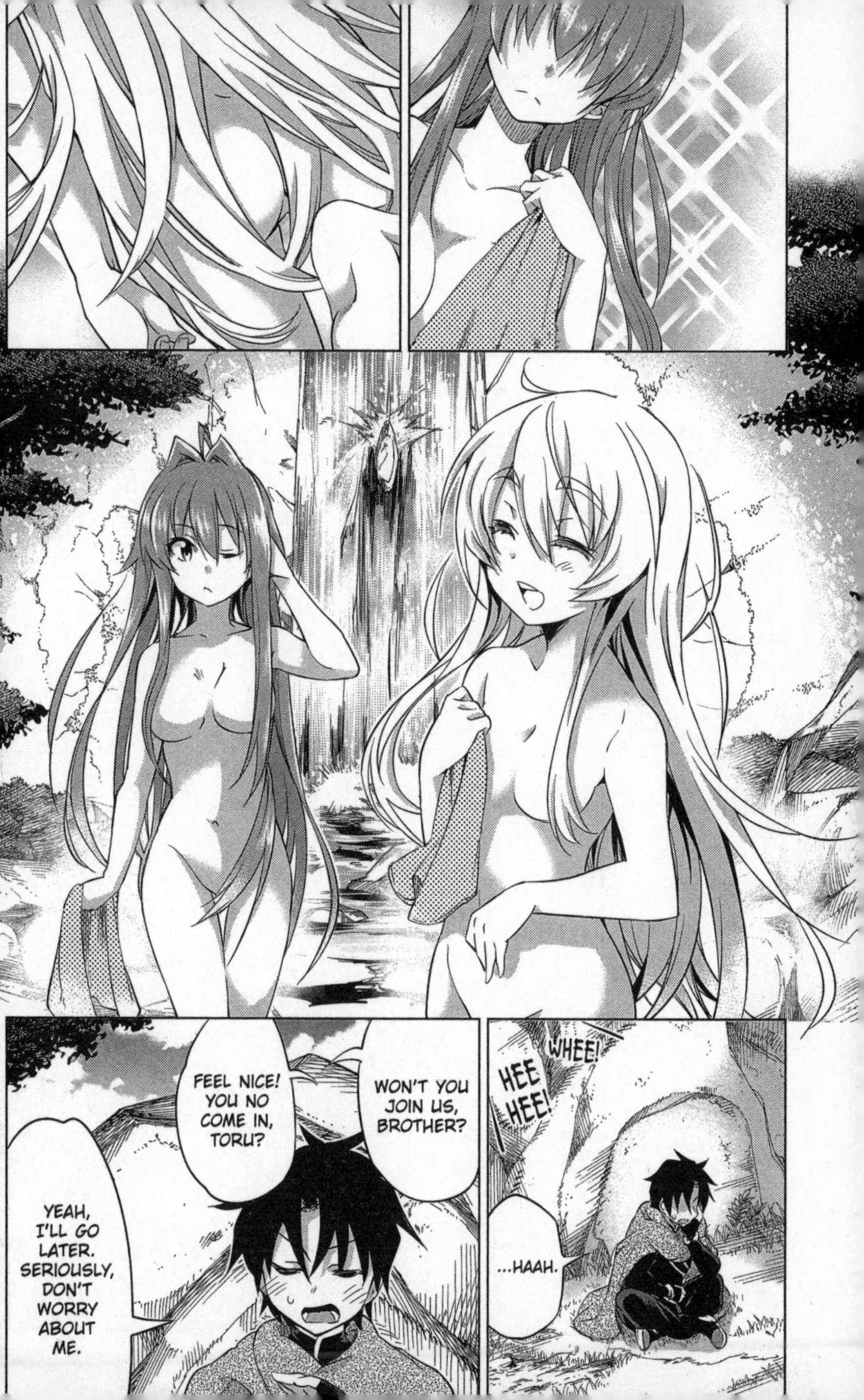
WHEE!
HEE HEE!
...HAAH.
WON'T YOU JOIN US, BROTHER?
FEEL NICE! YOU NO COME IN, TORU?
YEAH, I'LL GO LATER. SERIOUSLY, DON'T WORRY ABOUT ME.

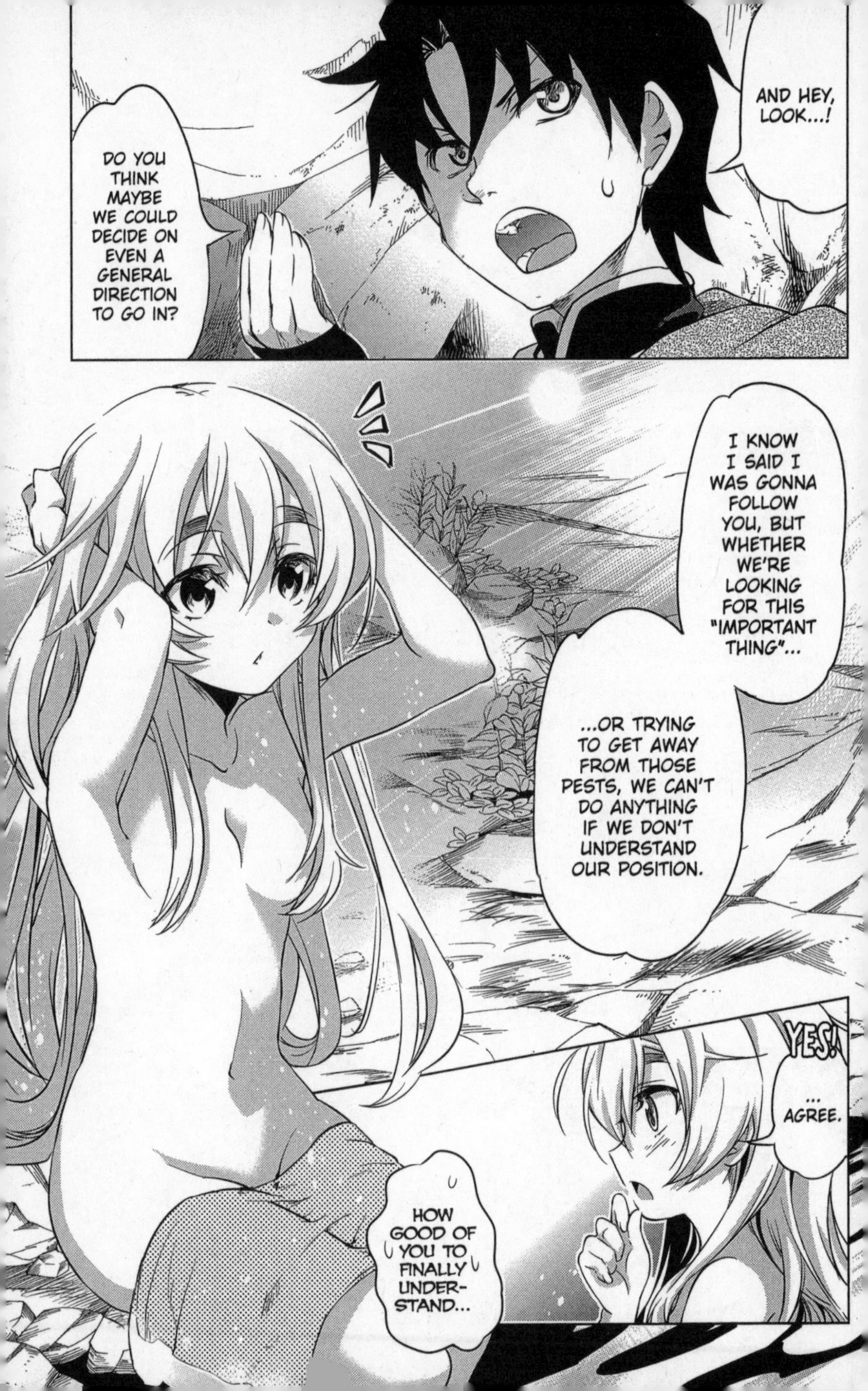
AND HEY, LOOK...!
DO YOU THINK MAYBE WE COULD DECIDE ON EVEN A GENERAL DIRECTION TO GO IN?
I KNOW I SAID I WAS GONNA FOLLOW YOU, BUT WHETHER WE'RE LOOKING FOR THIS "IMPORTANT THING"...
...OR TRYING TO GET AWAY FROM THOSE PESTS, WE CAN'T DO ANYTHING IF WE DON'T UNDERSTAND OUR POSITION.
YES!
... AGREE.
HOW GOOD OF YOU TO FINALLY UNDER-STAND...

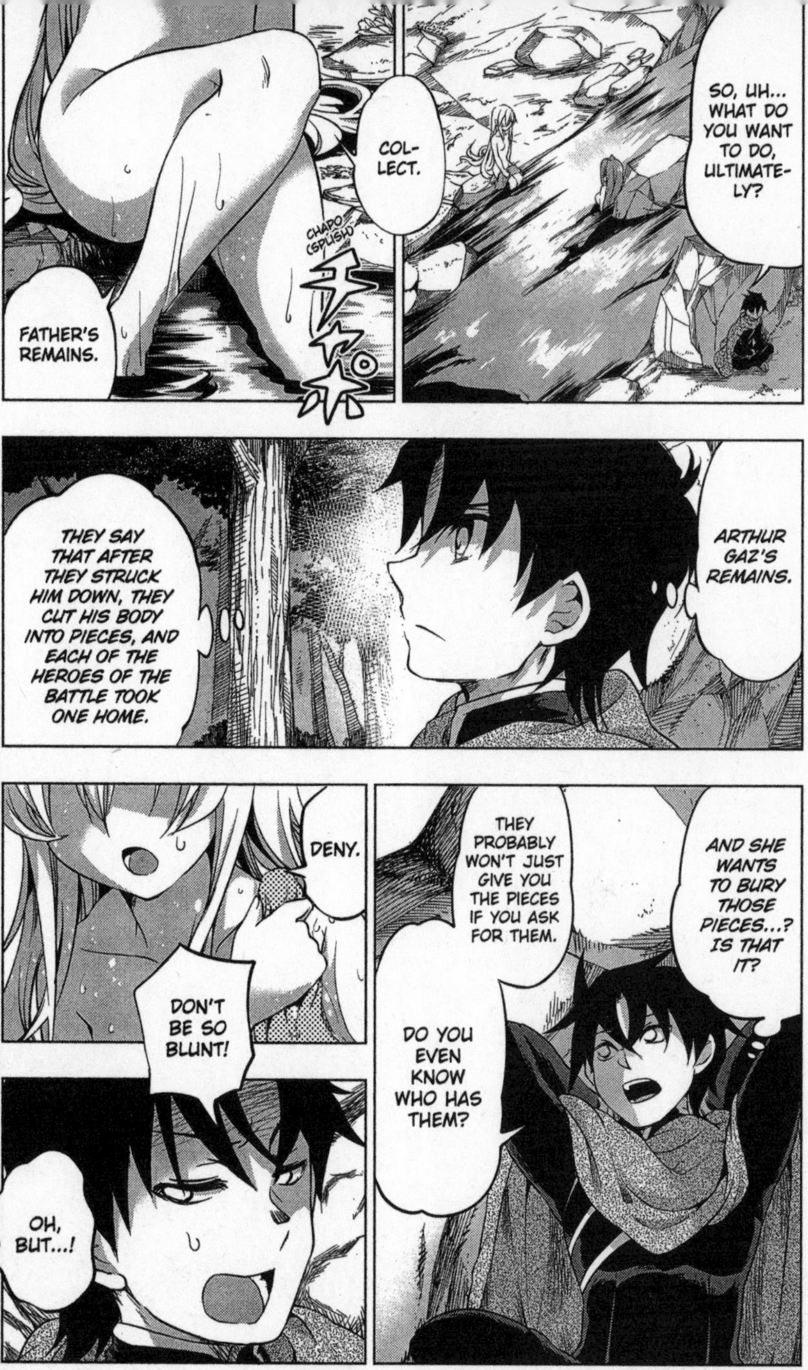

SO, UH... WHAT DO YOU WANT TO DO, ULTIMATE-LY?
COL-LECT.
CHAPO (SPLISH)
FATHER'S REMAINS.
ARTHUR GAZ'S REMAINS.
THEY SAY THAT AFTER THEY STRUCK HIM DOWN, THEY CUT HIS BODY INTO PIECES, AND EACH OF THE HEROES OF THE BATTLE TOOK ONE HOME.
AND SHE WANTS TO BURY THOSE PIECES...? IS THAT IT?
THEY PROBABLY WON'T JUST GIVE YOU THE PIECES IF YOU ASK FOR THEM.
DO YOU EVEN KNOW WHO HAS THEM?
DENY.
DON'T BE SO BLUNT!
OH, BUT...!

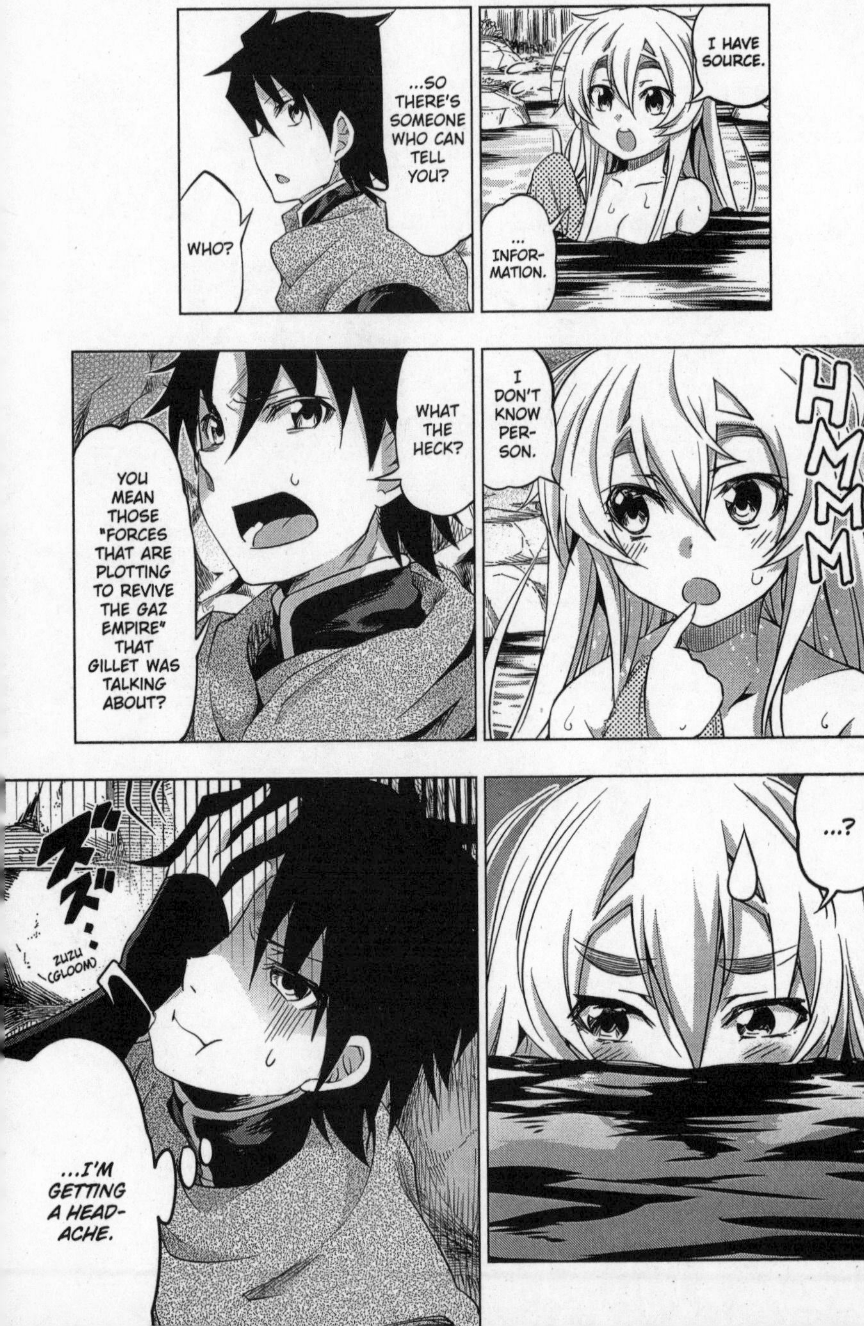
I HAVE SOURCE.
... INFORMATION.
...SO THERE'S SOMEONE WHO CAN TELL YOU?
WHO?
HMMM
I DON'T KNOW PERSON.
WHAT THE HECK?
YOU MEAN THOSE "FORCES THAT ARE PLOTTING TO REVIVE THE GAZ EMPIRE" THAT GILLET WAS TALKING ABOUT?
...?
ズズ…
ZUZU (GLOOM)
...I'M GETTING A HEADACHE.

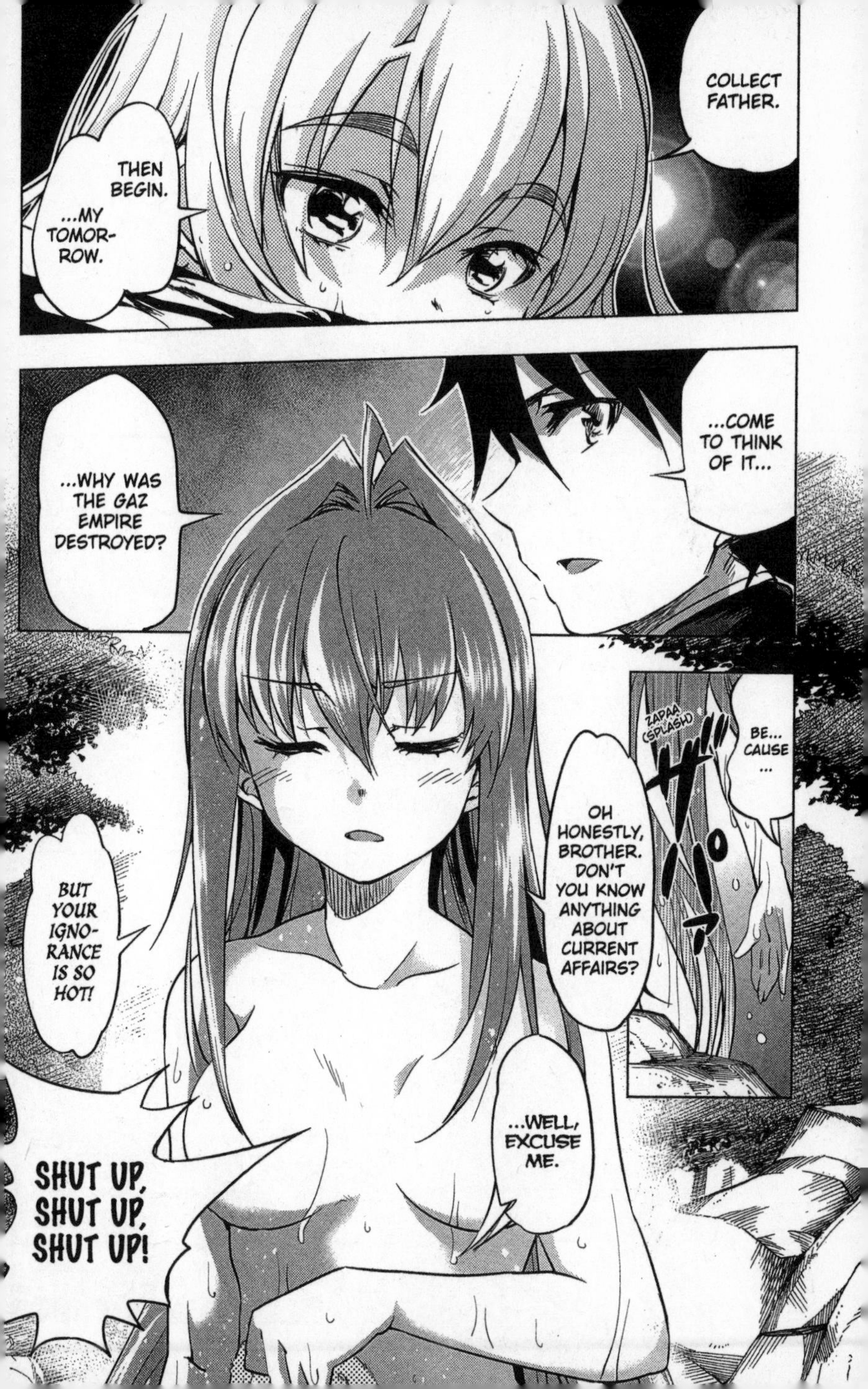
COLLECT FATHER.
THEN BEGIN.
...MY TOMOR-ROW.
...COME TO THINK OF IT...
...WHY WAS THE GAZ EMPIRE DESTROYED?
ZAPAA (SPLASH)
BE... CAUSE ...
OH HONESTLY, BROTHER. DON'T YOU KNOW ANYTHING ABOUT CURRENT AFFAIRS?
BUT YOUR IGNO-RANCE IS SO HOT!
...WELL, EXCUSE ME.
SHUT UP, SHUT UP, SHUT UP!

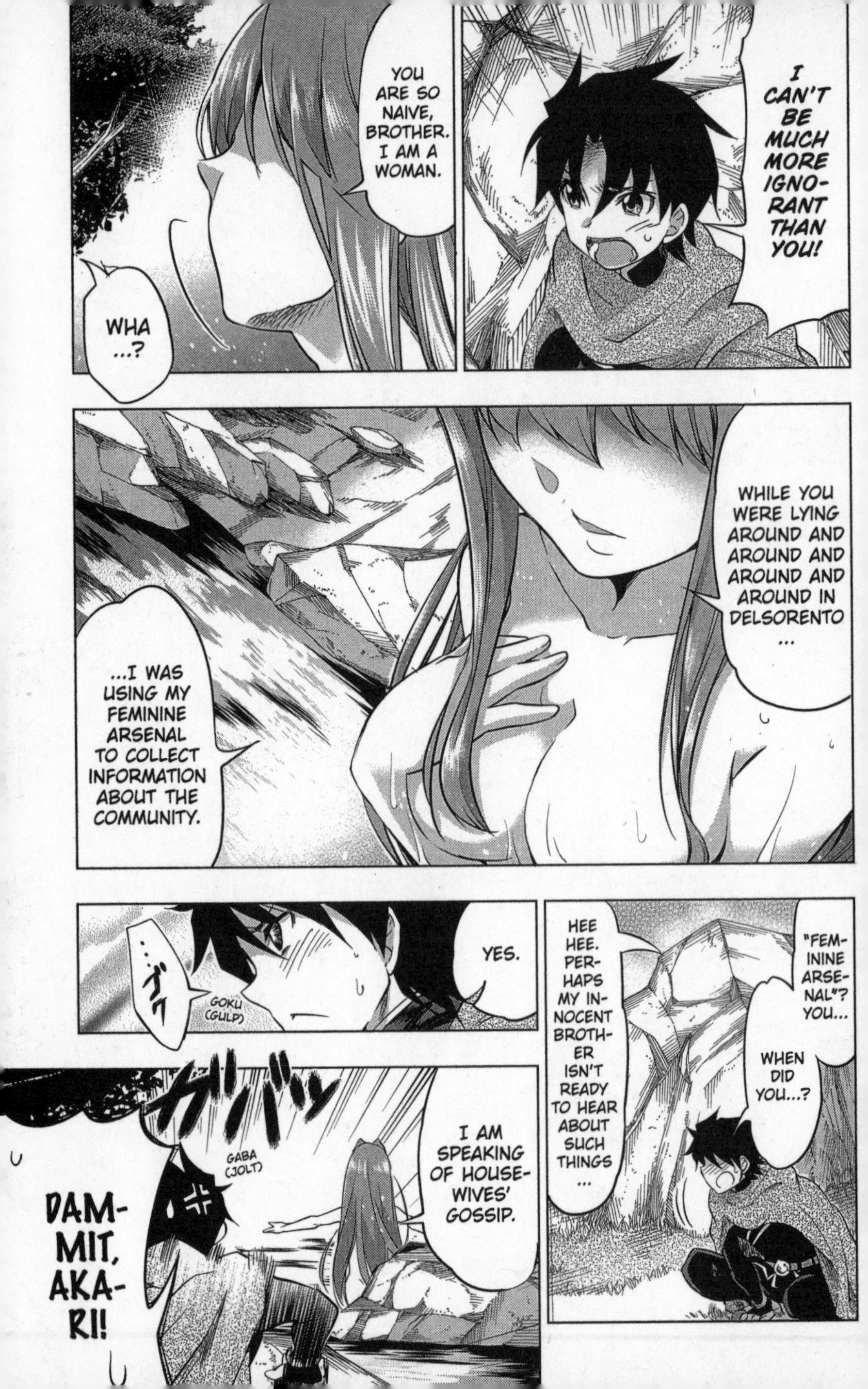
I CAN'T BE MUCH MORE IGNORANT THAN YOU!
YOU ARE SO NAIVE, BROTHER. I AM A WOMAN.
WHA...?
WHILE YOU WERE LYING AROUND AND AROUND AND AROUND AND AROUND IN DELSORENTO...
...I WAS USING MY FEMININE ARSENAL TO COLLECT INFORMATION ABOUT THE COMMUNITY.
"FEMININE ARSENAL"? YOU...
WHEN DID YOU...?
HEE HEE. PERHAPS MY INNOCENT BROTHER ISN'T READY TO HEAR ABOUT SUCH THINGS...
YES.
GOKU (GULP)
I AM SPEAKING OF HOUSEWIVES' GOSSIP.
GABA (JOLT)
DAMMIT, AKARI!

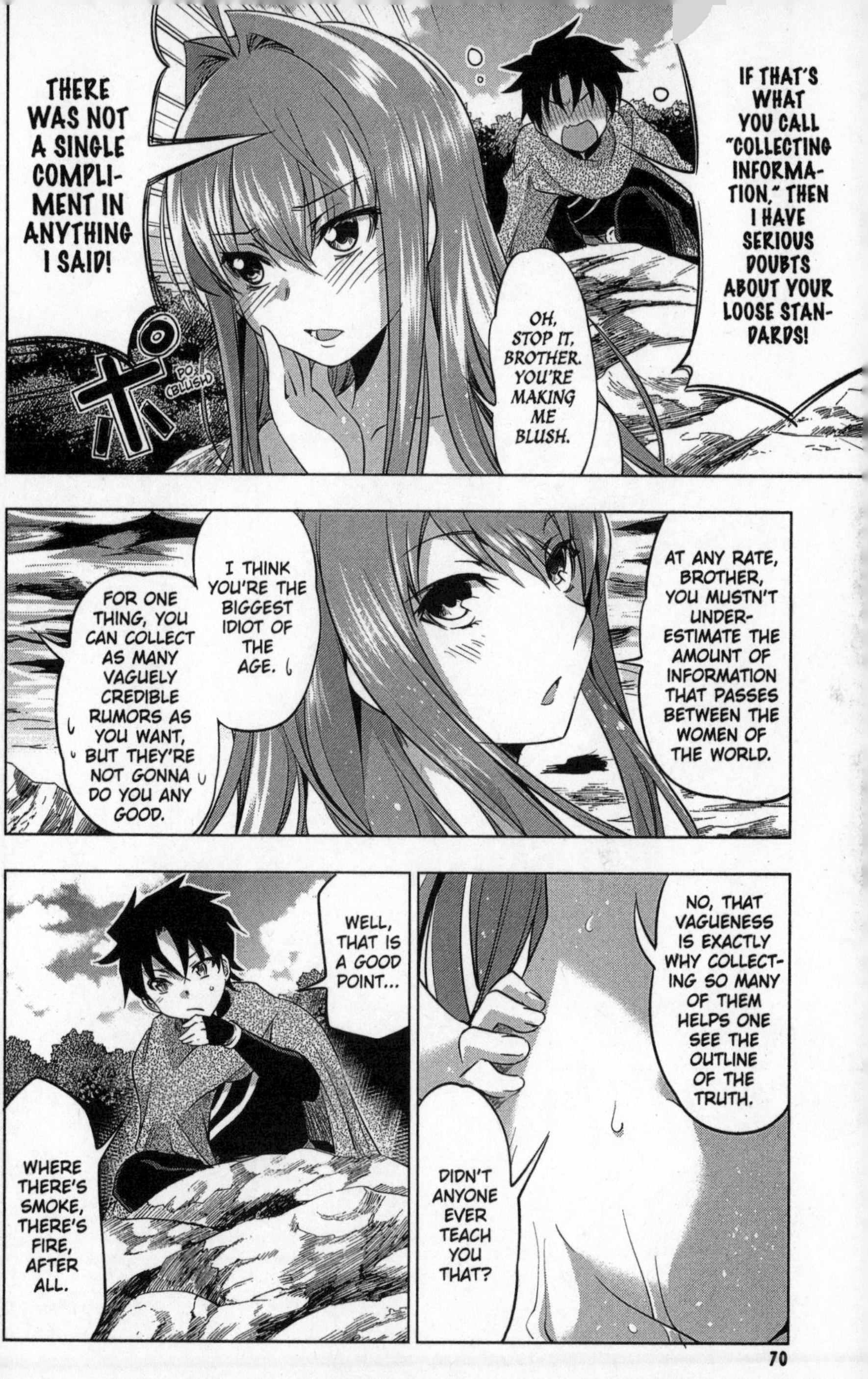
OH, STOP IT, BROTHER. YOU'RE MAKING ME BLUSH.
PO (BLUSH)
THERE WAS NOT A SINGLE COMPLIMENT IN ANYTHING I SAID!
IF THAT'S WHAT YOU CALL "COLLECTING INFORMATION," THEN I HAVE SERIOUS DOUBTS ABOUT YOUR LOOSE STANDARDS!
AT ANY RATE, BROTHER, YOU MUSTN'T UNDERESTIMATE THE AMOUNT OF INFORMATION THAT PASSES BETWEEN THE WOMEN OF THE WORLD.
I THINK YOU'RE THE BIGGEST IDIOT OF THE AGE.
FOR ONE THING, YOU CAN COLLECT AS MANY VAGUELY CREDIBLE RUMORS AS YOU WANT, BUT THEY'RE NOT GONNA DO YOU ANY GOOD.
NO, THAT VAGUENESS IS EXACTLY WHY COLLECTING SO MANY OF THEM HELPS ONE SEE THE OUTLINE OF THE TRUTH.
DIDN'T ANYONE EVER TEACH YOU THAT?
WELL, THAT IS A GOOD POINT...
WHERE THERE'S SMOKE, THERE'S FIRE, AFTER ALL.

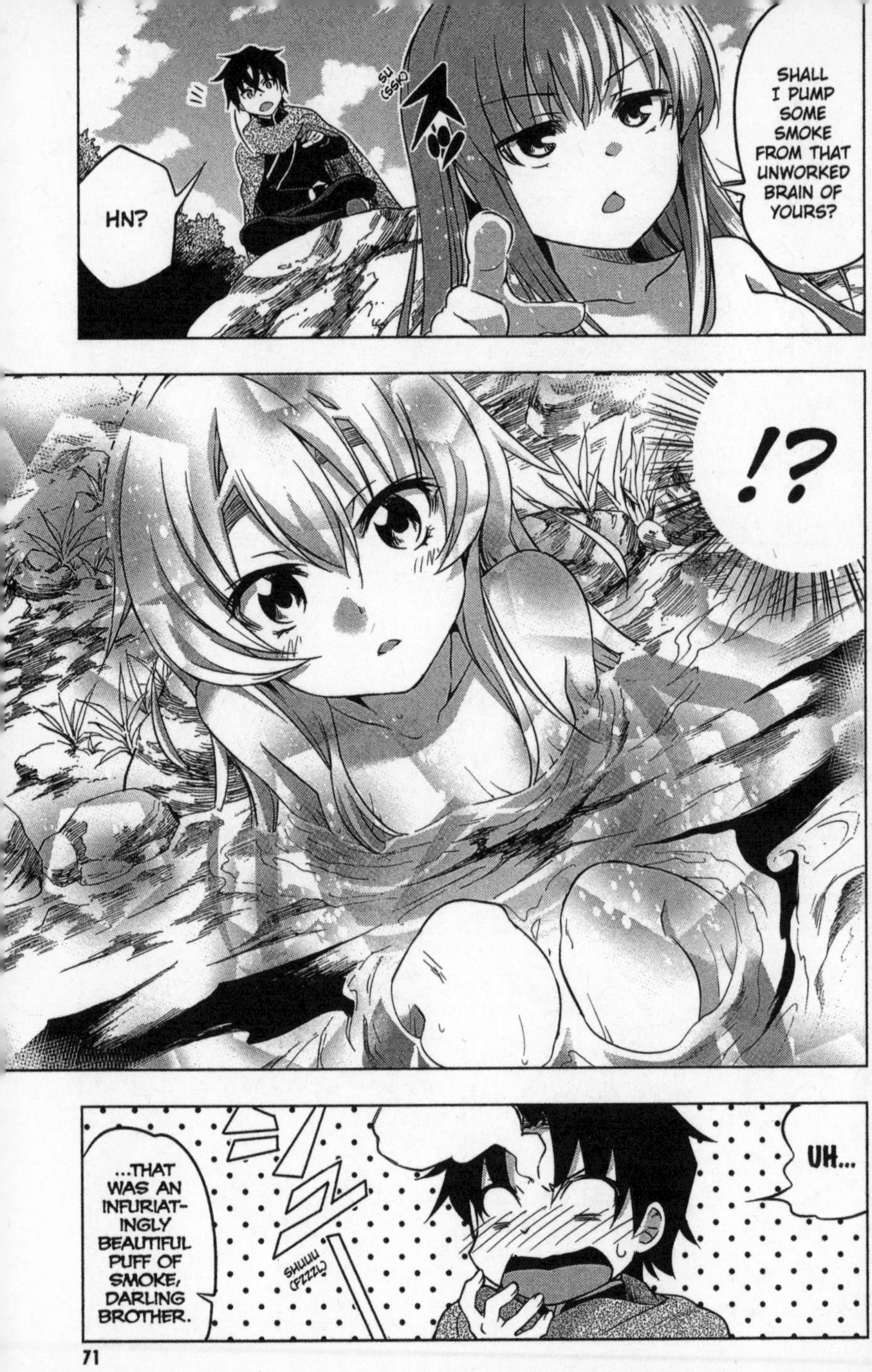
SHALL I PUMP SOME SMOKE FROM THAT UNWORKED BRAIN OF YOURS?
SU (SSK)
HN?
!?
UH...
SHUUU (FZZZL)
...THAT WAS AN INFURIATINGLY BEAUTIFUL PUFF OF SMOKE, DARLING BROTHER.

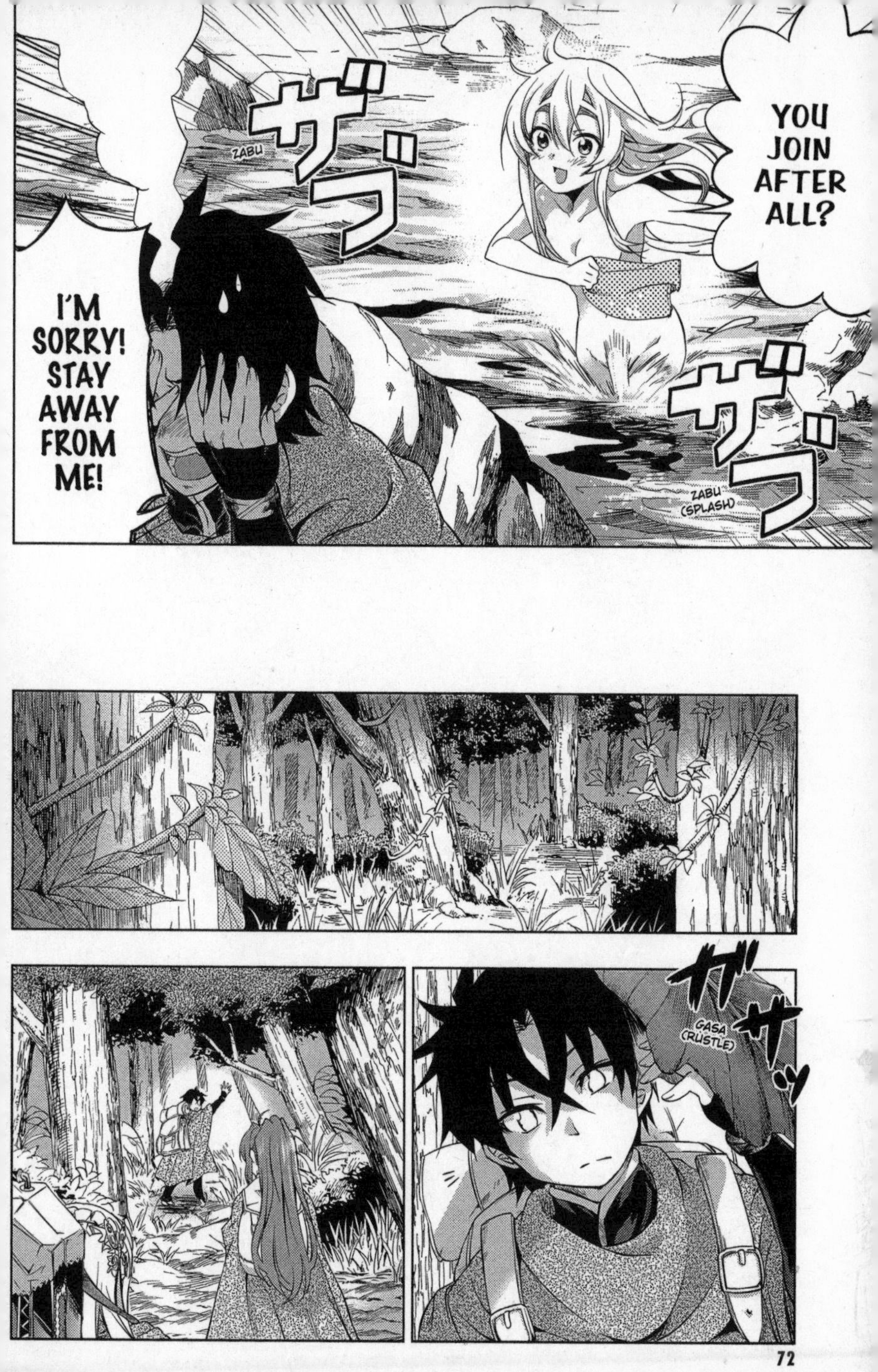
YOU JOIN AFTER ALL?
ZABU
ZABU (SPLASH)
I'M SORRY! STAY AWAY FROM ME!
GASA (RUSTLE)

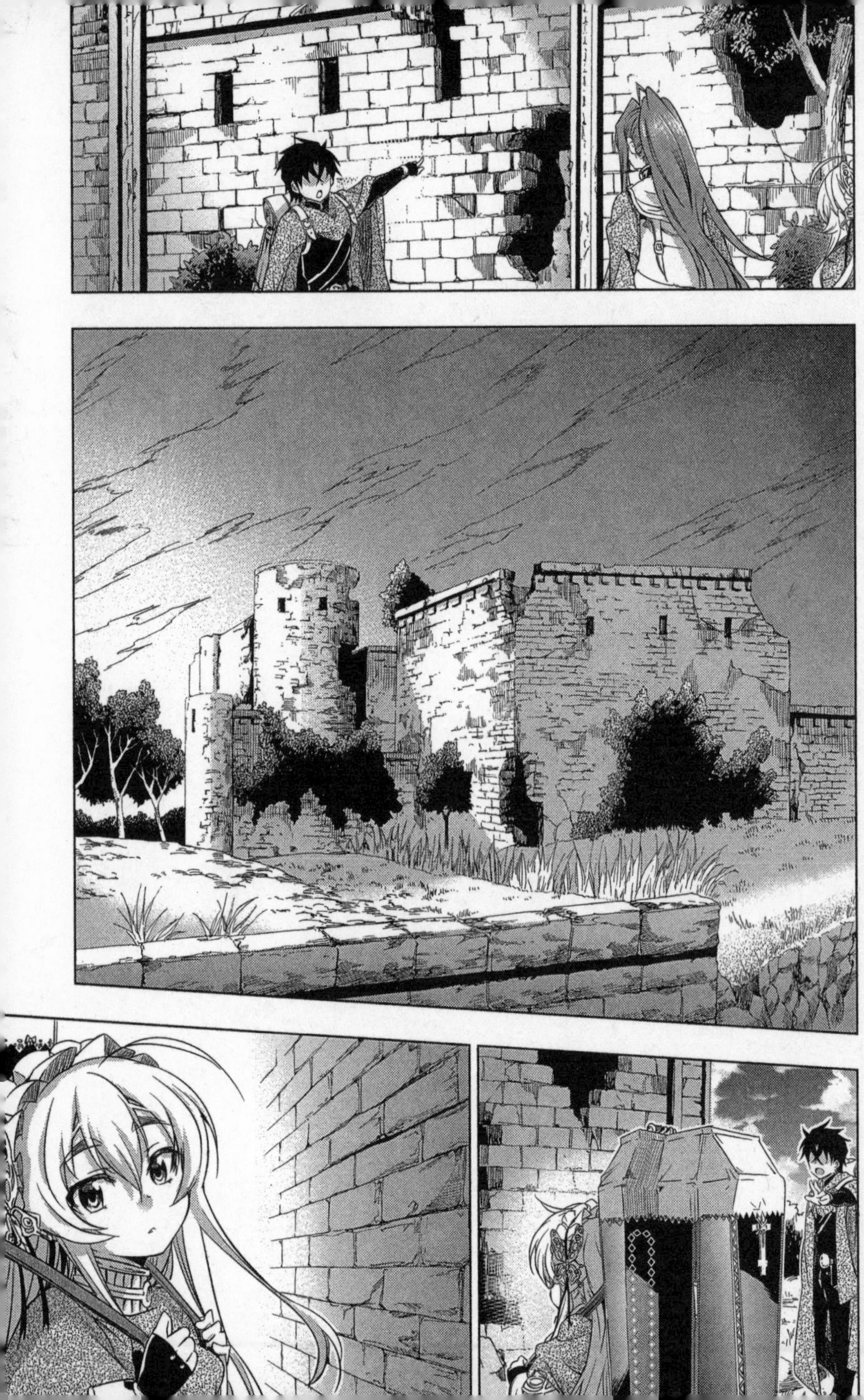

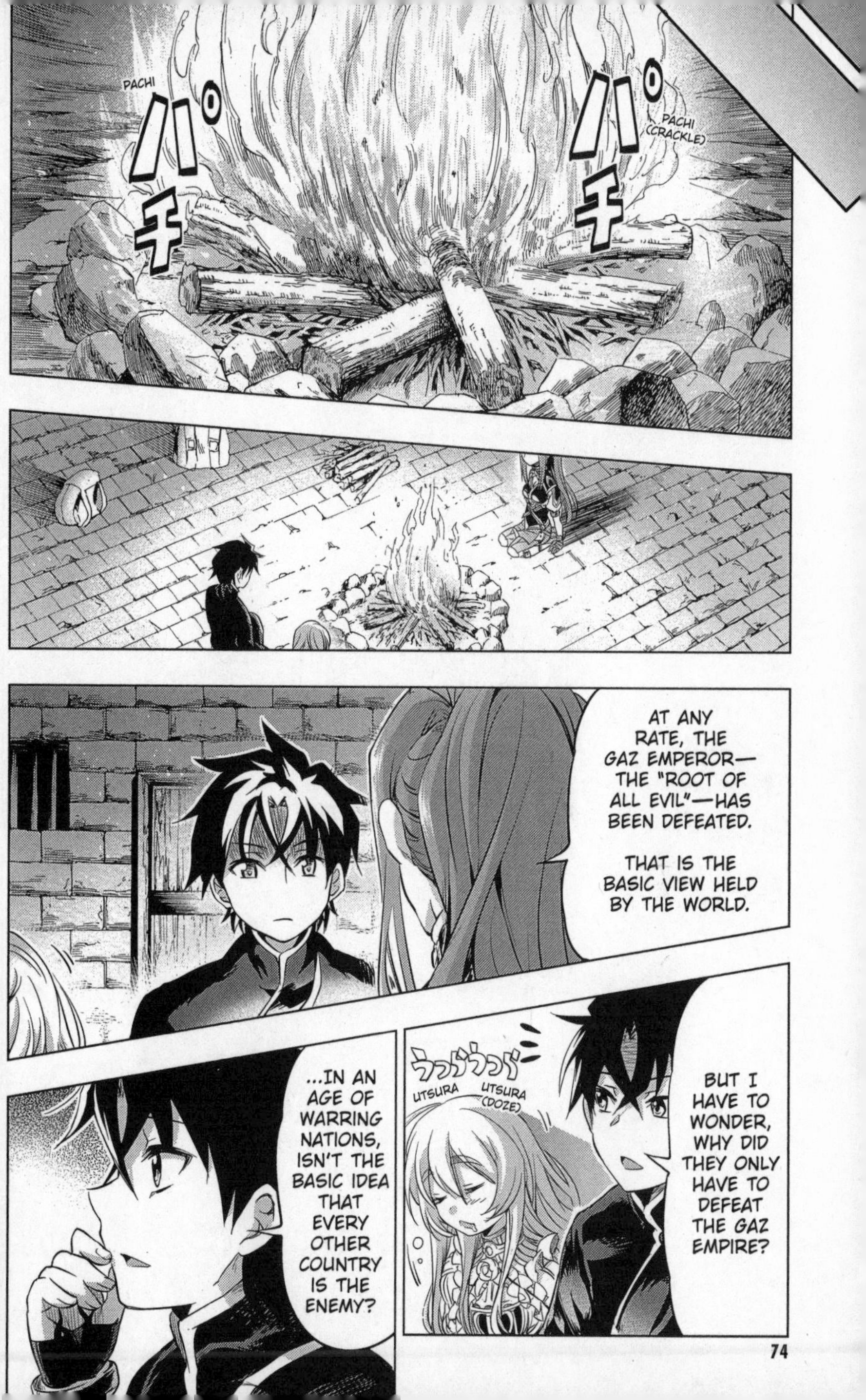
PACHI (CRACKLE)
PACHI
AT ANY RATE, THE GAZ EMPEROR—THE "ROOT OF ALL EVIL"—HAS BEEN DEFEATED.
THAT IS THE BASIC VIEW HELD BY THE WORLD.
BUT I HAVE TO WONDER, WHY DID THEY ONLY HAVE TO DEFEAT THE GAZ EMPIRE?
UTSURA UTSURA (DOZE)
...IN AN AGE OF WARRING NATIONS, ISN'T THE BASIC IDEA THAT EVERY OTHER COUNTRY IS THE ENEMY?

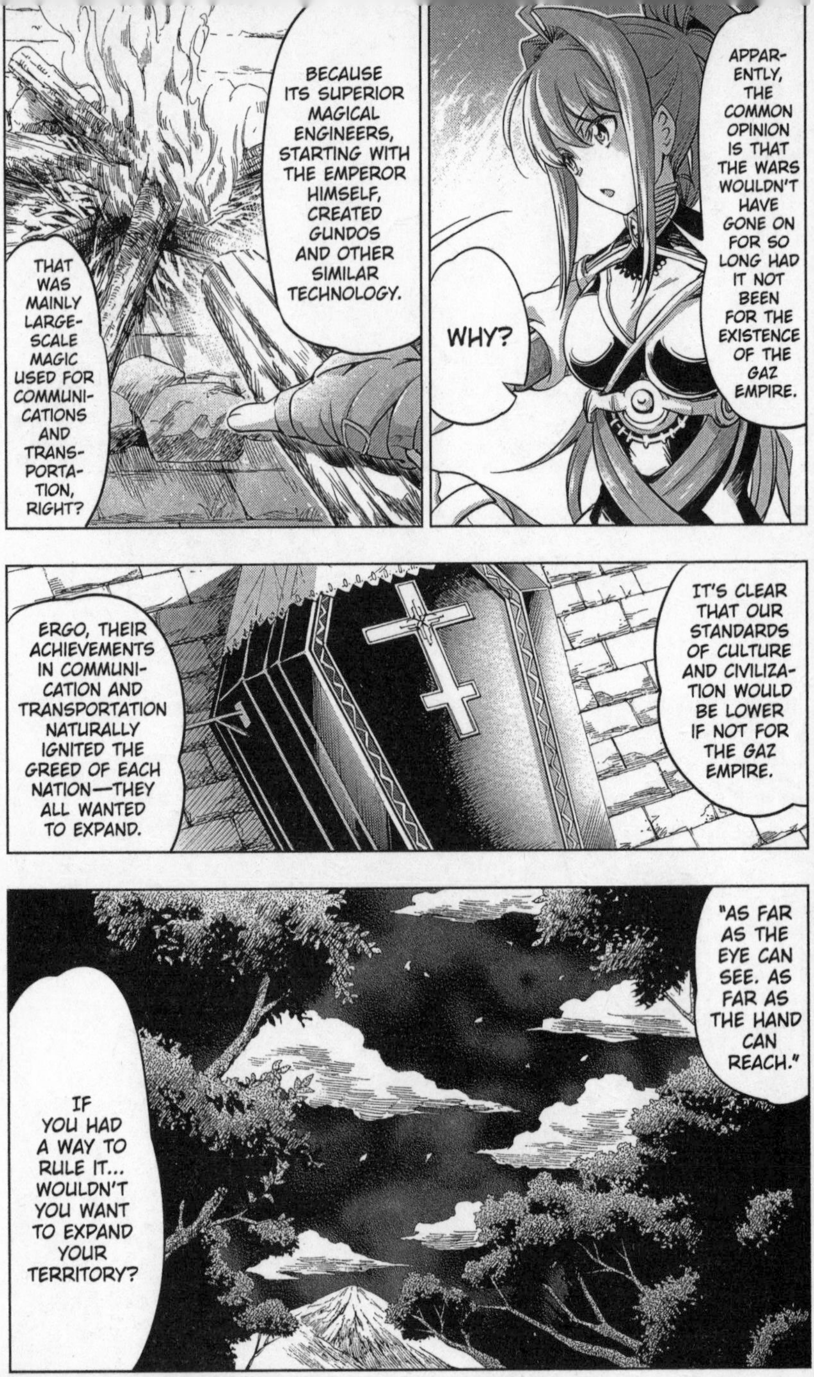
APPARENTLY, THE COMMON OPINION IS THAT THE WARS WOULDN'T HAVE GONE ON FOR SO LONG HAD IT NOT BEEN FOR THE EXISTENCE OF THE GAZ EMPIRE.
WHY?
BECAUSE ITS SUPERIOR MAGICAL ENGINEERS, STARTING WITH THE EMPEROR HIMSELF, CREATED GUNDOS AND OTHER SIMILAR TECHNOLOGY.
THAT WAS MAINLY LARGE-SCALE MAGIC USED FOR COMMUNICATIONS AND TRANSPORTATION, RIGHT?
IT'S CLEAR THAT OUR STANDARDS OF CULTURE AND CIVILIZATION WOULD BE LOWER IF NOT FOR THE GAZ EMPIRE.
ERGO, THEIR ACHIEVEMENTS IN COMMUNICATION AND TRANSPORTATION NATURALLY IGNITED THE GREED OF EACH NATION—THEY ALL WANTED TO EXPAND.
"AS FAR AS THE EYE CAN SEE. AS FAR AS THE HAND CAN REACH."
IF YOU HAD A WAY TO RULE IT... WOULDN'T YOU WANT TO EXPAND YOUR TERRITORY?

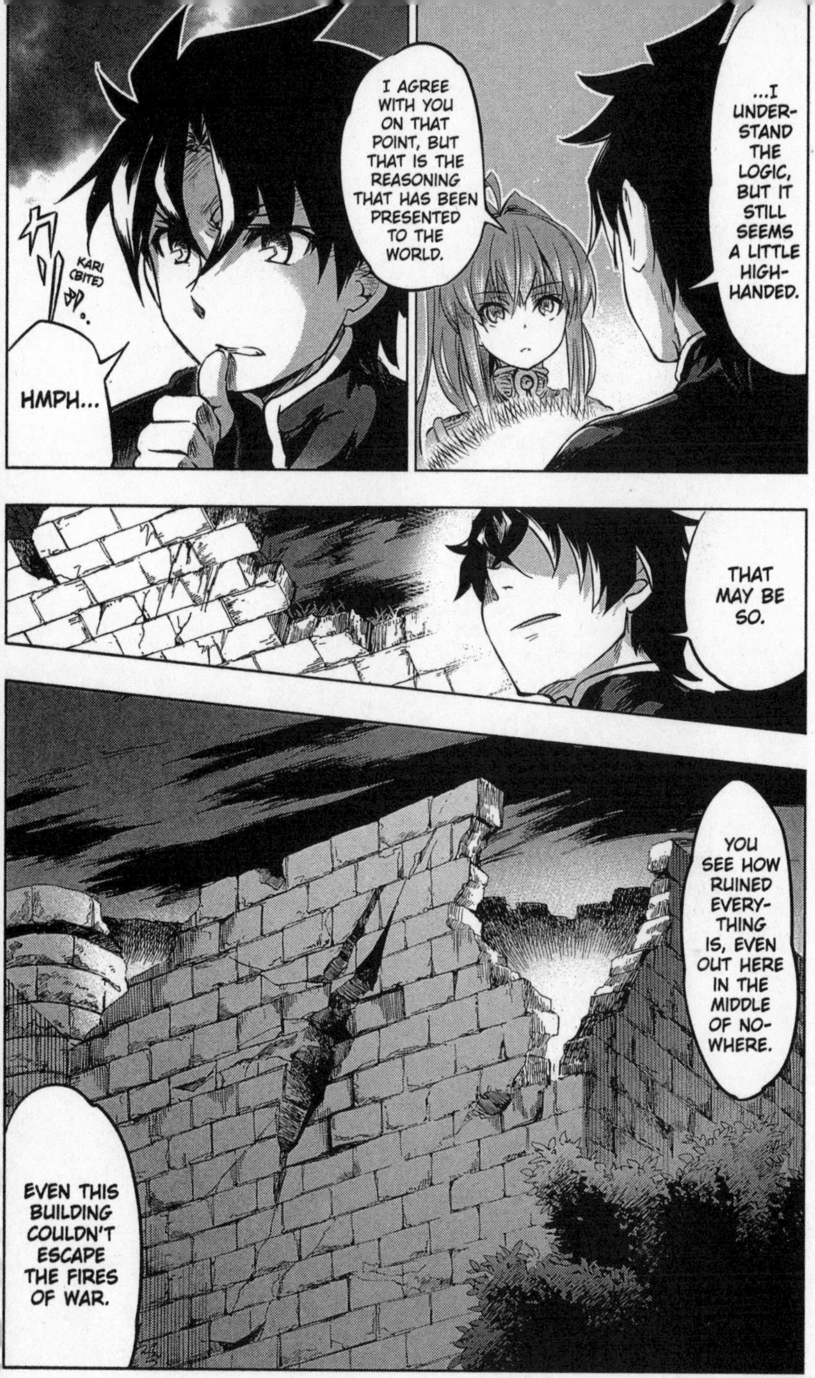
...I UNDERSTAND THE LOGIC, BUT IT STILL SEEMS A LITTLE HIGH-HANDED.
I AGREE WITH YOU ON THAT POINT, BUT THAT IS THE REASONING THAT HAS BEEN PRESENTED TO THE WORLD.
KARI (BITE)
HMPH...
THAT MAY BE SO.
YOU SEE HOW RUINED EVERYTHING IS, EVEN OUT HERE IN THE MIDDLE OF NOWHERE.
EVEN THIS BUILDING COULDN'T ESCAPE THE FIRES OF WAR.

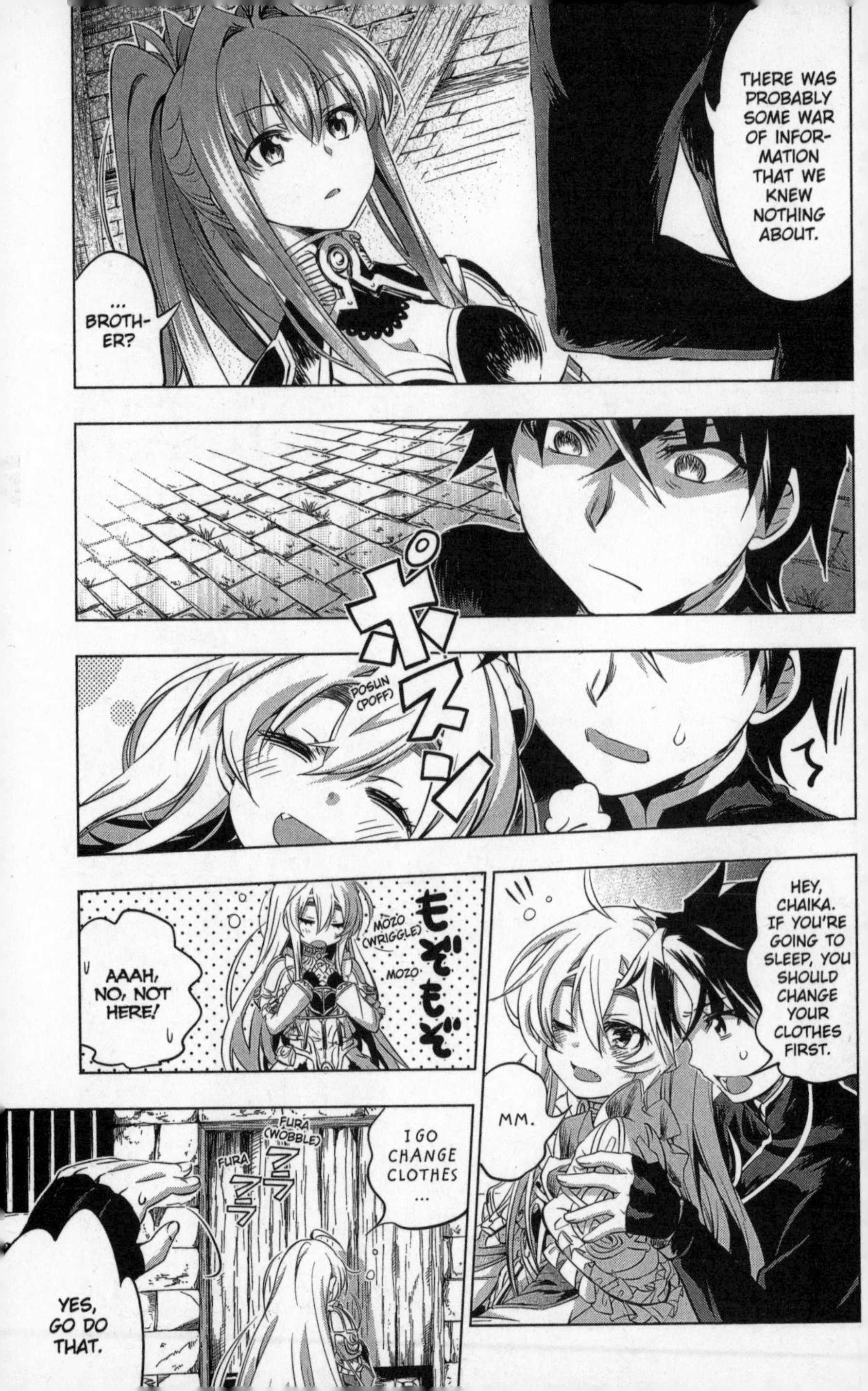

THERE WAS PROBABLY SOME WAR OF INFORMATION THAT WE KNEW NOTHING ABOUT.
... BROTHER?
ポスン
POSUN (POFF)
HEY, CHAIKA. IF YOU'RE GOING TO SLEEP, YOU SHOULD CHANGE YOUR CLOTHES FIRST.
MM.
もぞもぞ
MOZO (WRIGGLE)
MOZO
AAAH, NO, NOT HERE!
I GO CHANGE CLOTHES ...
フラフラ
FURA (WOBBLE)
FURA
YES, GO DO THAT.

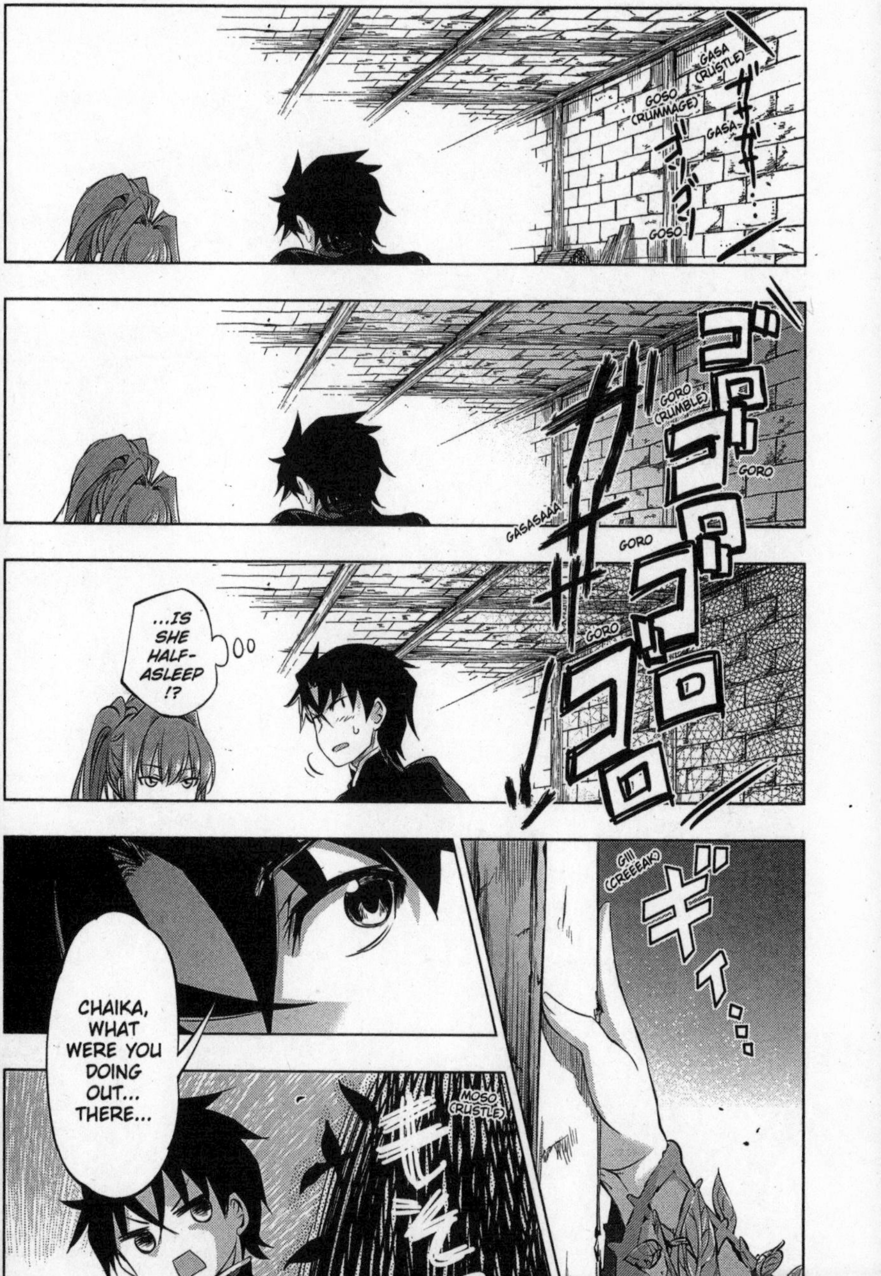
GASA (RUSTLE)
GASA
GOSO (RUMMAGE)
GOSO
GORO (RUMBLE)
GORO
GORO
GASASAAA
GORO
...IS SHE HALF-ASLEEP!?
GIII (CREEEAK)
CHAIKA, WHAT WERE YOU DOING OUT... THERE...
MOSO (RUSTLE)

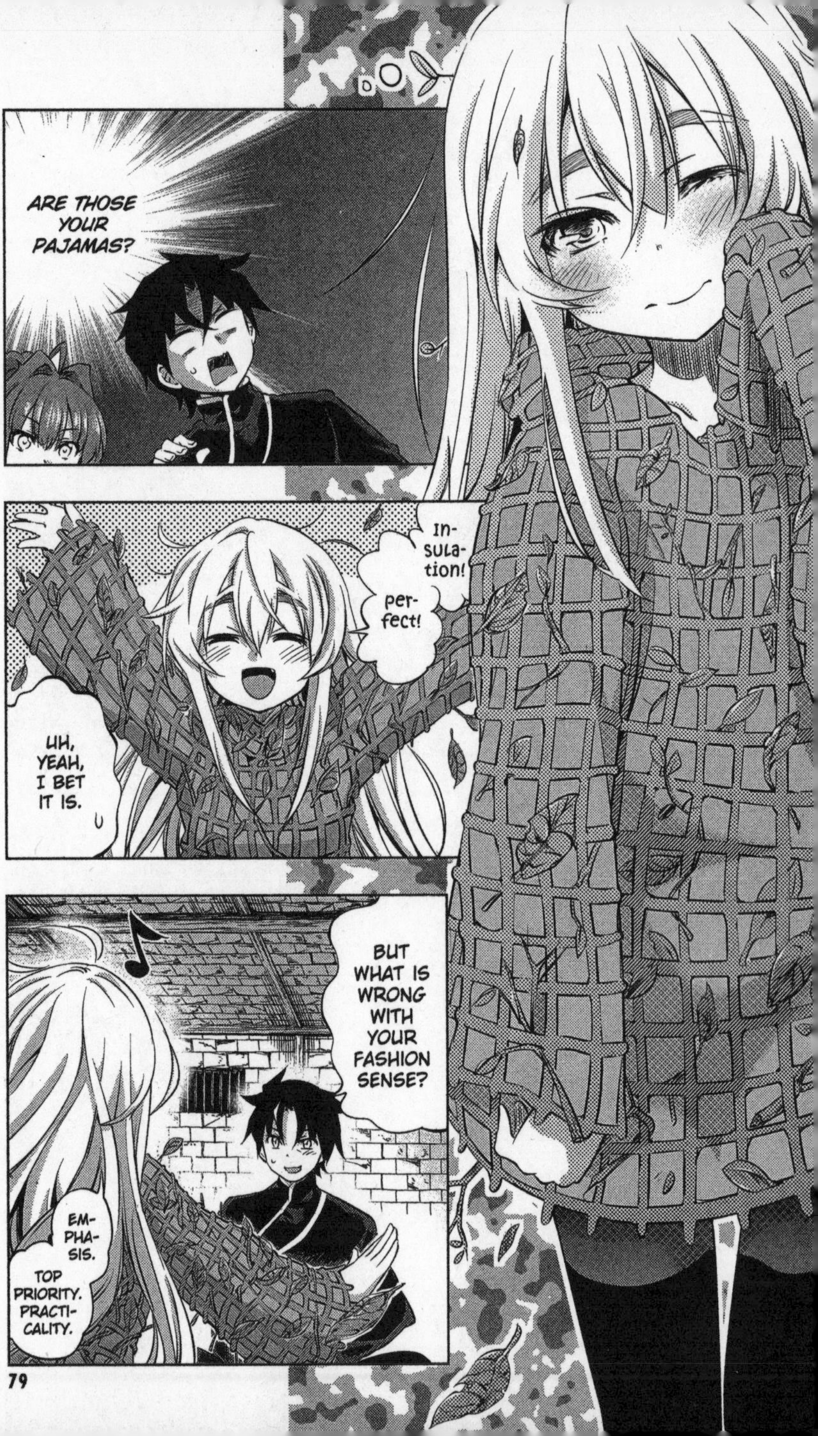
DO
ARE THOSE YOUR PAJAMAS?
In-sula-tion!
per-fect!
UH, YEAH, I BET IT IS.
BUT WHAT IS WRONG WITH YOUR FASHION SENSE?
EM-PHA-SIS.
TOP PRIORITY. PRACTI-CALITY.

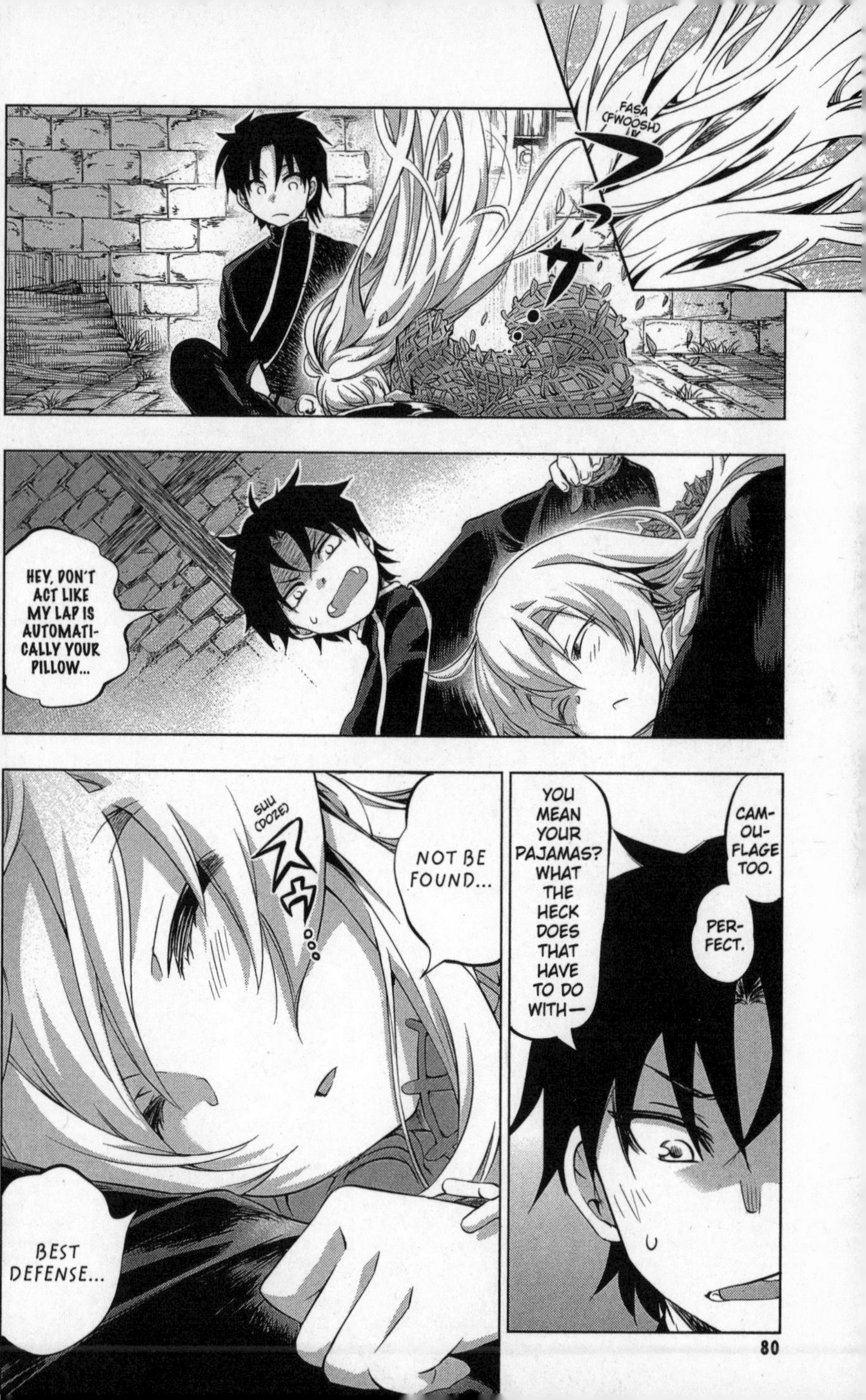
FASA (FWOOSH)
HEY, DON'T ACT LIKE MY LAP IS AUTOMATICALLY YOUR PILLOW...
CAMOUFLAGE TOO.
PERFECT.
YOU MEAN YOUR PAJAMAS? WHAT THE HECK DOES THAT HAVE TO DO WITH—
NOT BE FOUND...
SUU (DOZE)
BEST DEFENSE...

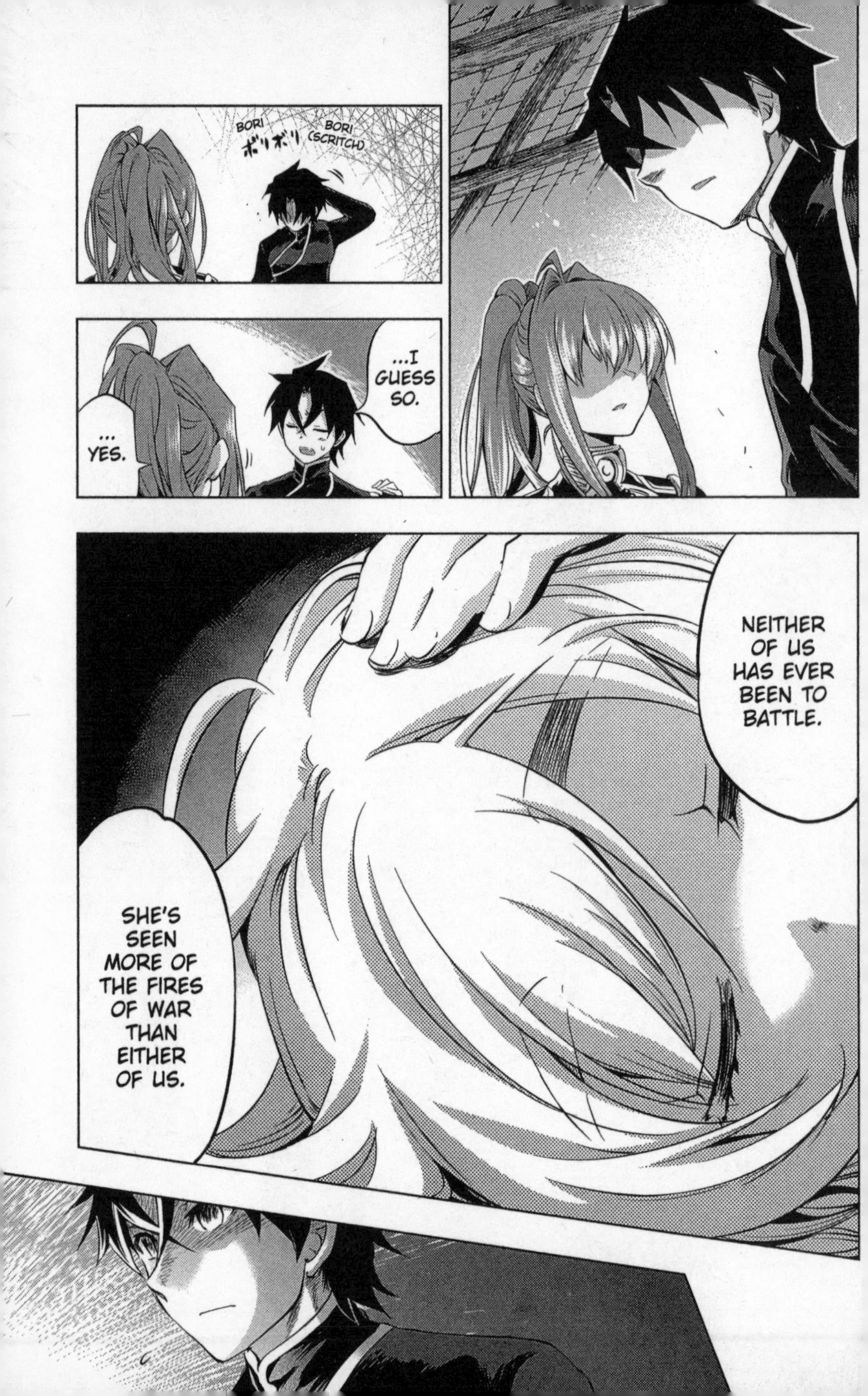
BORI BORI (SCRITCH)
ボリボリ
...I GUESS SO.
... YES.
NEITHER OF US HAS EVER BEEN TO BATTLE.
SHE'S SEEN MORE OF THE FIRES OF WAR THAN EITHER OF US.

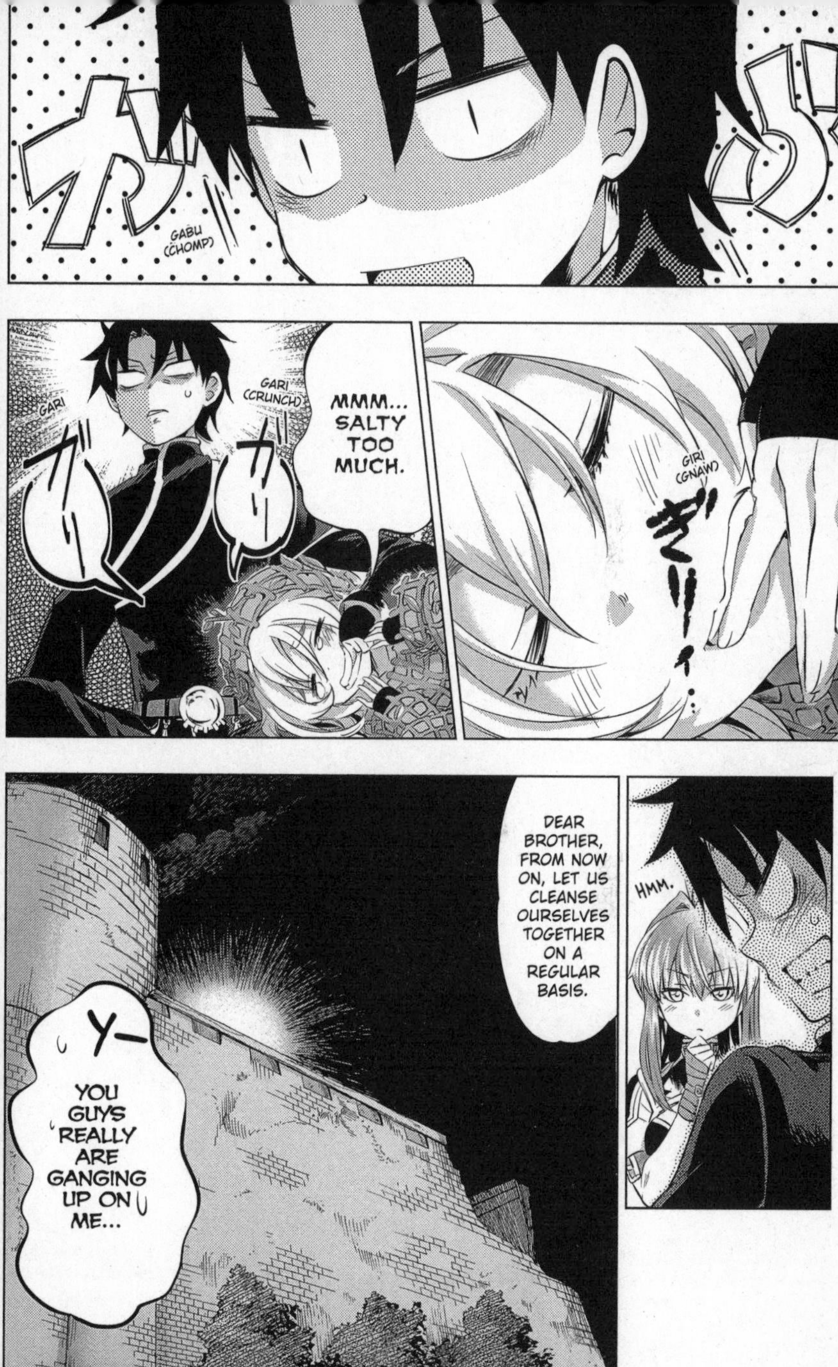
GABU (CHOMP)
GIRI (GNAW)
MMM... SALTY TOO MUCH.
GARI (CRUNCH)
GARI
DEAR BROTHER, FROM NOW ON, LET US CLEANSE OURSELVES TOGETHER ON A REGULAR BASIS.
HMM.
Y-
YOU GUYS REALLY ARE GANGING UP ON ME...

episode 13: END

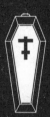

CHAIKA: THE COFFIN PRINCESS

episode 14: Dominica

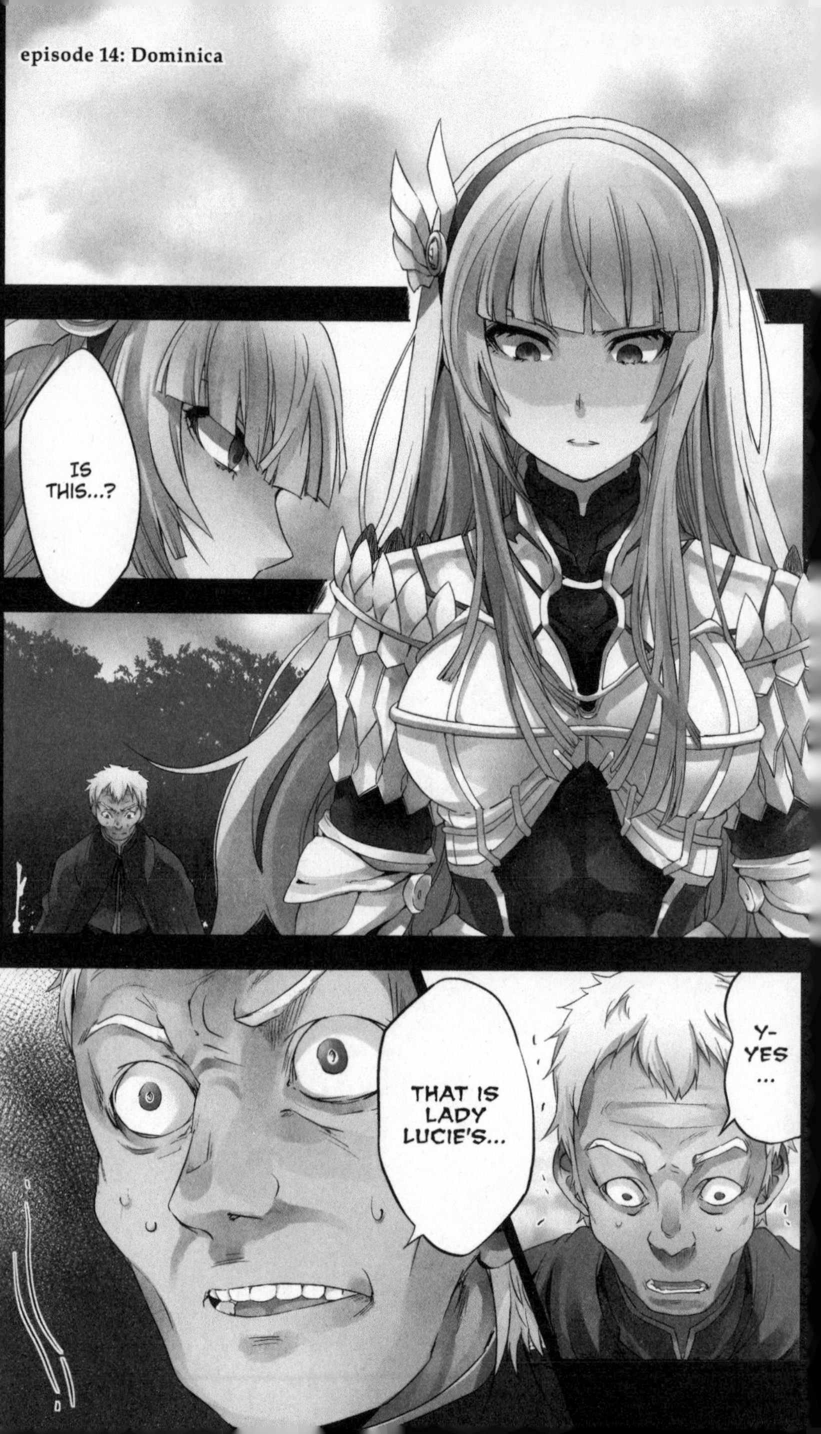
IS THIS...?
Y-YES...
THAT IS LADY LUCIE'S...

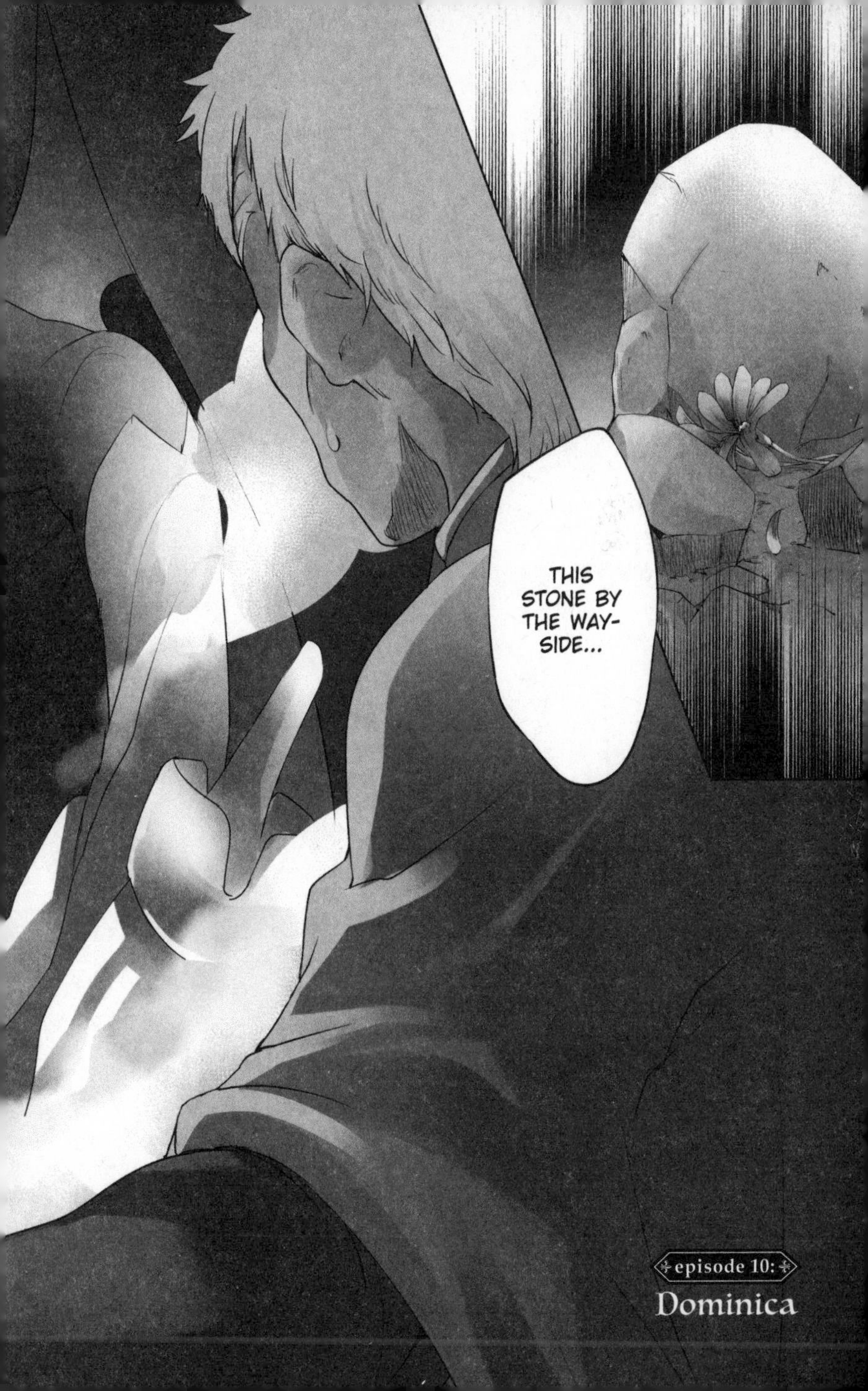
THIS STONE BY THE WAY-SIDE...
episode 10:
Dominica

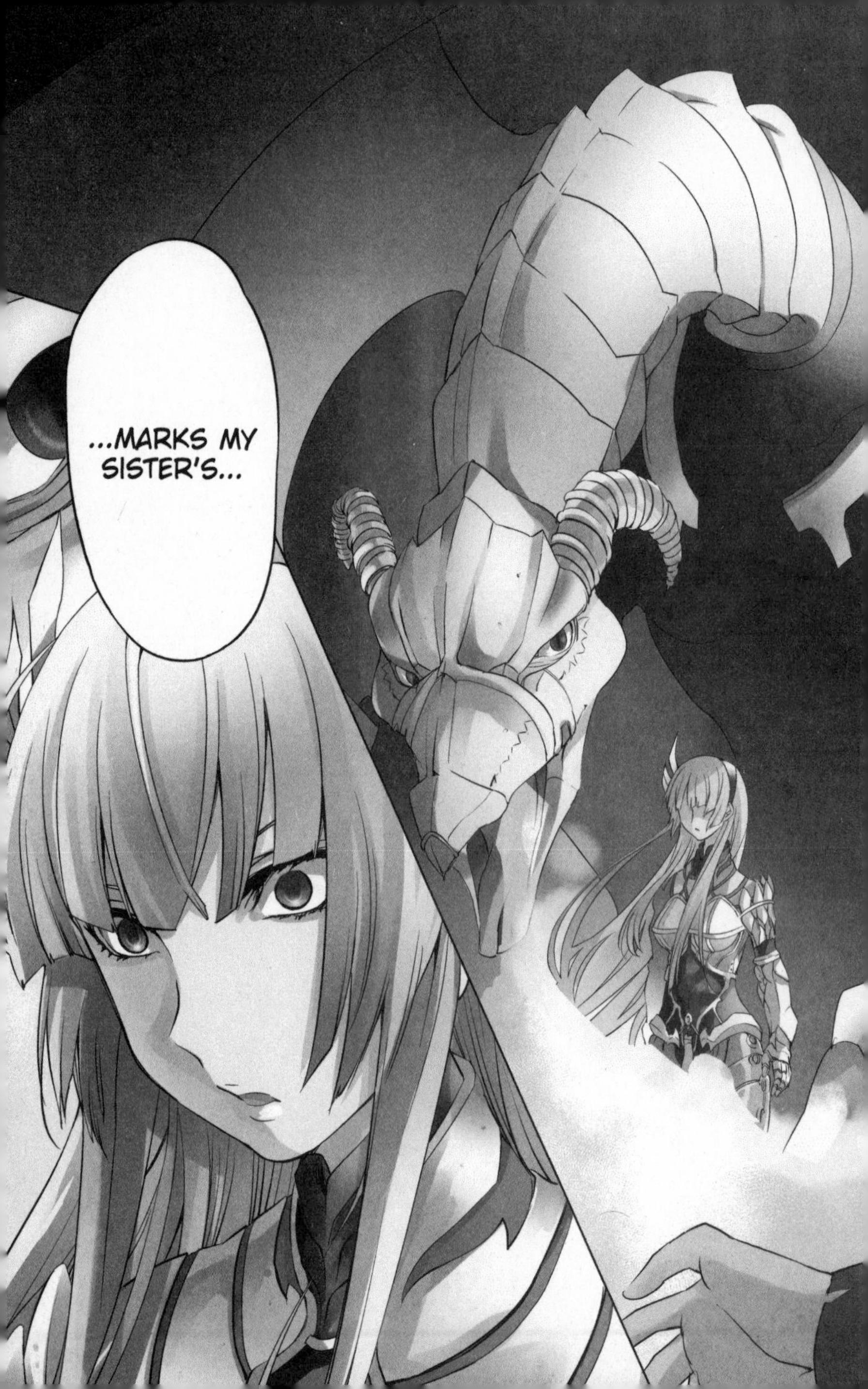
...MARKS MY SISTER'S...

CHAIKA: THE COFFIN PRINCESS

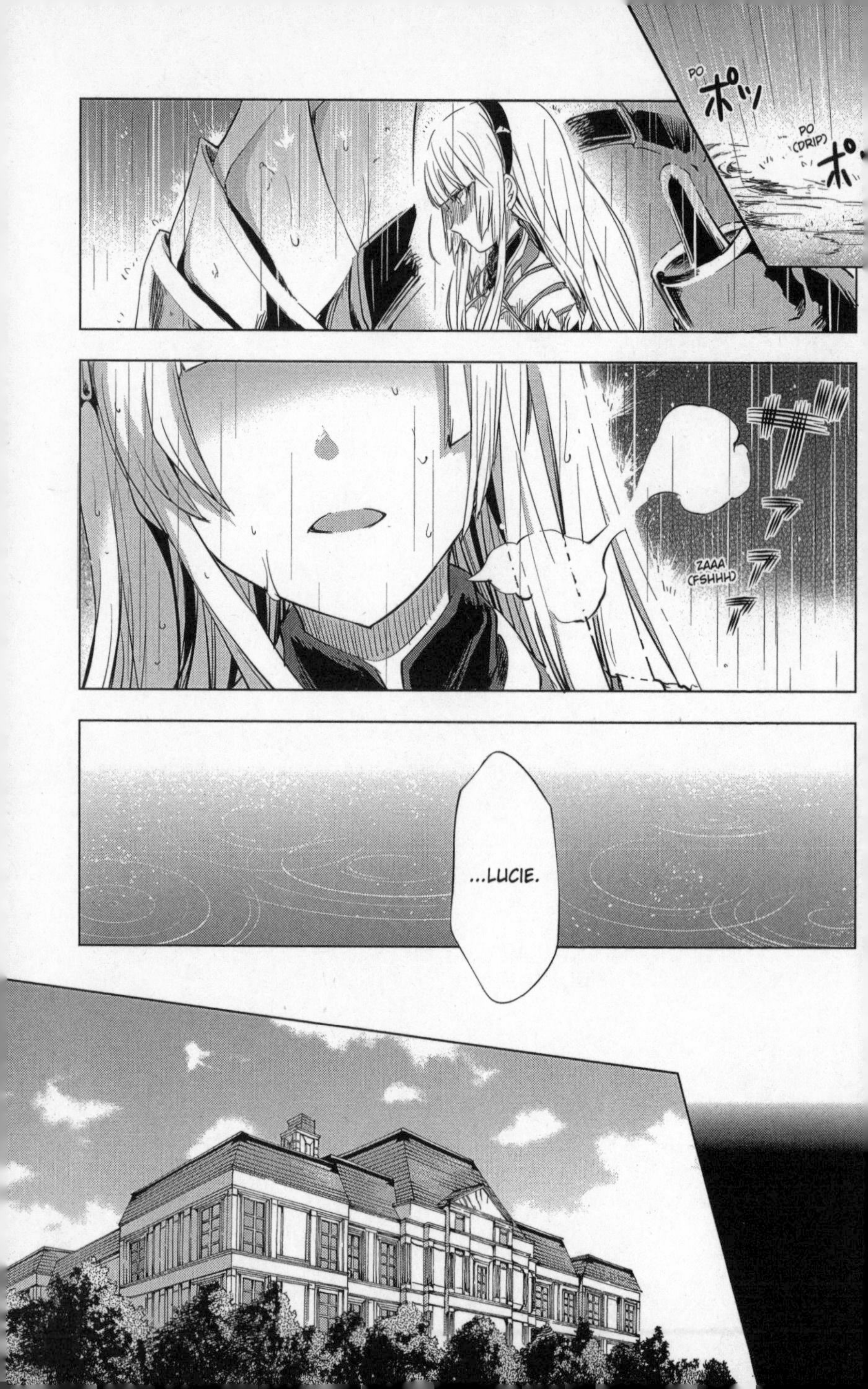
PO ポッ
PO (DRIP) ポ
ZAAA (FSHHH) ザァァァァ
...LUCIE.

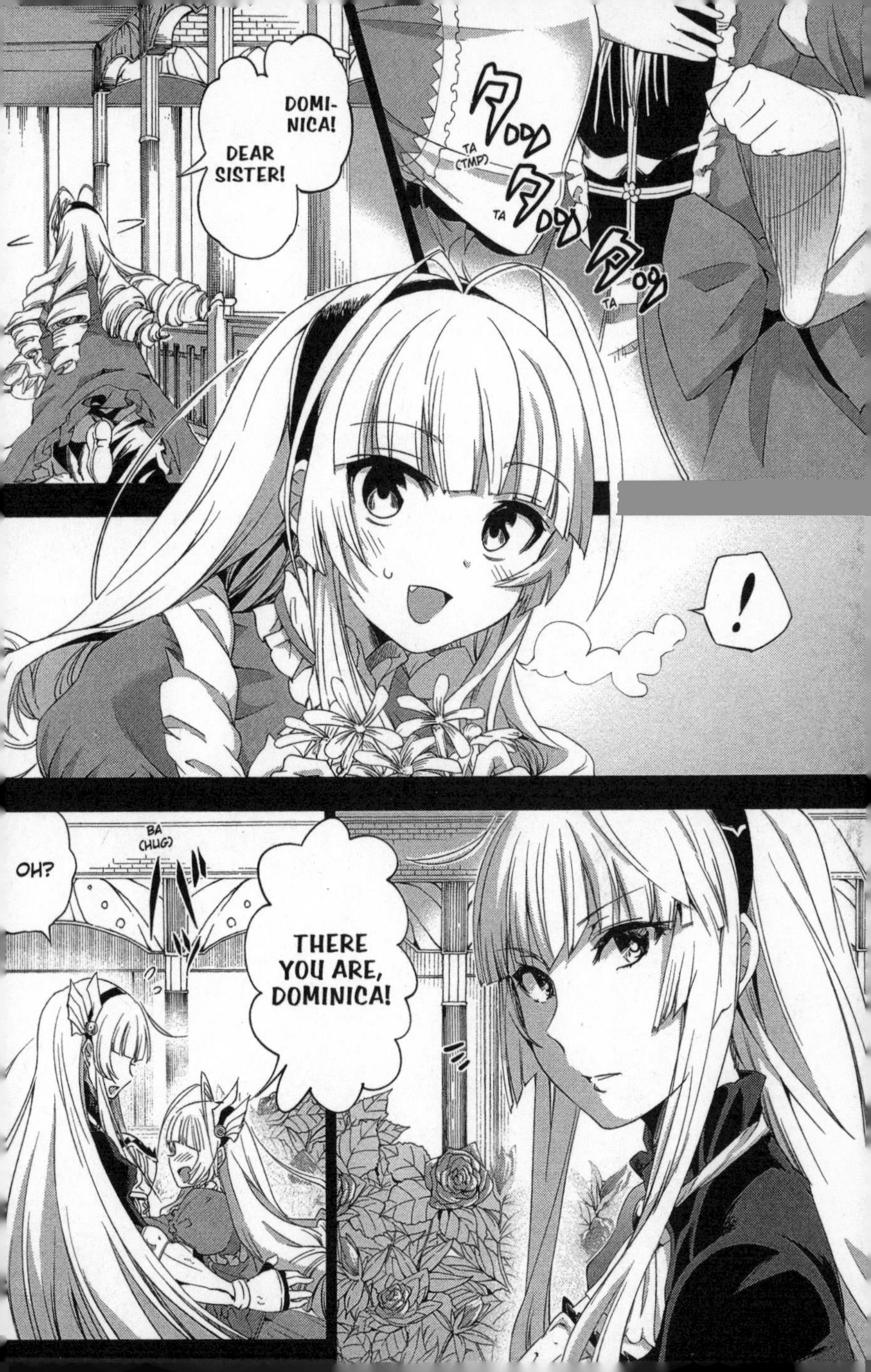
TA (TMP)
TA
TA
DOMI-NICA!
DEAR SISTER!
!
BA (HUG)
THERE YOU ARE, DOMINICA!
OH?

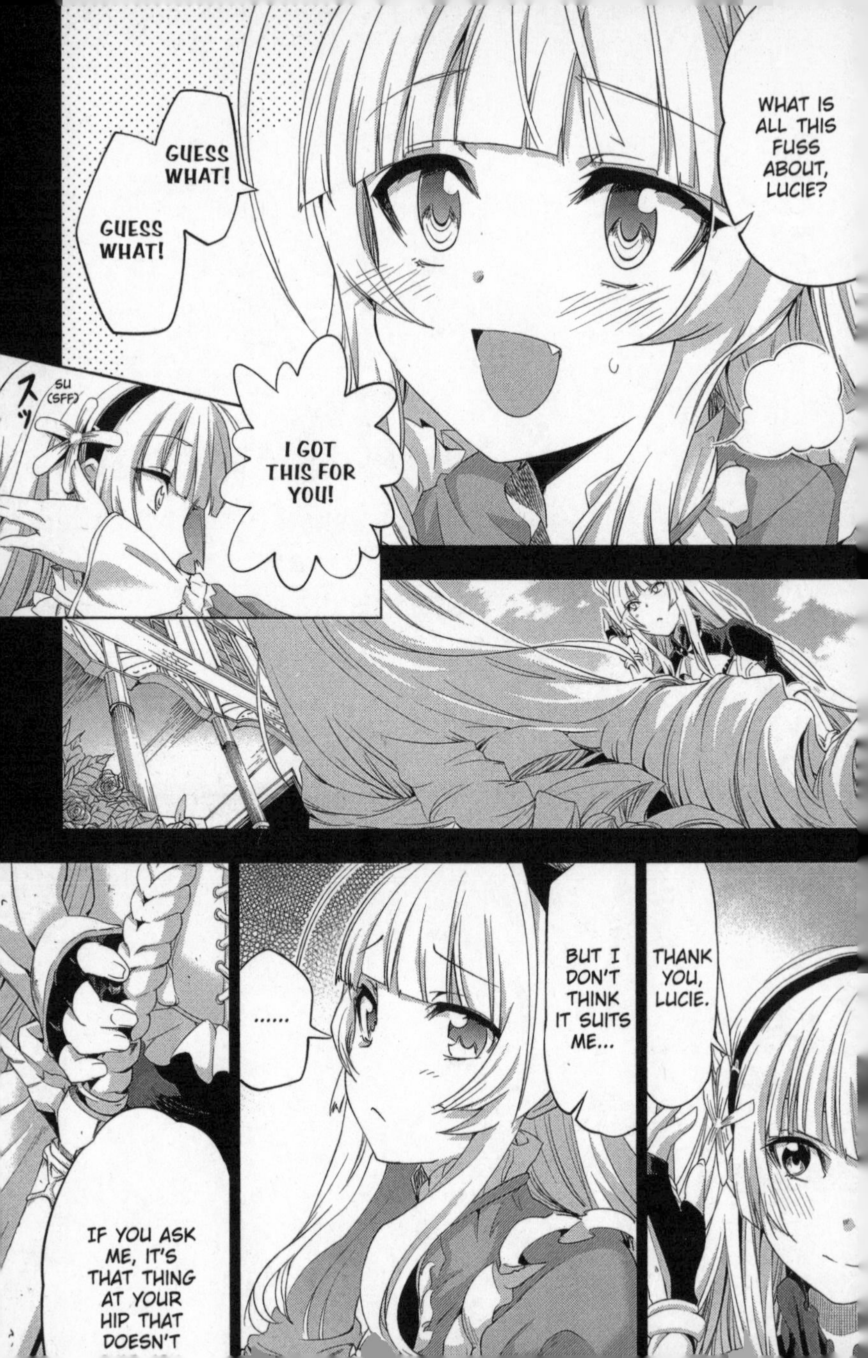
WHAT IS ALL THIS FUSS ABOUT, LUCIE?
GUESS WHAT!
GUESS WHAT!
I GOT THIS FOR YOU!
スッ
SU (SFF)
THANK YOU, LUCIE.
BUT I DON'T THINK IT SUITS ME...
......
IF YOU ASK ME, IT'S THAT THING AT YOUR HIP THAT DOESN'T

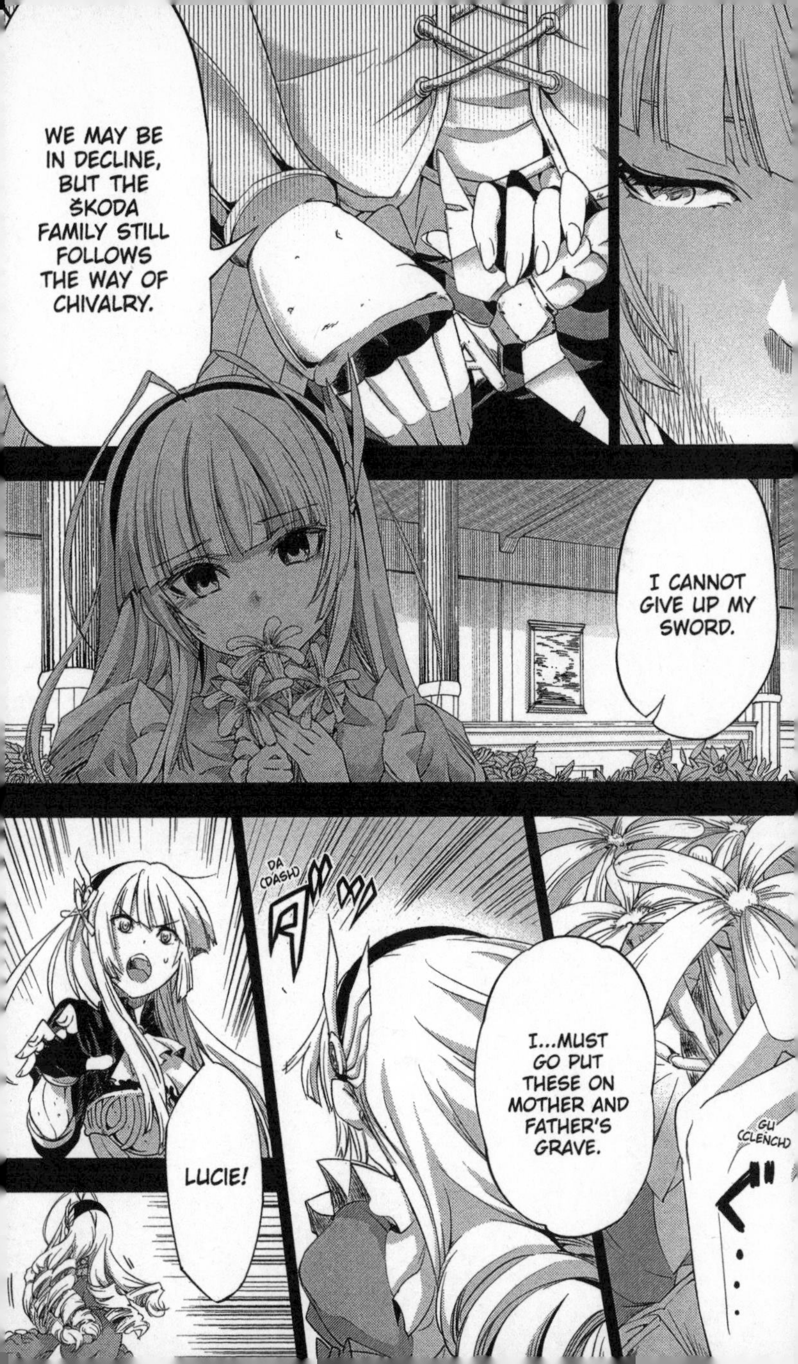

WE MAY BE IN DECLINE, BUT THE ŠKODA FAMILY STILL FOLLOWS THE WAY OF CHIVALRY.
I CANNOT GIVE UP MY SWORD.
GU (CLENCH)
...
I...MUST GO PUT THESE ON MOTHER AND FATHER'S GRAVE.
DA (DASH)
LUCIE!

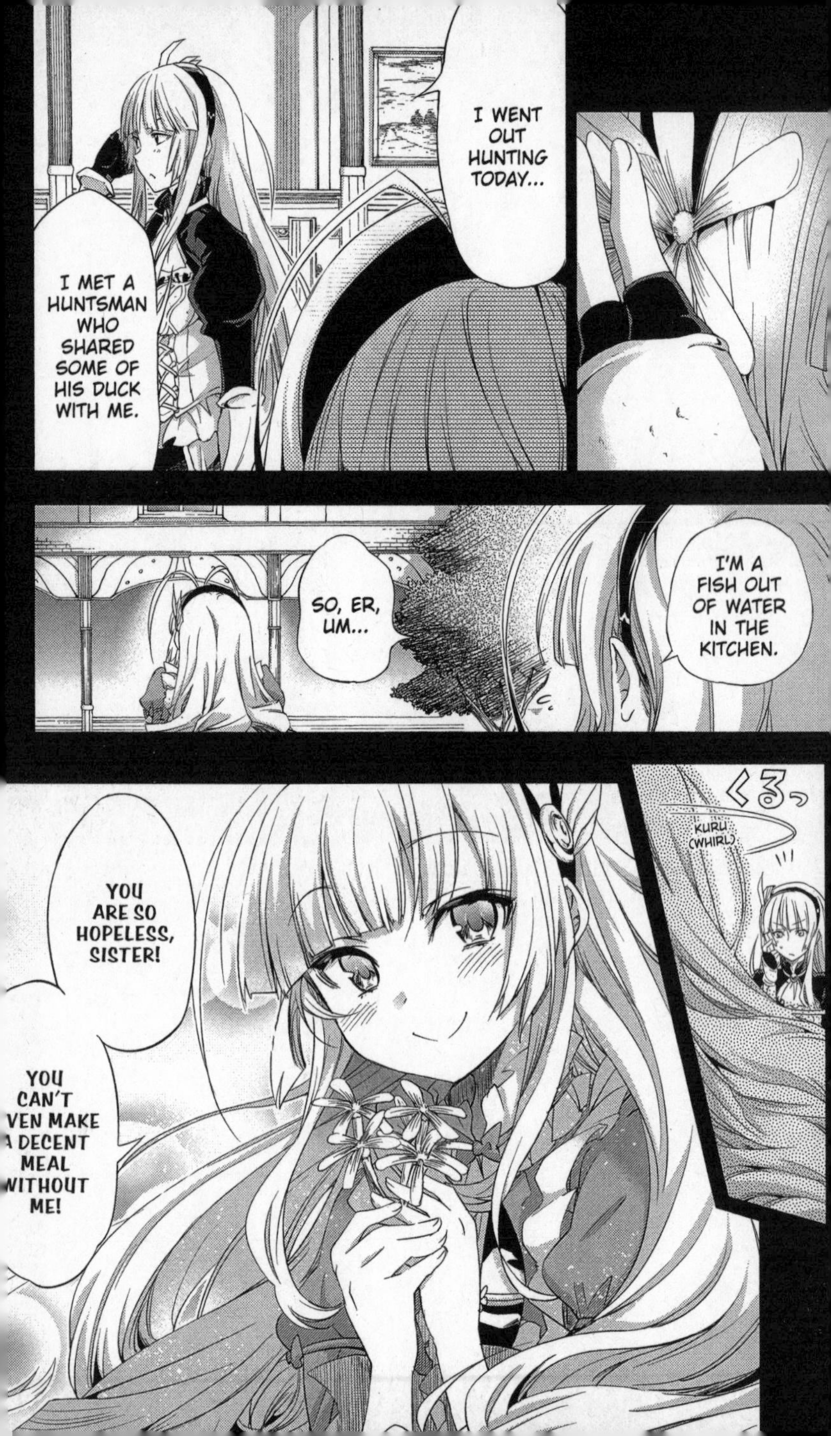

I WENT OUT HUNTING TODAY...
I MET A HUNTSMAN WHO SHARED SOME OF HIS DUCK WITH ME.
I'M A FISH OUT OF WATER IN THE KITCHEN.
SO, ER, UM...
くるっ
KURU (WHIRL)
YOU ARE SO HOPELESS, SISTER!
YOU CAN'T VEN MAKE A DECENT MEAL WITHOUT ME!

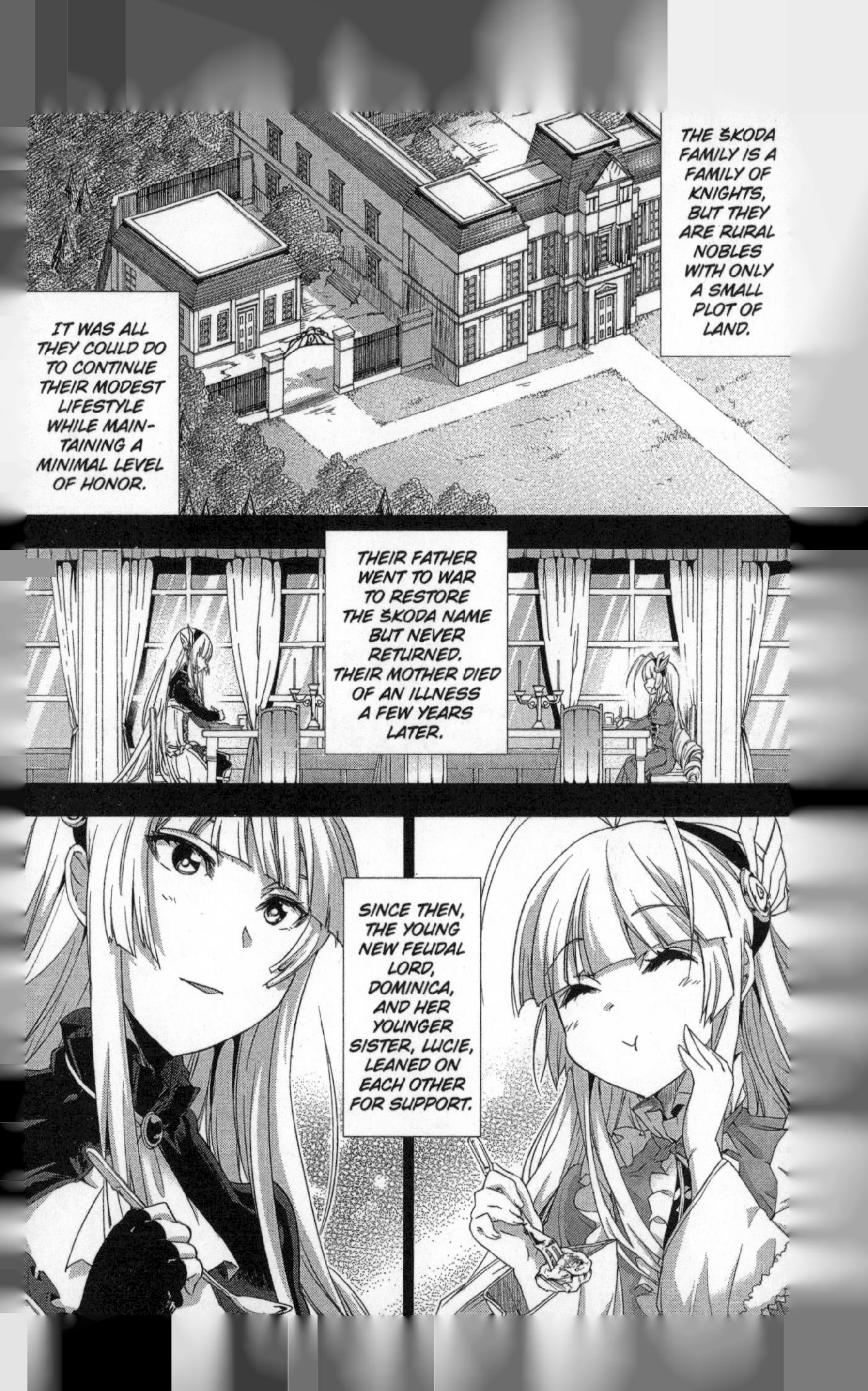
THE ŠKODA FAMILY IS A FAMILY OF KNIGHTS, BUT THEY ARE RURAL NOBLES WITH ONLY A SMALL PLOT OF LAND.
IT WAS ALL THEY COULD DO TO CONTINUE THEIR MODEST LIFESTYLE WHILE MAIN-TAINING A MINIMAL LEVEL OF HONOR.
THEIR FATHER WENT TO WAR TO RESTORE THE ŠKODA NAME BUT NEVER RETURNED. THEIR MOTHER DIED OF AN ILLNESS A FEW YEARS LATER.
SINCE THEN, THE YOUNG NEW FEUDAL LORD, DOMINICA, AND HER YOUNGER SISTER, LUCIE, LEANED ON EACH OTHER FOR SUPPORT.

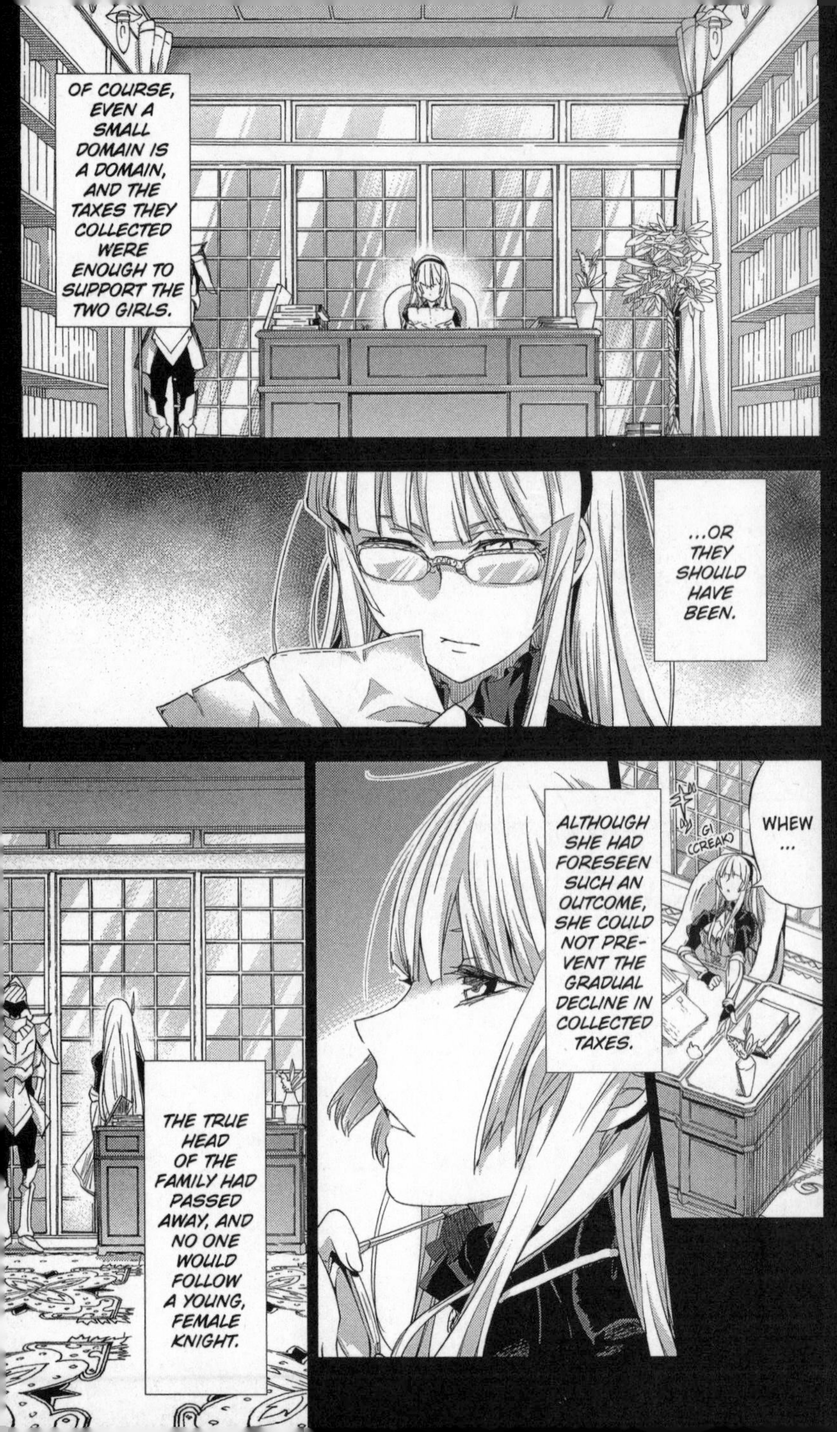
OF COURSE, EVEN A SMALL DOMAIN IS A DOMAIN, AND THE TAXES THEY COLLECTED WERE ENOUGH TO SUPPORT THE TWO GIRLS.
...OR THEY SHOULD HAVE BEEN.
WHEW ...
GI (CREAK)
ALTHOUGH SHE HAD FORESEEN SUCH AN OUTCOME, SHE COULD NOT PRE-VENT THE GRADUAL DECLINE IN COLLECTED TAXES.
THE TRUE HEAD OF THE FAMILY HAD PASSED AWAY, AND NO ONE WOULD FOLLOW A YOUNG, FEMALE KNIGHT.

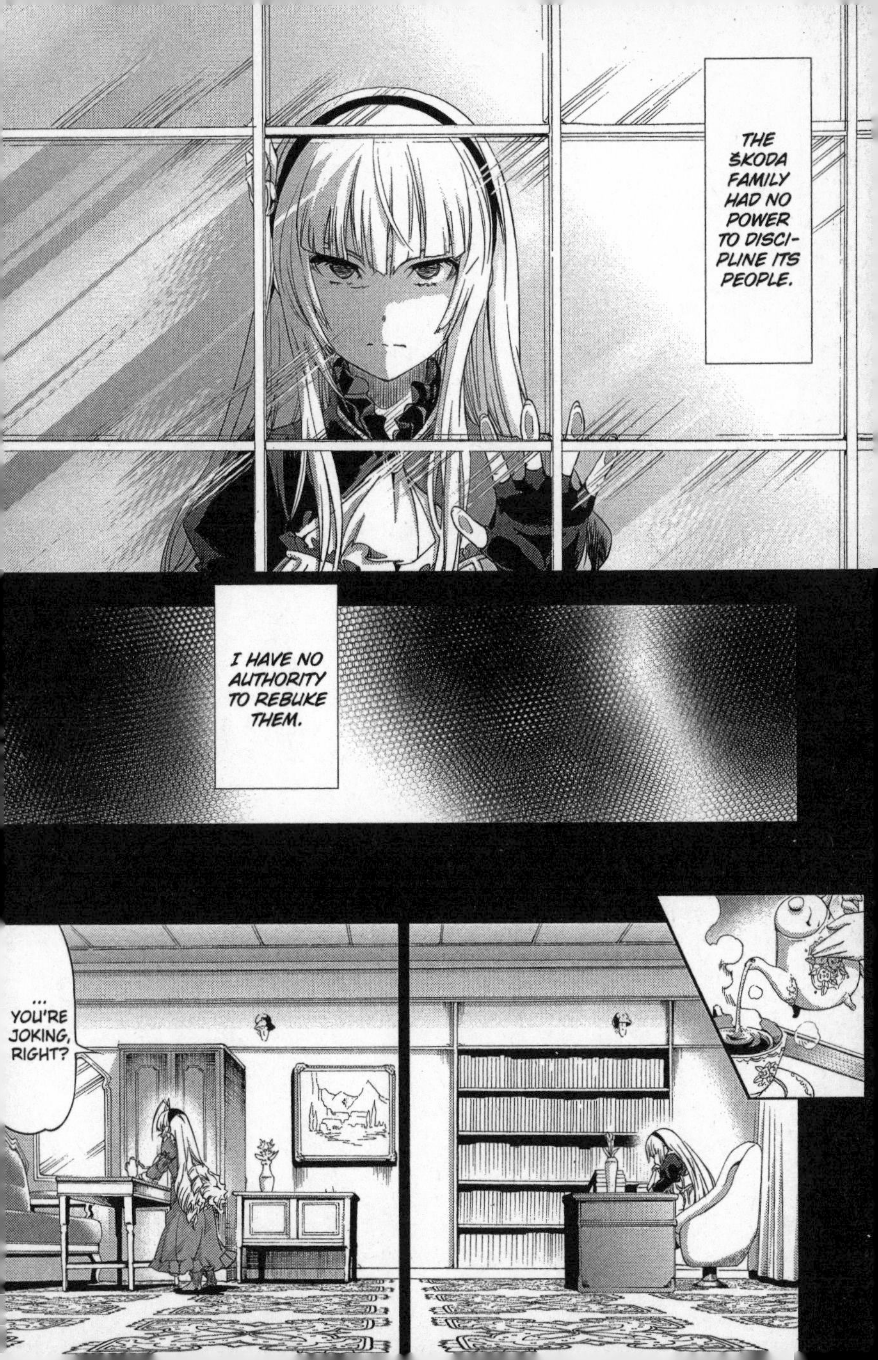
THE ŠKODA FAMILY HAD NO POWER TO DISCI-PLINE ITS PEOPLE.
I HAVE NO AUTHORITY TO REBUKE THEM.
... YOU'RE JOKING, RIGHT?

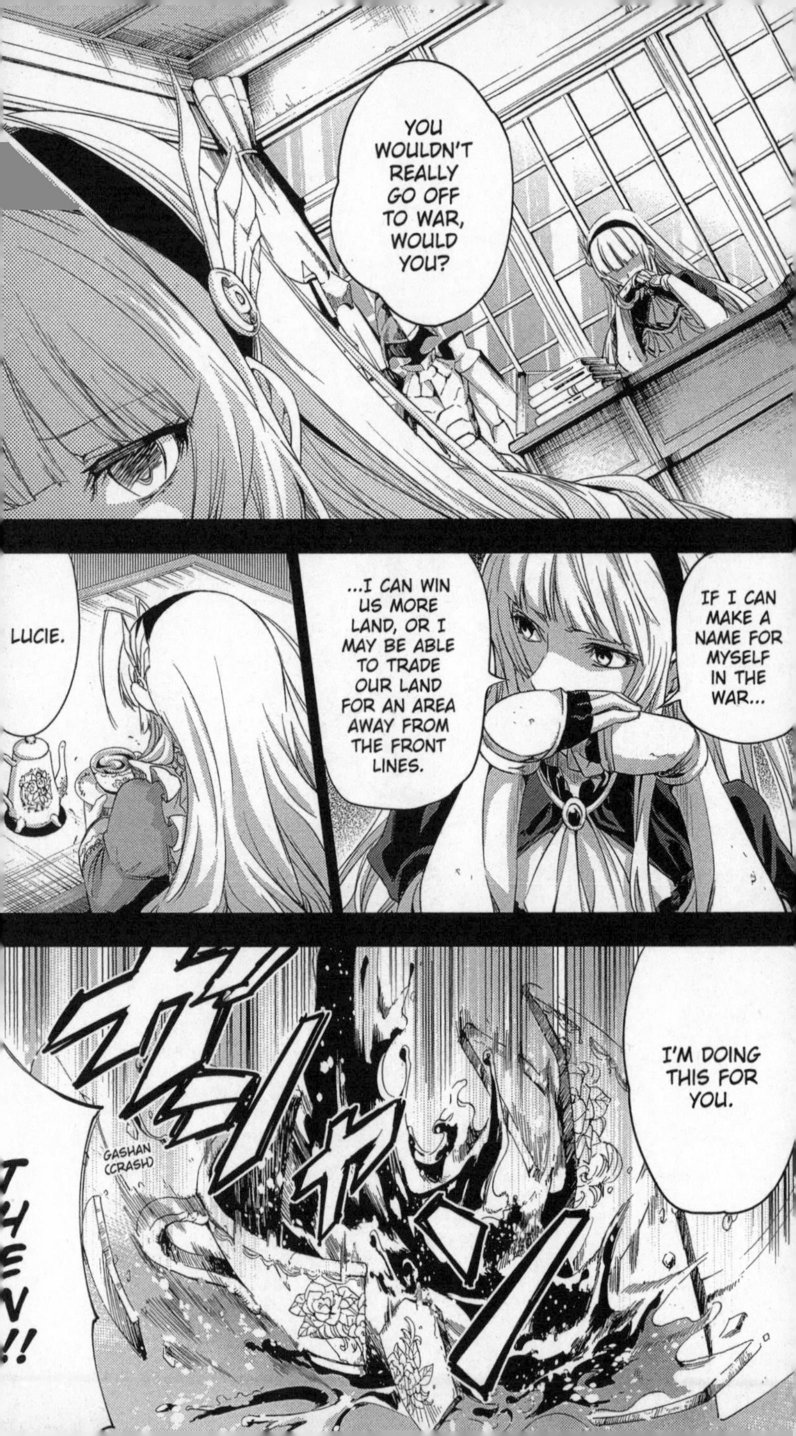
YOU WOULDN'T REALLY GO OFF TO WAR, WOULD YOU?
IF I CAN MAKE A NAME FOR MYSELF IN THE WAR...
...I CAN WIN US MORE LAND, OR I MAY BE ABLE TO TRADE OUR LAND FOR AN AREA AWAY FROM THE FRONT LINES.
LUCIE.
I'M DOING THIS FOR YOU.
GASHAN (CRASH)
THEV!!

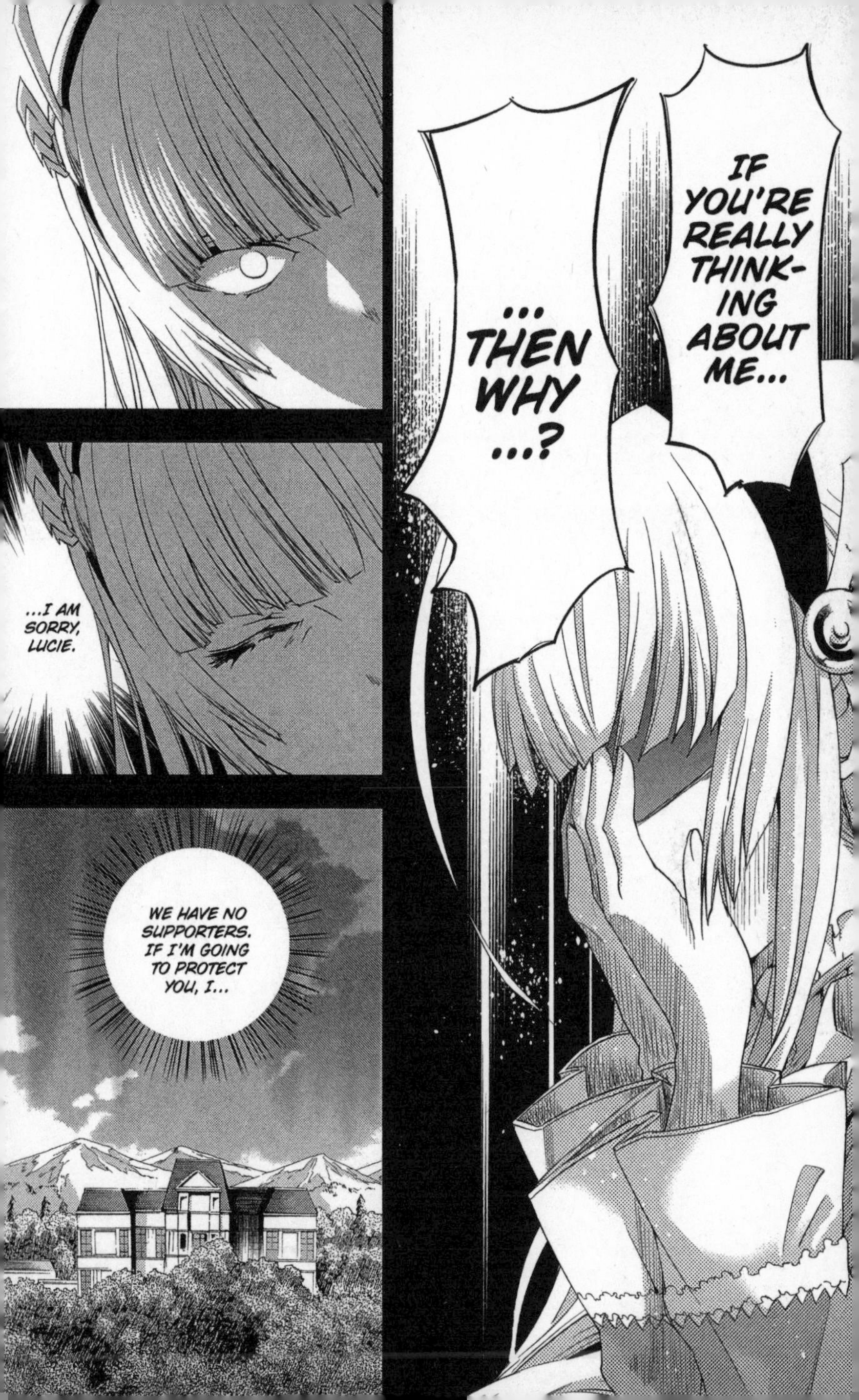
IF YOU'RE REALLY THINKING ABOUT ME...
...THEN WHY...?
...I AM SORRY, LUCIE.
WE HAVE NO SUPPORTERS. IF I'M GOING TO PROTECT YOU, I...

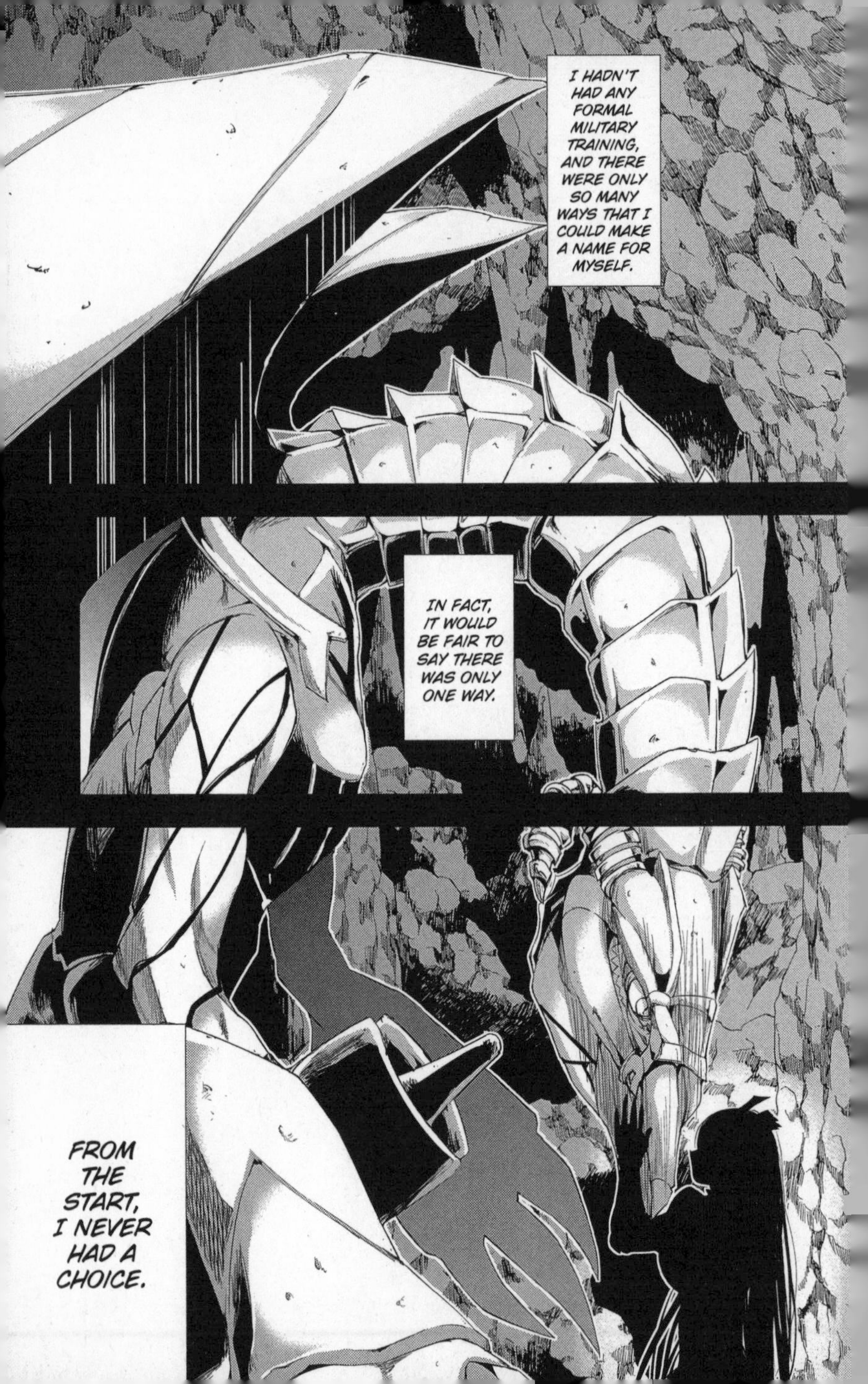
I HADN'T HAD ANY FORMAL MILITARY TRAINING, AND THERE WERE ONLY SO MANY WAYS THAT I COULD MAKE A NAME FOR MYSELF.
IN FACT, IT WOULD BE FAIR TO SAY THERE WAS ONLY ONE WAY.
FROM THE START, I NEVER HAD A CHOICE.

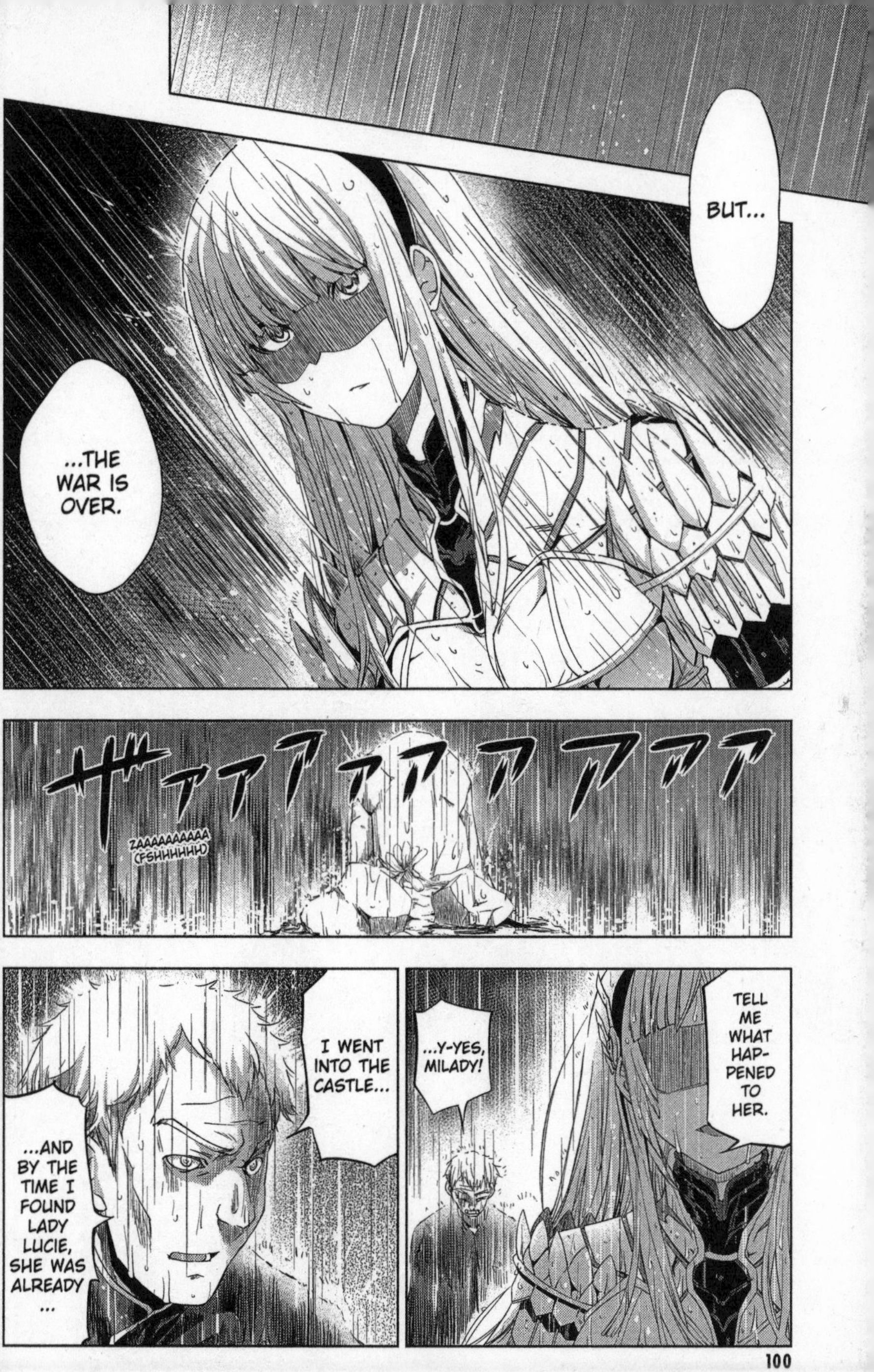
BUT...
...THE WAR IS OVER.
ザァァァァァァァァ
ZAAAAAAAAAA (FSHHHHHH)
TELL ME WHAT HAP-PENED TO HER.
...Y-YES, MILADY!
I WENT INTO THE CASTLE...
...AND BY THE TIME I FOUND LADY LUCIE, SHE WAS ALREADY ...

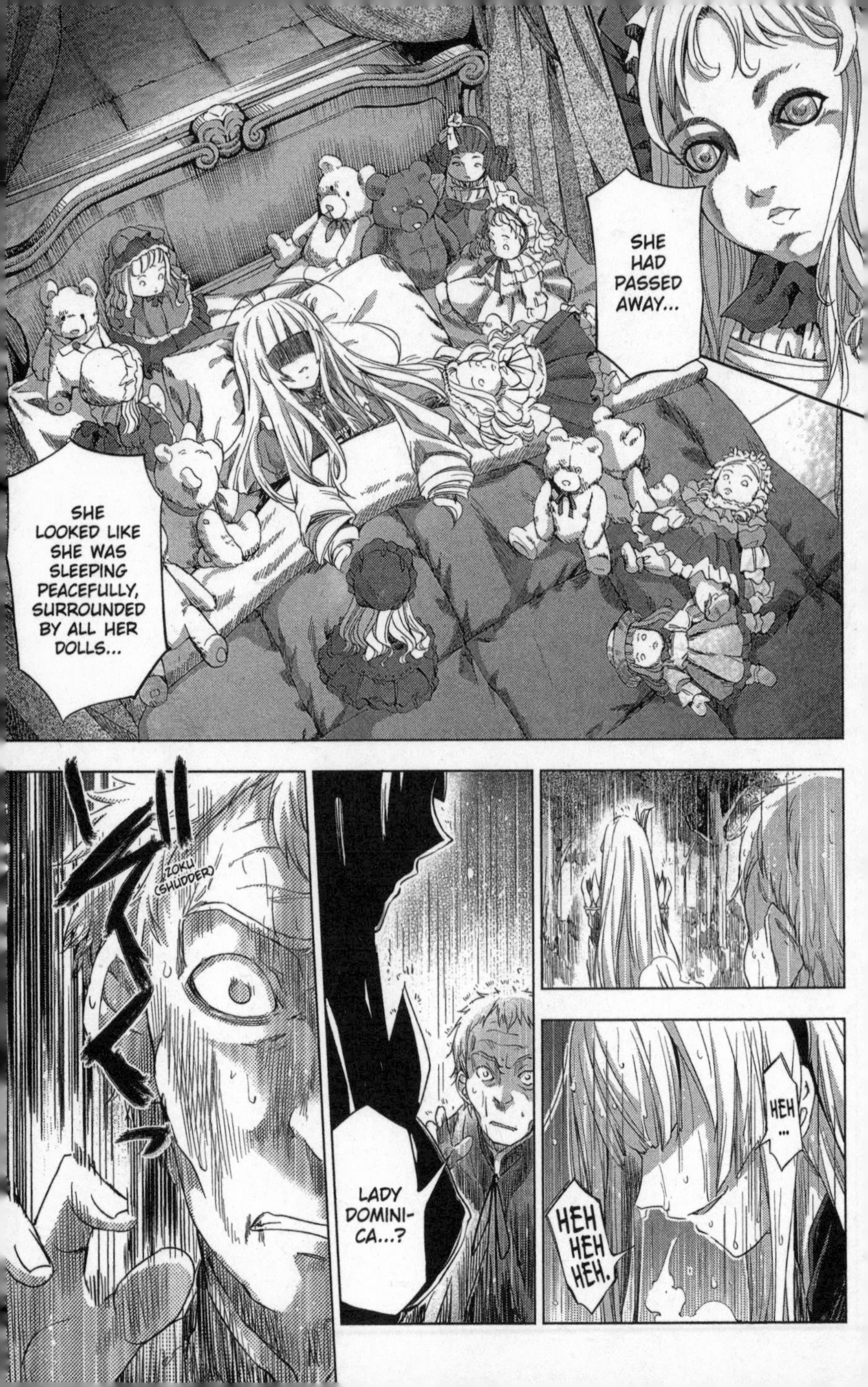
SHE HAD PASSED AWAY...
SHE LOOKED LIKE SHE WAS SLEEPING PEACEFULLY, SURROUNDED BY ALL HER DOLLS...
HEH...
HEH HEH HEH.
LADY DOMINICA...?
ZOKU (SHUDDER)

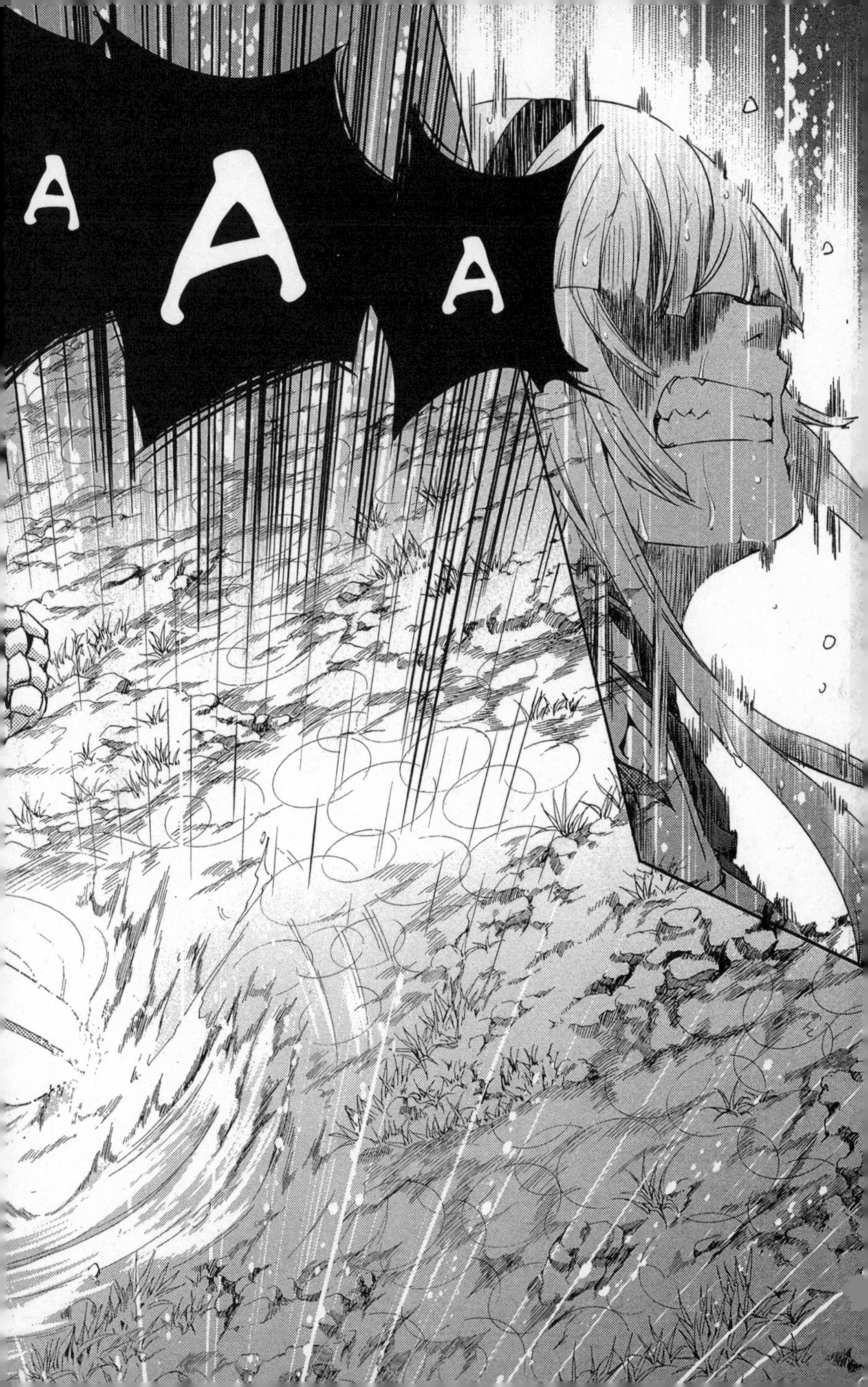
A A A

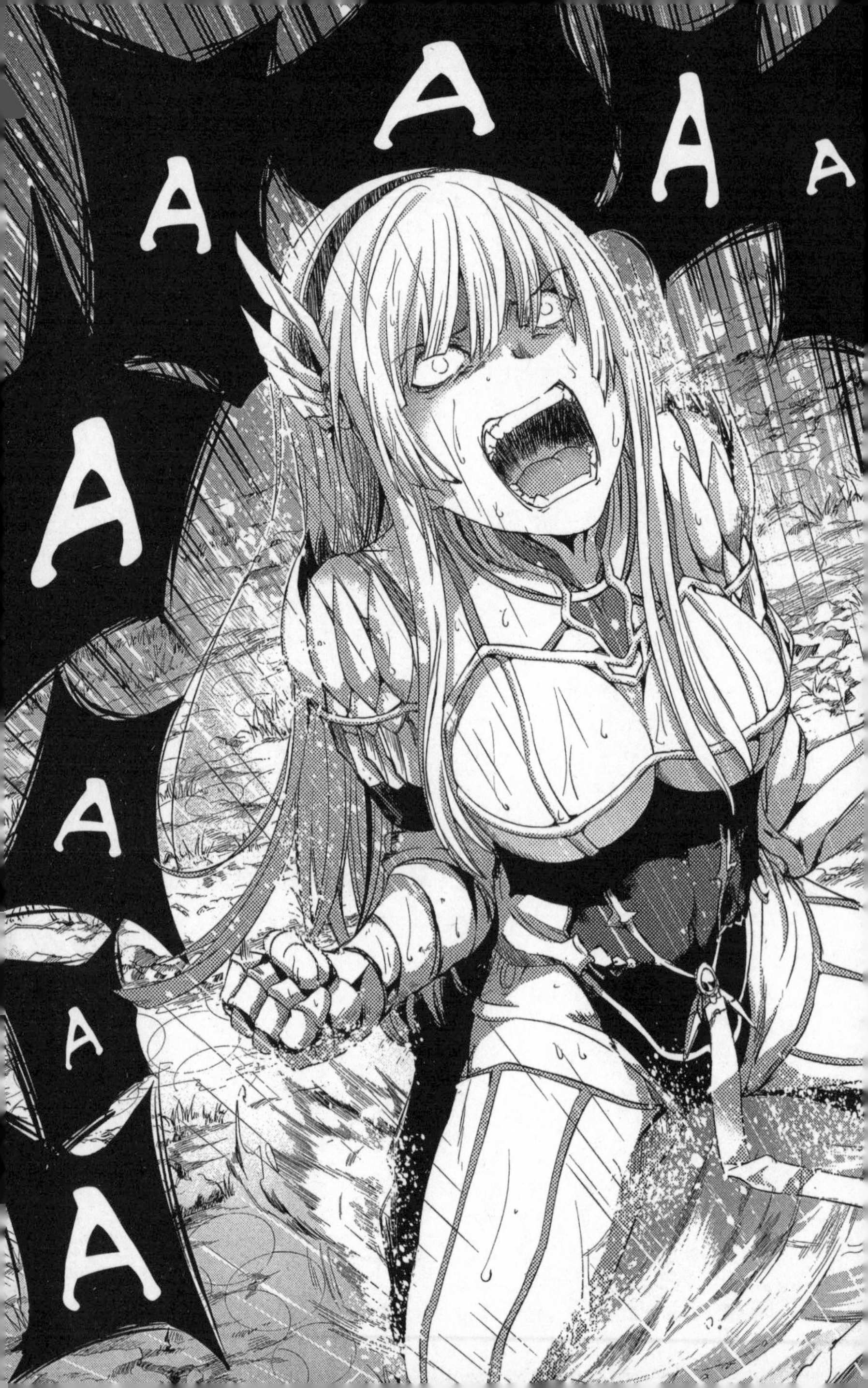
AAAAAAAA

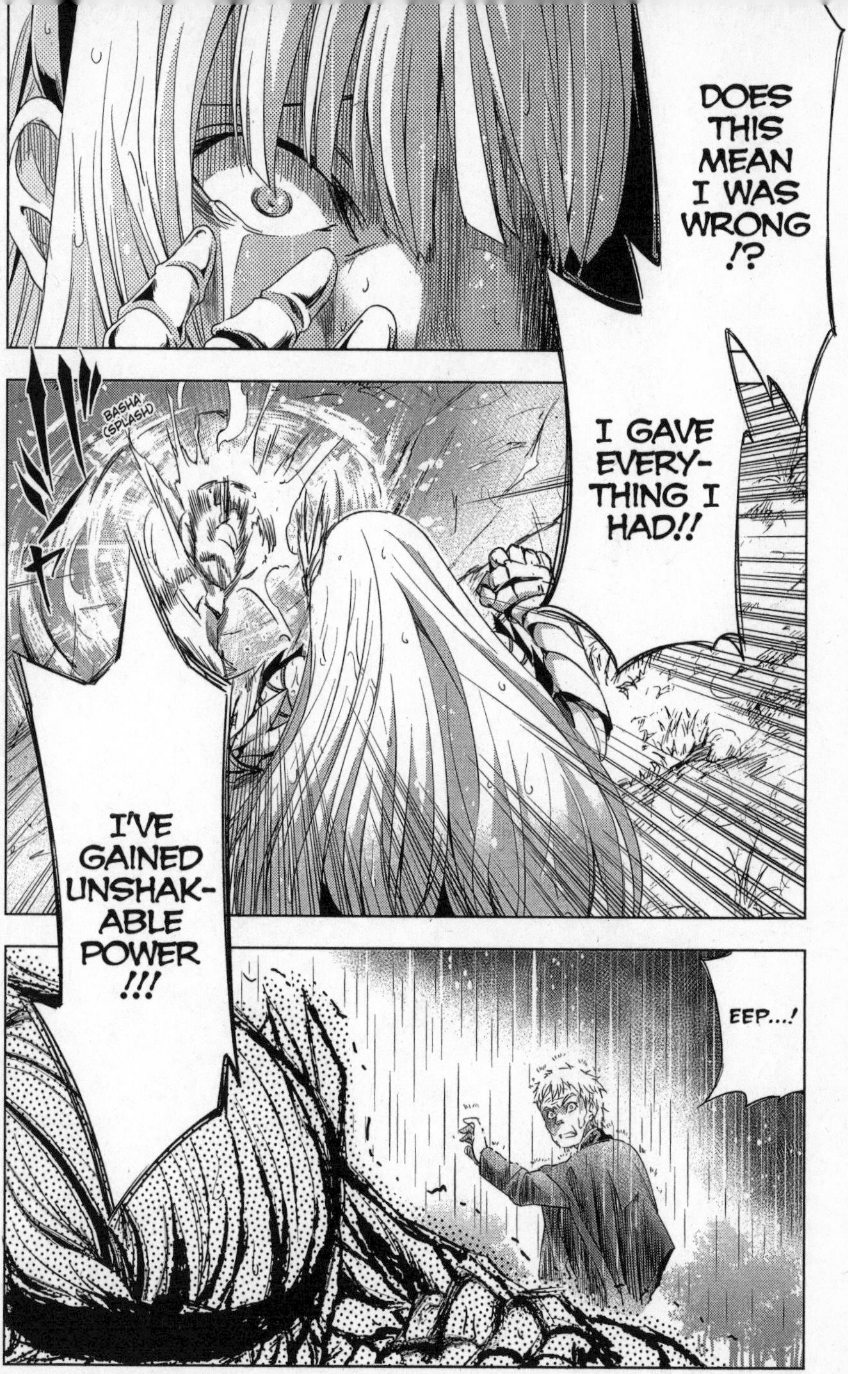
DOES THIS MEAN I WAS WRONG !?
I GAVE EVERY-THING I HAD!!
BASHA (SPLASH)
I'VE GAINED UNSHAK-ABLE POWER !!!
EEP...!

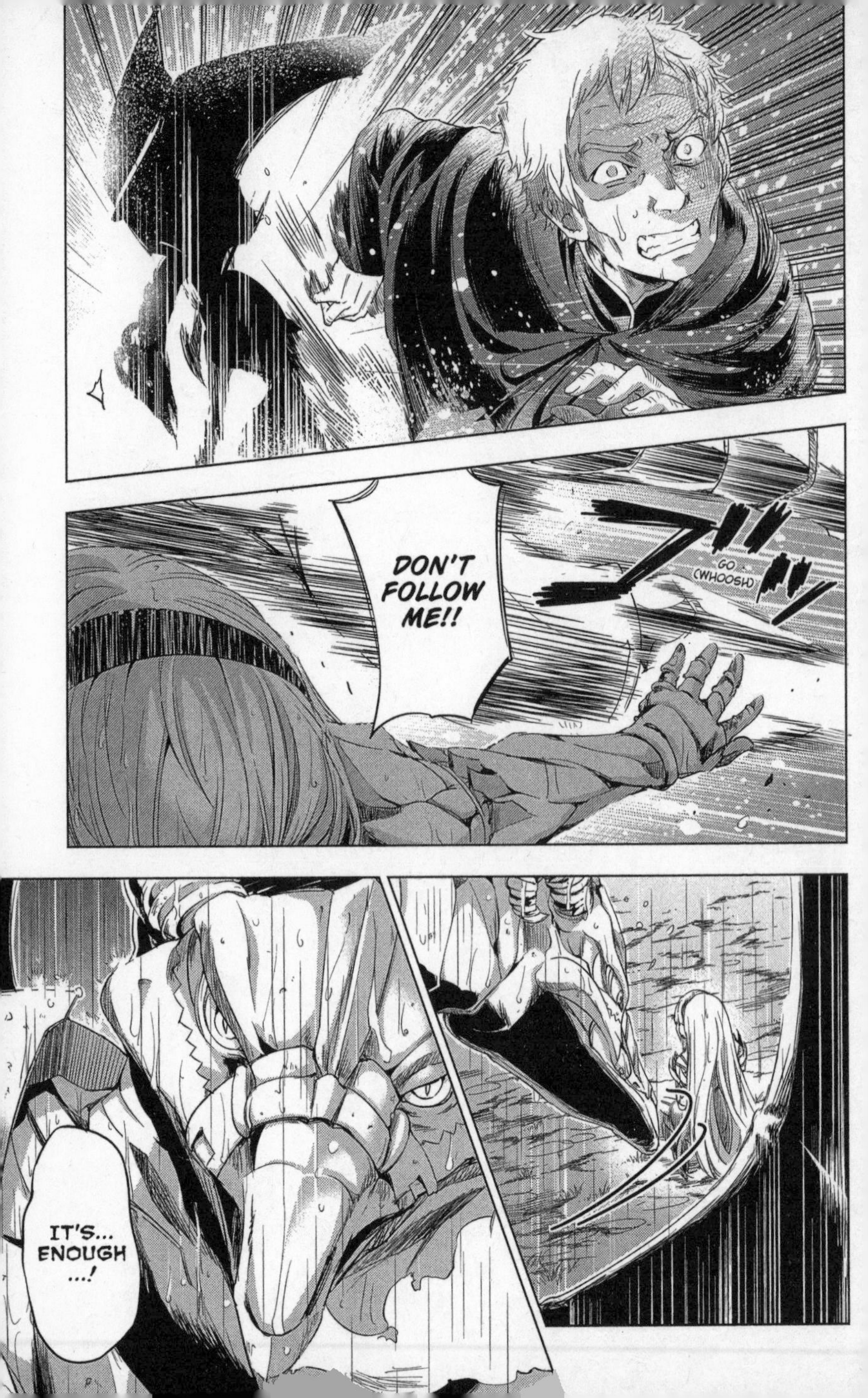
GO (WHOOSH)
DON'T FOLLOW ME!!
IT'S... ENOUGH ...!

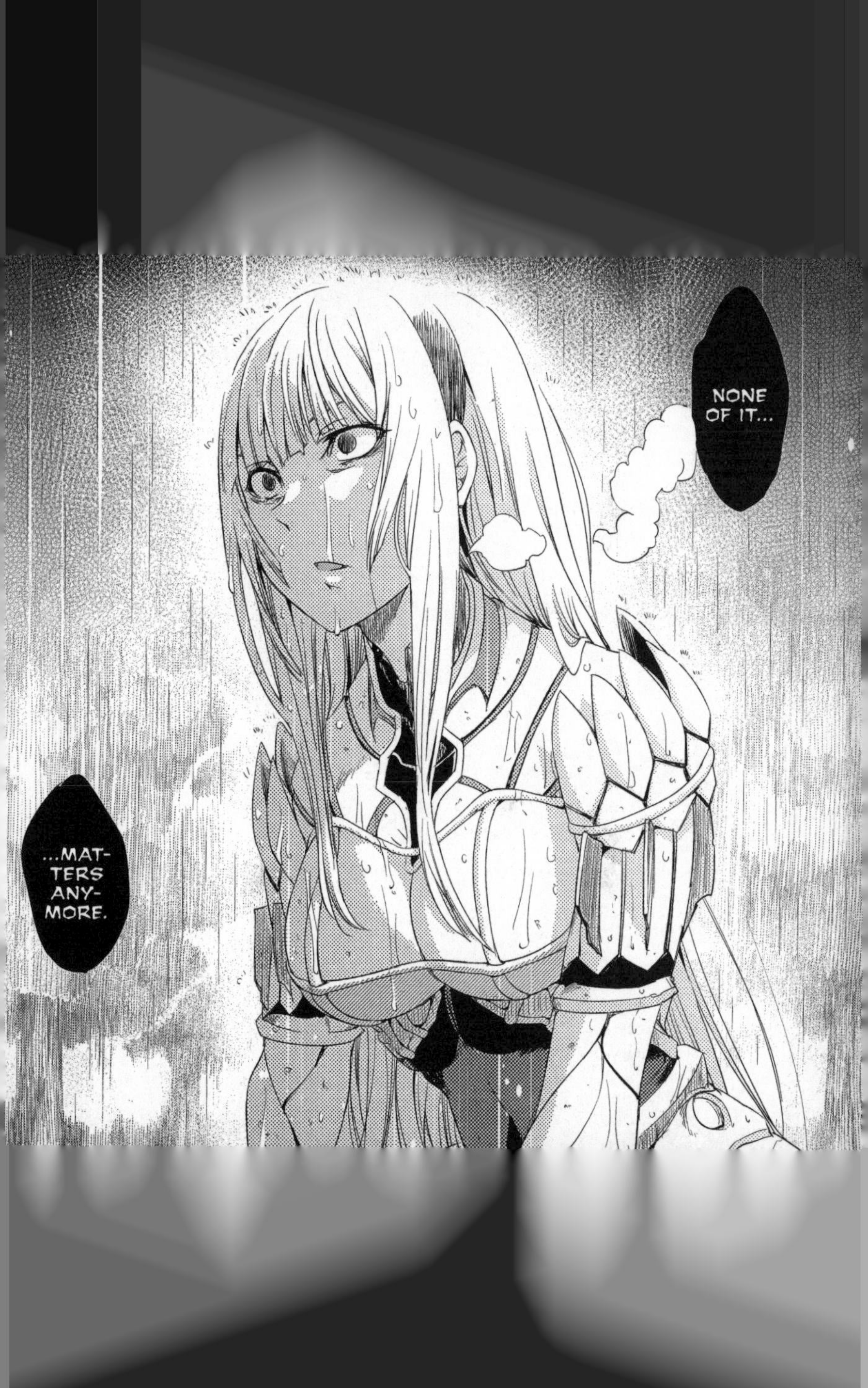
NONE OF IT...
...MAT-TERS ANY-MORE.

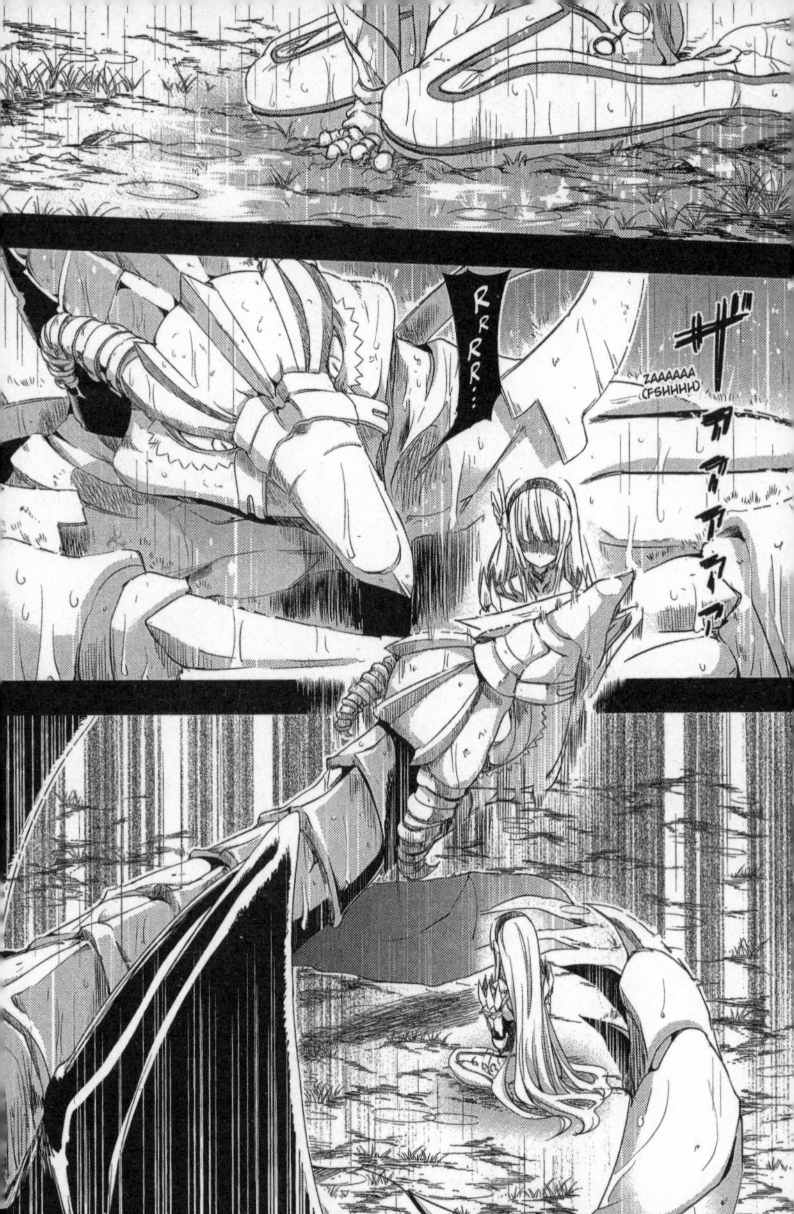
ザアアアアア
ZAAAAAA (FSHHHH)
RRRR...

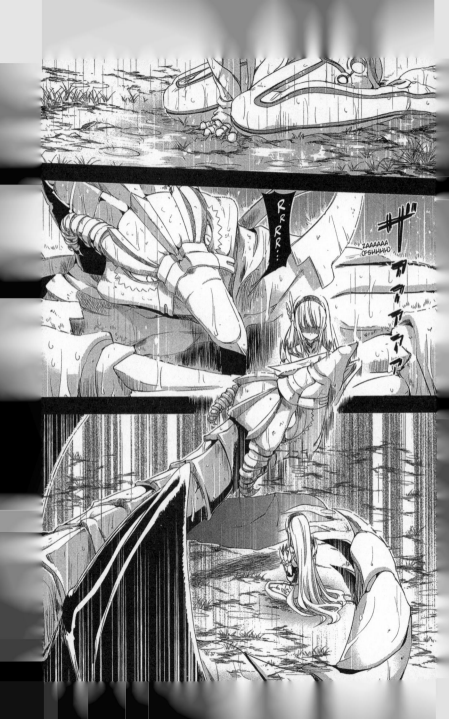

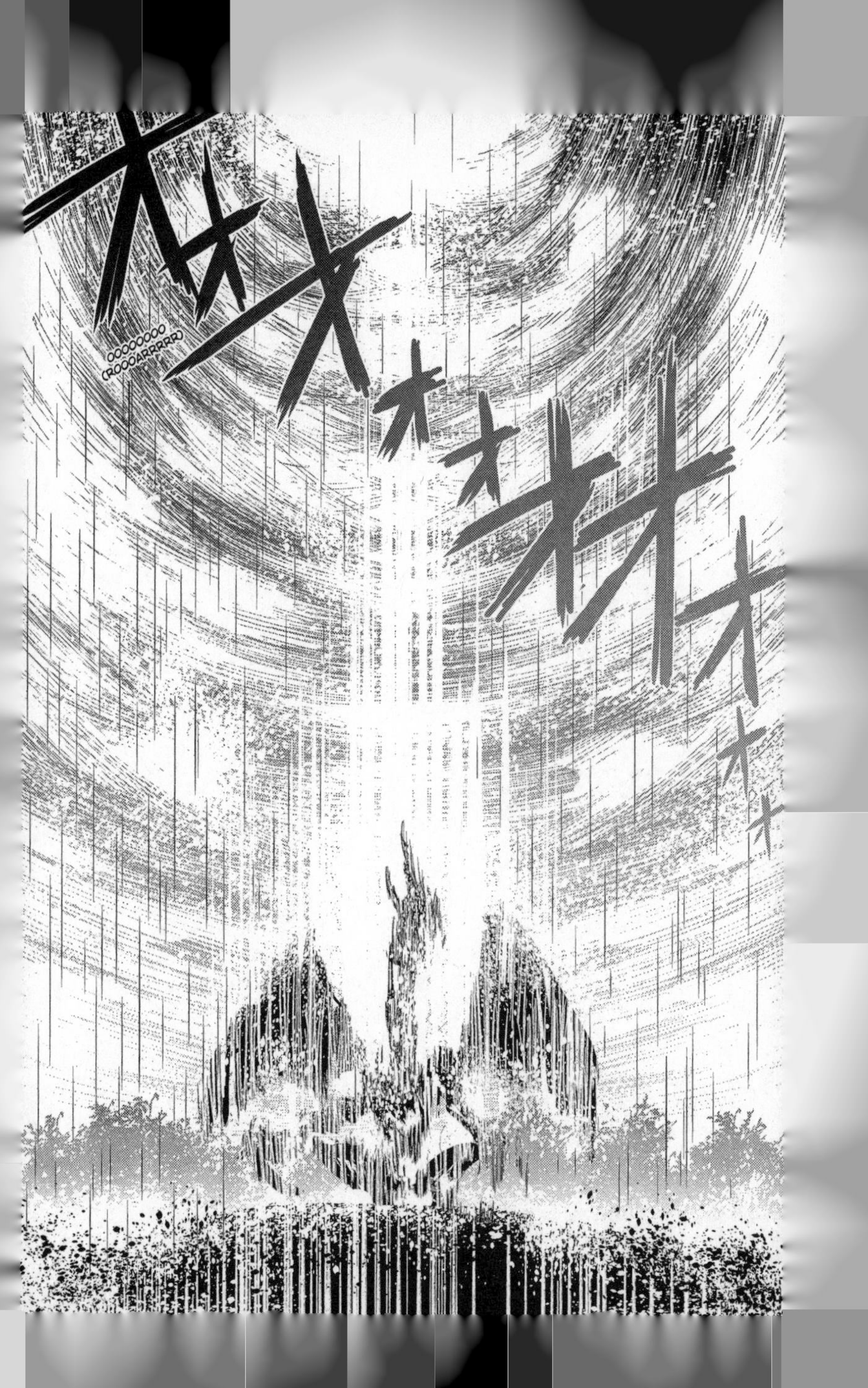
OOOOOOOOO
(ROOOARRRRR)

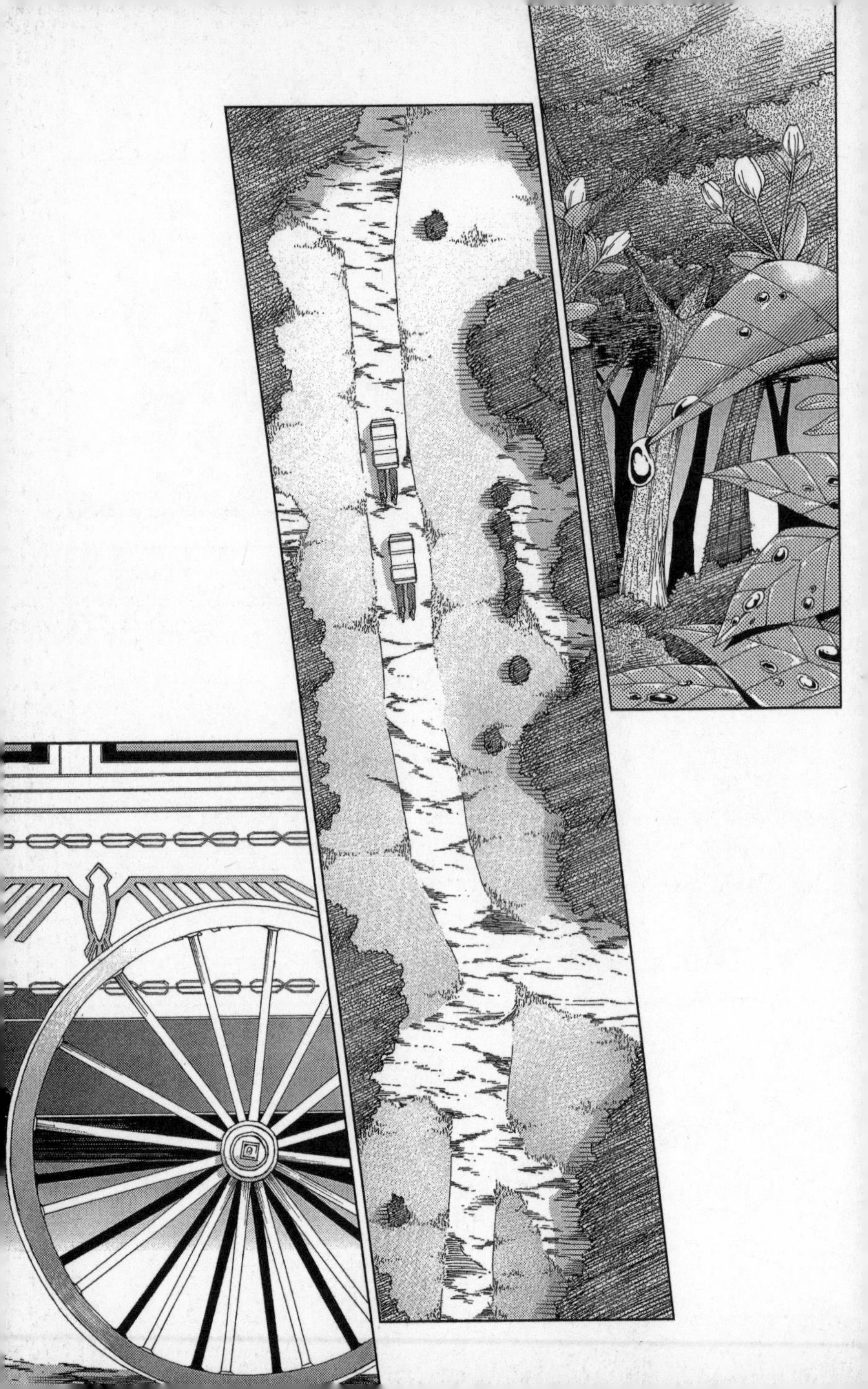

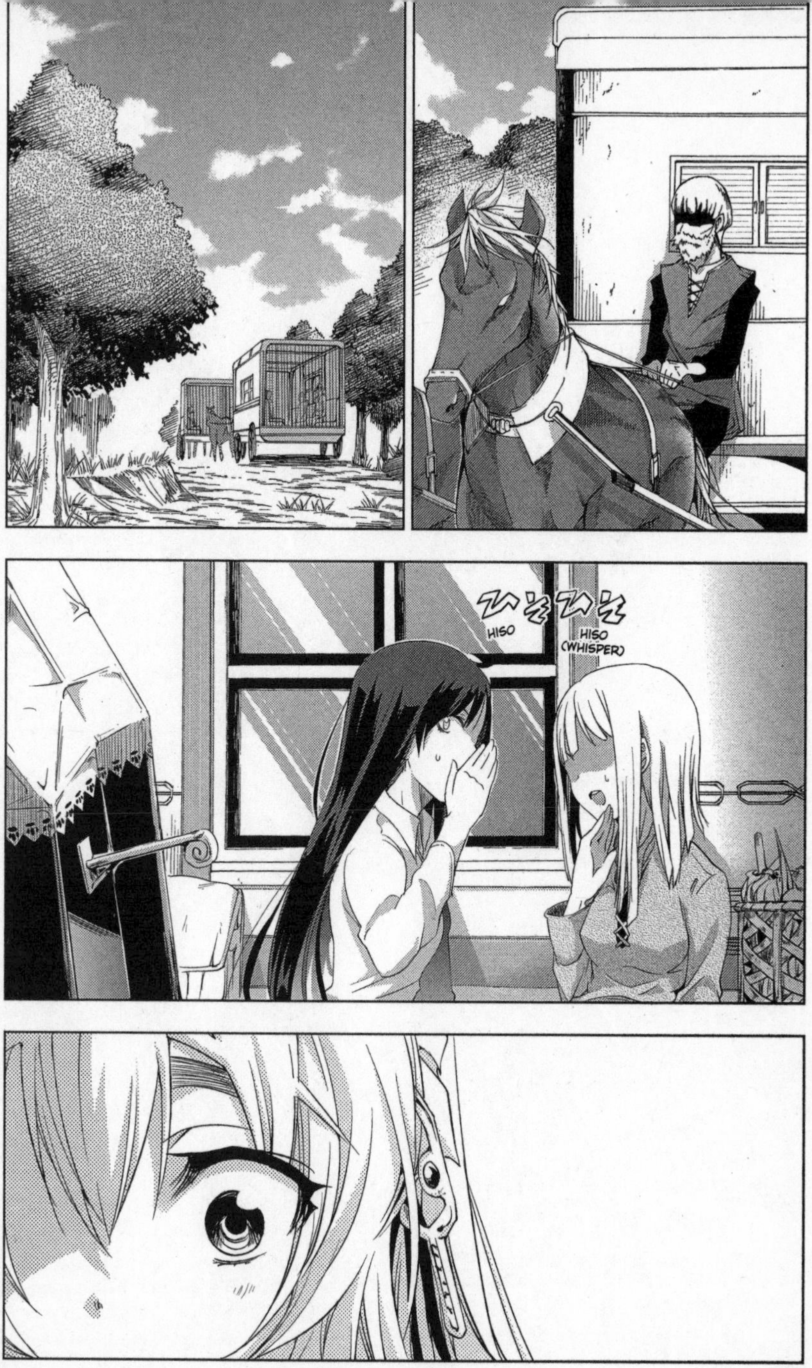
ひそひそ
HISO
HISO
(WHISPER)

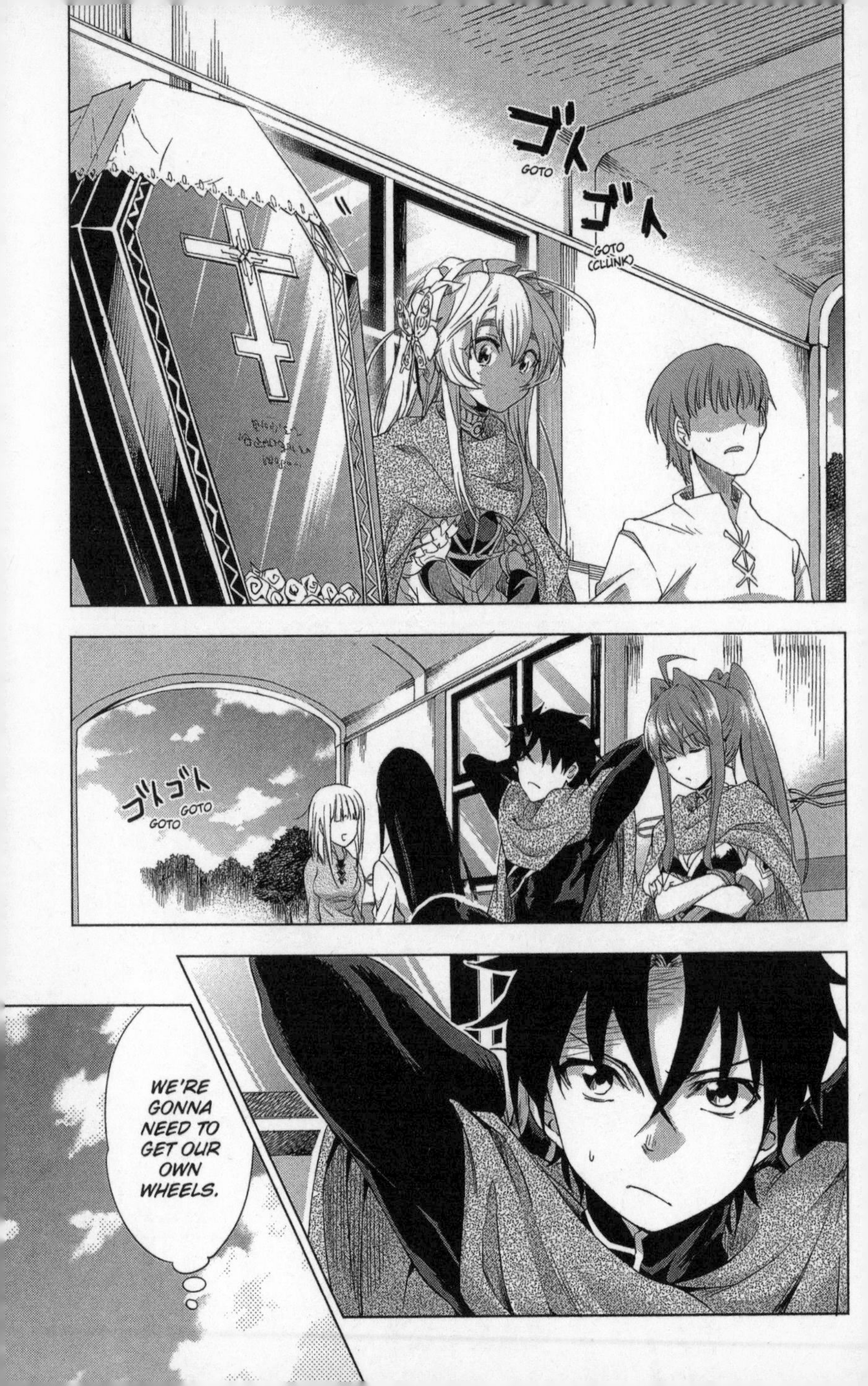
ゴト GOTO
ゴト GOTO (CLUNK)
ゴトゴト GOTO GOTO
WE'RE GONNA NEED TO GET OUR OWN WHEELS.

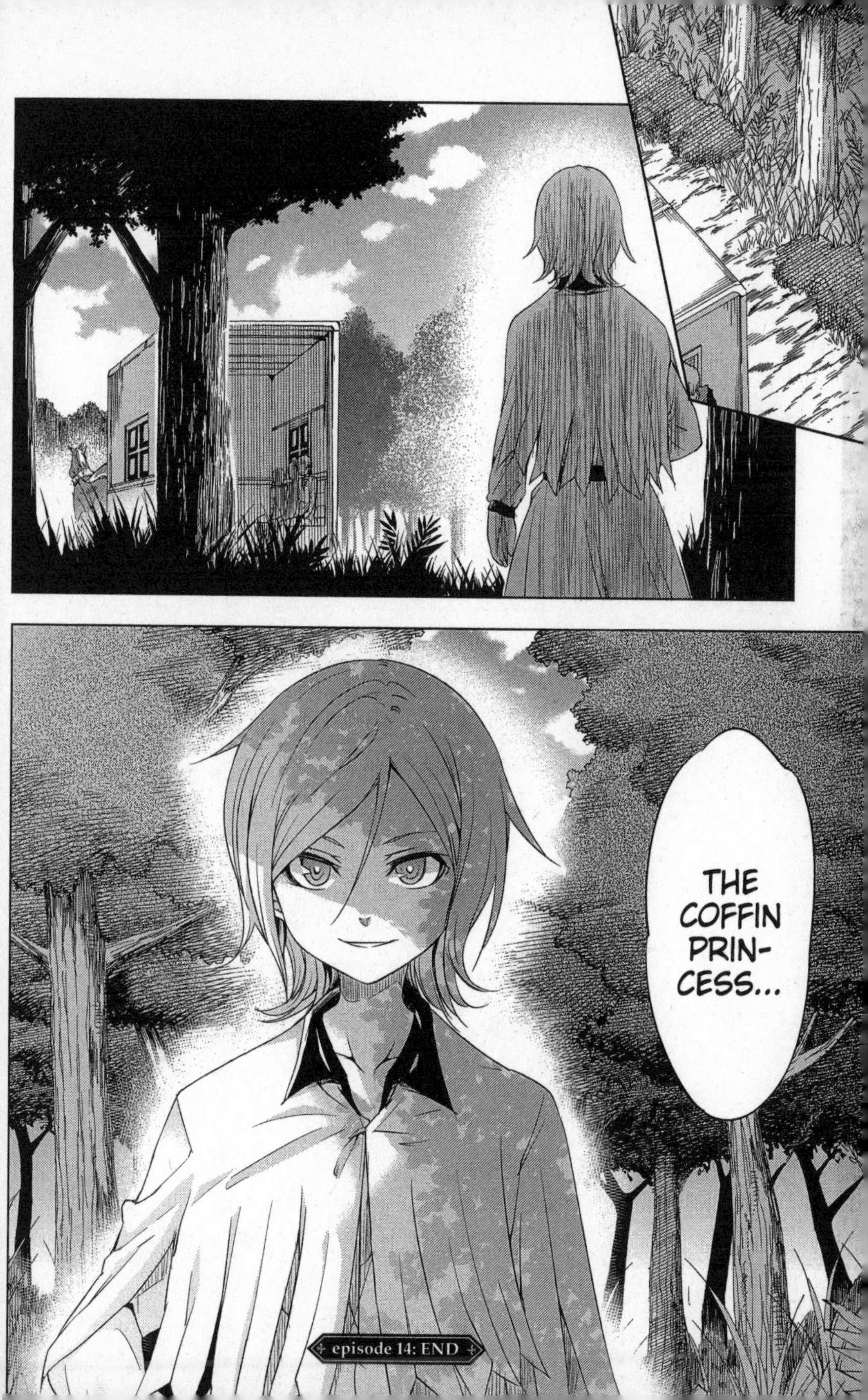
THE COFFIN PRIN-CESS...
episode 14: END

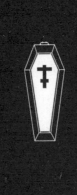

CHAIKA: THE COFFIN PRINCESS

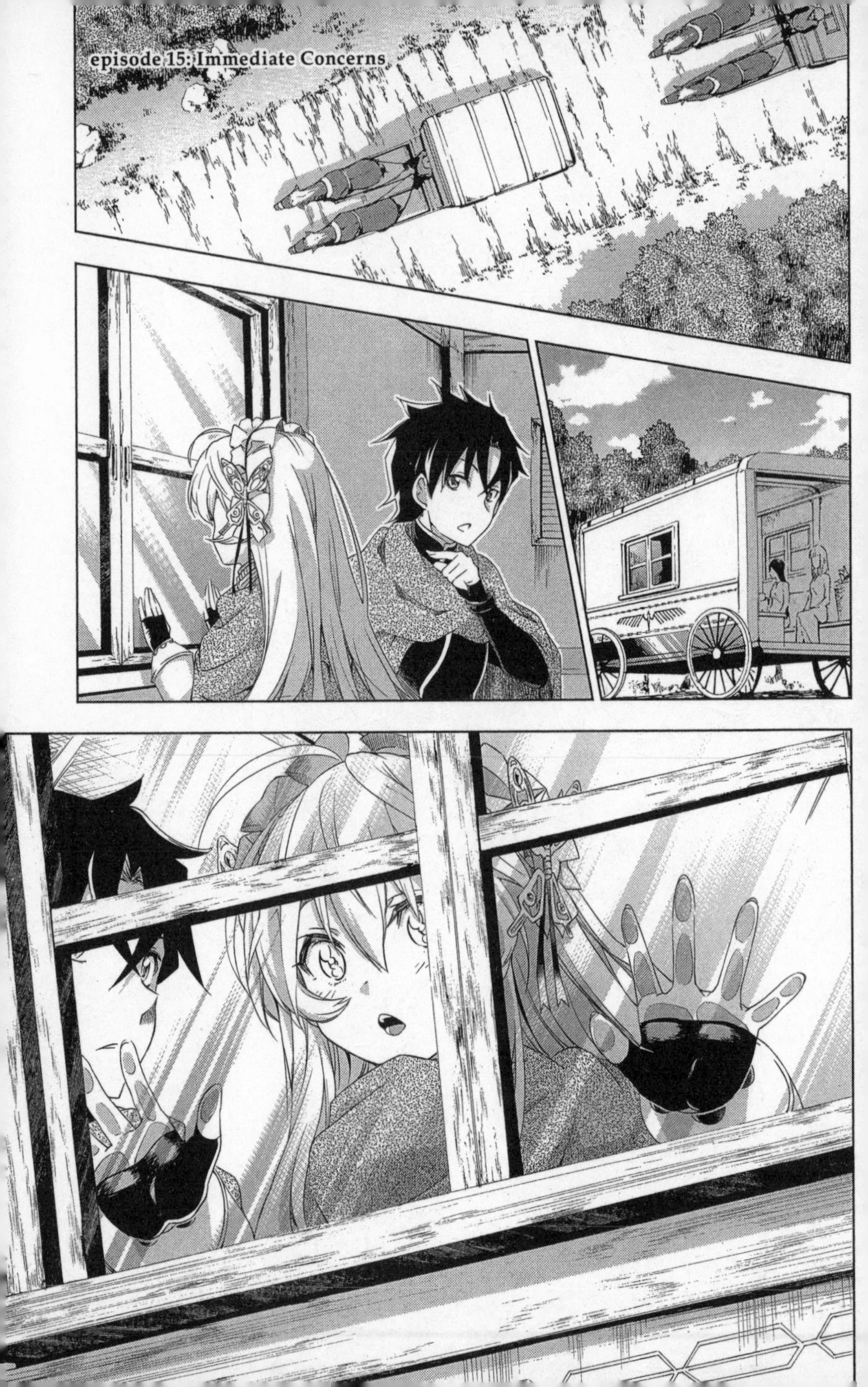
episode 15: Immediate Concerns

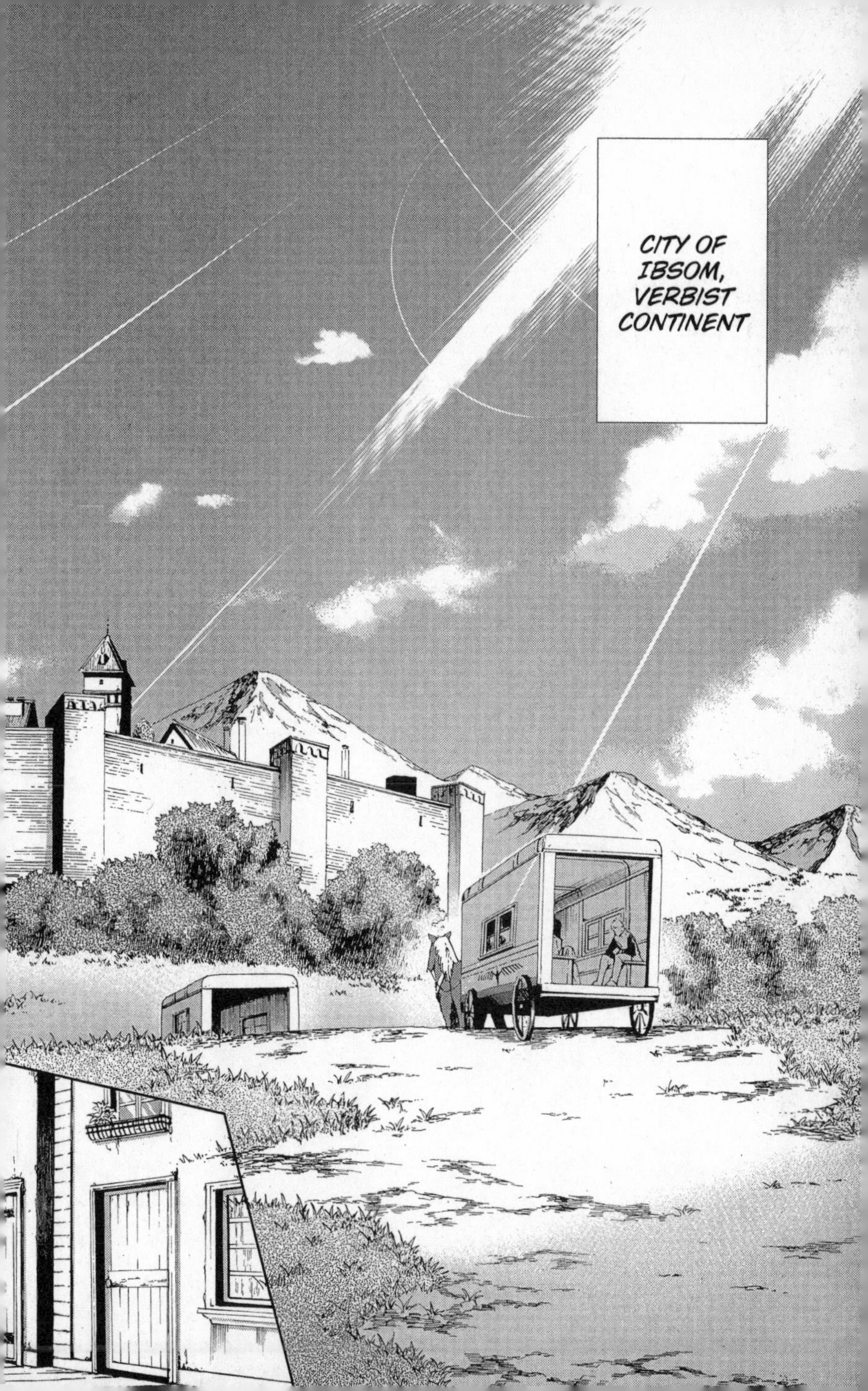
CITY OF IBSOM, VERBIST CONTINENT

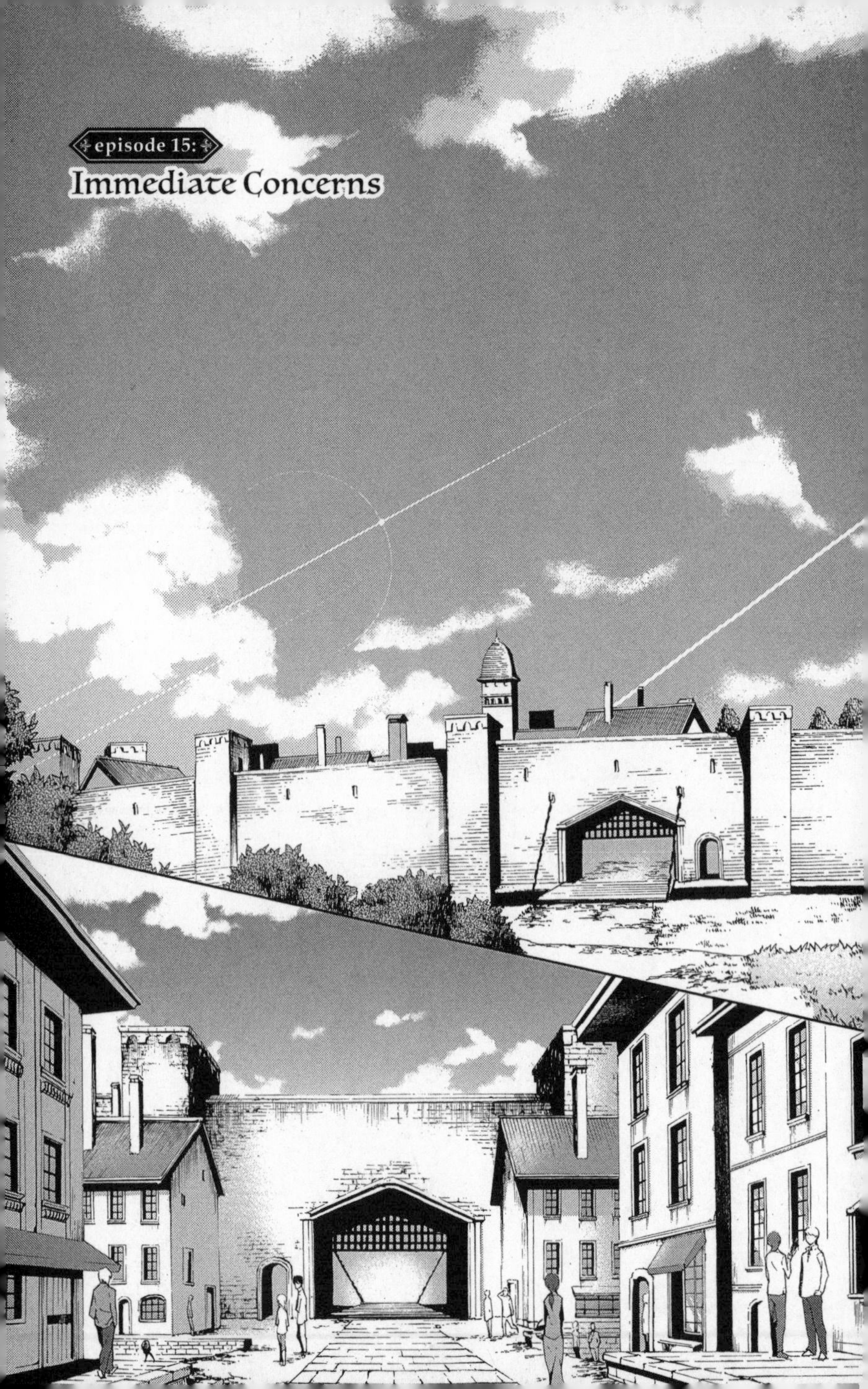
episode 15:
Immediate Concerns

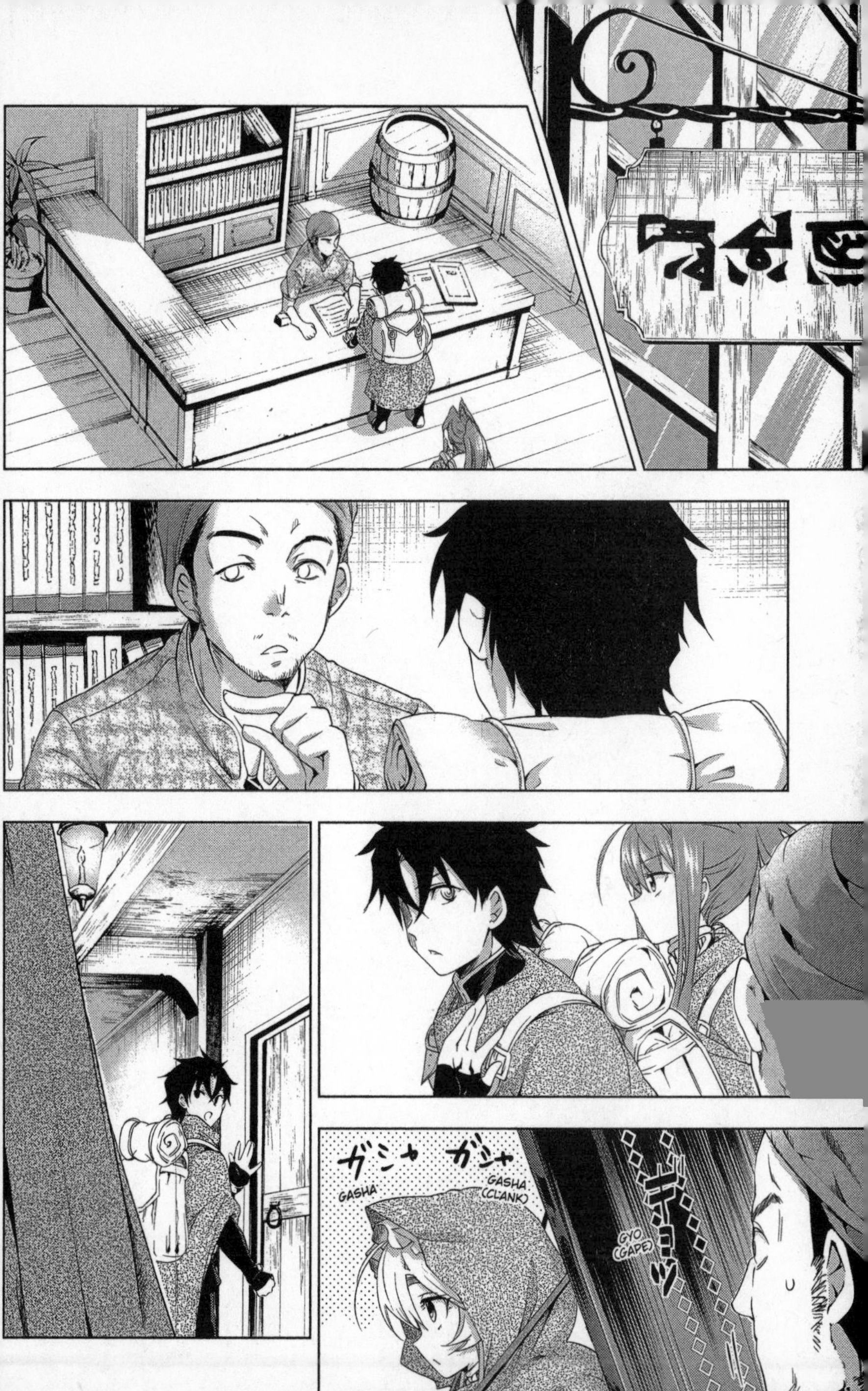
ギョッ
GYO (GAPE)
ガシャ ガシャ
GASHA
GASHA (CLANK)

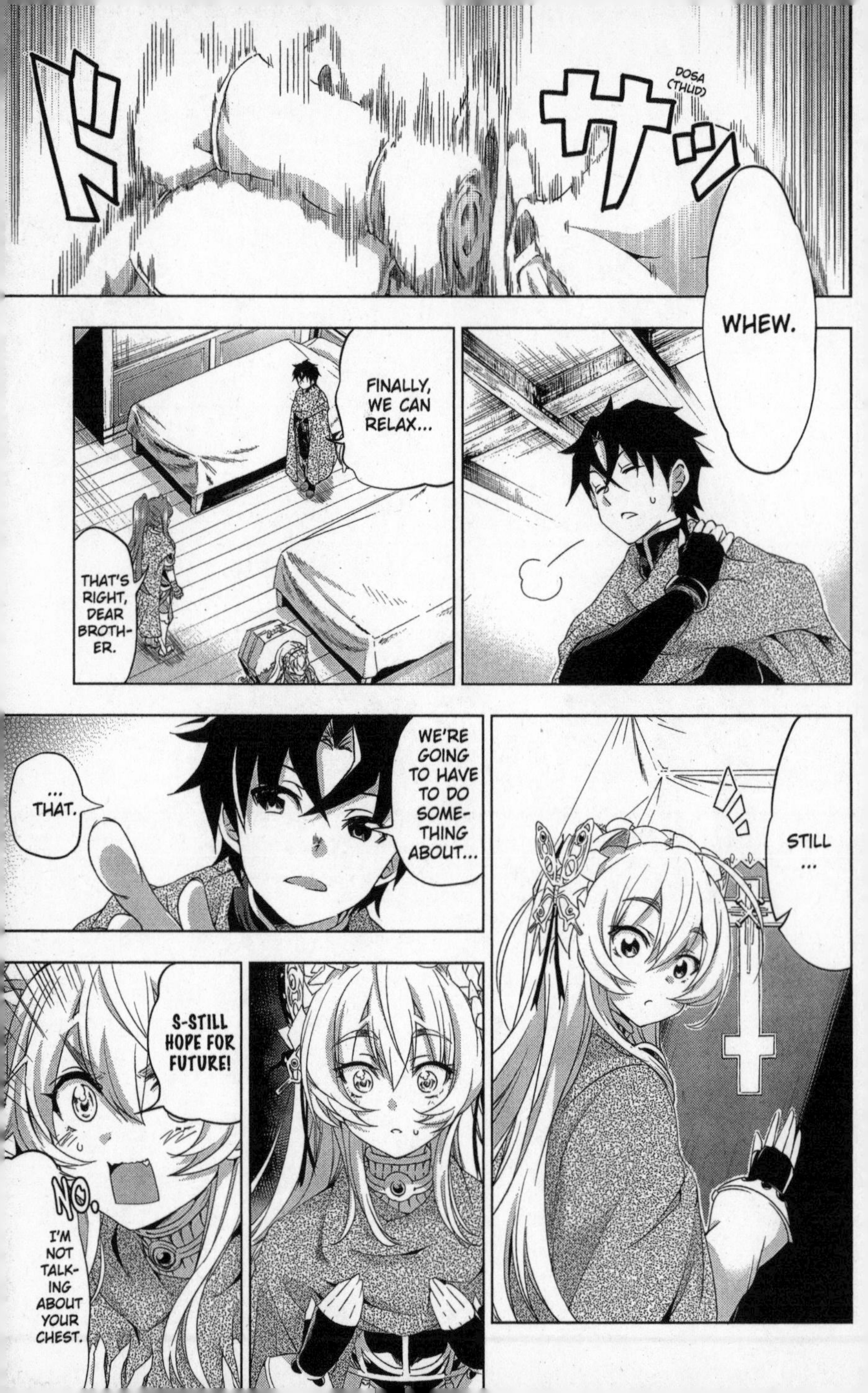
ドサッ
DOSA (THUD)
WHEW.
FINALLY, WE CAN RELAX...
THAT'S RIGHT, DEAR BROTHER.
STILL ...
WE'RE GOING TO HAVE TO DO SOMETHING ABOUT...
... THAT.
S-STILL HOPE FOR FUTURE!
NO.
I'M NOT TALKING ABOUT YOUR CHEST.

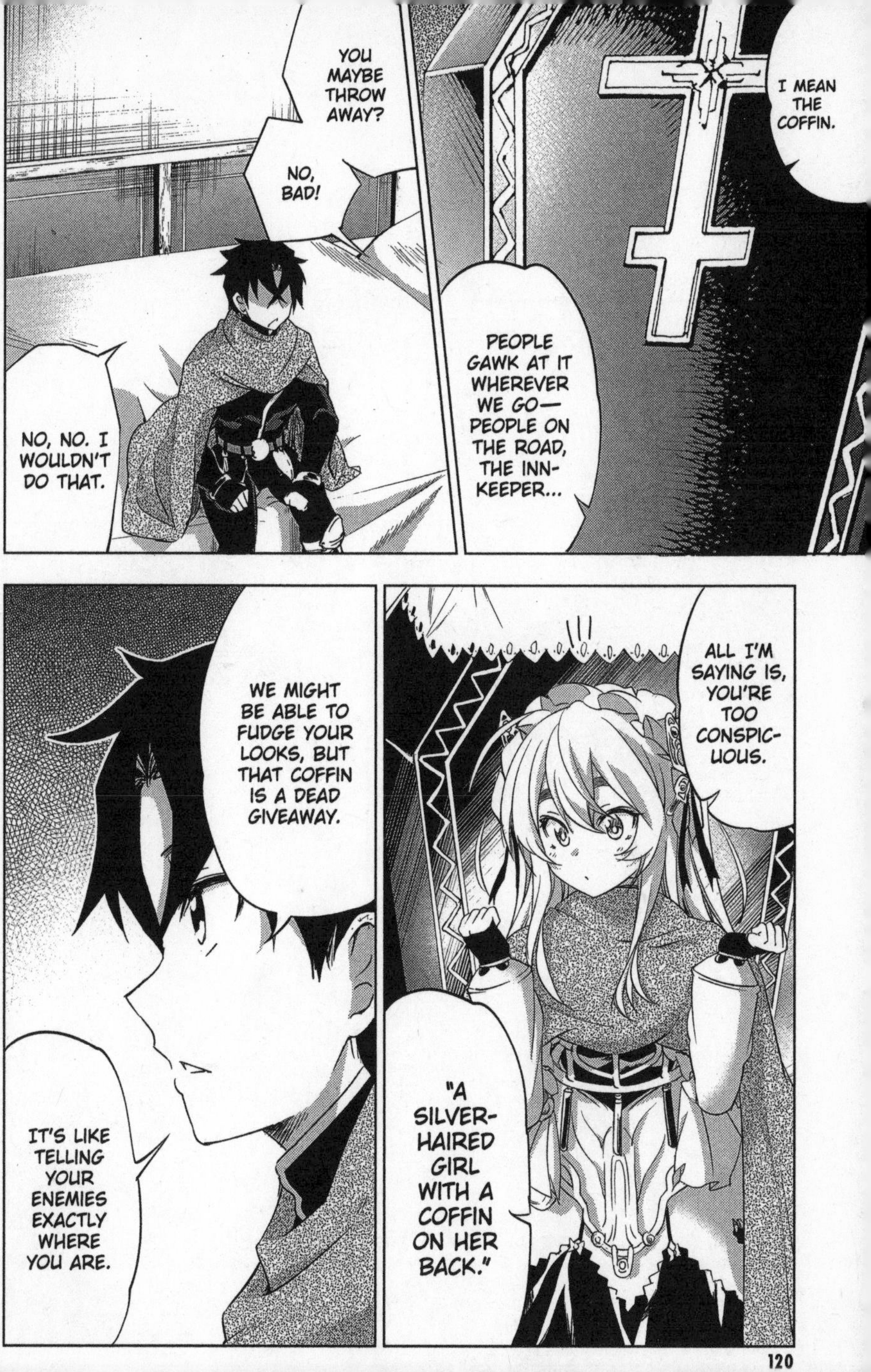
I MEAN THE COFFIN.
PEOPLE GAWK AT IT WHEREVER WE GO—PEOPLE ON THE ROAD, THE INN-KEEPER...
YOU MAYBE THROW AWAY?
NO, BAD!
NO, NO. I WOULDN'T DO THAT.
ALL I'M SAYING IS, YOU'RE TOO CONSPICUOUS.
"A SILVER-HAIRED GIRL WITH A COFFIN ON HER BACK."
WE MIGHT BE ABLE TO FUDGE YOUR LOOKS, BUT THAT COFFIN IS A DEAD GIVEAWAY.
IT'S LIKE TELLING YOUR ENEMIES EXACTLY WHERE YOU ARE.

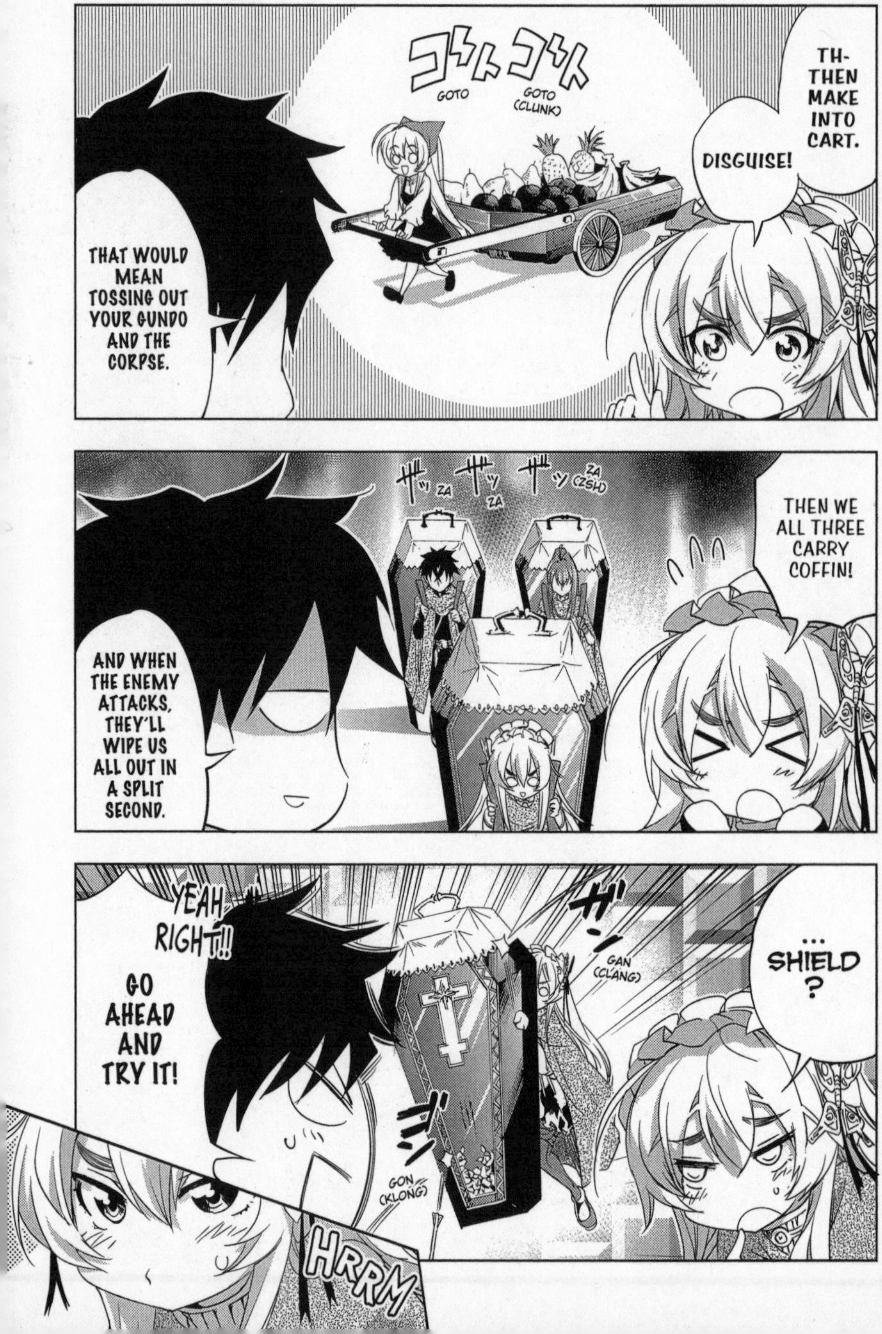
TH-THEN MAKE INTO CART.
DISGUISE!
コトコト
GOTO GOTO (CLUNK)
THAT WOULD MEAN TOSSING OUT YOUR GUNDO AND THE CORPSE.
THEN WE ALL THREE CARRY COFFIN!
ザッ ZA ザッ ZA ザッ ZA (ZSH)
AND WHEN THE ENEMY ATTACKS, THEY'LL WIPE US ALL OUT IN A SPLIT SECOND.
... SHIELD?
ガン
GAN (CLANG)
YEAH RIGHT!!
GO AHEAD AND TRY IT!
ゴン
GON (KLONG)
HRRM

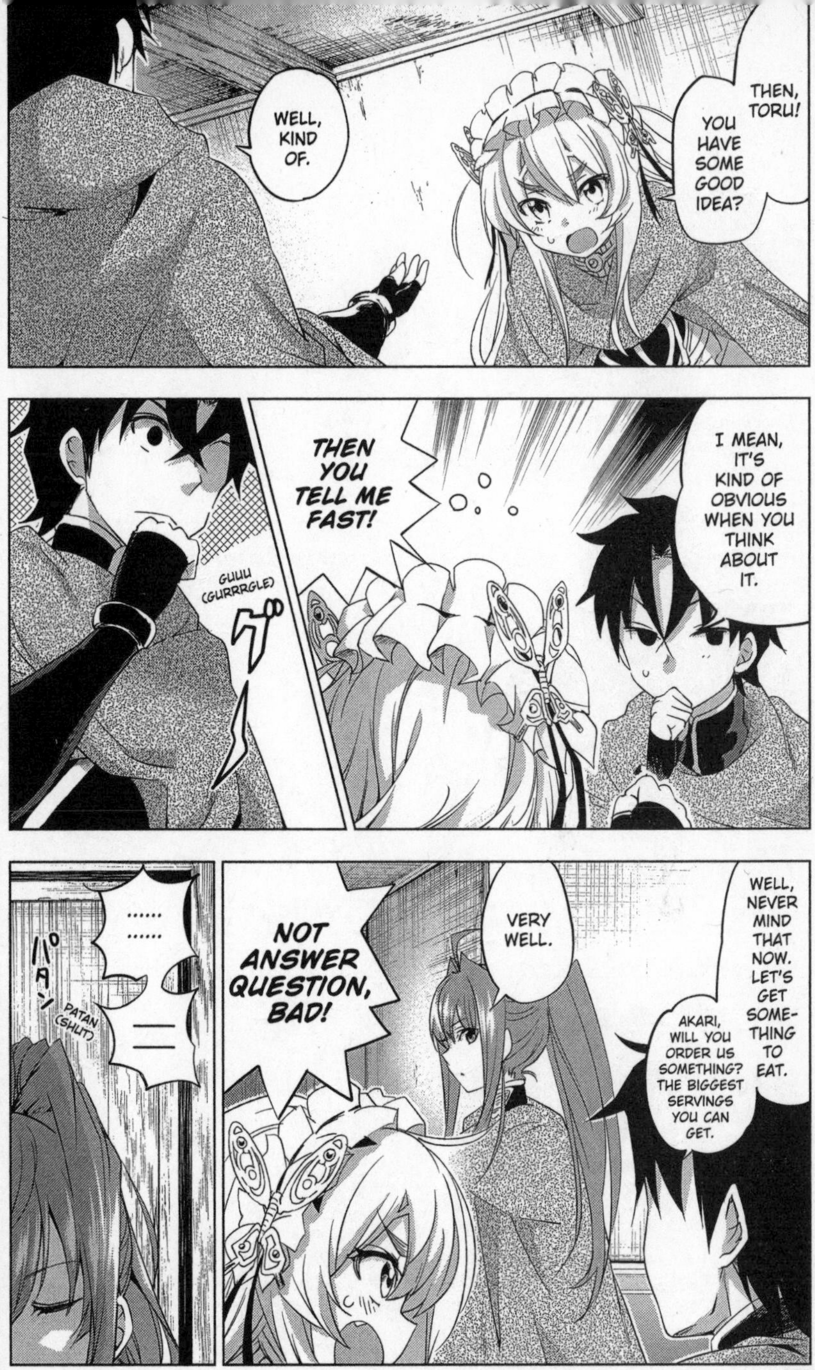
THEN, TORU!
YOU HAVE SOME GOOD IDEA?
WELL, KIND OF.
I MEAN, IT'S KIND OF OBVIOUS WHEN YOU THINK ABOUT IT.
THEN YOU TELL ME FAST!
GUUU (GURRRGLE)
WELL, NEVER MIND THAT NOW. LET'S GET SOME-THING TO EAT.
AKARI, WILL YOU ORDER US SOMETHING? THE BIGGEST SERVINGS YOU CAN GET.
VERY WELL.
NOT ANSWER QUESTION, BAD!
PATAN (SHUT)
......
......
——

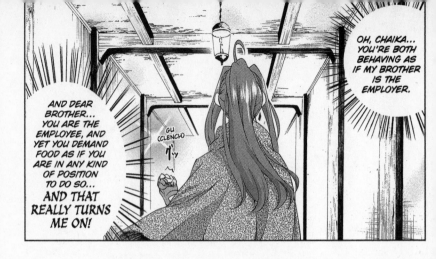

OH, CHAIKA... YOU'RE BOTH BEHAVING AS IF MY BROTHER IS THE EMPLOYER.

AND DEAR BROTHER... YOU ARE THE EMPLOYEE, AND YET YOU DEMAND FOOD AS IF YOU ARE IN ANY KIND OF POSITION TO DO SO... AND THAT REALLY TURNS ME ON!

GU (CLENCH)

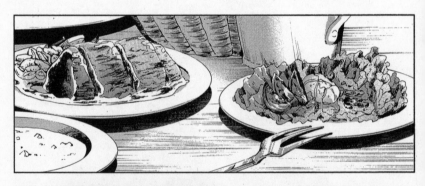

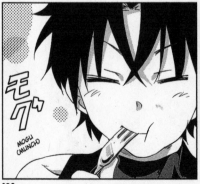

MOGU (MUNCH)

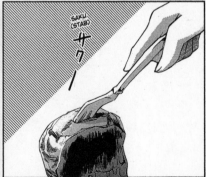

SAKU (STAB)

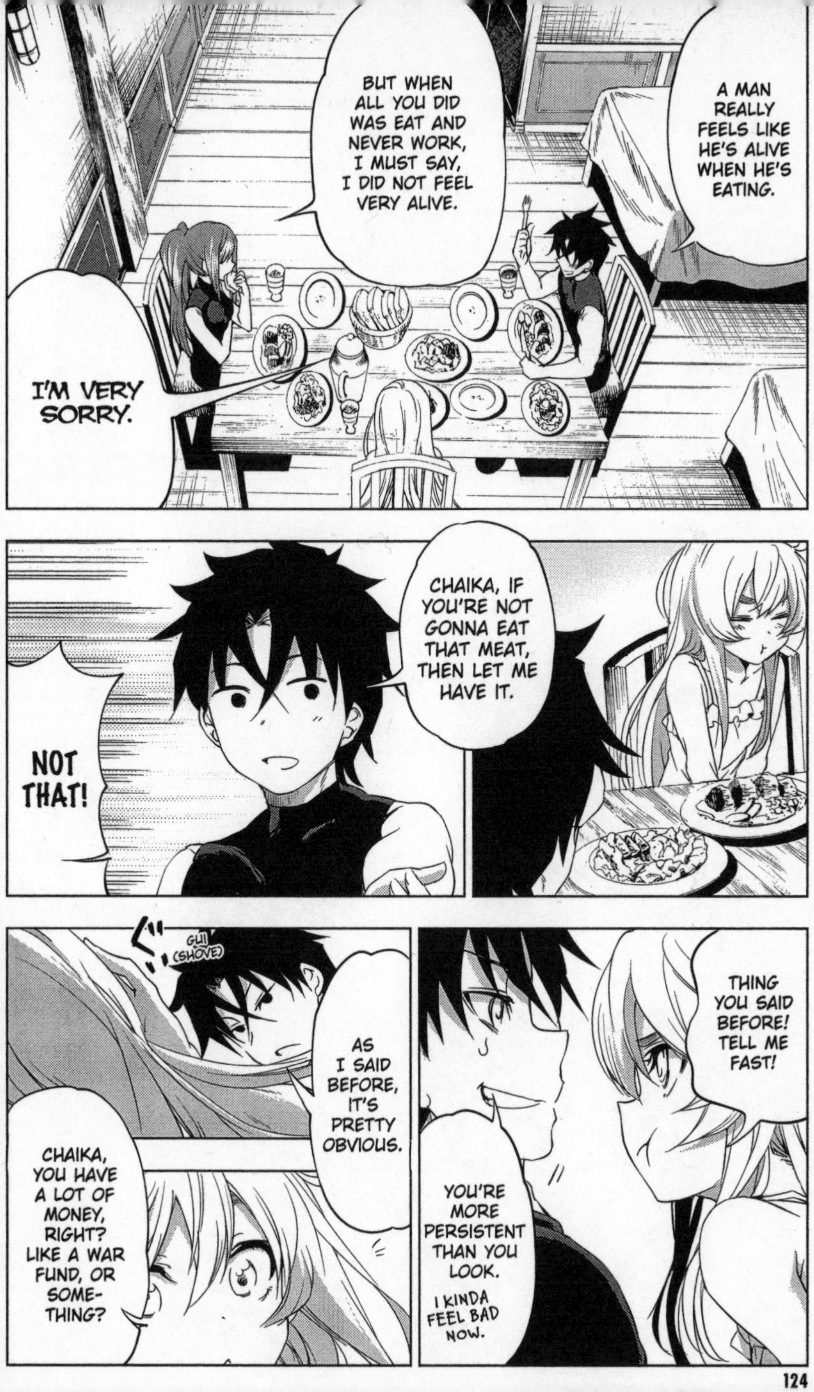
A MAN REALLY FEELS LIKE HE'S ALIVE WHEN HE'S EATING.
BUT WHEN ALL YOU DID WAS EAT AND NEVER WORK, I MUST SAY, I DID NOT FEEL VERY ALIVE.
I'M VERY SORRY.
CHAIKA, IF YOU'RE NOT GONNA EAT THAT MEAT, THEN LET ME HAVE IT.
NOT THAT!
THING YOU SAID BEFORE! TELL ME FAST!
YOU'RE MORE PERSISTENT THAN YOU LOOK.
I KINDA FEEL BAD NOW.
GUI (SHOVE)
AS I SAID BEFORE, IT'S PRETTY OBVIOUS.
CHAIKA, YOU HAVE A LOT OF MONEY, RIGHT? LIKE A WAR FUND, OR SOME-THING?

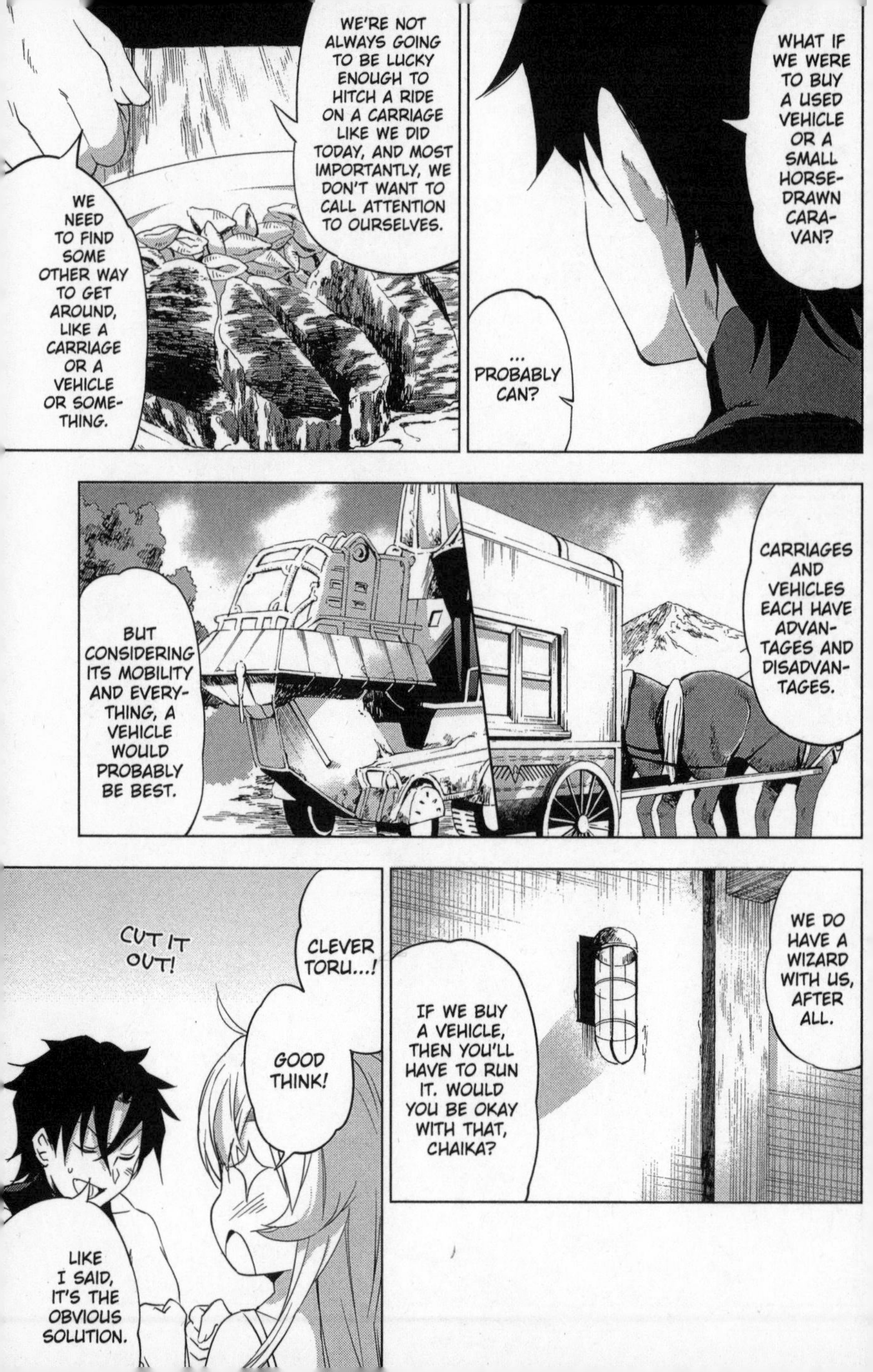
WHAT IF WE WERE TO BUY A USED VEHICLE OR A SMALL HORSE-DRAWN CARA-VAN?
... PROBABLY CAN?
WE'RE NOT ALWAYS GOING TO BE LUCKY ENOUGH TO HITCH A RIDE ON A CARRIAGE LIKE WE DID TODAY, AND MOST IMPORTANTLY, WE DON'T WANT TO CALL ATTENTION TO OURSELVES.
WE NEED TO FIND SOME OTHER WAY TO GET AROUND, LIKE A CARRIAGE OR A VEHICLE OR SOME-THING.
CARRIAGES AND VEHICLES EACH HAVE ADVAN-TAGES AND DISADVAN-TAGES.
BUT CONSIDERING ITS MOBILITY AND EVERY-THING, A VEHICLE WOULD PROBABLY BE BEST.
WE DO HAVE A WIZARD WITH US, AFTER ALL.
IF WE BUY A VEHICLE, THEN YOU'LL HAVE TO RUN IT. WOULD YOU BE OKAY WITH THAT, CHAIKA?
CLEVER TORU...!
CUT IT OUT!
GOOD THINK!
LIKE I SAID, IT'S THE OBVIOUS SOLUTION.

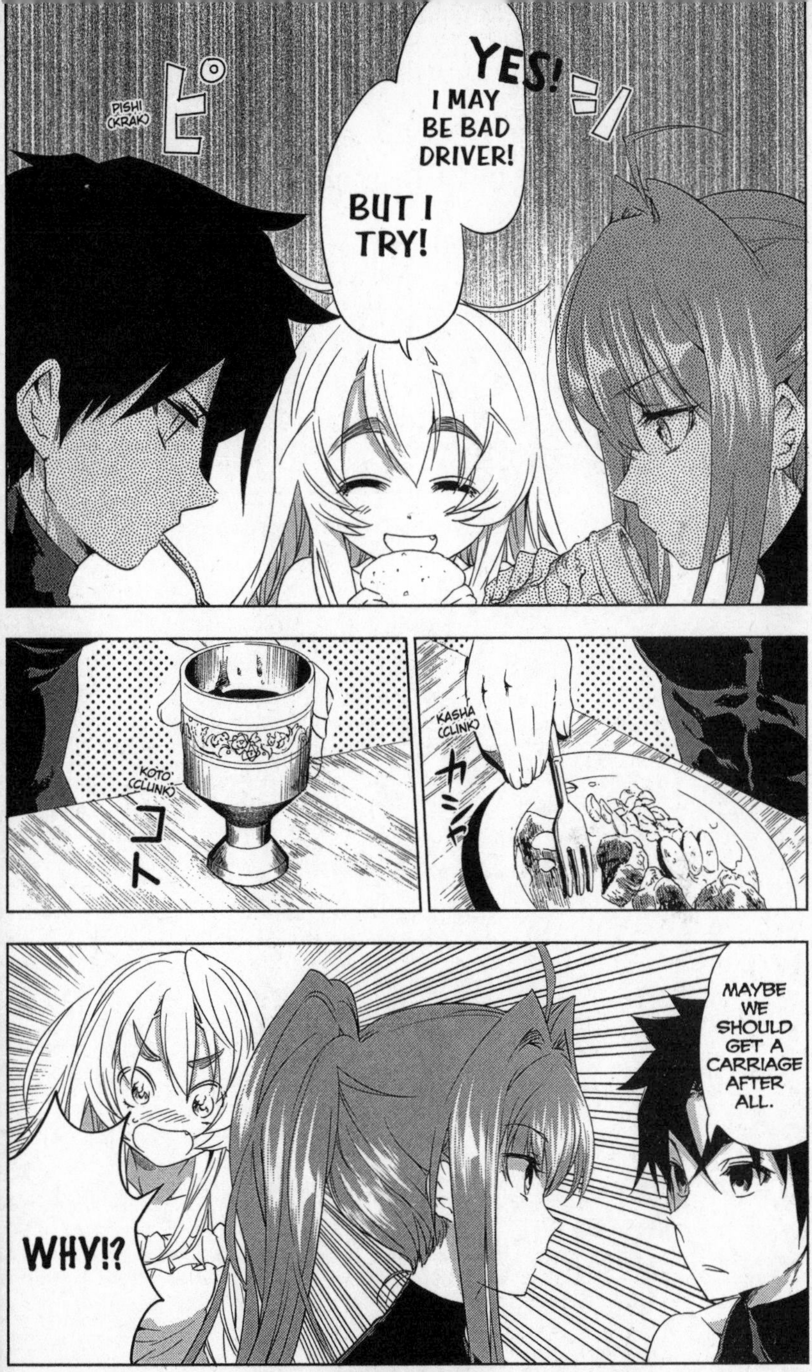
YES! ニノ
I MAY BE BAD DRIVER!
BUT I TRY!
ピ
PISH! (KRAK)
カシャ
KASHA (CLINK)
コト
KOTO (CLINK)
MAYBE WE SHOULD GET A CARRIAGE AFTER ALL.
WHY!?

episode 15: END

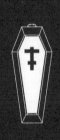

CHAIKA: THE COFFIN PRINCESS

episode 16: Collaborator

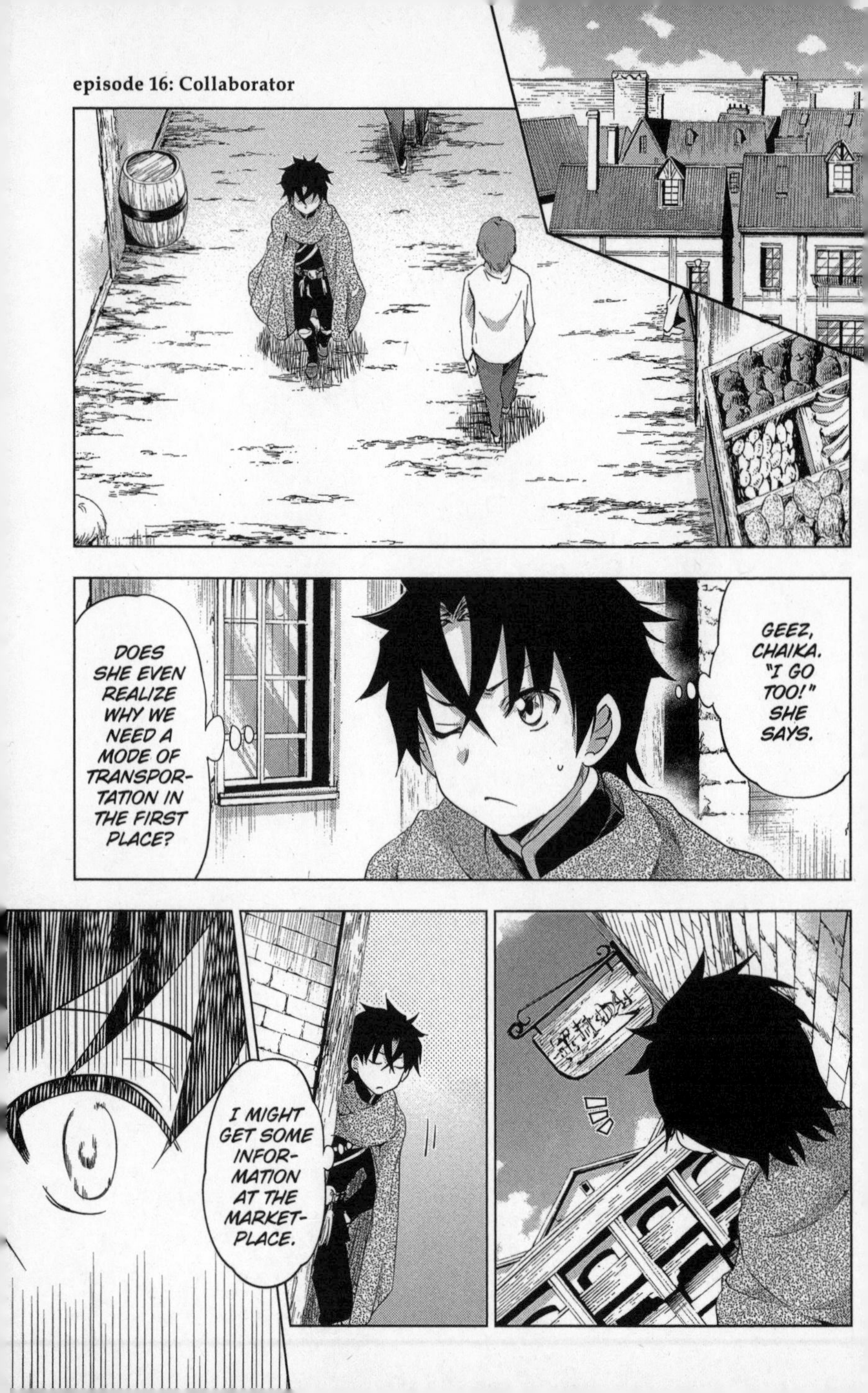

GEEZ, CHAIKA. "I GO TOO!" SHE SAYS.
DOES SHE EVEN REALIZE WHY WE NEED A MODE OF TRANSPORTATION IN THE FIRST PLACE?
I MIGHT GET SOME INFORMATION AT THE MARKETPLACE.

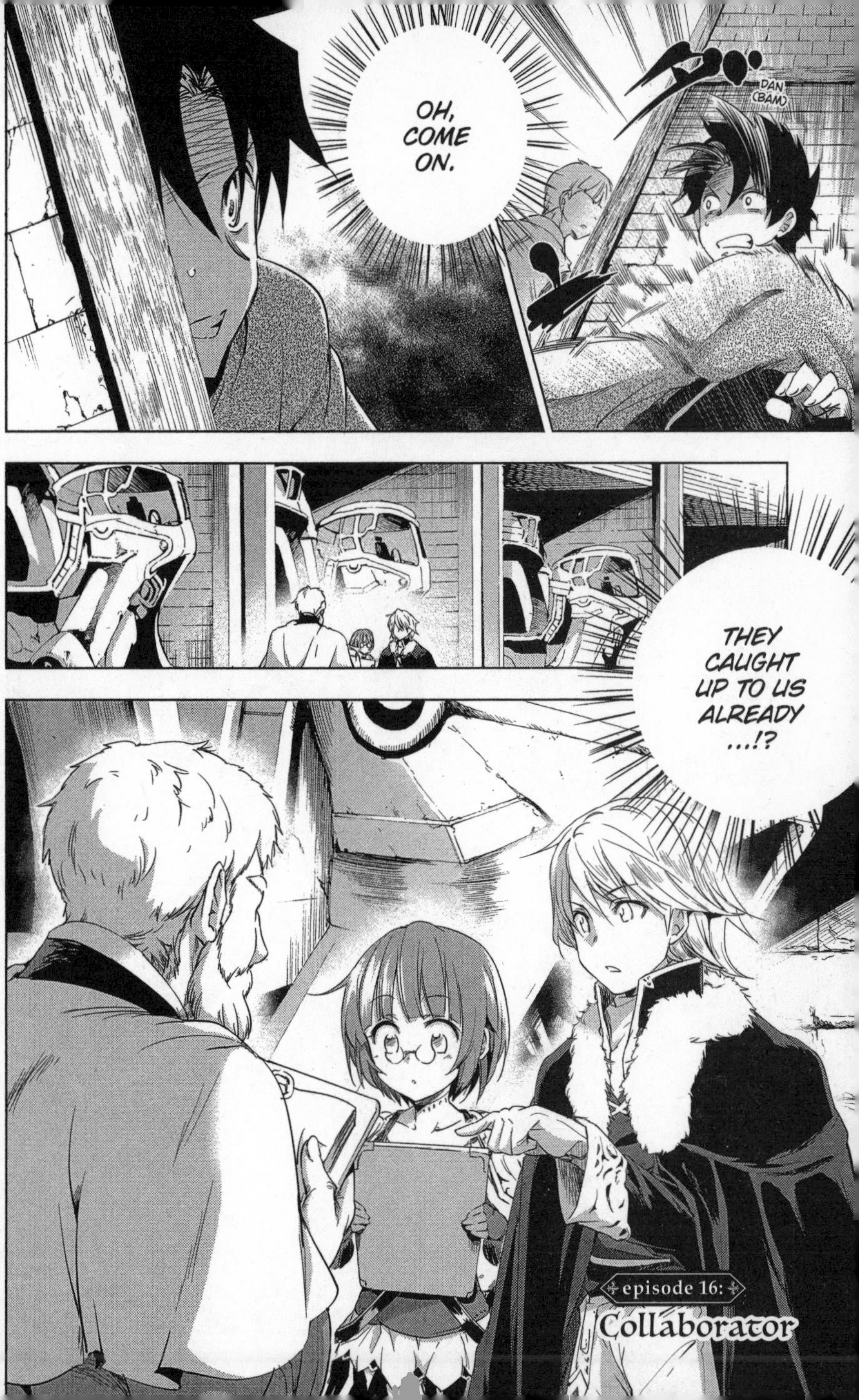
DAN
(BAM)
OH, COME ON.
THEY CAUGHT UP TO US ALREADY ...!?
episode 16:
Collaborator

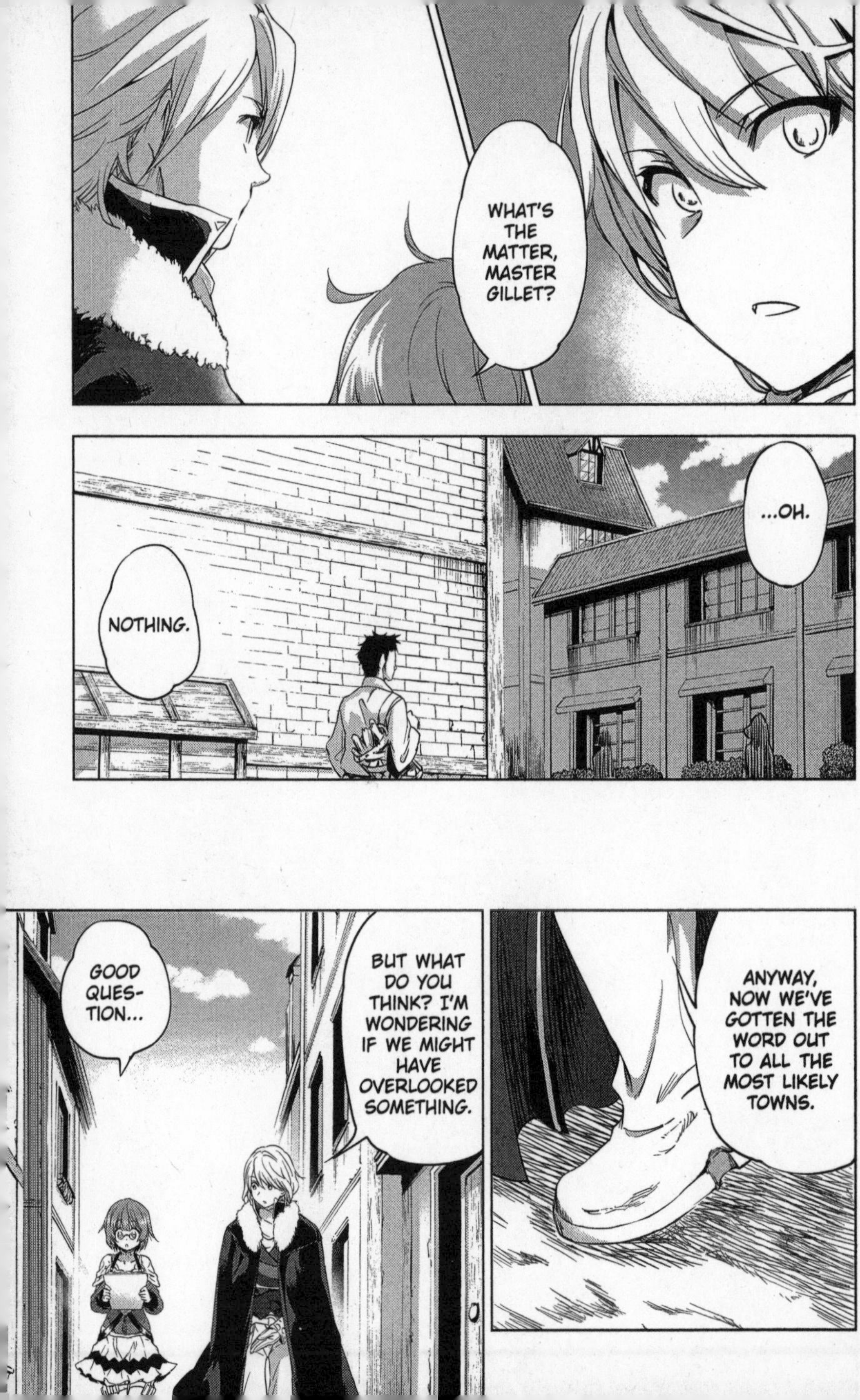
WHAT'S THE MATTER, MASTER GILLET?
...OH.
NOTHING.
ANYWAY, NOW WE'VE GOTTEN THE WORD OUT TO ALL THE MOST LIKELY TOWNS.
BUT WHAT DO YOU THINK? I'M WONDERING IF WE MIGHT HAVE OVERLOOKED SOMETHING.
GOOD QUES-TION...

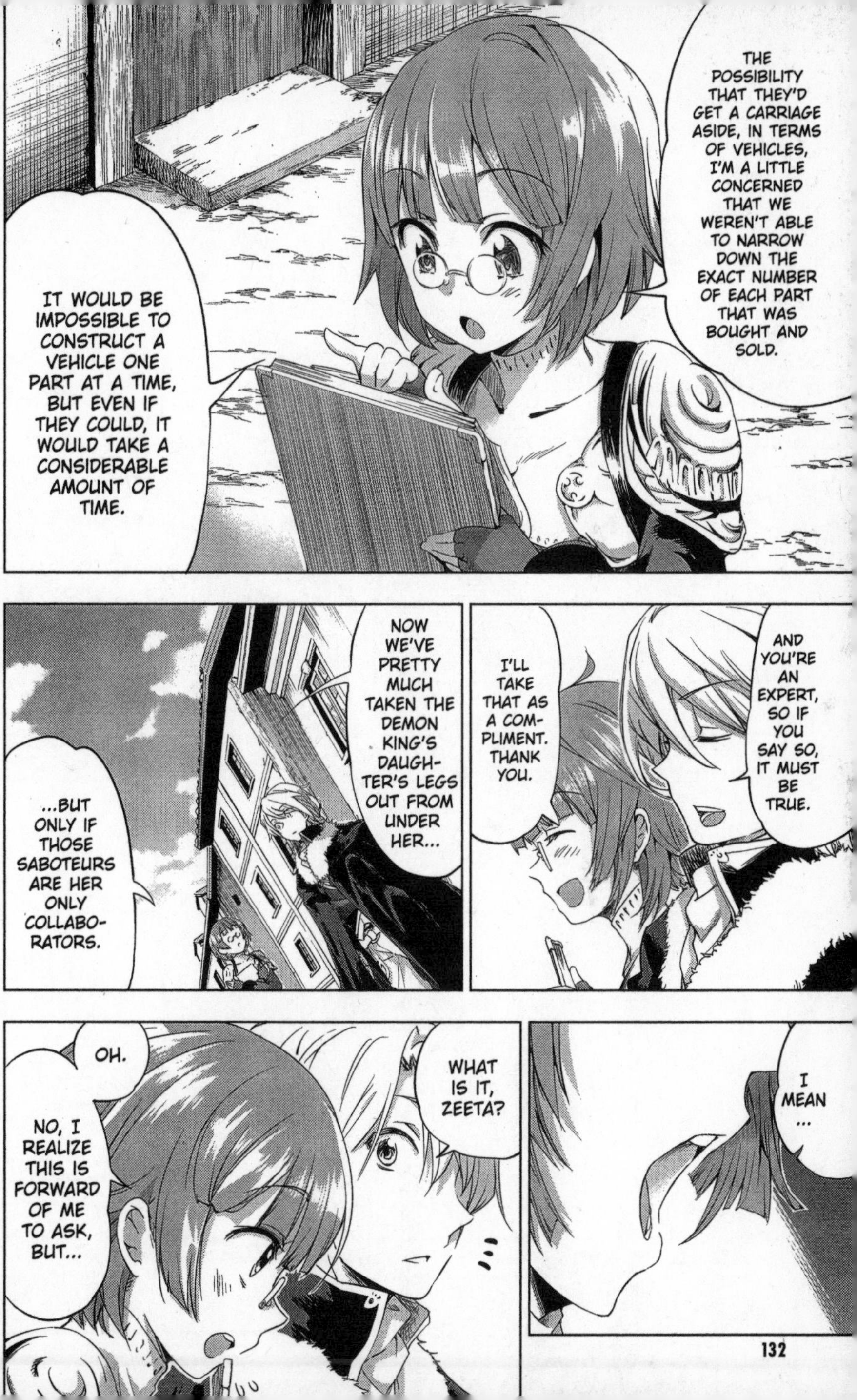
IT WOULD BE IMPOSSIBLE TO CONSTRUCT A VEHICLE ONE PART AT A TIME, BUT EVEN IF THEY COULD, IT WOULD TAKE A CONSIDERABLE AMOUNT OF TIME.
THE POSSIBILITY THAT THEY'D GET A CARRIAGE ASIDE, IN TERMS OF VEHICLES, I'M A LITTLE CONCERNED THAT WE WEREN'T ABLE TO NARROW DOWN THE EXACT NUMBER OF EACH PART THAT WAS BOUGHT AND SOLD.
NOW WE'VE PRETTY MUCH TAKEN THE DEMON KING'S DAUGHTER'S LEGS OUT FROM UNDER HER...
...BUT ONLY IF THOSE SABOTEURS ARE HER ONLY COLLABORATORS.
AND YOU'RE AN EXPERT, SO IF YOU SAY SO, IT MUST BE TRUE.
I'LL TAKE THAT AS A COMPLIMENT. THANK YOU.
OH.
WHAT IS IT, ZEETA?
NO, I REALIZE THIS IS FORWARD OF ME TO ASK, BUT...
I MEAN ...

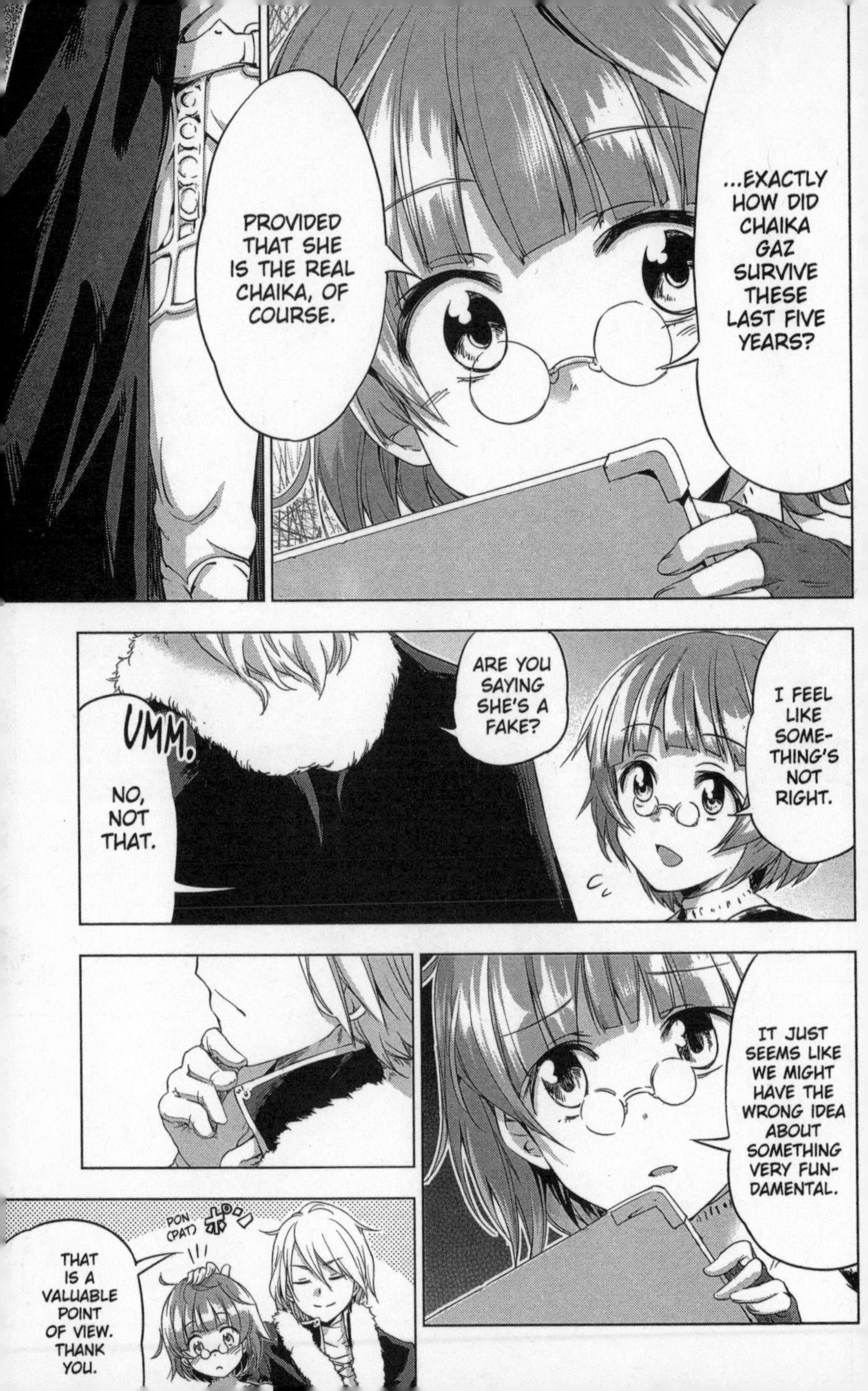
...EXACTLY HOW DID CHAIKA GAZ SURVIVE THESE LAST FIVE YEARS?
PROVIDED THAT SHE IS THE REAL CHAIKA, OF COURSE.
I FEEL LIKE SOME-THING'S NOT RIGHT.
ARE YOU SAYING SHE'S A FAKE?
UMM.
NO, NOT THAT.
IT JUST SEEMS LIKE WE MIGHT HAVE THE WRONG IDEA ABOUT SOMETHING VERY FUN-DAMENTAL.
PON (PAT)
THAT IS A VALUABLE POINT OF VIEW. THANK YOU.

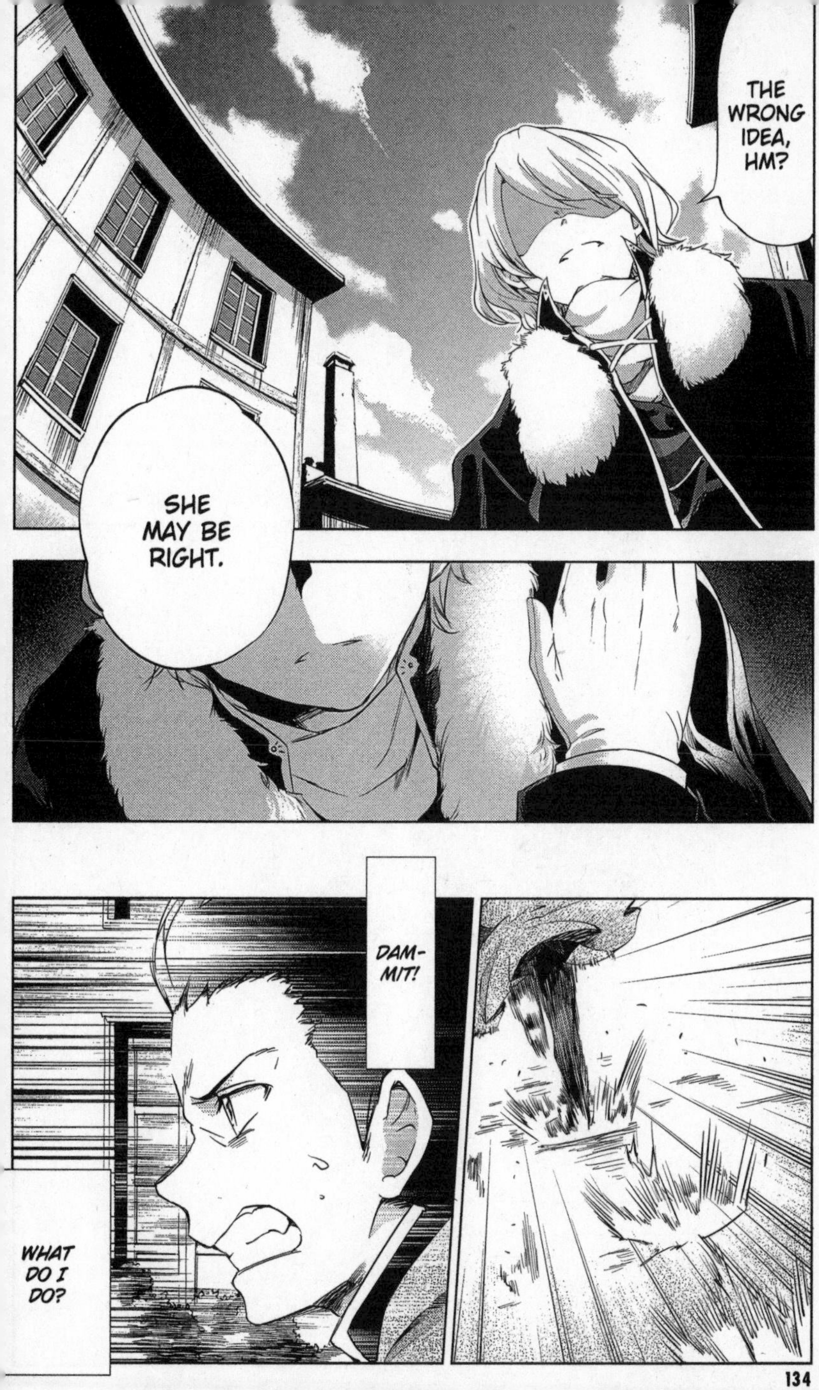
THE WRONG IDEA, HM?
SHE MAY BE RIGHT.
DAM-MIT!
WHAT DO I DO?

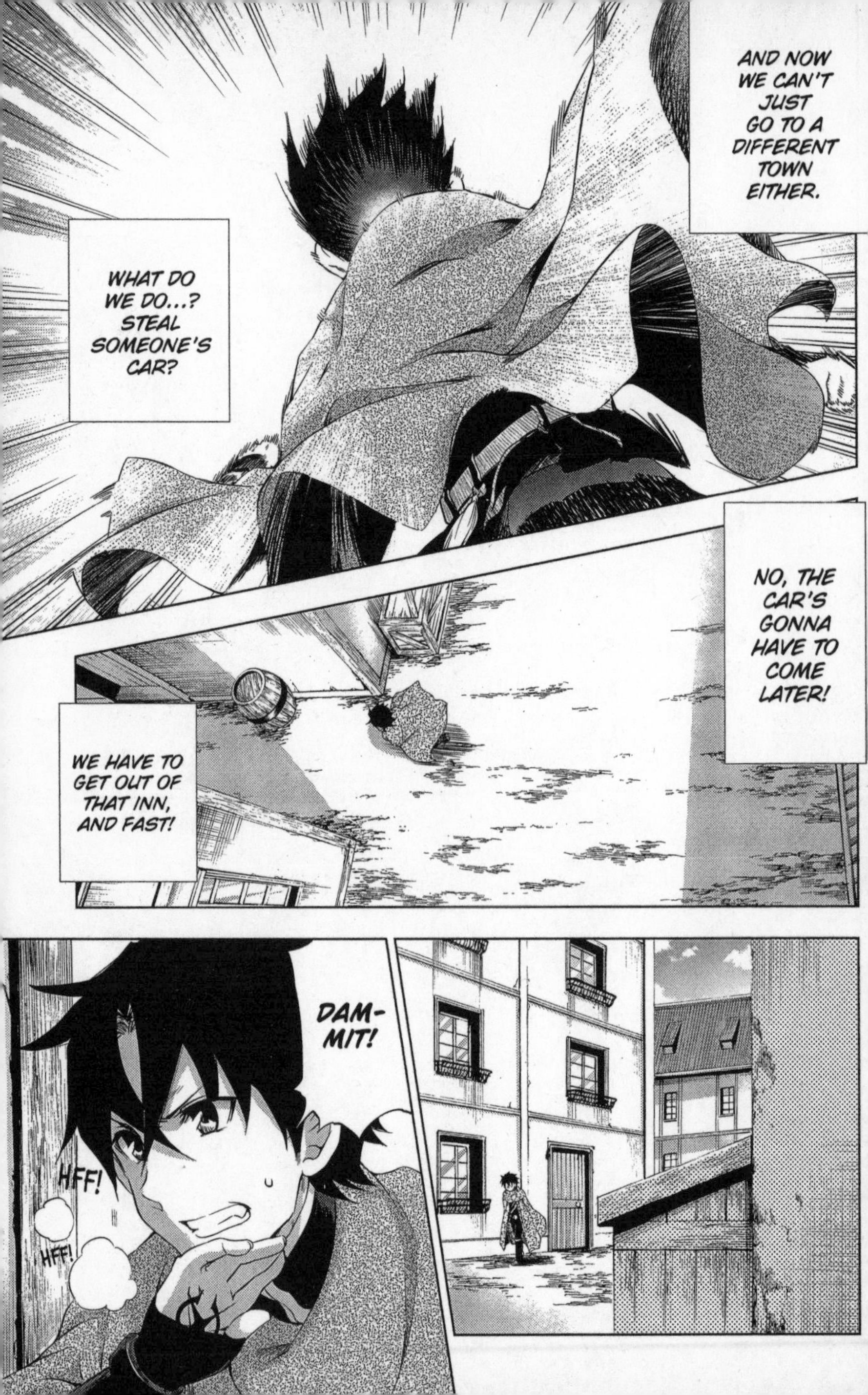
AND NOW WE CAN'T JUST GO TO A DIFFERENT TOWN EITHER.
WHAT DO WE DO...? STEAL SOMEONE'S CAR?
NO, THE CAR'S GONNA HAVE TO COME LATER!
WE HAVE TO GET OUT OF THAT INN, AND FAST!
DAM-MIT!
HFF!
HFF!

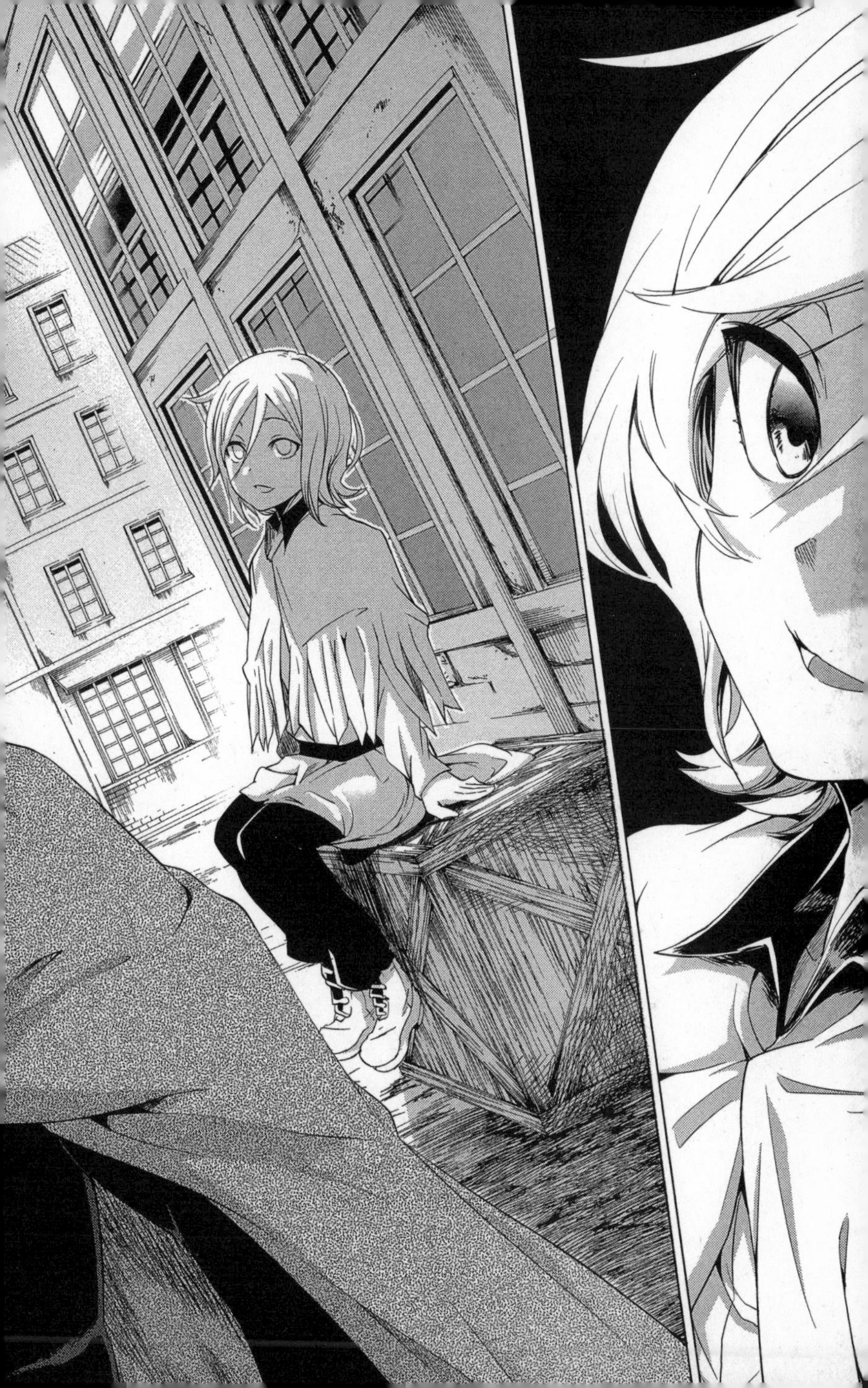

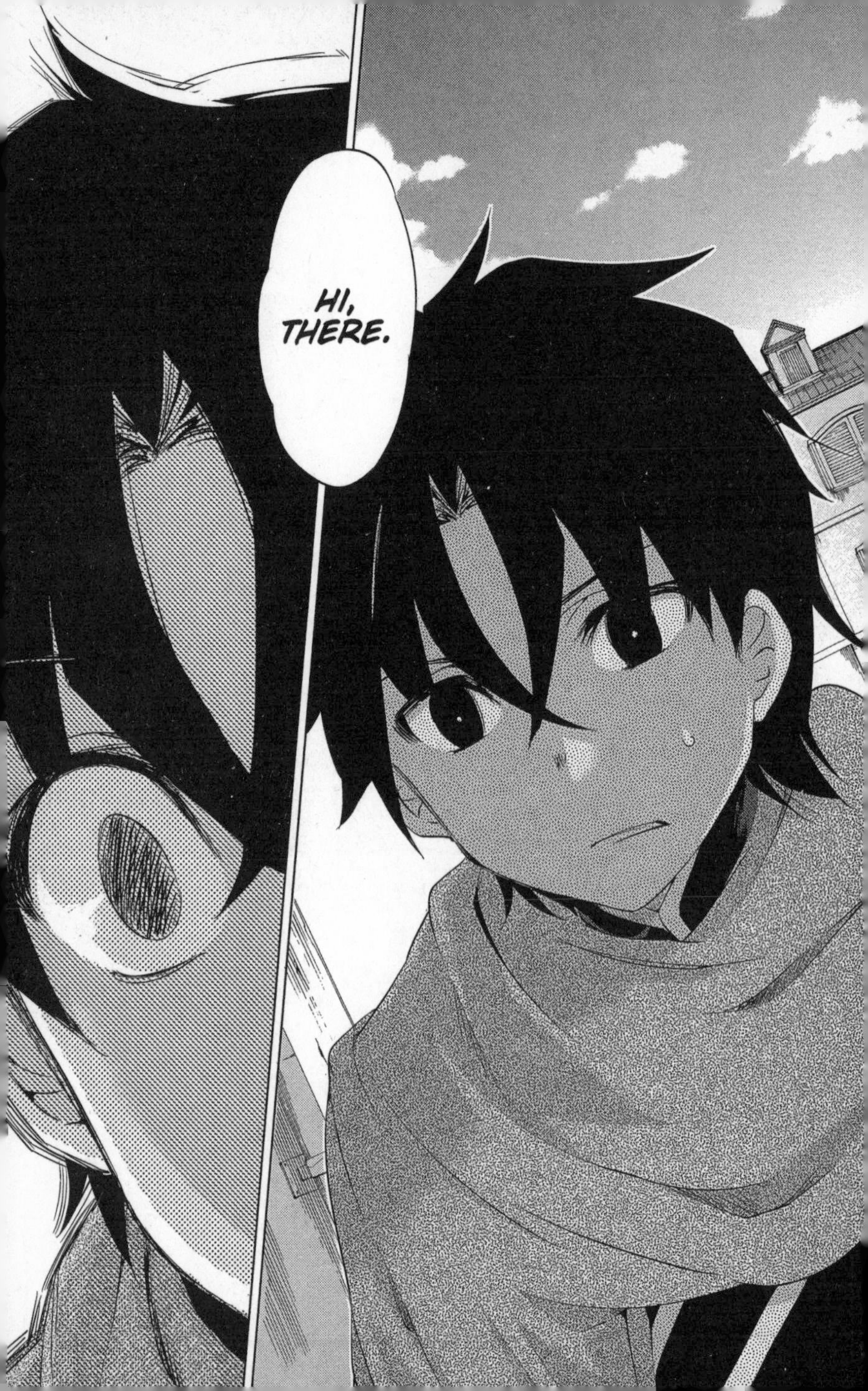
HI, THERE.

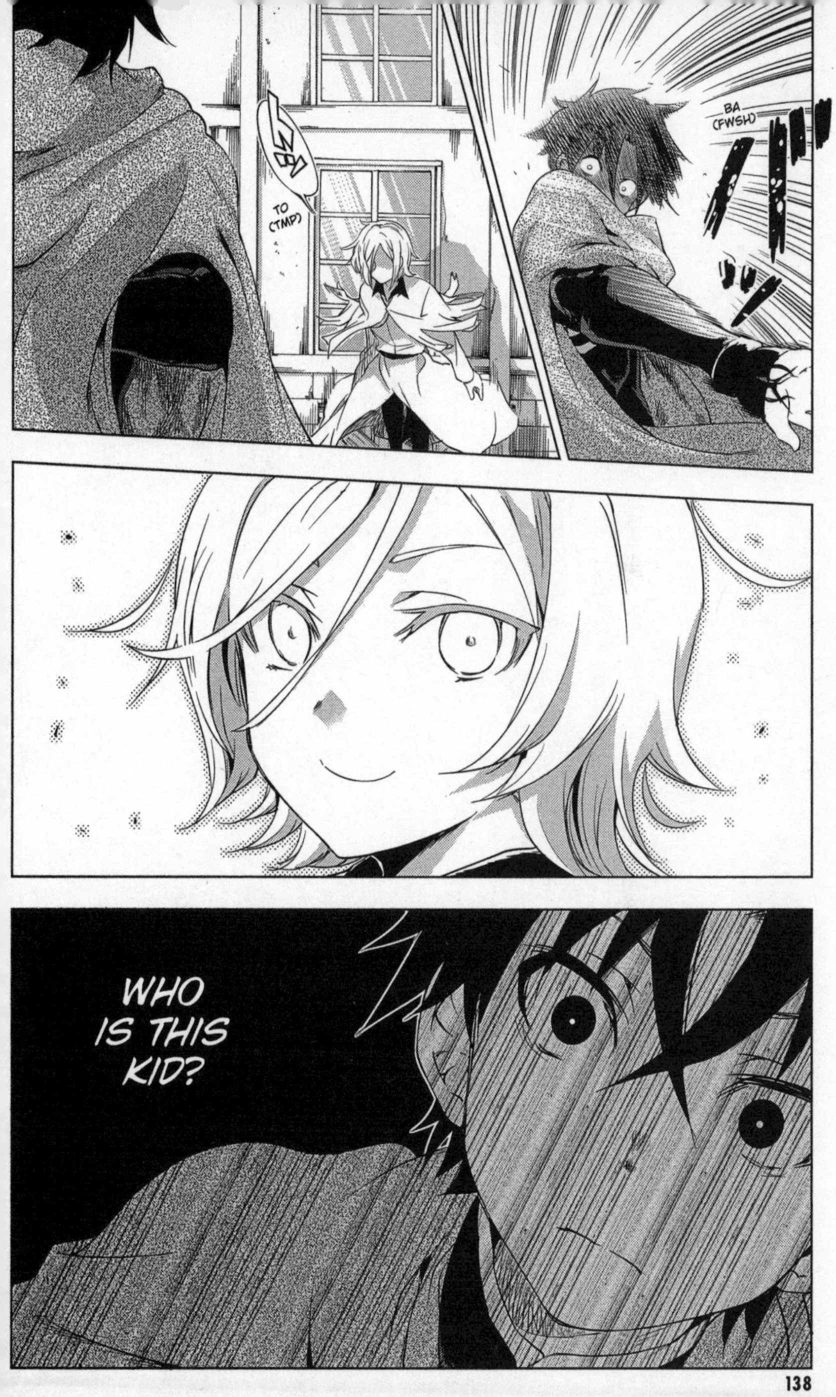
BA (FWSH)
TO (TMP)
WHO IS THIS KID?

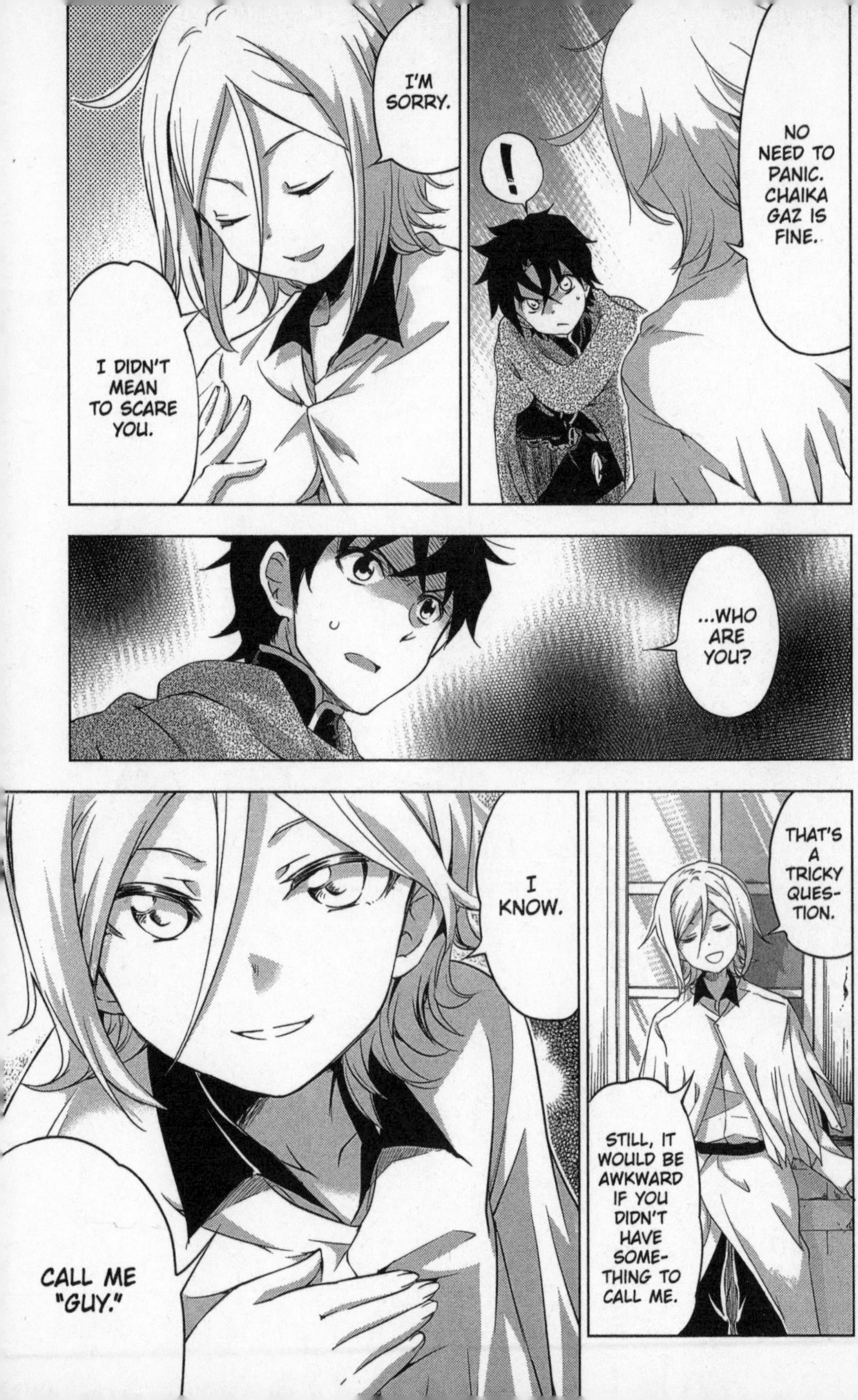
NO NEED TO PANIC. CHAIKA GAZ IS FINE.
!
I'M SORRY.
I DIDN'T MEAN TO SCARE YOU.
...WHO ARE YOU?
THAT'S A TRICKY QUES-TION.
STILL, IT WOULD BE AWKWARD IF YOU DIDN'T HAVE SOME-THING TO CALL ME.
I KNOW.
CALL ME "GUY."

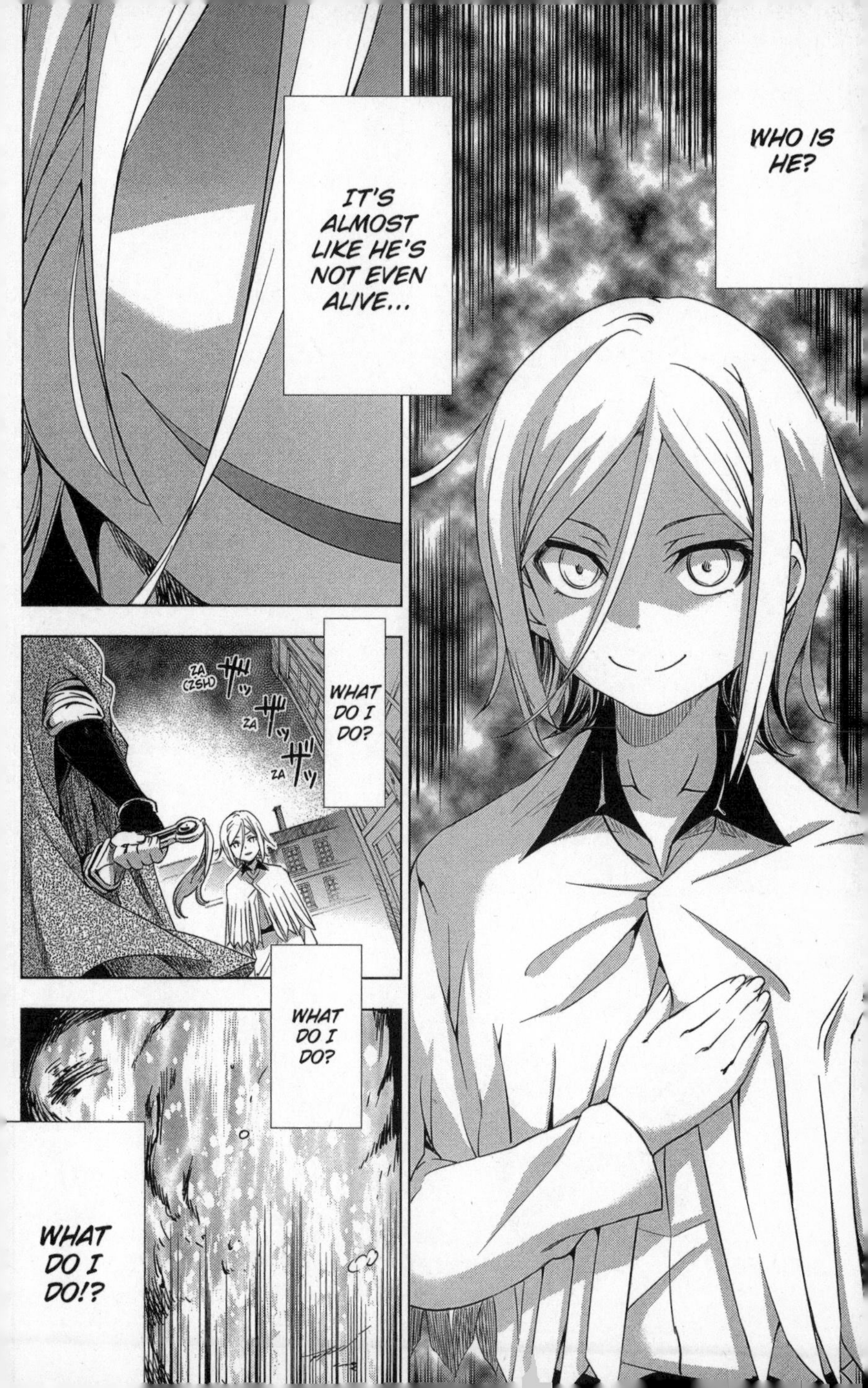

WHO IS HE?
IT'S ALMOST LIKE HE'S NOT EVEN ALIVE...
WHAT DO I DO?
ザッ ZA (ZSH)
ザッ ZA
ザッ ZA
WHAT DO I DO?
WHAT DO I DO!?

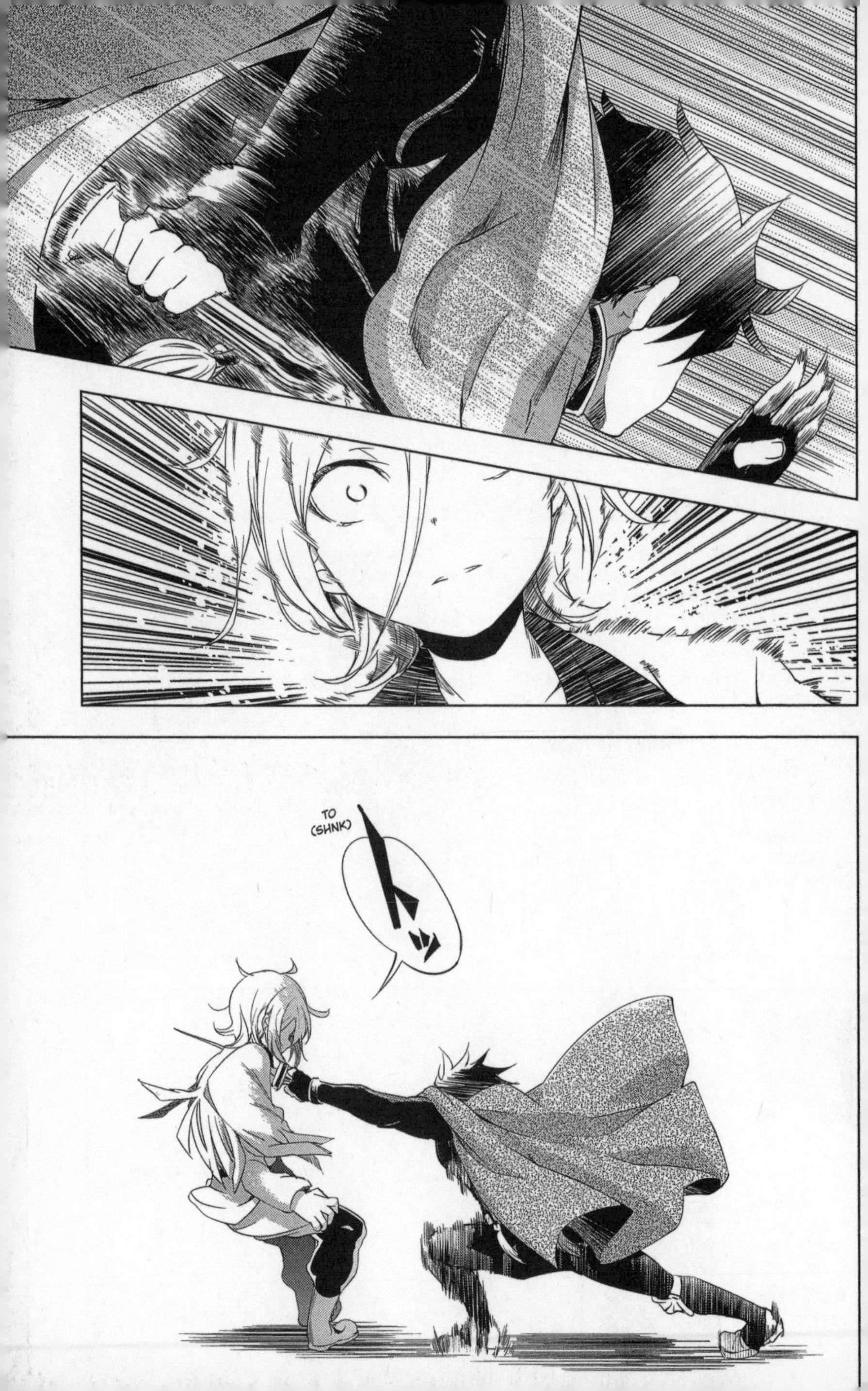
TO
(SHNK)

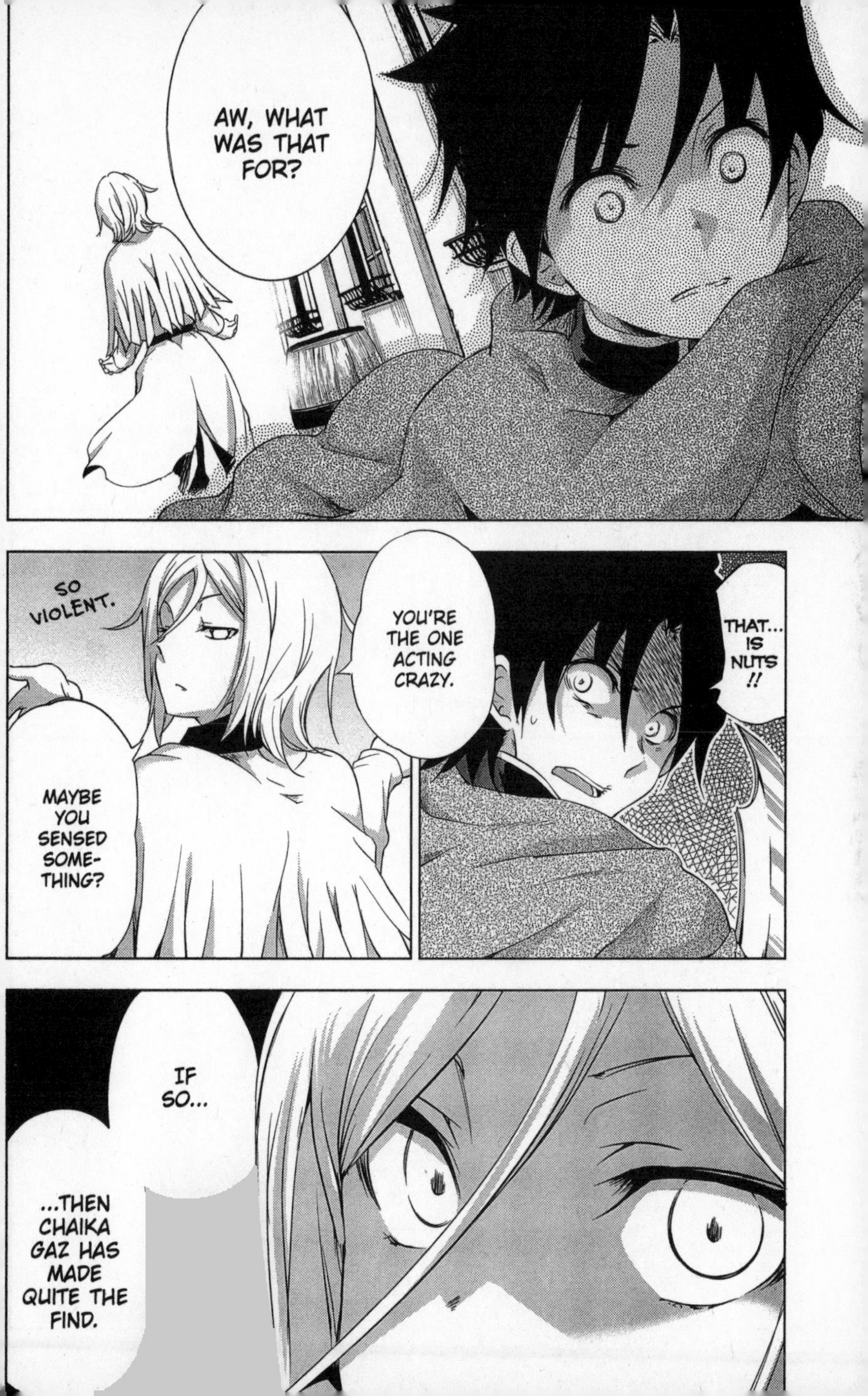
AW, WHAT WAS THAT FOR?
THAT... IS NUTS!!
YOU'RE THE ONE ACTING CRAZY.
SO VIOLENT.
MAYBE YOU SENSED SOME-THING?
IF SO...
...THEN CHAIKA GAZ HAS MADE QUITE THE FIND.

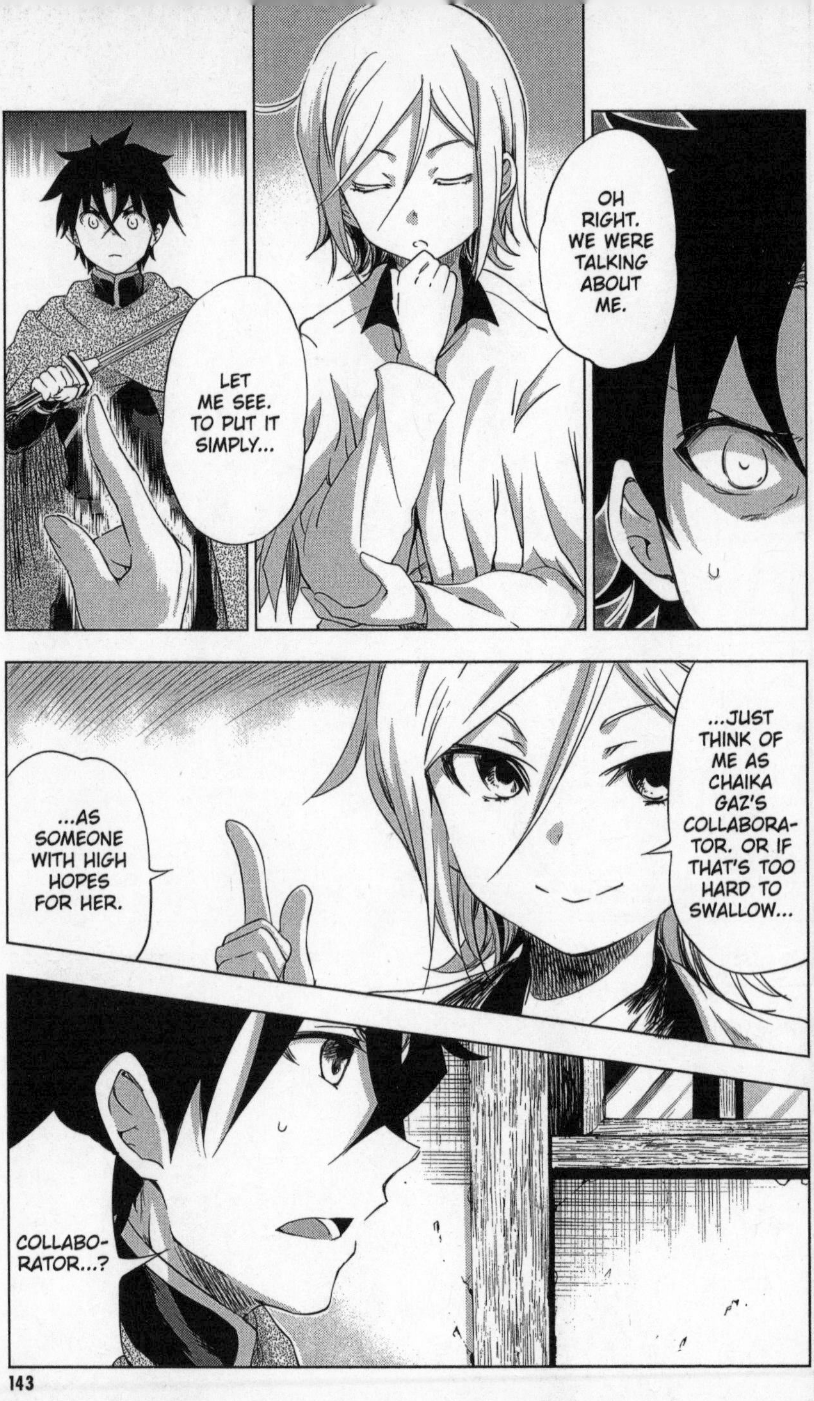
OH RIGHT. WE WERE TALKING ABOUT ME.
LET ME SEE. TO PUT IT SIMPLY...
...JUST THINK OF ME AS CHAIKA GAZ'S COLLABORA-TOR. OR IF THAT'S TOO HARD TO SWALLOW...
...AS SOMEONE WITH HIGH HOPES FOR HER.
COLLABO-RATOR...?

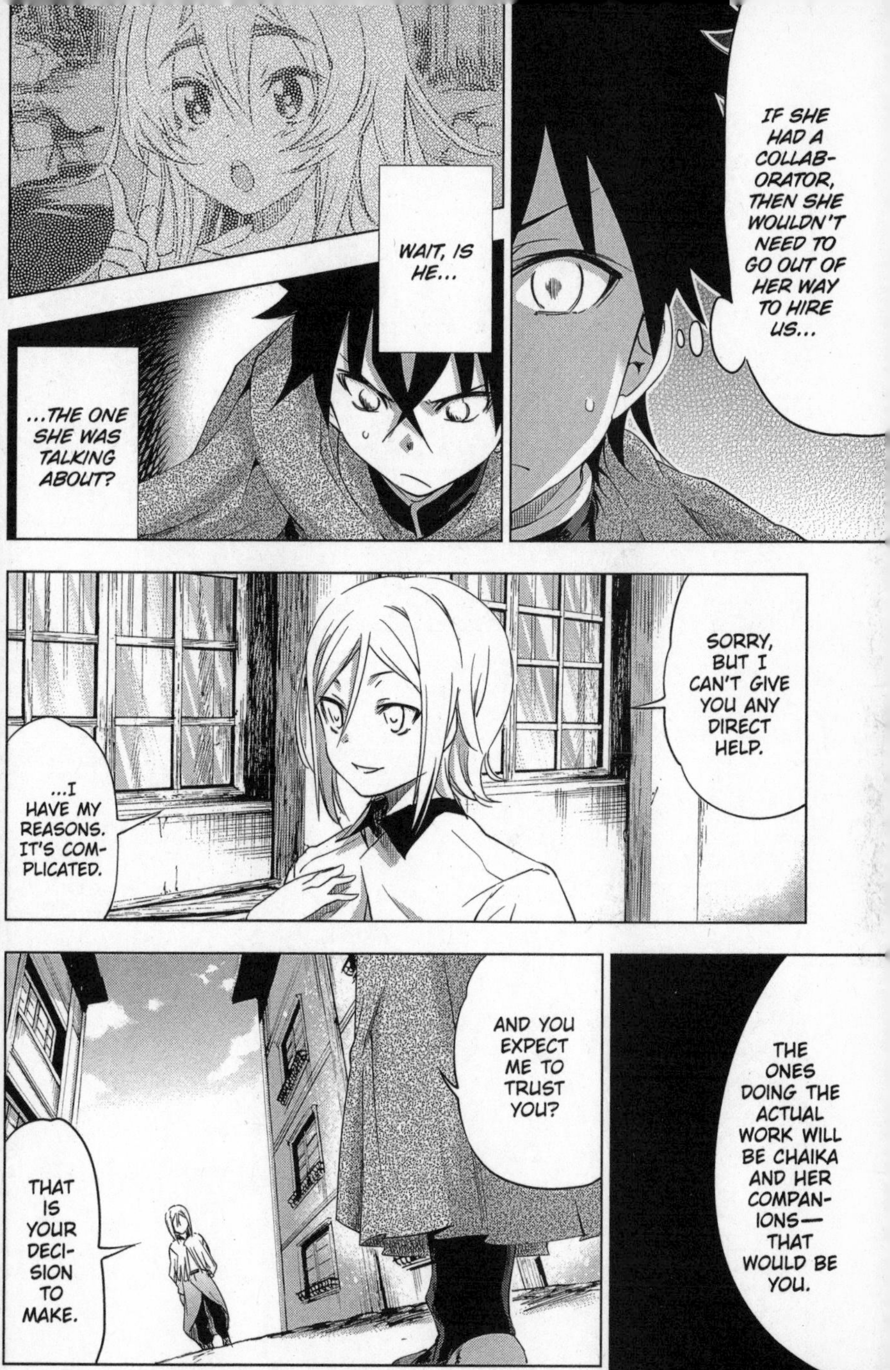
IF SHE HAD A COLLAB-ORATOR, THEN SHE WOULDN'T NEED TO GO OUT OF HER WAY TO HIRE US...
WAIT, IS HE...
...THE ONE SHE WAS TALKING ABOUT?
SORRY, BUT I CAN'T GIVE YOU ANY DIRECT HELP.
...I HAVE MY REASONS. IT'S COM-PLICATED.
THE ONES DOING THE ACTUAL WORK WILL BE CHAIKA AND HER COMPAN-IONS—THAT WOULD BE YOU.
AND YOU EXPECT ME TO TRUST YOU?
THAT IS YOUR DECI-SION TO MAKE.

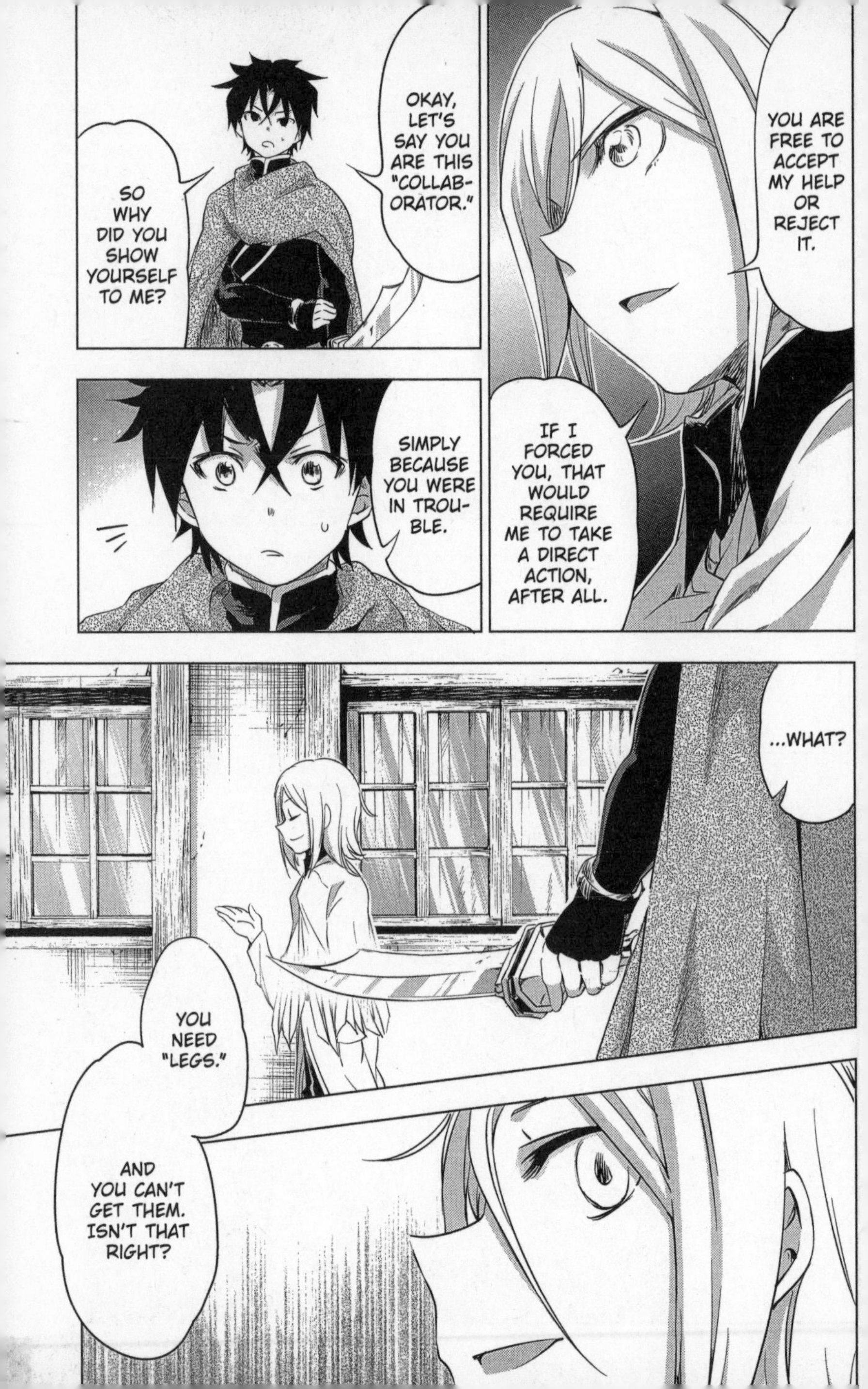
YOU ARE FREE TO ACCEPT MY HELP OR REJECT IT.
IF I FORCED YOU, THAT WOULD REQUIRE ME TO TAKE A DIRECT ACTION, AFTER ALL.
OKAY, LET'S SAY YOU ARE THIS "COLLAB-ORATOR."
SO WHY DID YOU SHOW YOURSELF TO ME?
SIMPLY BECAUSE YOU WERE IN TROU-BLE.
...WHAT?
YOU NEED "LEGS."
AND YOU CAN'T GET THEM. ISN'T THAT RIGHT?

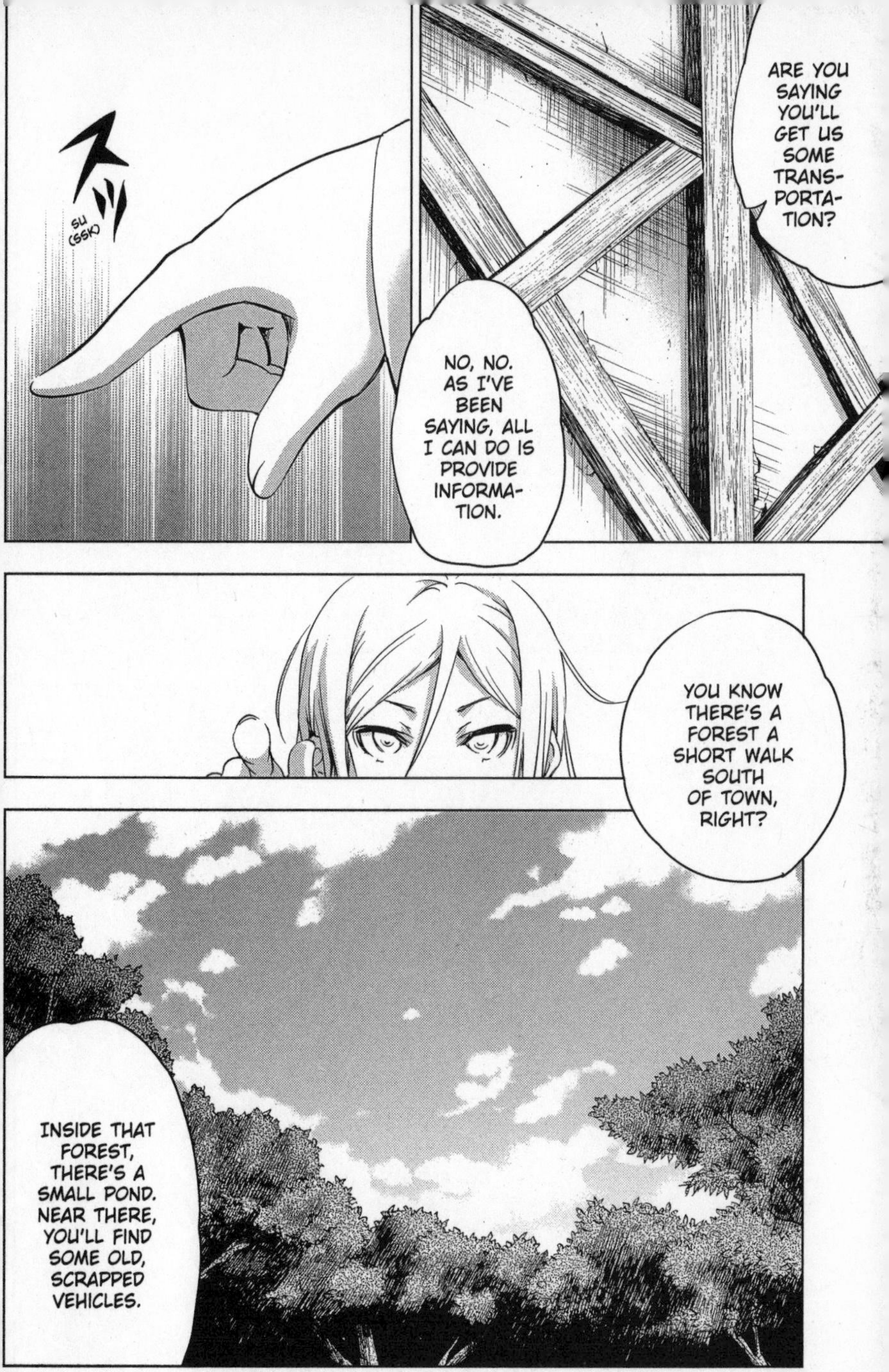
ARE YOU SAYING YOU'LL GET US SOME TRANSPORTATION?
NO, NO. AS I'VE BEEN SAYING, ALL I CAN DO IS PROVIDE INFORMATION.
スッ
SU (SSK)
YOU KNOW THERE'S A FOREST A SHORT WALK SOUTH OF TOWN, RIGHT?
INSIDE THAT FOREST, THERE'S A SMALL POND. NEAR THERE, YOU'LL FIND SOME OLD, SCRAPPED VEHICLES.

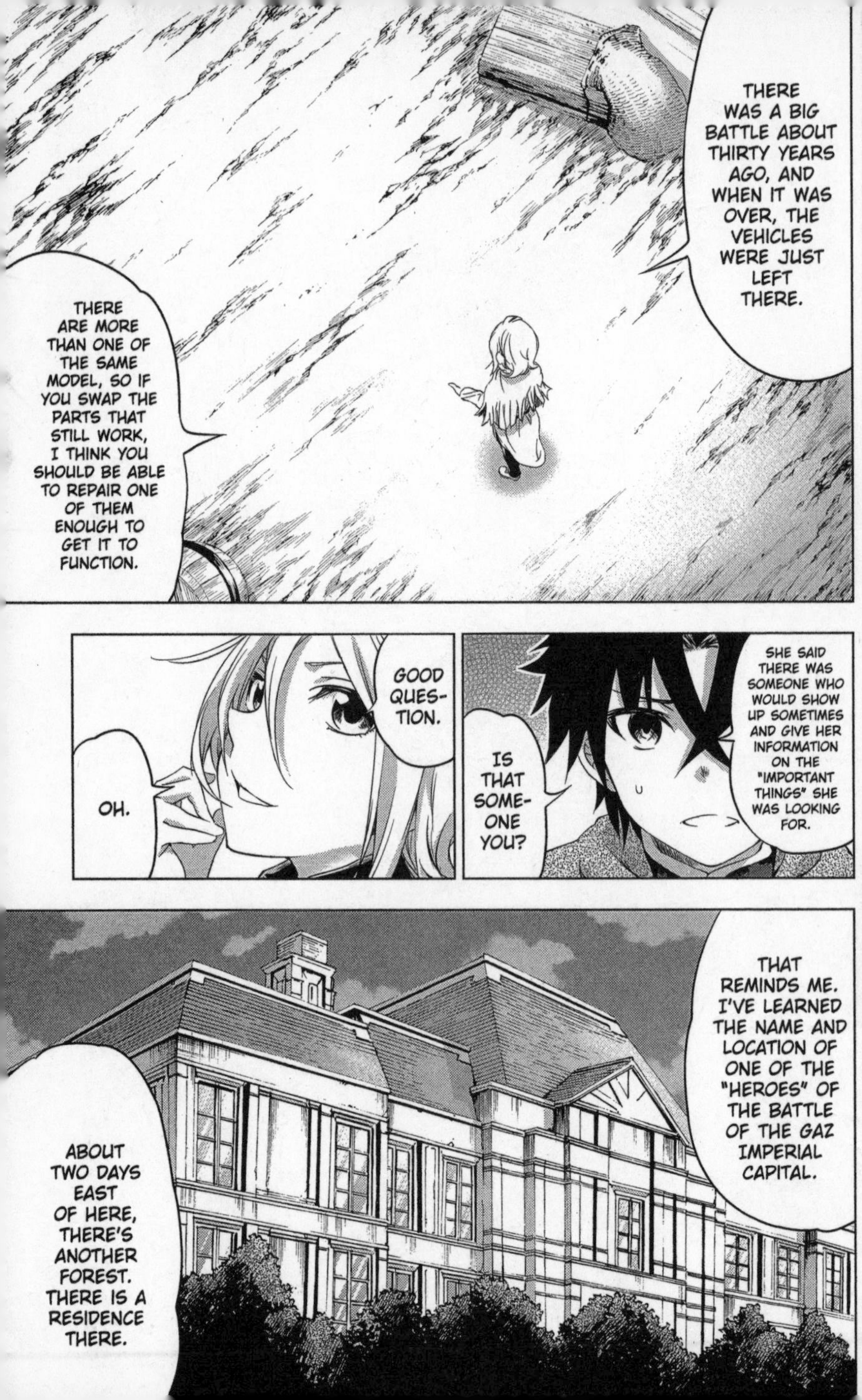
THERE WAS A BIG BATTLE ABOUT THIRTY YEARS AGO, AND WHEN IT WAS OVER, THE VEHICLES WERE JUST LEFT THERE.
THERE ARE MORE THAN ONE OF THE SAME MODEL, SO IF YOU SWAP THE PARTS THAT STILL WORK, I THINK YOU SHOULD BE ABLE TO REPAIR ONE OF THEM ENOUGH TO GET IT TO FUNCTION.
SHE SAID THERE WAS SOMEONE WHO WOULD SHOW UP SOMETIMES AND GIVE HER INFORMATION ON THE "IMPORTANT THINGS" SHE WAS LOOKING FOR.
IS THAT SOMEONE YOU?
GOOD QUESTION.
OH.
THAT REMINDS ME. I'VE LEARNED THE NAME AND LOCATION OF ONE OF THE "HEROES" OF THE BATTLE OF THE GAZ IMPERIAL CAPITAL.
ABOUT TWO DAYS EAST OF HERE, THERE'S ANOTHER FOREST. THERE IS A RESIDENCE THERE.

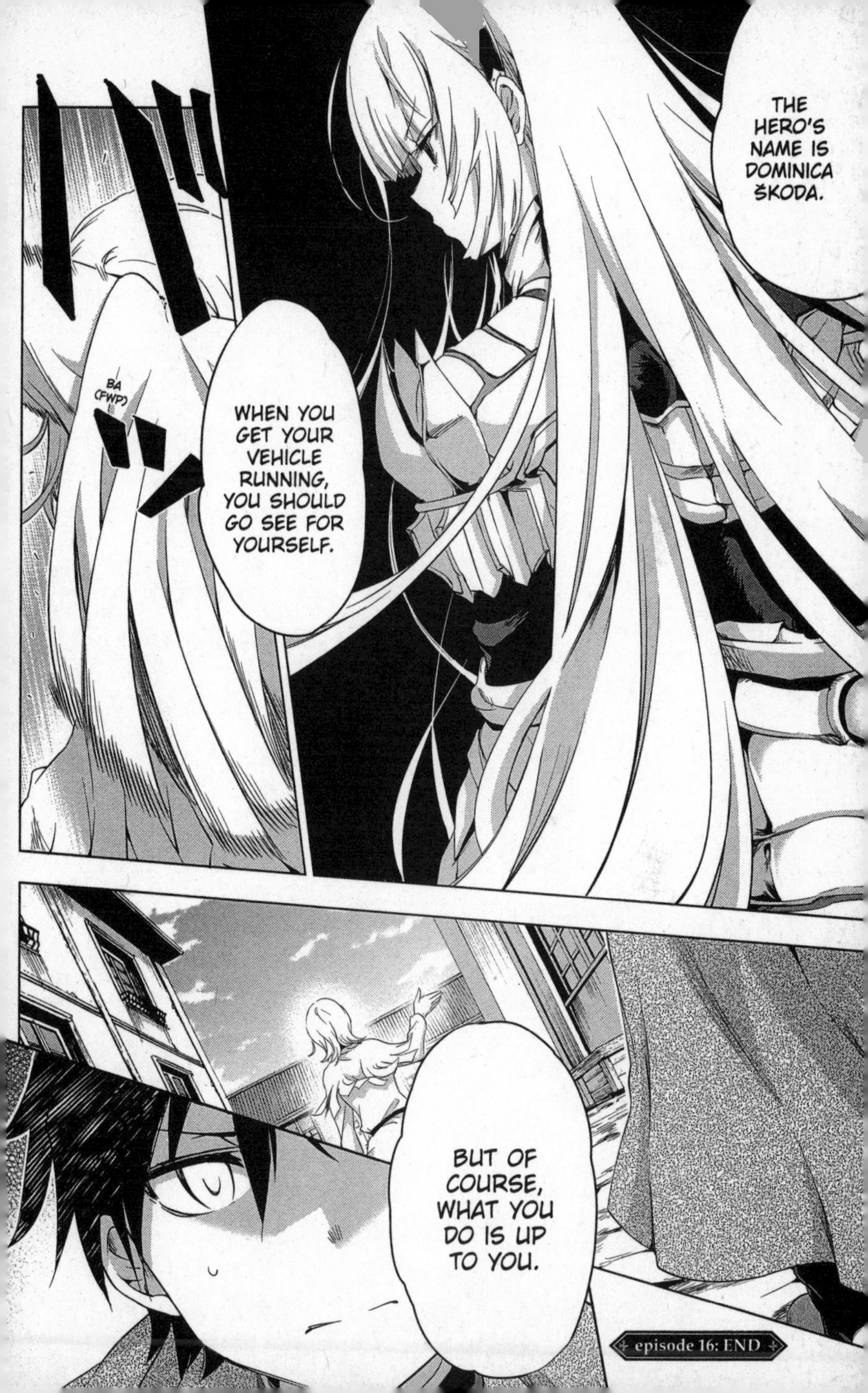
THE HERO'S NAME IS DOMINICA ŠKODA.
WHEN YOU GET YOUR VEHICLE RUNNING, YOU SHOULD GO SEE FOR YOURSELF.
BA (FWP)
BUT OF COURSE, WHAT YOU DO IS UP TO YOU.
episode 16: END

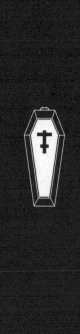

CHAIKA: THE COFFIN PRINCESS

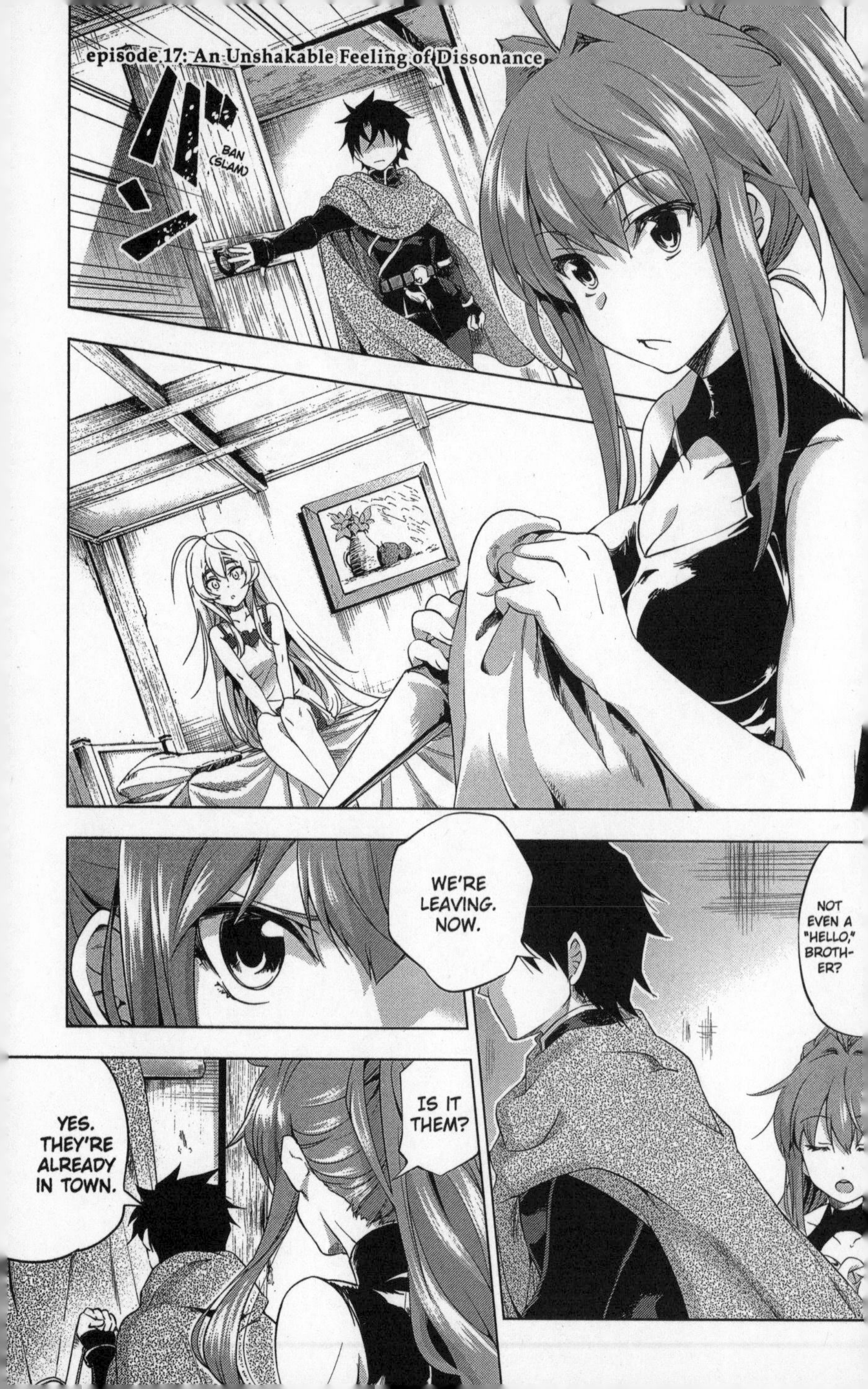
episode 17: An Unshakable Feeling of Dissonance
BAN (SLAM)
NOT EVEN A "HELLO," BROTHER?
WE'RE LEAVING. NOW.
IS IT THEM?
YES. THEY'RE ALREADY IN TOWN.

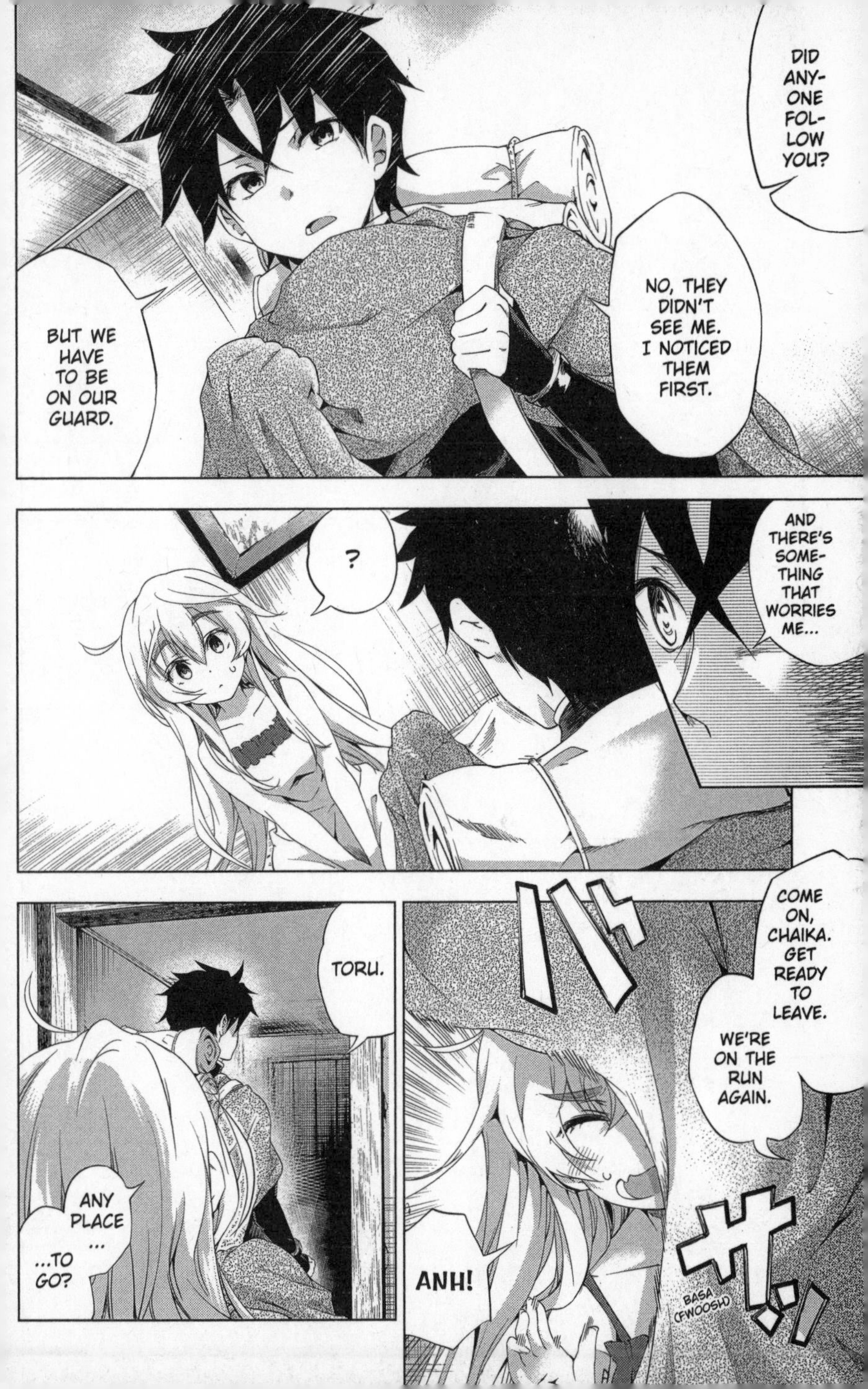
DID ANYONE FOLLOW YOU?
NO, THEY DIDN'T SEE ME. I NOTICED THEM FIRST.
BUT WE HAVE TO BE ON OUR GUARD.
AND THERE'S SOMETHING THAT WORRIES ME...
?
COME ON, CHAIKA. GET READY TO LEAVE.
WE'RE ON THE RUN AGAIN.
BASA (FWOOSH)
ANH!
TORU.
ANY PLACE ...
...TO GO?

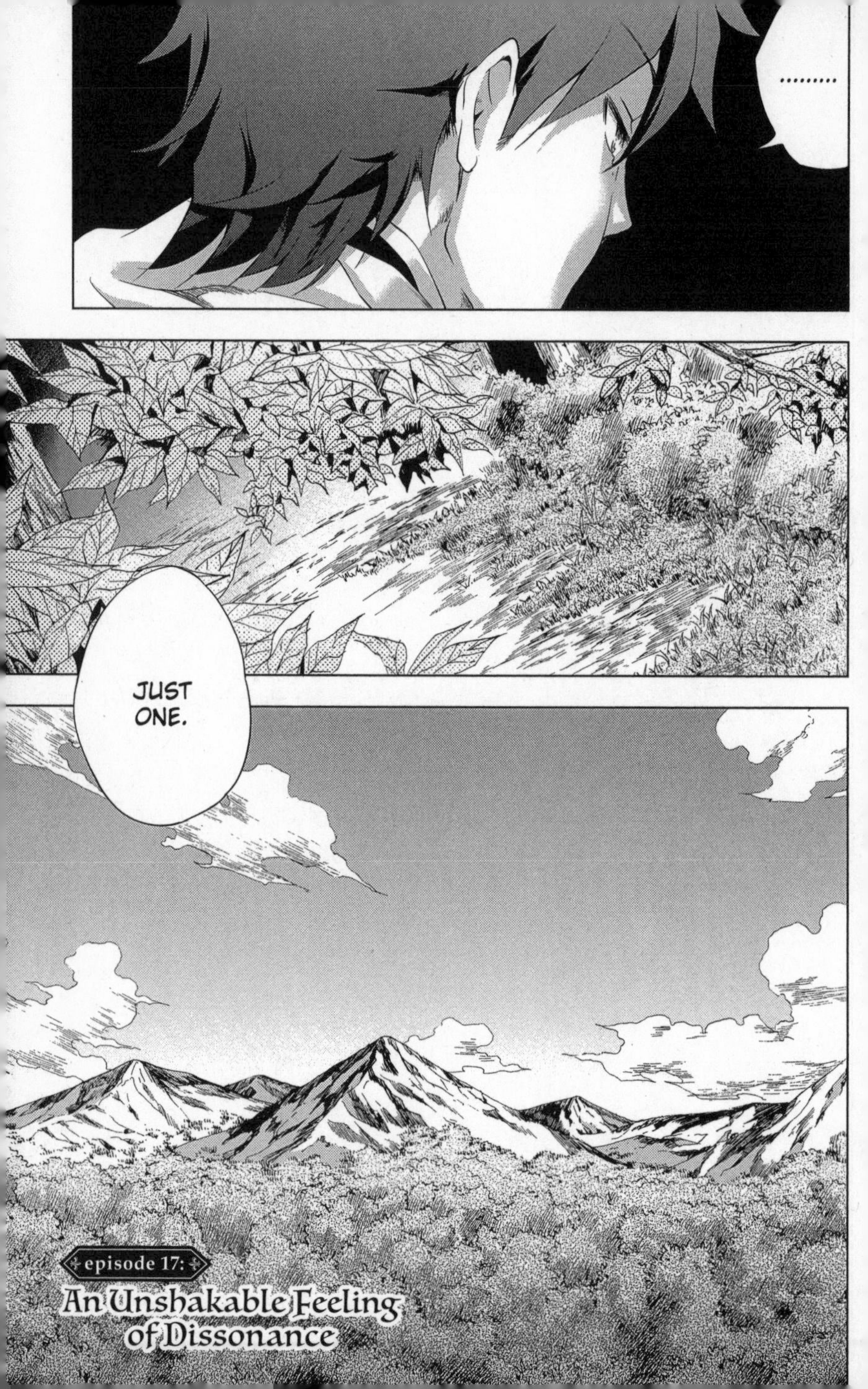
....
JUST ONE.
episode 17:
An Unshakable Feeling of Dissonance

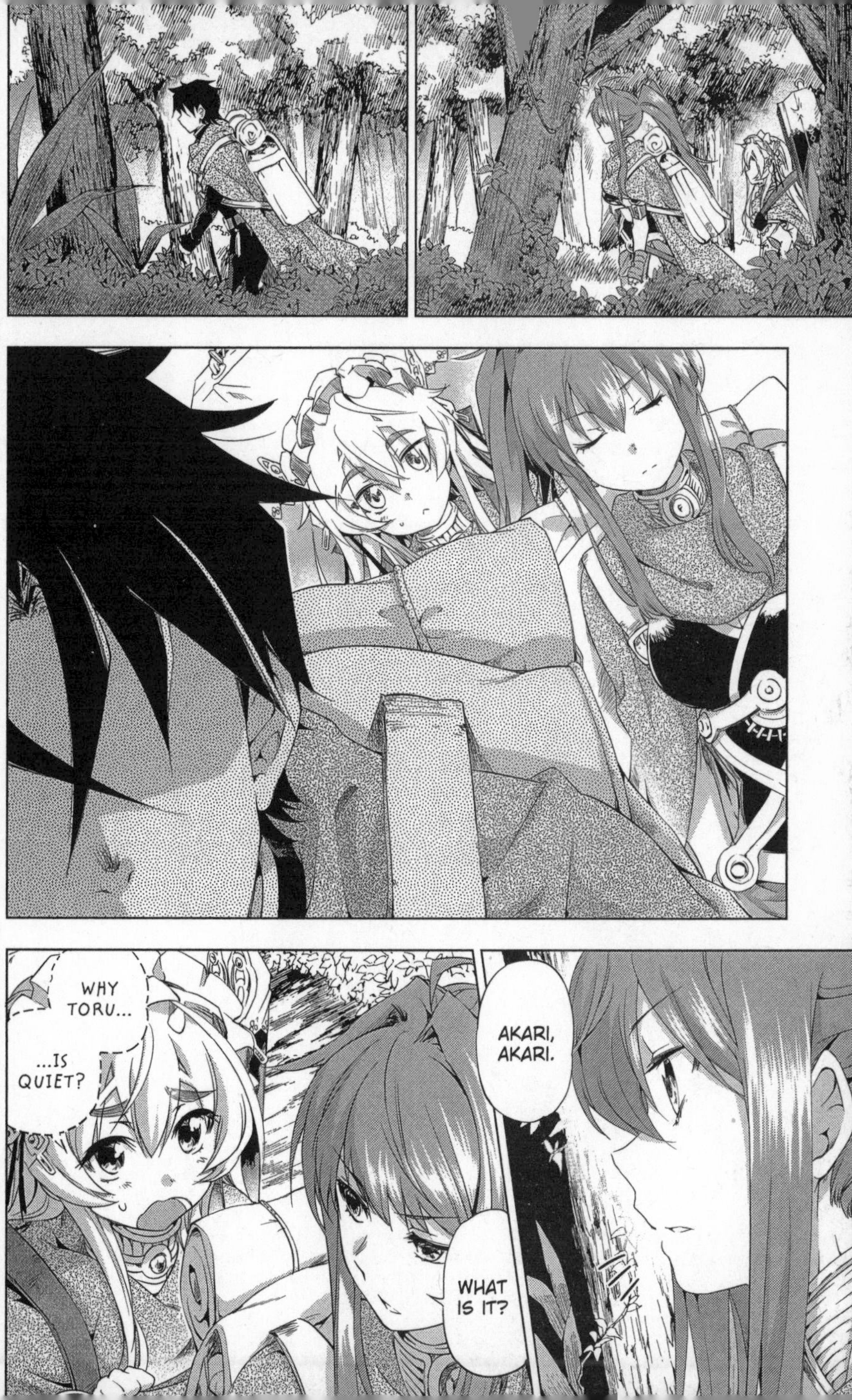
AKARI, AKARI.
WHAT IS IT?
WHY TORU... ...IS QUIET?

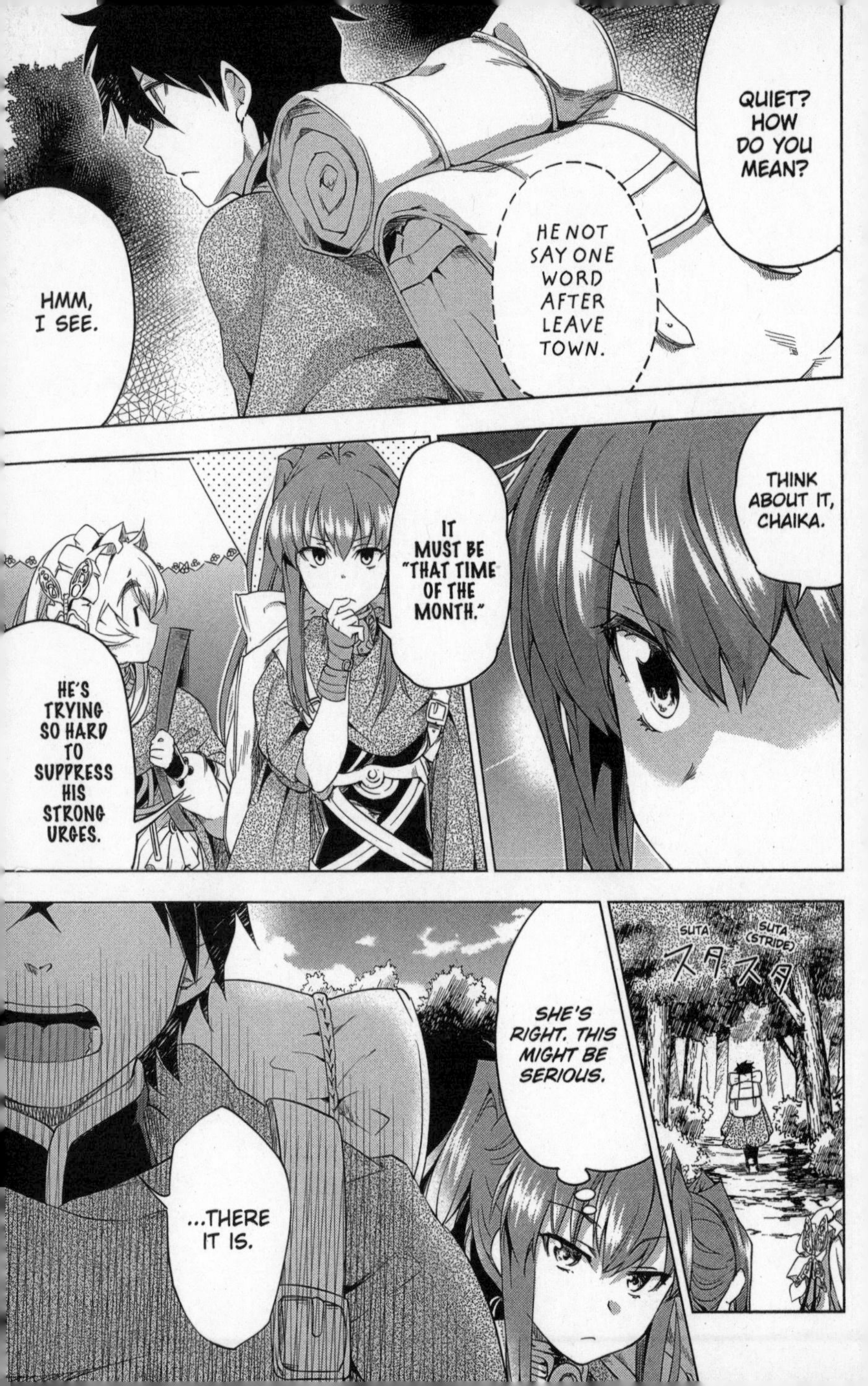
QUIET? HOW DO YOU MEAN?
HE NOT SAY ONE WORD AFTER LEAVE TOWN.
HMM, I SEE.
THINK ABOUT IT, CHAIKA.
IT MUST BE "THAT TIME OF THE MONTH."
HE'S TRYING SO HARD TO SUPPRESS HIS STRONG URGES.
スタスタ
SUTA SUTA (STRIDE)
SHE'S RIGHT. THIS MIGHT BE SERIOUS.
...THERE IT IS.

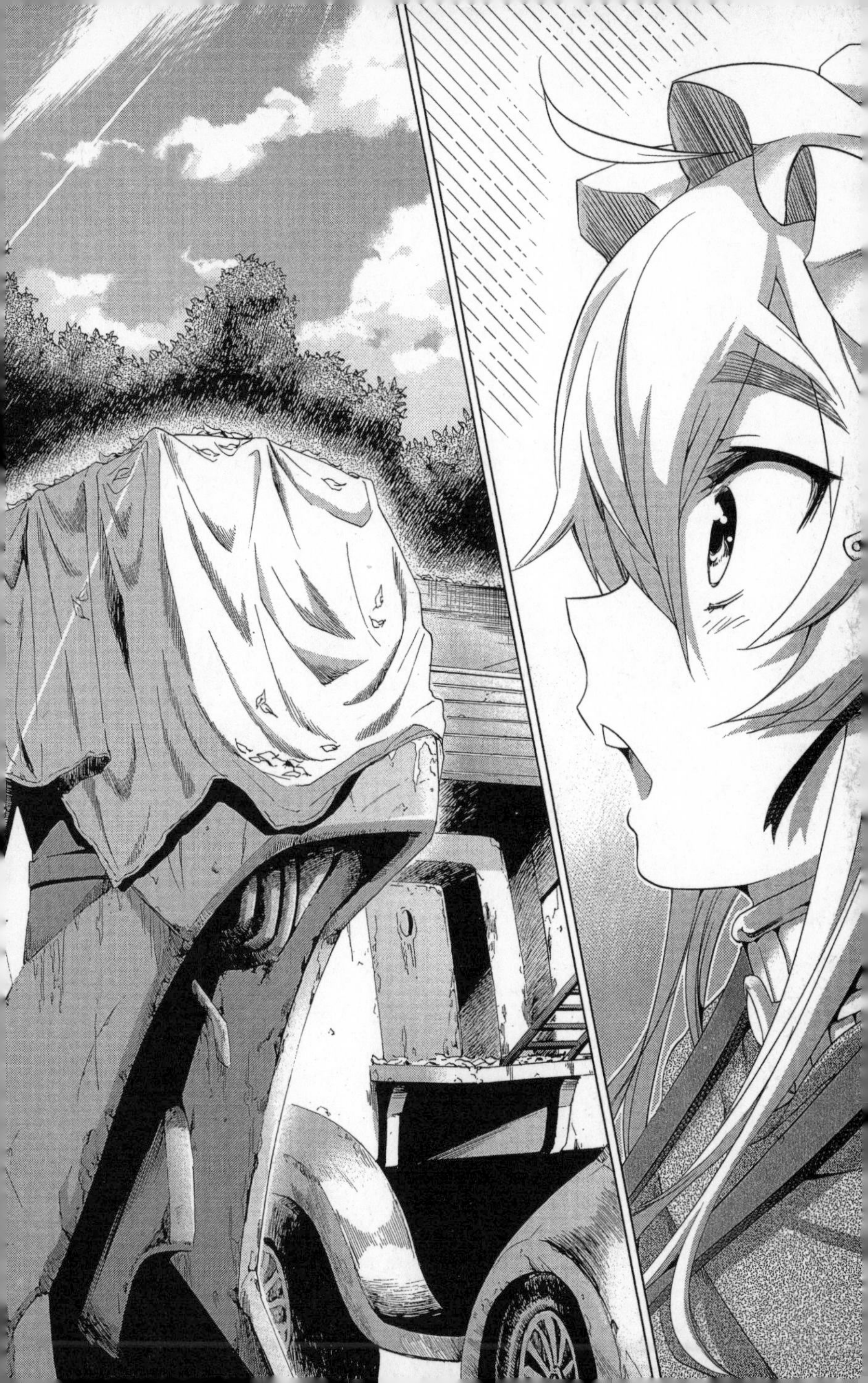

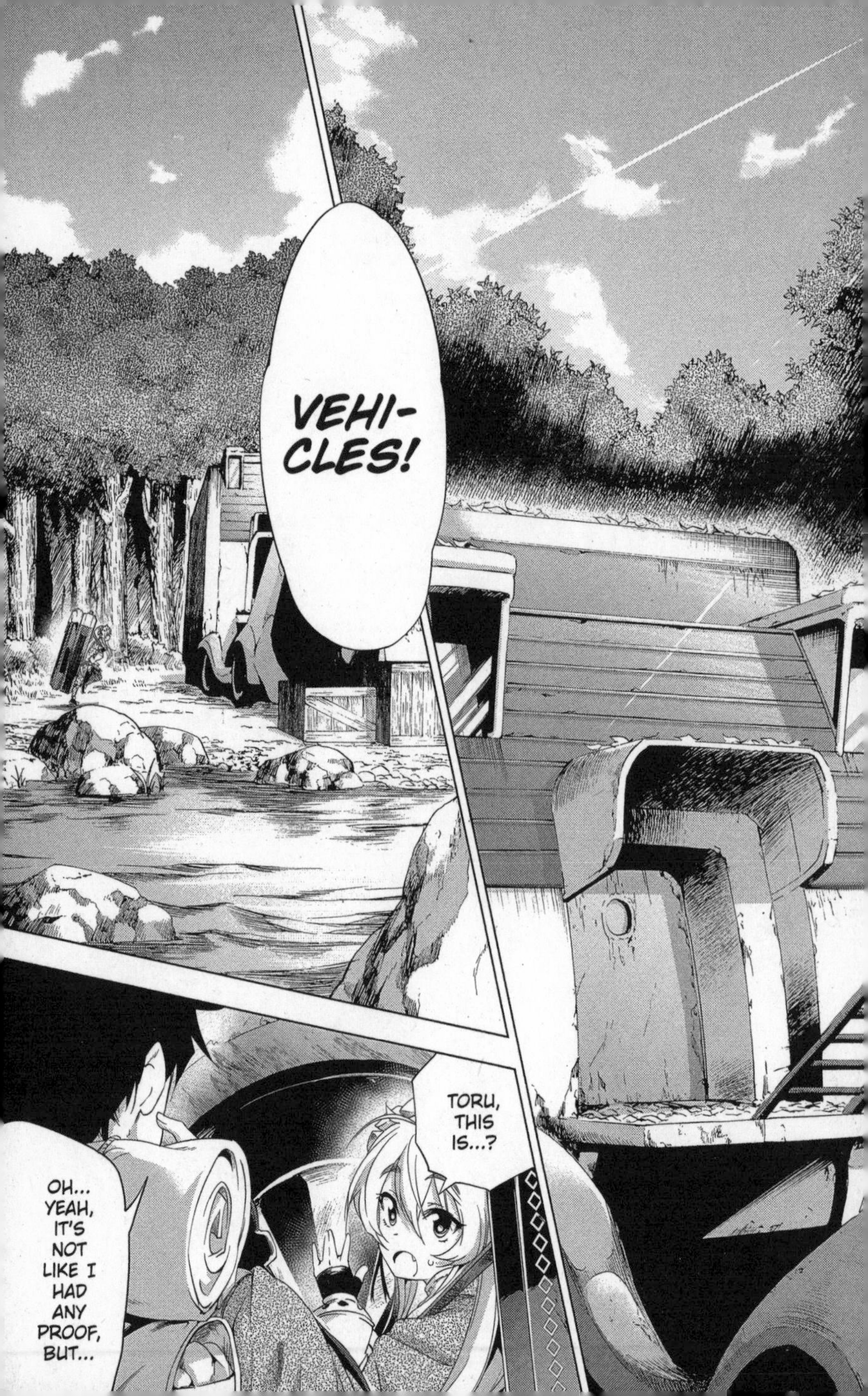
VEHI-
CLES!
TORU, THIS IS...?
OH... YEAH, IT'S NOT LIKE I HAD ANY PROOF, BUT...

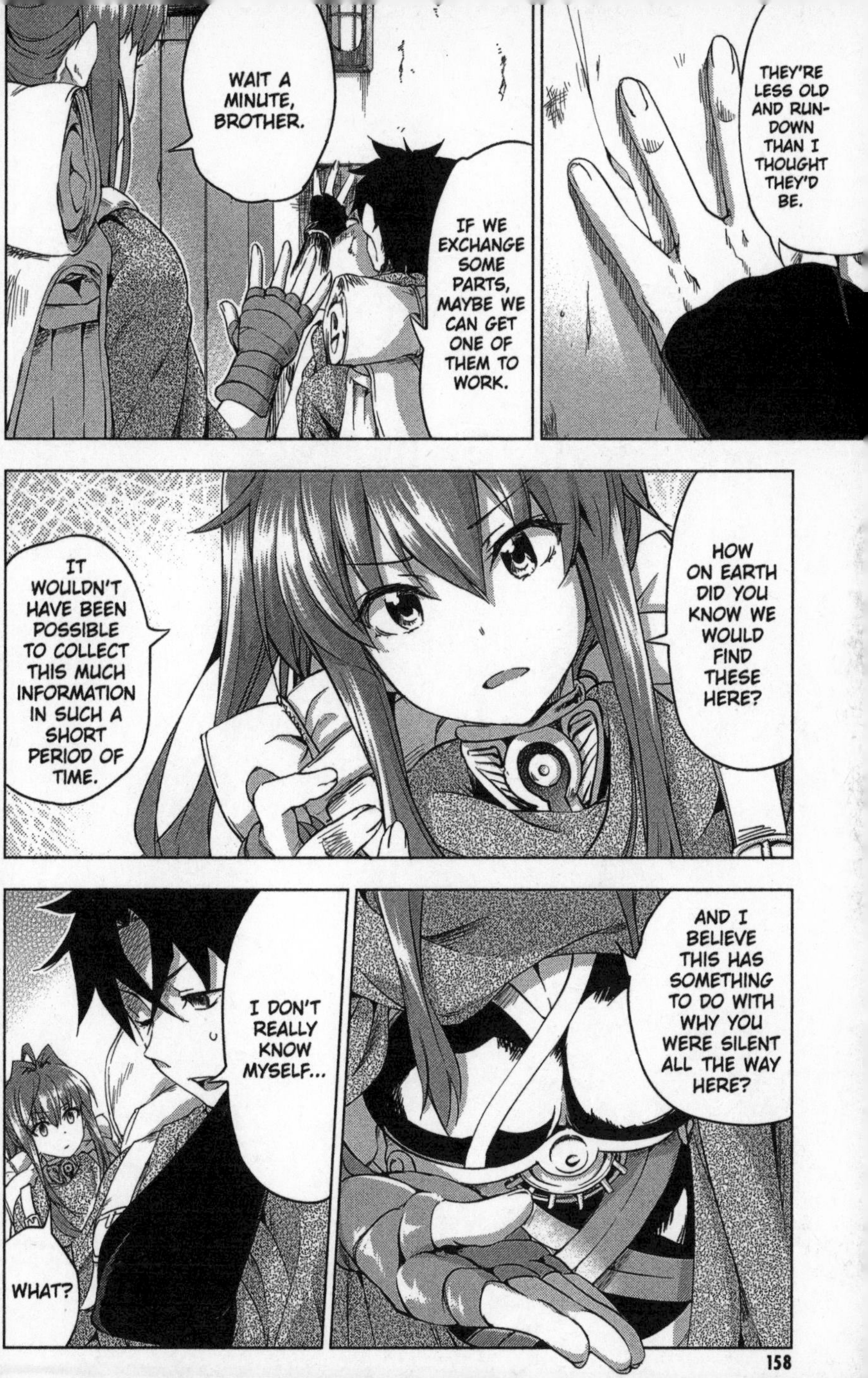
THEY'RE LESS OLD AND RUN-DOWN THAN I THOUGHT THEY'D BE.
IF WE EXCHANGE SOME PARTS, MAYBE WE CAN GET ONE OF THEM TO WORK.
WAIT A MINUTE, BROTHER.
HOW ON EARTH DID YOU KNOW WE WOULD FIND THESE HERE?
IT WOULDN'T HAVE BEEN POSSIBLE TO COLLECT THIS MUCH INFORMATION IN SUCH A SHORT PERIOD OF TIME.
AND I BELIEVE THIS HAS SOMETHING TO DO WITH WHY YOU WERE SILENT ALL THE WAY HERE?
I DON'T REALLY KNOW MYSELF...
WHAT?

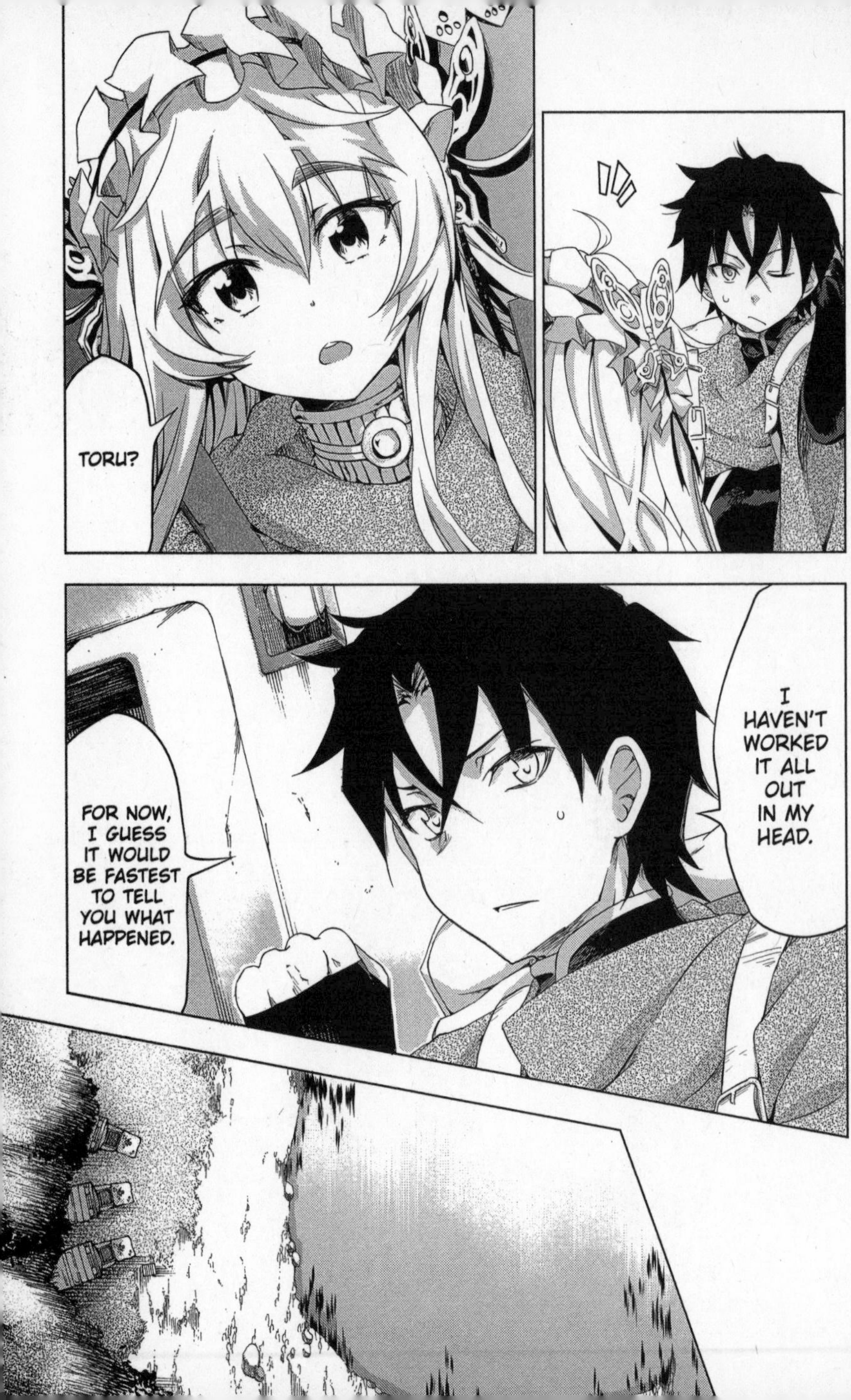
TORU?
I HAVEN'T WORKED IT ALL OUT IN MY HEAD.
FOR NOW, I GUESS IT WOULD BE FASTEST TO TELL YOU WHAT HAPPENED.

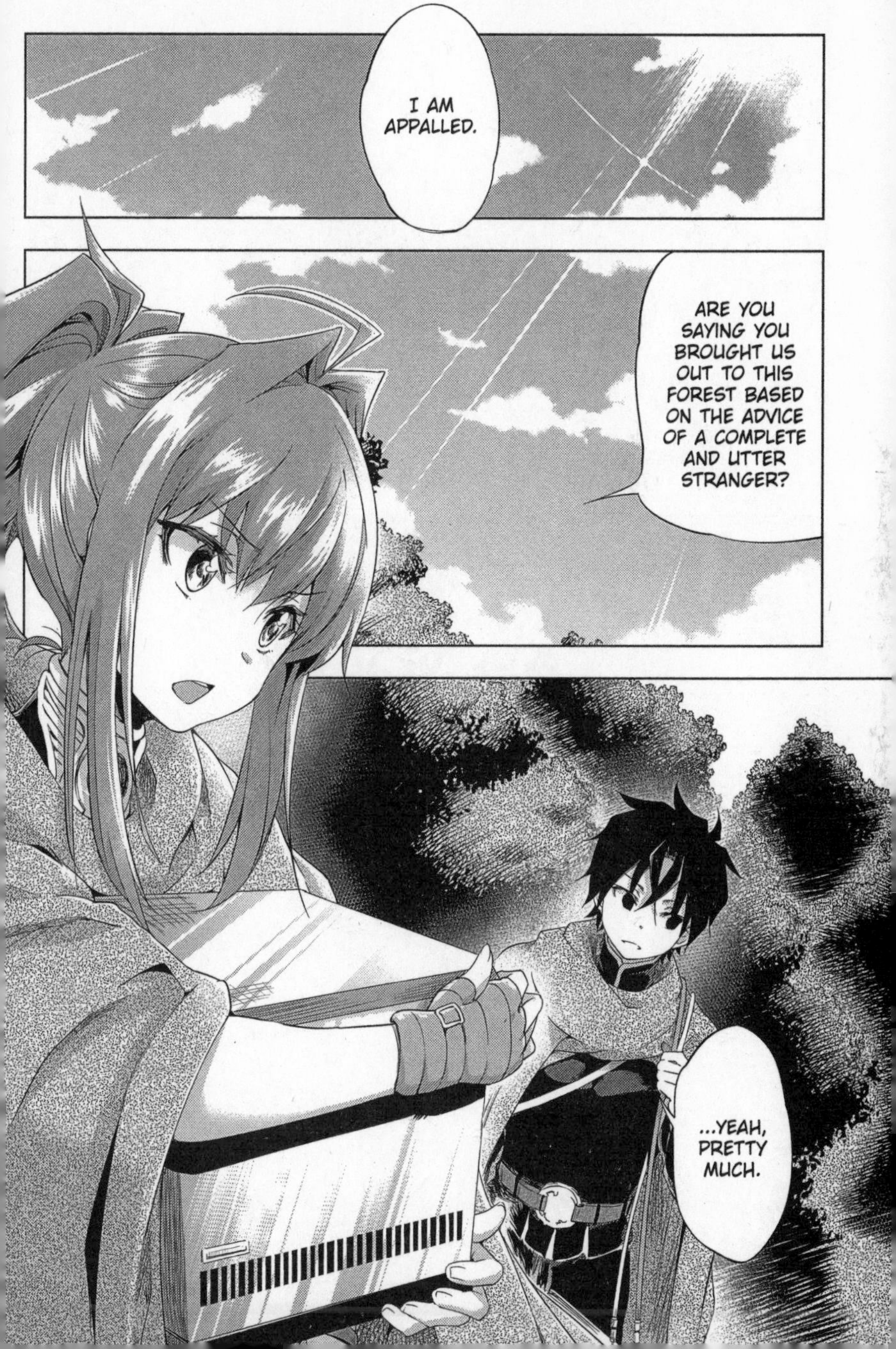
I AM APPALLED.
ARE YOU SAYING YOU BROUGHT US OUT TO THIS FOREST BASED ON THE ADVICE OF A COMPLETE AND UTTER STRANGER?
...YEAH, PRETTY MUCH.

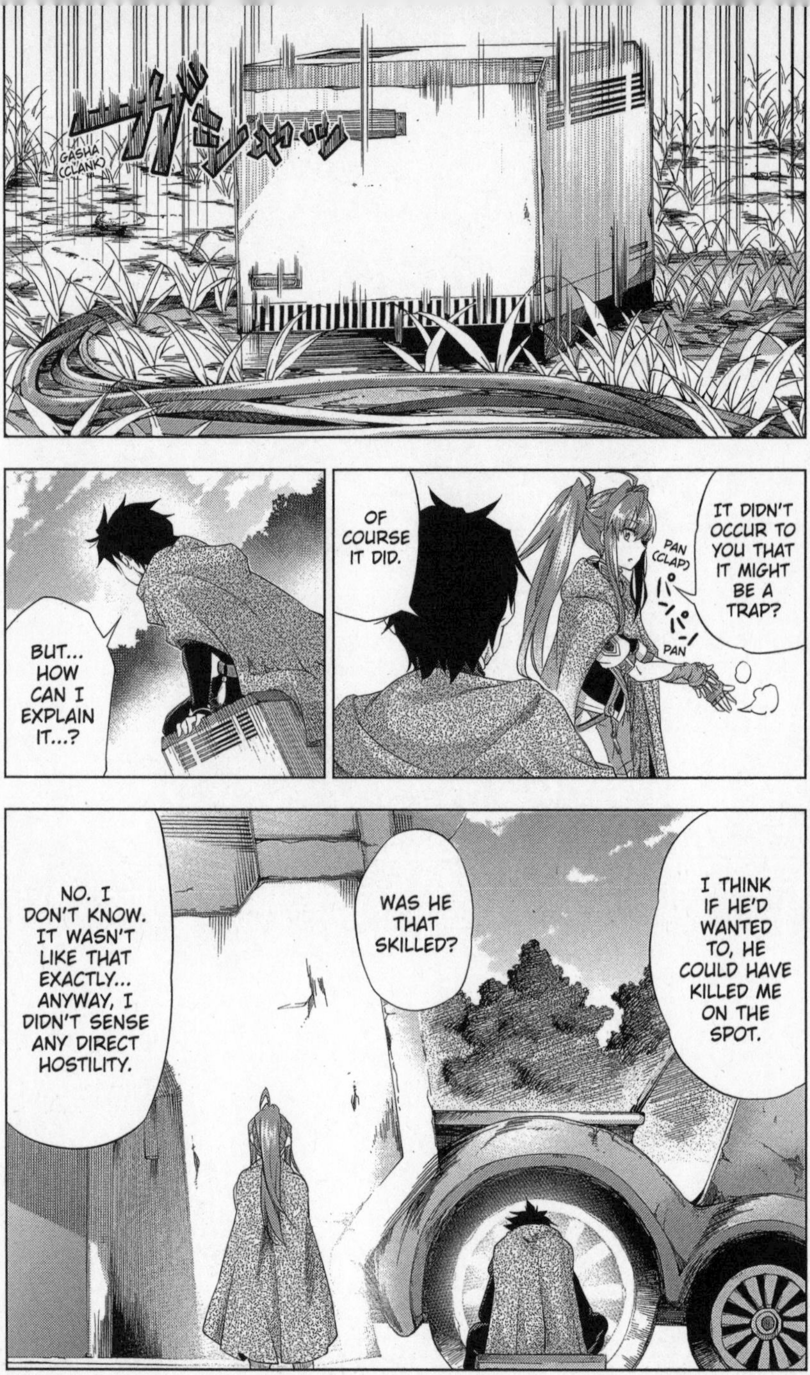
ガシャーン
GASHA (CLANK)
IT DIDN'T OCCUR TO YOU THAT IT MIGHT BE A TRAP?
パンパン
PAN (CLAP)
PAN
OF COURSE IT DID.
BUT... HOW CAN I EXPLAIN IT...?
I THINK IF HE'D WANTED TO, HE COULD HAVE KILLED ME ON THE SPOT.
WAS HE THAT SKILLED?
NO. I DON'T KNOW. IT WASN'T LIKE THAT EXACTLY... ANYWAY, I DIDN'T SENSE ANY DIRECT HOSTILITY.

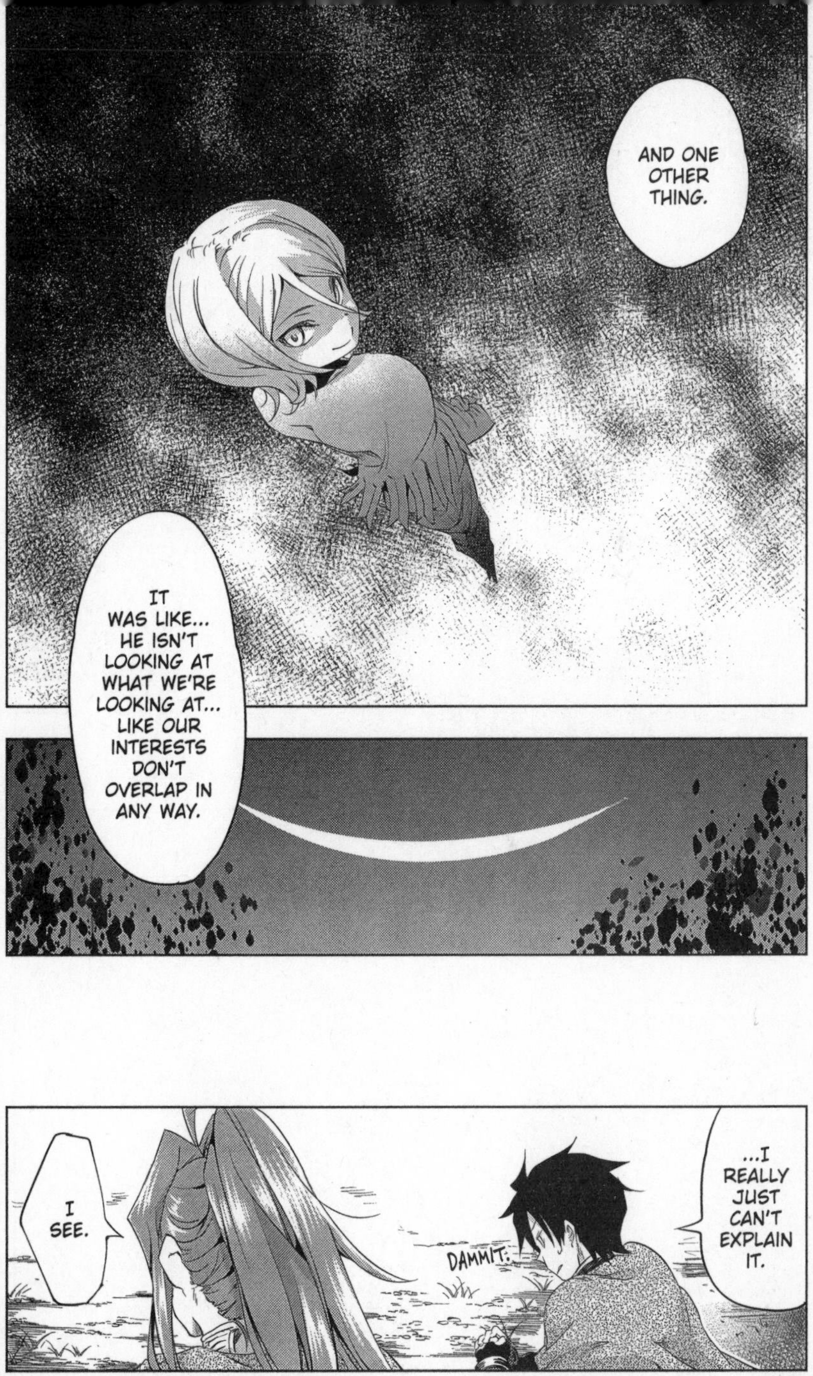
AND ONE OTHER THING.
IT WAS LIKE... HE ISN'T LOOKING AT WHAT WE'RE LOOKING AT... LIKE OUR INTERESTS DON'T OVERLAP IN ANY WAY.
...I REALLY JUST CAN'T EXPLAIN IT.
DAMMIT.
I SEE.

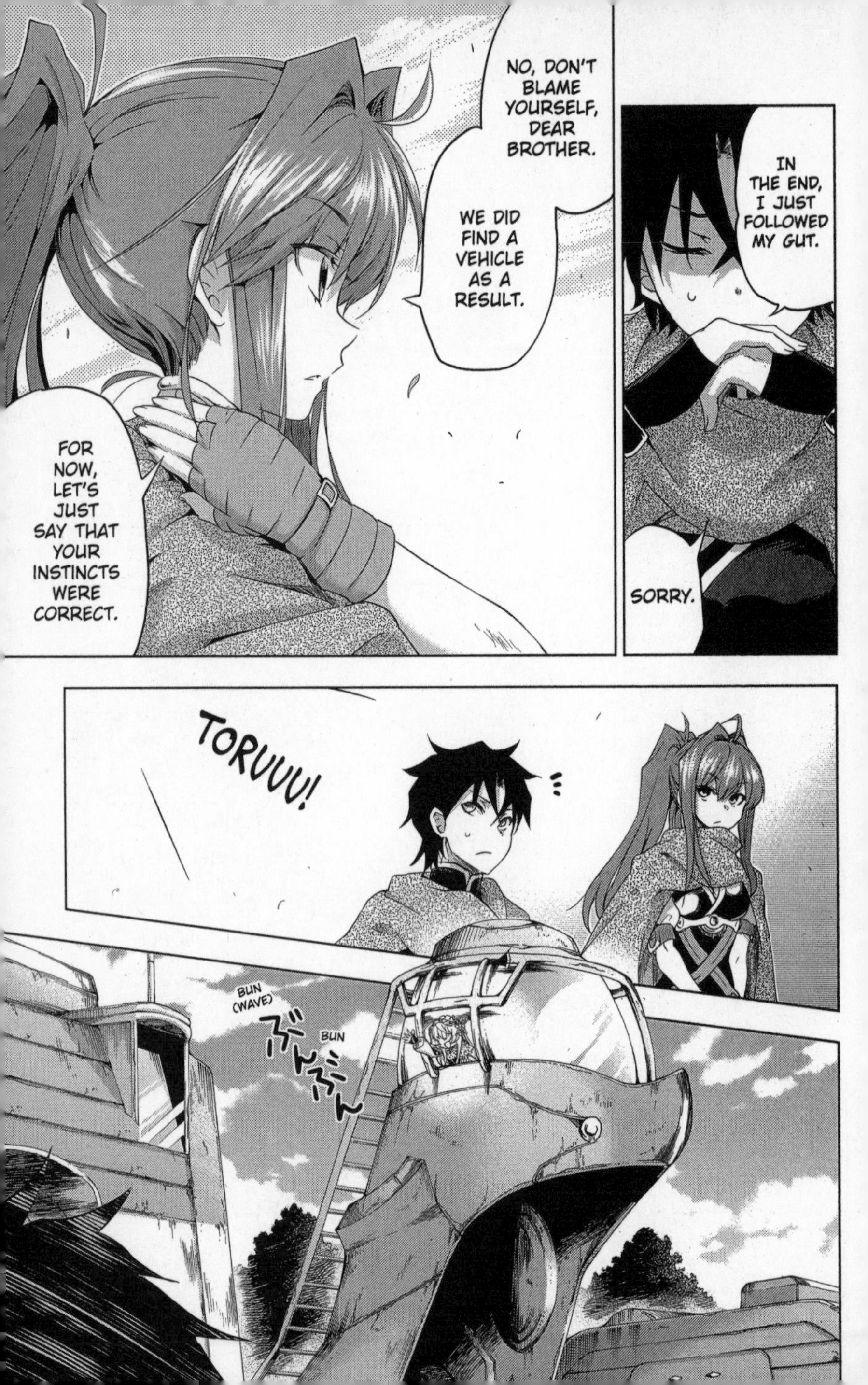
IN THE END, I JUST FOLLOWED MY GUT.
SORRY.
NO, DON'T BLAME YOURSELF, DEAR BROTHER.
WE DID FIND A VEHICLE AS A RESULT.
FOR NOW, LET'S JUST SAY THAT YOUR INSTINCTS WERE CORRECT.
TORUVUU!
BUN (WAVE)
ぶんぶん
BUN

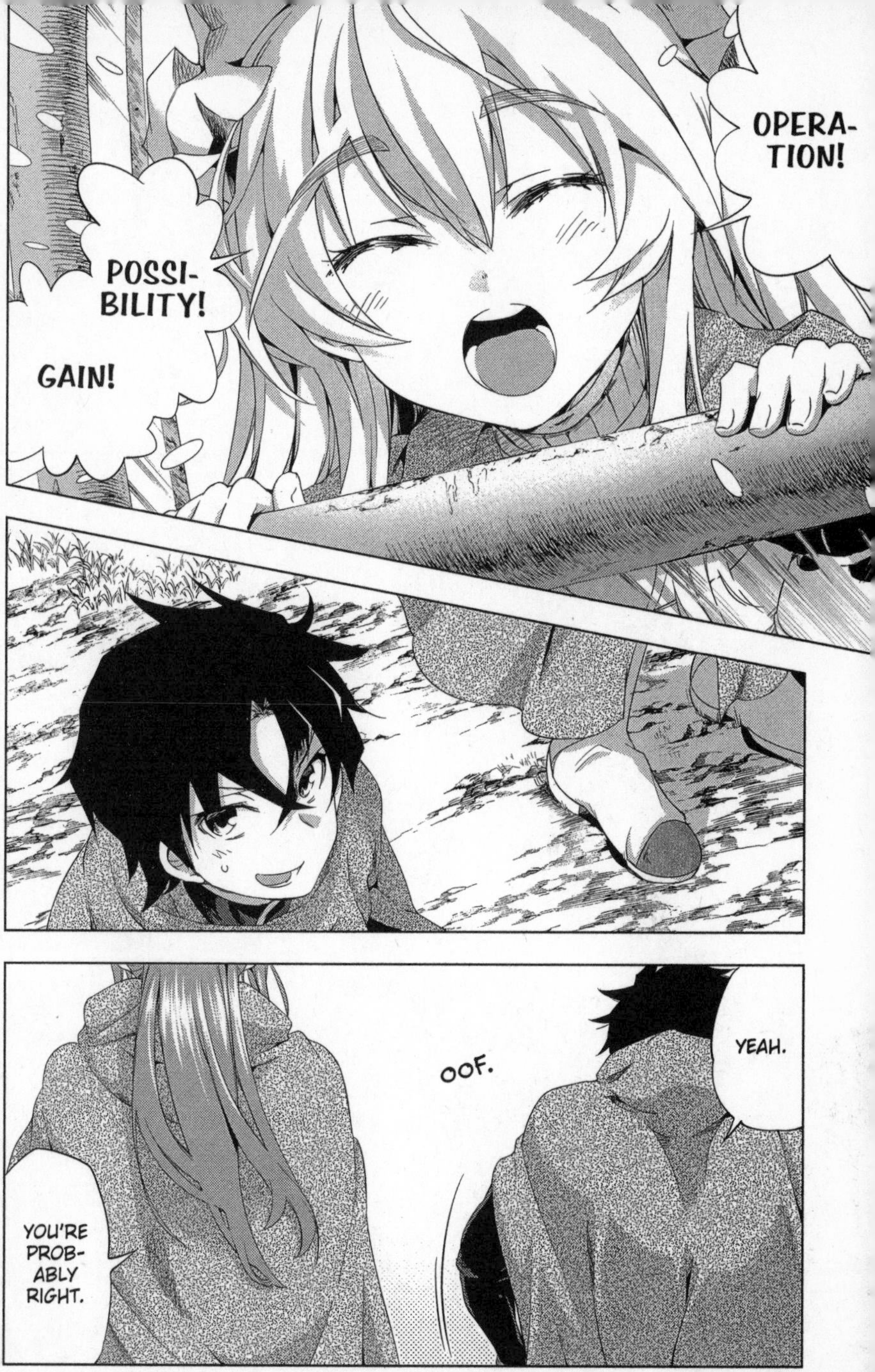
OPERA-TION!
POSSI-BILITY!
GAIN!
YEAH.
OOF.
YOU'RE PROB-ABLY RIGHT.

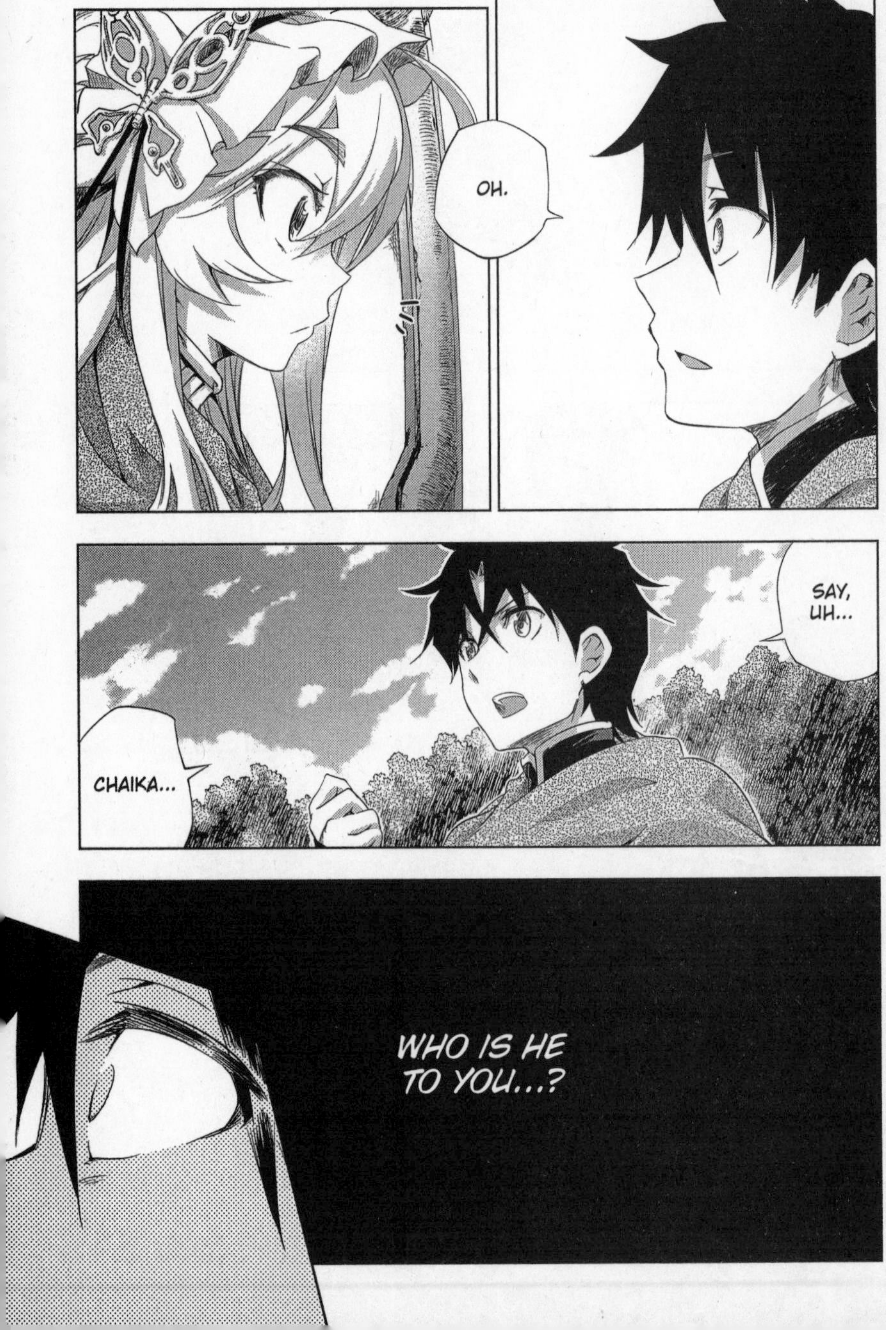
OH.
SAY, UH...
CHAIKA...
WHO IS HE TO YOU...?

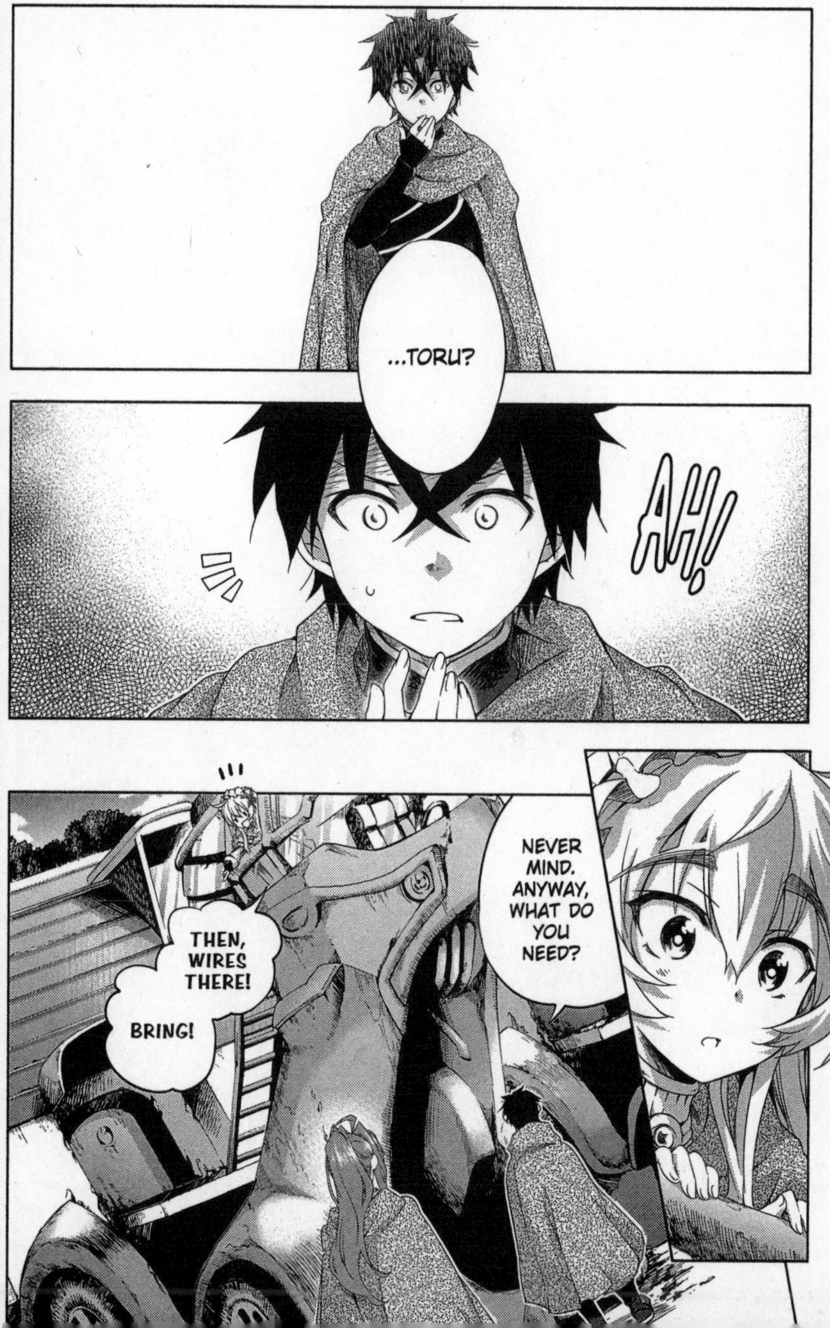
...TORU?
AH!
NEVER MIND. ANYWAY, WHAT DO YOU NEED?
THEN, WIRES THERE!
BRING!

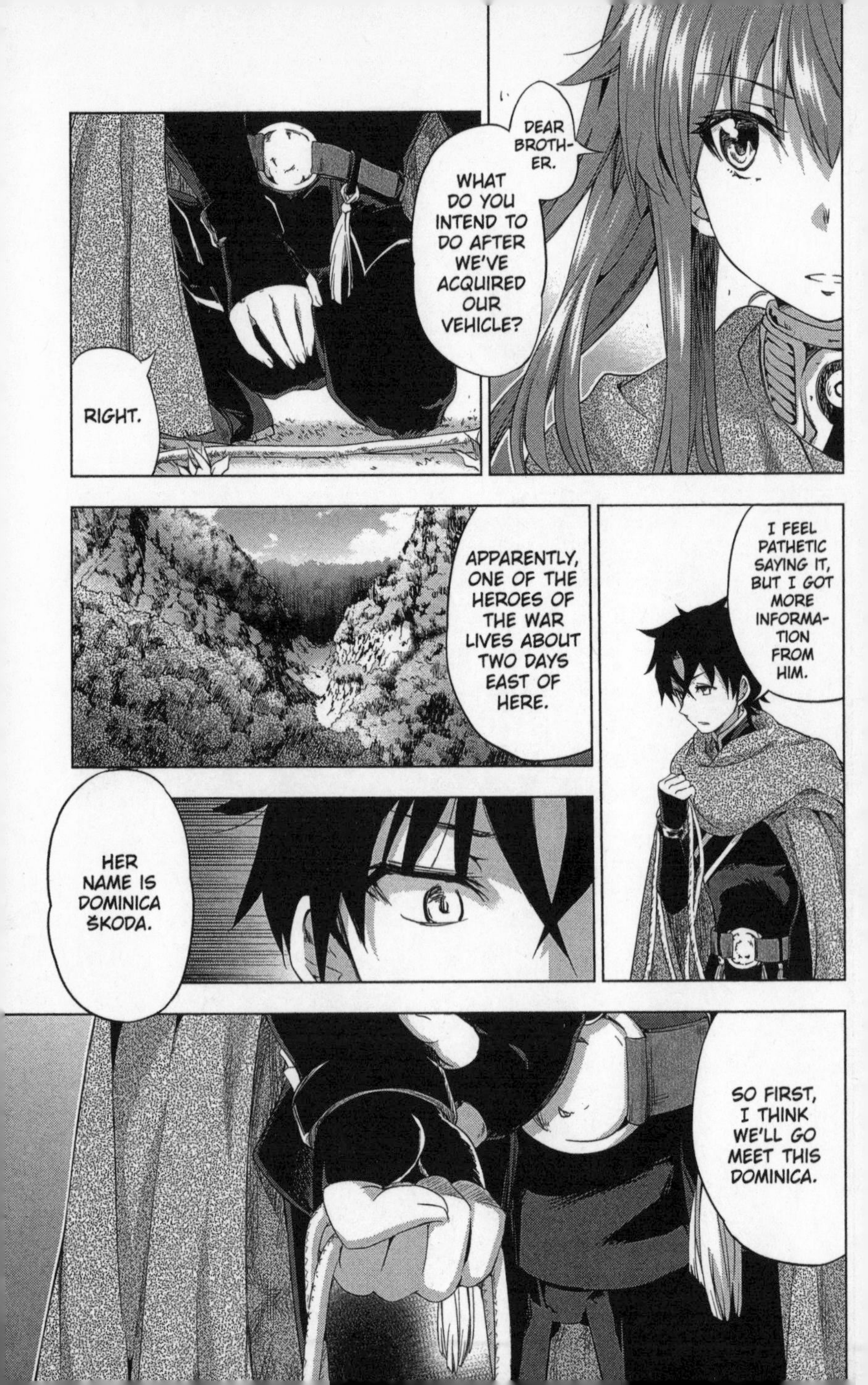
DEAR BROTHER.
WHAT DO YOU INTEND TO DO AFTER WE'VE ACQUIRED OUR VEHICLE?
RIGHT.
I FEEL PATHETIC SAYING IT, BUT I GOT MORE INFORMATION FROM HIM.
APPARENTLY, ONE OF THE HEROES OF THE WAR LIVES ABOUT TWO DAYS EAST OF HERE.
HER NAME IS DOMINICA ŠKODA.
SO FIRST, I THINK WE'LL GO MEET THIS DOMINICA.

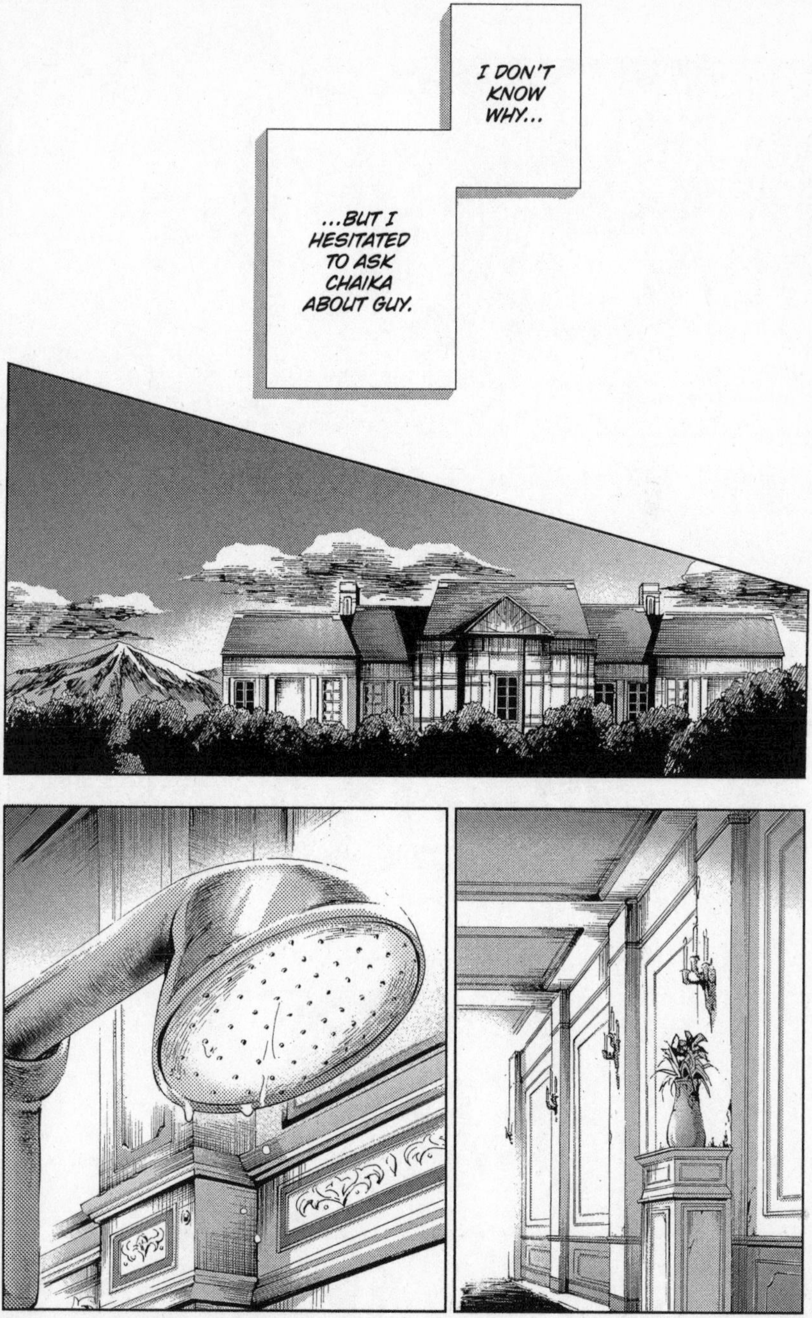
I DON'T KNOW WHY...
...BUT I HESITATED TO ASK CHAIKA ABOUT GUY.

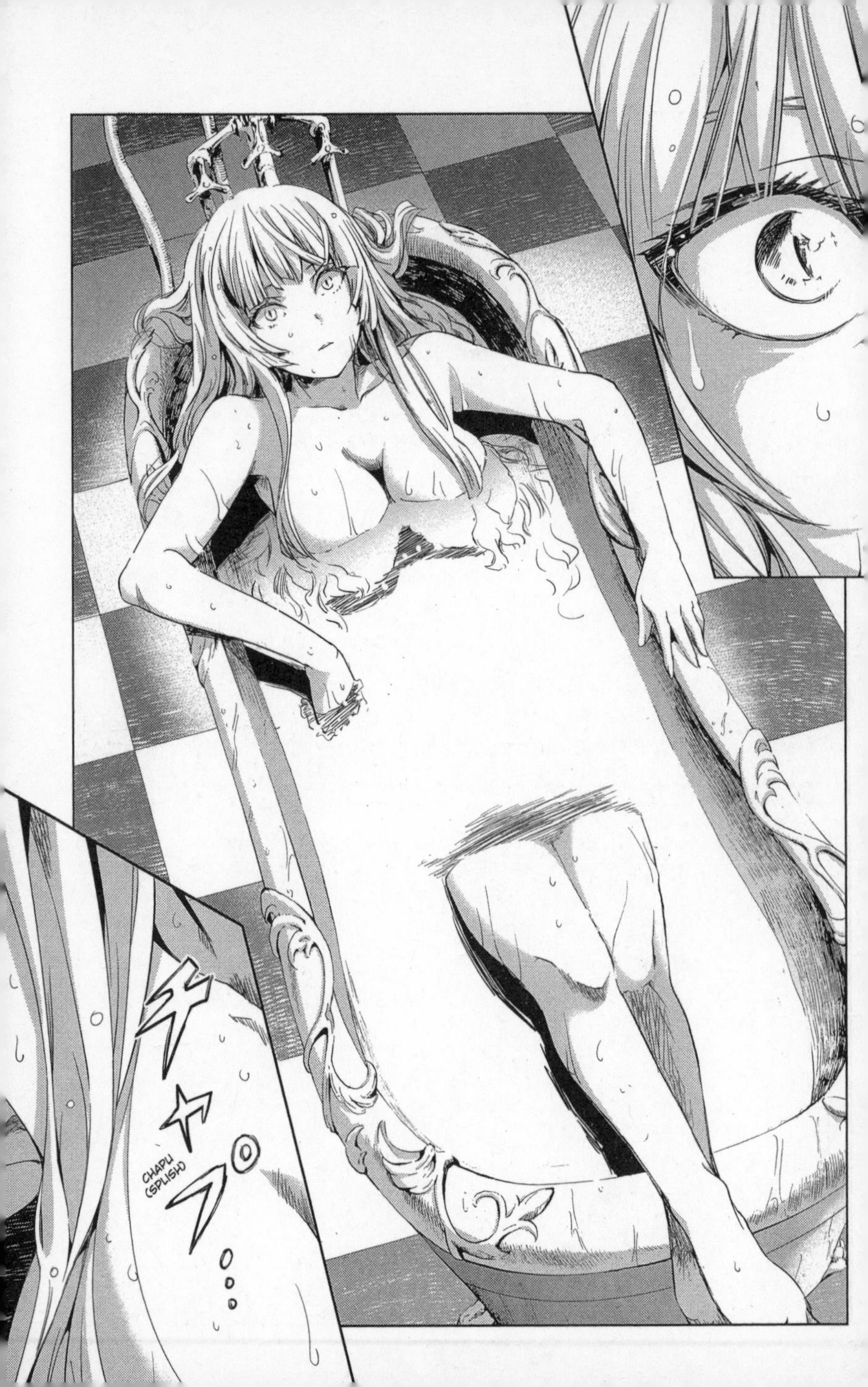
チャプ…
CHAPU (SPLISH)

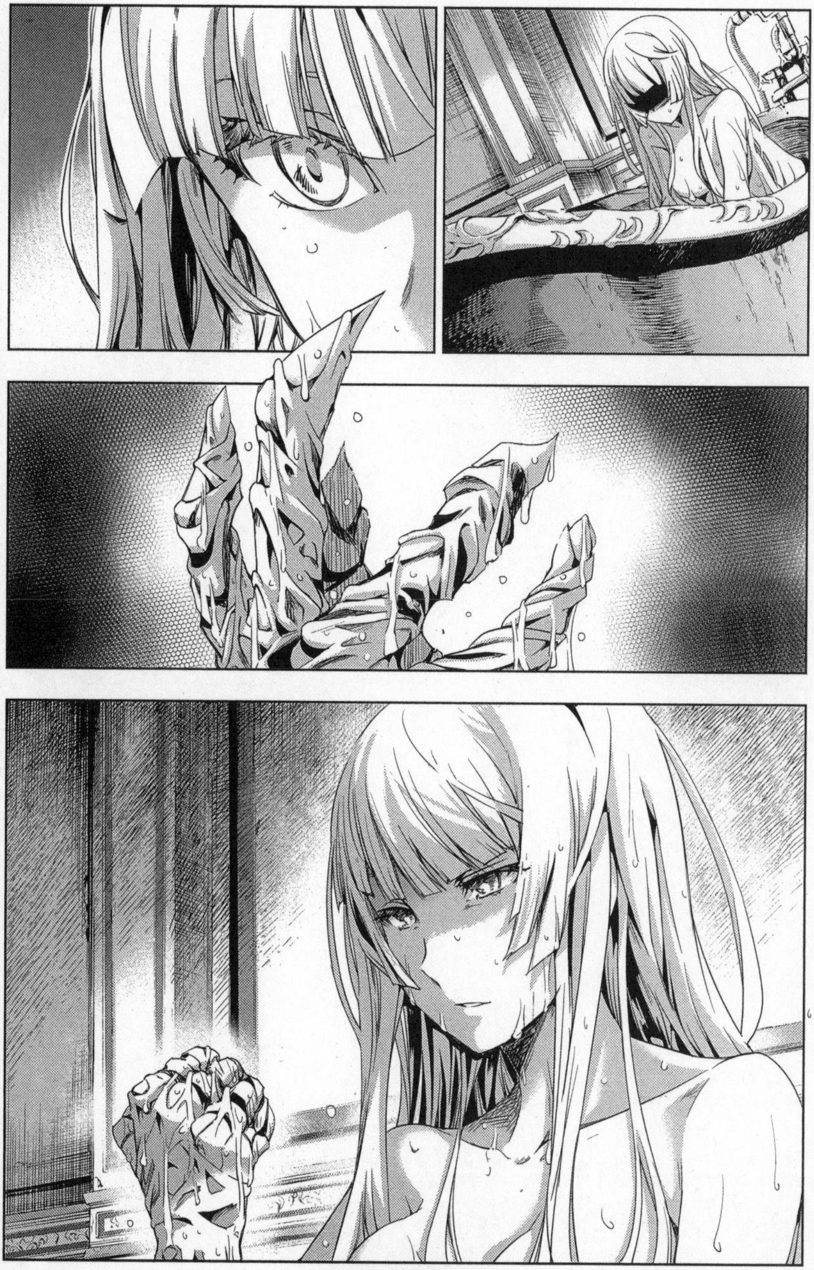

episode 17: END

CHAIKA: THE COFFIN PRINCESS

from Ichirou Sakaki

THERE ARE SOME BIG RISKS IN ADAPTING A MANGA VERSION OF SOMETHING ELSE. MANGA IS A DIFFERENT MEDIUM OF EXPRESSION, SO IF YOU'RE TOO FAITHFUL TO THE ORIGINAL FORMAT, YOU LOSE SOME OF THE BALANCE NEEDED IN MANGA. BUT IF YOU COMPLETELY IGNORE THE ORIGINAL AND JUST WRITE WHATEVER YOU WANT, THEN FANS OF THE ORIGINAL WILL CRITICIZE YOU FOR THAT. IT ACTUALLY HAS A PRETTY HIGH DIFFICULTY LEVEL; THERE IS NO CLEAR RIGHT ANSWER. IN THAT SENSE, SAKAYAMA-SAN'S MANGA VERSION CONFORMS TO THE NOVEL BUT SEAMLESSLY WEAVES ORIGINAL ELEMENTS ALL THROUGHOUT, AND WHAT SURPRISES ME IS HOW NATURALLY SAKAYAMA-SAN ACCOMPLISHES THIS AMAZING FEAT. ESPECIALLY THE WAY HE WRITES THE DIALOGUE—IT'S THE SAME AS WRITING A NOVEL IN THE SENSE THAT IT INVOLVES EXPRESSION THROUGH THE WRITTEN WORD, AND THE SECOND YOU GET CARELESS ABOUT IT, THE READER IMMEDIATELY THINKS, "THAT'S NOT RIGHT." BUT HE'S MASTERED EVEN AKARI'S UNIQUE TURN OF PHRASE, AND IT ALMOST SEEMS LIKE HE'S PORTRAYING *CHAIKA: THE COFFIN PRINCESS* BETTER THAN THE ORIGINAL. I THINK IT MUST BE VERY DIFFICULT TO MAINTAIN THIS DENSITY, THIS QUALITY, IN A MAGAZINE SERIES, BUT AS THE ORIGINAL AUTHOR, I AM FILLED WITH GRATITUDE THAT HE DOES.

ICHIROU SAKAKI

from Namaniku ATK

WORKING AWAY FROM HOME
AFTERWORD
WHOA...
CONGRATULATIONS ON RELEASING VOLUME THREE!! I CAN'T TAKE MY EYES OFF OF IT, ANTICIPATING THE FUTURE EXPLOITS OF THE LONG-AWAITED, LARGE-BUSTED CHAIKA CHARACTERS (MONOTONE VOICE)!
BA-BAM!

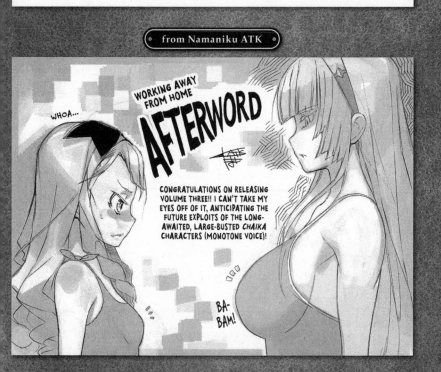

CONGRATULATIONS! VOLUME 3!

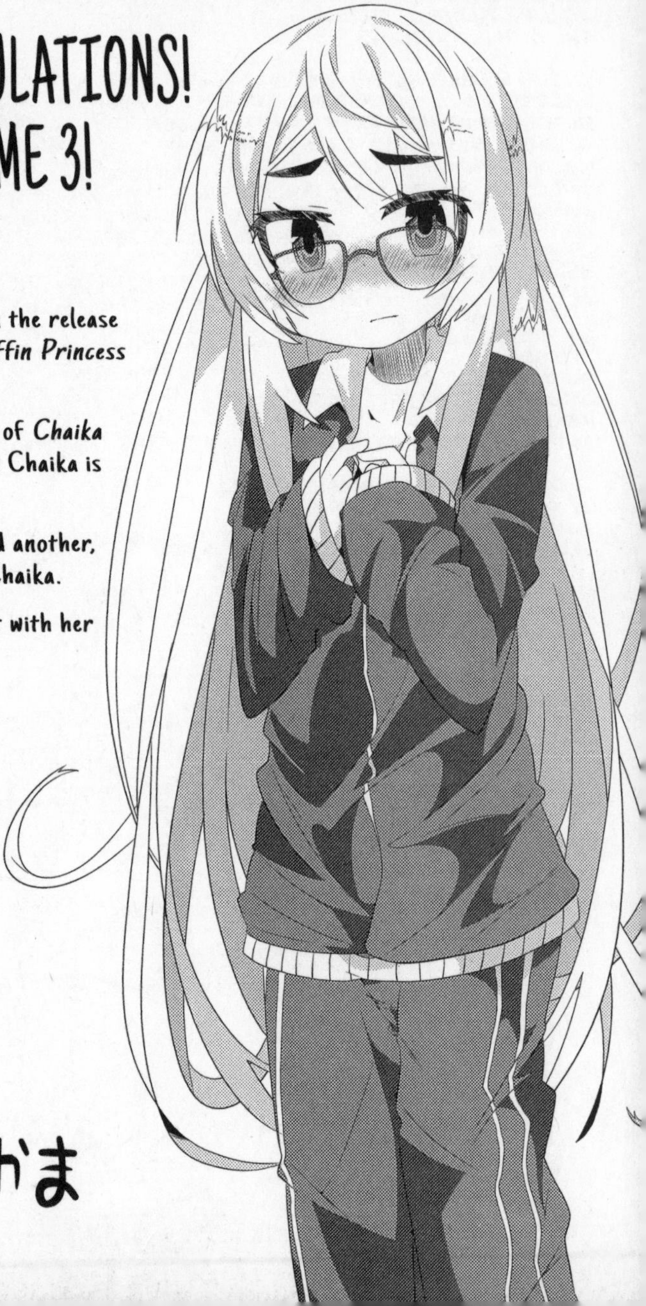

Congratulations on the release of *Chaika: The Coffin Princess* Volume Three!

The manga version of *Chaika* is so much fun, and Chaika is so cute!

After one thing and another, I drew an indoor Chaika.

I'd like to hang out with her inside...

KANIKAMA
かにかま

THANK YOU FOR BUYING VOLUME THREE OF CHAIKA: THE COFFIN PRINCESS.

IN THIS VOLUME, THE CONFLICT WITH GILLET'S TEAM COMES TO A TEMPORARY CLOSE, AND WE MOVE RIGHT INTO A NEW ARC. THIS VOLUME TAKES PLACE AROUND VOLUME TWO OF THE NOVELS, BUT I TOOK THE LIBERTY OF WRITING ONE CHAPTER THAT'S NEARLY ALL ORIGINAL MATERIAL. THOUGH IT COULD BE THAT I WAS JUST SPEWING OUT MY OWN APPETITES FOR FANTASY MANGA—WHICH IS TO SAY, IF IT'S A FANTASY MANGA, THERE HAS TO BE A BATHING SCENE...! I USUALLY FOLLOW THE ORIGINAL STORY FAITHFULLY WHEN DRAWING THIS SERIES, SO NOW THAT I'VE TRIED IT, I BOW MY HEAD AT HOW HARD IT IS TO COME UP WITH YOUR OWN STORIES.

AND THERE ARE NEW CHARACTERS IN THIS VOLUME, SO I HOPE I CAN FILL THE NEXT VOLUME WITH ALL KINDS OF NEW MATERIAL.

AND SAKAKI-SENSEI, NAMANIKU-SENSEI, AND KANIKAMA-SENSEI, THANK YOU FOR CONTRIBUTING!

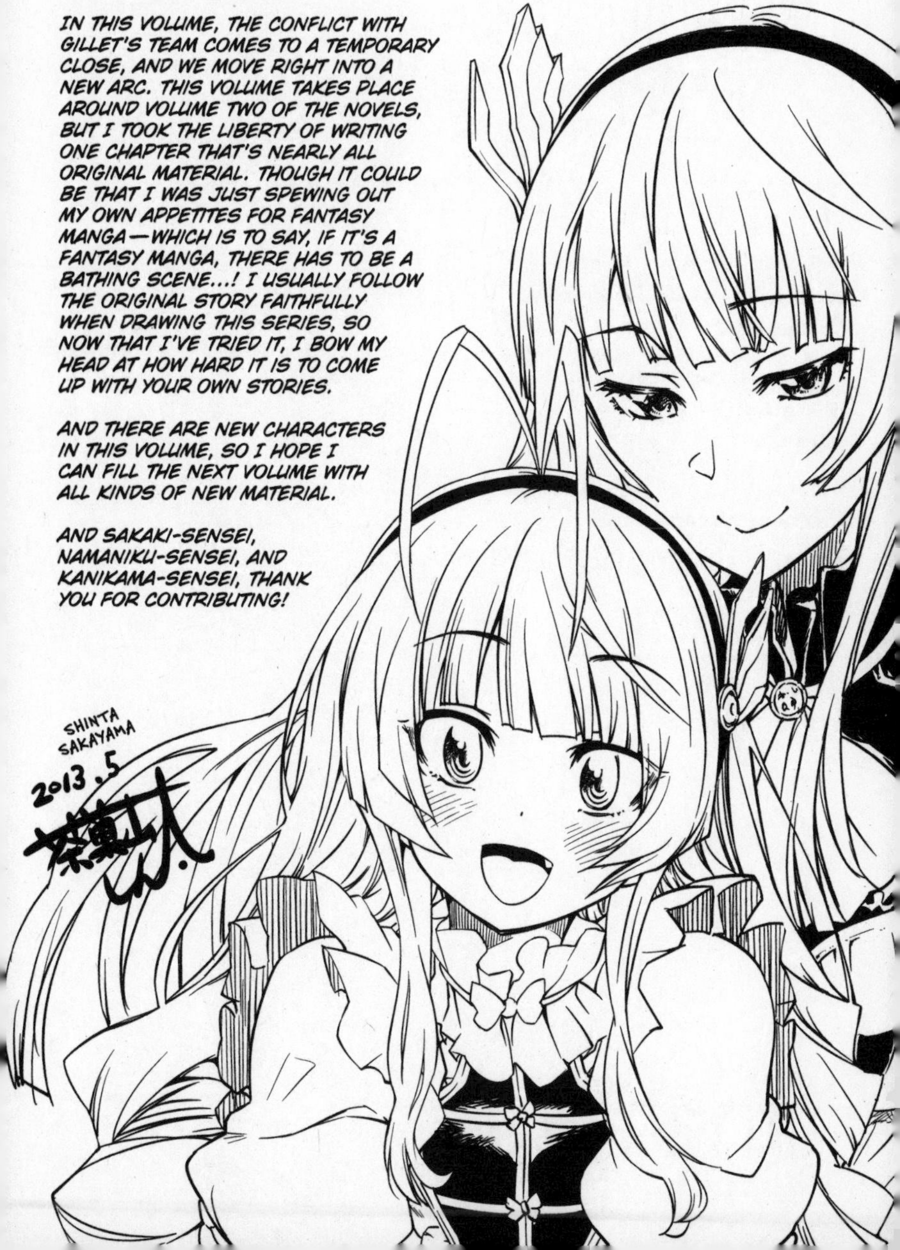
SHINTA
SAKAYAMA
2013.5

CHAIKA: THE COFFIN PRINCESS

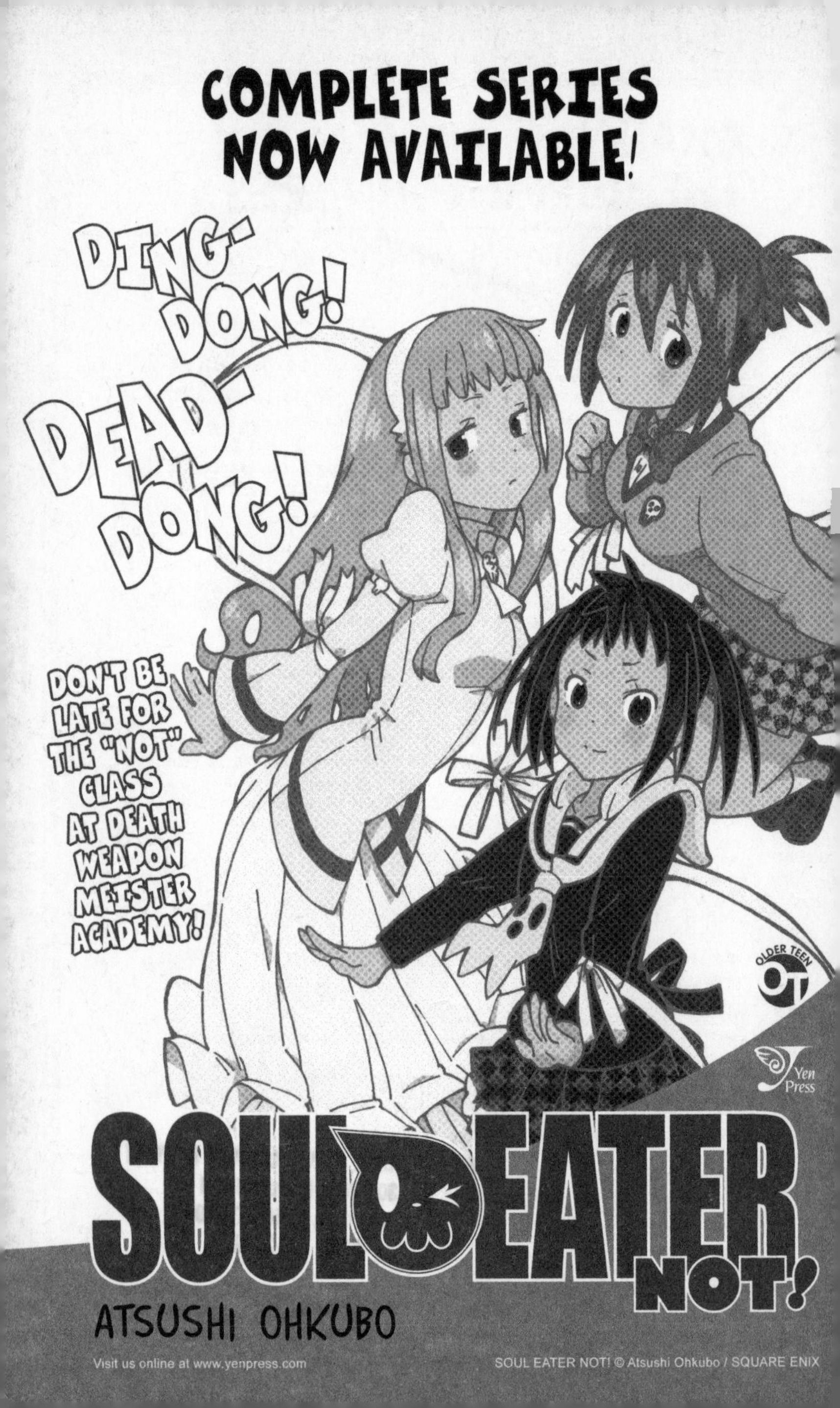

COMPLETE SERIES NOW AVAILABLE!
DING-DONG!
DEAD-DONG!
DON'T BE LATE FOR THE "NOT" CLASS AT DEATH WEAPON MEISTER ACADEMY!
OLDER TEEN OT
Yen Press
SOUL EATER NOT!
ATSUSHI OHKUBO
Visit us online at www.yenpress.com
SOUL EATER NOT! © Atsushi Ohkubo / SQUARE ENIX

CHAIKA: THE COFFIN PRINCESS ❸

Original Story By: ICHIROU SAKAKI
Manga: SHINTA SAKAYAMA
Character Design: Namaniku ATK (Nitroplus)

Translation: Athena and Alethea Nibley
Lettering: Abigail Blackman

HITSUGI NO CHAIKA Volume 3
©Ichirou Sakaki, Nitroplus
©Shinta SAKAYAMA 2013
Edited by KADOKAWA SHOTEN. First published in Japan in 2013 by KADOKAWA CORPORATION, Tokyo. English translation rights arranged with KADOKAWA CORPORATION, Tokyo through TUTTLE-MORI AGENCY, INC., Tokyo.

Translation © 2015 by Hachette Book Group, Inc.

Yen Press
Hachette Book Group
1290 Avenue of the Americas
New York, NY 10104

www.hachettebookgroup.com
www.yenpress.com

Yen Press is an imprint of Hachette Book Group, Inc.
The Yen Press name and logo are trademarks of Hachette Book Group, Inc.

The publisher is not responsible for websites (or their content) that are not owned by the publisher.

First Yen Press Edition: December 20⁙

ISBN: 978-0-316-26379-5

10 9 8 7 6 5 4 3 2 1

BVG

Printed in the United States of America

D1227086